ALGONQUIN BOOKS

Dear Reader,

If you're a longtime Larry Watson fan, I suspect it's for the same reasons that I am: his characters, though they are distinctly different—and sometimes damnable—are rendered with great empathy, no matter their past crimes. His landscapes, always the landscapes of the great West, are vast and beautiful and in the blood of his characters. He refuses to back away from subjects and perspectives that many of us would like to avoid. And above all, he's a hell of a storyteller.

So I'm tremendously excited to publish his new novel, *As Good as Gone*, where Larry Watson is at the peak of his storytelling powers. Calvin Sidey has left his family to live a life of self-reliance out on the prairie. Years later he returns—one of the last of the old cowboys. But in the 1960s a seismic shift in American culture has begun, and well-meaning Calvin is now a dangerous man. In this profoundly moving novel, Watson captures our fascination with and longing for the Old West and its heroes; he challenges our understanding of loyalty and justice; and he forces us to examine the consequences of individualism.

Whether you're a longtime fan or a first-time reader, I hope you'll agree that *As Good as Gone*, both tough and tender, is a stunning achievement. I am so pleased to put it in your hands.

Sincerely,

Kathy Pories
Senior Editor

AS GOOD AS GONE

ALSO BY LARRY WATSON

Let Him Go
American Boy
Sundown, Yellow Moon
Orchard
Laura
White Crosses
Justice
Montana 1948
In a Dark Time

AS GOOD AS GONE

A NOVEL

Larry Watson

ALGONQUIN BOOKS
OF CHAPEL HILL
2016

Published by
Algonquin Books of Chapel Hill
Post Office Box 2225
Chapel Hill, North Carolina 27515-2225

a division of
Workman Publishing
225 Varick Street
New York, New York 10014

This is a work of fiction. While, as in all fiction, the literary perceptions and in-sights are based on experience, all names, characters, places, and incidents either are products of the author's imagination or are used fictitiously.

LIBRARY OF CONGRESS CATALOGING-IN-PUBLICATION DATA

[TK]

10 9 8 7 6 5 4 3 2 1
First Edition

for Susan

ONE

IIIIIIIIIIIIIIIIIIIIIIIIIII

He's watching, Bill Sidey thinks. My father is watching me at this very moment. But Bill can't take his eyes off the road, a steep, twisting two-track trail that winds down from the top of the butte to the canyon floor.

A juniper bush scratches the side of the car and Bill winces. Something that sounds more solid than weeds scrapes along the undercarriage. But there's nothing Bill can do other than keep the tires in the ruts and feather the brakes to make sure he doesn't lose control on his descent.

And sure enough, when the road finally levels off and Bill permits himself a look farther ahead, he sees the figure that he's sure has been there all along. A tall, lean white-haired man stands in the open doorway of a twenty-foot house trailer, his hands jammed in the pockets of his faded Levi's. Calvin Sidey, Bill's father. A hawk with prey in sight could not watch more intently.

Bill parks next to the familiar old Ford truck, yet his father makes no move to come forward. Bill climbs out of the car, and when he slams the door behind him, it sets up an echo that bounces from one canyon wall to the other.

He lives here, Bill thinks, so he can see the enemy approach. It's the same thought he's had on the other occasions when he's driven out to his father's home, but this time Bill wonders if even he has that status in his father's eyes.

His father calls out warily, "I didn't know you were coming."

To that Bill has no response. His father doesn't have a telephone. He picks up his mail no more than once or twice a week. How can anyone, son or stranger, notify Calvin Sidey of an impending visit?

His father tries again. "What brings you out this way?"

And that's Calvin Sidey in a sentence: Let's get to it. Well, that suits Bill too. When he looks toward his father, Bill has to shield his eyes against the sun glinting off the trailer's aluminum siding.

"I've got a favor to ask."

His father steps back inside the trailer, but since he doesn't shut and lock the door behind him, Bill understands that he's supposed to follow.

The trailer's interior, even with windows open on every side, must be fifteen degrees hotter than the July afternoon that's already topped ninety degrees. "Can I get you a cup of coffee?" his father asks.

"Coffee? Jesus. No. A glass of water? Please."

The trailer is exactly as Bill remembers it, and why not. It's likely that nothing more than the calendar page has changed since Bill was last here, though he can't recall when that might have been. His father has his life stripped down to the essentials, and for everything that's left he has a hook, shelf, bin, drawer, peg, or rack. Bill guesses that in the cupboard there are no more than one or at most two plates, bowls, glasses, and cups. In the same cupboard will be a can of coffee, a box of oatmeal, a few cans of soup and beans, lard, crackers, flour, sugar, salt, and pepper. Above the two burner stove hang a sauce pan and a frying pan. On a shelf above the neatly made bed is a short row of books, and though Bill can't see the titles, he doesn't have to. These are his father's copies of Virgil, Horace, Juvenal, Ovid, Cicero, Catullus, and Pliny. The homemade gun rack above the door holds his Winchester lever-action .30-30, a twelve-gauge Remington pump shotgun, and a fishing pole. And there's that calendar, hanging right next to the door. It's this year's and the page is turned to the correct month, but Bill wonders if his father knows the date. Even if he does, the day surely doesn't mean "holiday" to him the way it does for most Americans, though it's hard to imagine a man who values independence more than Calvin Sidey.

Bill stands by the small kitchen table, but since his father has not invited him to sit down, Bill doesn't pull out one of the two chairs. And why two, Bill wonders, since his father lives alone and never has guests.

From a pitcher on the counter Calvin Sidey pours water into a glass, then sets the glass on the table next to an open book. Bill can't decipher any of the words on the page because the book is in Latin, a subject Bill never studied in school but which his father has never stopped studying and translating. Also on the table is an ashtray containing a few butts of hand-rolled cigarettes.

Bill brings the glass to his lips and drinks. The water isn't very cold and it has a brassy odor.

"Why don't you move this trailer, Dad? That stand of cotton-woods can't be more than fifty yards away, and if you were parked over there, you'd have some shade."

His father crosses his arms. "You said you had a favor to ask."

Bill is sweating in these close quarters, and he loosens his tie and collar. "Marjorie needs an operation."

"Uh-huh."

"She has to have a hysterectomy. It's an operation to—"

"I know what a hysterectomy is. What I don't know is why you felt you had to come out here and tell me about it in person. How serious is this?"

"She has . . . not tumors, exactly. But growths, painful growths."

"All right," his father says. "I'm sorry to hear this. But you drove all the way out here . . . What's the favor you need?"

"Do you mind if I sit down?" Bill asks, then pulls out a chair before his father can answer.

There's an odor in the trailer that Bill can't quite place, a smell reminiscent of gasoline or fresh paint. He looks around to see if his father has recently painted or varnished something. Then it comes to him. Kerosene. Lacking electricity, his father relies on candles or kerosene lamps. It's 1963, but in many ways his father is living in the nineteenth century. Of course it's stifling inside the trailer, Bill thinks. His father doesn't even have a fan to stir the heat or a refrigerator to keep food cold. And not far from the trailer is an outhouse . . .

"There's a doctor in Missoula who'll perform the operation," Bill says. "Carole—you remember Marjorie's sister?—had the same condition as Marjorie. Same symptoms. Same tests. Apparently it's something that runs in the family. And Carole had the surgery. Before then, she'd tried everything, and she says if it wasn't for the operation, she'd still be suffering."

"Most women would just bite down hard and wait for the misery to pass. Which it will."

"*Most* women?"

"In my experience."

"Something of an expert, are you, Dad?"

His father ignores this question. "Marjorie has to go to Missoula? I know Gladstone's got doctors who can perform a hysterectomy."

Bill has to smile. His father is still loyal to Gladstone, though he turned his back on the town almost thirty years ago.

"How about Mitch McCoy?" his father says. "Last I heard he was still practicing."

"The last you heard? When was that? Dr. McCoy is in a nursing home in Miles City."

"Mitchell McCoy? Are you sure?"

The heat, the long drive, his father's questions . . . Bill Sidey suddenly feels tired. He leans on his hand and rubs his eyes. "Yeah, Dad. I'm sure. Look, I can't pretend to explain it very well. Apparently the Missoula doctor has a special procedure. He doesn't take out the entire womb or something. The point is, Marjorie wants the operation. She *needs* the operation."

"And I reckon you're all set for her to have what she needs."

"We're leaving in a few days."

"Uh-huh."

Bill inhales deeply and then exhales, but the heat seems to prevent his breath from traveling far. "That's what I wanted to ask you about, Dad. Would you be willing to stay with the kids while Marjorie and I are in Missoula?"

His father involuntarily takes a step back. "Have you spoken to your sister about this?"

"Jeanette and I have sort of lost touch. I assume she's still in New Hampshire. We send the Christmas and birthday cards there and they don't come back undeliverable. Of course, we don't get any acknowledgment from her either. How about you?" Bill asks, though he's certain of the answer. "Do you hear from her?"

His father gives a quick shake of his head.

"What I'm asking you for," says Bill, "wouldn't be more than a week. At most."

"You're traveling in a few days, you say?"

He's trying to find a way to say no, Bill thinks. He's out of practice, and he can't find a reason quick enough. Why doesn't he come right out and say it—they're not my kids or my responsibility. He could say it when the children were his own, so what's stopping him now? Suddenly, Bill, who all his life has felt diminished in this man's presence, feels an odd surge of power.

"Ann and Will," says Bill. "In case you're trying to recall their names. Ann's seventeen and Will's eleven."

"I know my grandchildren's names."

"Ann's working at J. C. Penney this summer," Bill continues. "That's why I'm asking you for this favor. Ordinarily Ann could take care of her brother. And take care of the house. But with the hours she's working, Will would be alone too much of the day."

From out of his shirt pocket, his father takes a packet of cigarette papers, and when he looks around for his tin of Sir Walter Raleigh, Bill hurries to offer his father one of his own Camels. The men light their cigarettes, and while this action has given his father an extra minute to think, it's less time than he would have had rolling his own.

"Have you been working, Dad?" There, Bill thinks, he has opened a door through which his father can escape. He can simply excuse himself by saying he has the obligations of a job.

"Not since last fall," his father says. "I helped George Tell move his herd down from summer pasture. I'm sure he moved them back up last month, but I didn't hear from him. Before that? I don't recall."

"We *could* hire a babysitter," Bill says. "A college girl home for the summer perhaps. Though that might embarrass Ann, someone there so close to her age. Or maybe we could find a farm girl. But you know the house, Dad. And the business. And you're—"

Bill isn't sure why he suddenly stops short of uttering the word, especially since it's the word that he came here to say to his father.

"I'm what?"

"Family," says Bill, relieved that the word didn't snag on the way out.

His father draws deep on the Camel, lets the smoke drift from his nostrils, then examines the cigarette as if he's never smoked a tailor-made before. "When did you say you're leaving?" he says.

"Sunday. Right after church. And Dad? I'm not asking you to do anything with the kids. Just to be there. Just in case."

His father walks to the trailer door, opens it, and flicks his cigarette outside. "I'll be there Saturday," he says.

His father remains in the doorway, his hand on the handle of the screen door. Just as Bill understood earlier that he was supposed to follow his father inside the trailer, now he understands that he's expected to leave. "I'll look for you then," Bill says.

He steps out into the shadowless sunlight, and though the air's not moving outside the trailer any more than it was inside—it's the rare calm day in this part of Montana—Bill feels as though his first breath outdoors goes right to the bottom of his lungs.

"And Bill," his father calls after him. "Don't put anyone out of their room. I'll fix up a little space in the basement."

"The basement? Dad . . ."

"It'll be cooler down there."

Cooler? Bill thinks but doesn't say. Yet you live here?

"And it'll give me some privacy," his father adds.

Privacy for what? Bill thinks. "Whatever you say, Dad. I'll see you Saturday."

FROM INSIDE THE TRAILER, Calvin watches his son drive away. He wonders why he said yes to his son's request, which, he can't help noting, was offered without a please and accepted without a thank-you. Hadn't he banished long ago any feelings of obligation to others? Did he say yes simply because of blood? Could he have said no to anyone but his son? Or is this solitary life less endurable than he believes? Maybe he would have listened to any request that tried to bring him back inside the human circle. Well, no point in speculating. He said yes.

The car is out of sight now, but he can hear it, the engine laboring hard as it tries to crest the butte. Shift down, God damn it, Calvin thinks. Though Bill has climbed plenty of hills without his father's help.

Calvin walks back to the table. He stands over the book he'd been reading earlier. He flips pages until he comes to a poem he knows well. The words are in Latin, but in English he recites softly, "Now he is treading that dark road to the place from which they say no one has ever returned." Calvin has to smile to himself. Such portentous lines for a bird.

TWO

||||||||||||||||||||||||

There, right behind those rocks just breaking the river's surface, at the spot where the water swirls and seems to back up on itself, Bill keeps casting. He knows there's deep water there, cool depths that walleye, pike, and bass prefer in this weather. He's thrown spoons, spinners, poppers, jigs, and damn near everything else in his tackle box into this section of the Elk River, but he hasn't had a hit yet.

Not that he minds; he's merely killing time, putting off that inevitable moment when he has to return home and tell his wife about the trip he's taken today. He recalls something that Beverly Lodge once said: "Men—once they have an excuse to go, they're liable to stay gone." He didn't think her remark applied to him, but maybe he's no different from the other men who are in no hurry to go home at the end of the day, the men who would rather stop for a drink or two at the Elks Club or the VFW rather than go see their wives and children.

Bill reels in his line, the current's tug strong enough that he can almost believe he has a fish on the other end. No such luck. Well, he's fished the hell out of this stretch of the river.

He walks perhaps a quarter of a mile upstream, the setting sun throwing his shadow far ahead until it vanishes in the darkening tall grass. He heads for a grove of cottonwoods not far away, a spot on the river he knows well, and not only because he's fished these waters so often over the years. There the river swings wide and slow. Twenty years ago Bill thought he might lose his life there.

That was the summer of 1943, when he and Sleepy Bryant and Chuck McMahon were told they were likely to ship out before the month was out. In the meantime, they fished the Elk River at every opportunity. On that particular day they had driven farther from Gladstone than usual, out to a stretch of river where they'd heard fish were biting. They parked their car near a narrow rickety wooden bridge, and they worked their way downriver to this shady grove. They'd also worked their way through the better part of a case of beer, and by late afternoon Bill left the fishing to his friends and lay down under a cottonwood for a nap.

He woke to the sound of two words—*Don't move*—and Bill's first thought was that a rattlesnake was nearby, and he made sure he moved nothing but his eyes.

Which revealed to him a figure aiming a pump-action .22 at him.

The rifle was in the hands of a teenager, maybe fourteen or fifteen, and tall and sunburned. The hair curling out from his battered straw hat was so blond it was almost white, and the hat was pulled low and cast his eyes entirely in shadow. Over his shoulder he called out to someone Bill couldn't see, "Hey, if I shoot this one here, we can bury him on the spot."

Another voice, deeper and more serious, answered, "Bury him? What in hell for?"

The voice attached itself to another tall blond in a straw hat. He was older than the man pointing the rifle at Bill, and there wasn't much doubt they were brothers. The most important similarity, however, was that he too was armed. His carbine was pointed at Sleepy and Chuck, marching up from the riverbank with their hands raised over their heads.

The younger man asked his brother, "Should I have this one here stick his hands up too?"

"He's laying down, for Christ's sake. He don't need his hands up."

"Was this land posted or something?" Sleepy asked. "We didn't see any signs. We parked up by the road and hiked down here."

"We know where you parked your goddamn car," the older brother said. "And you don't fish around here without we say so."

"You don't own this river," Chuck said. Sleepy's tone had been conciliatory, but Chuck could barely contain his anger. "We don't need your permission to fish here."

"Then how come you got your hands in the air like a scared sonofabitch?"

That remark brought a giggle from the younger brother. For some reason, his good humor was especially frightening. The older brother's surly attitude seemed more in keeping with the situation; the younger one's laughter was the behavior of someone whose next action could not be predicted.

Still lying flat in the cottonwood's shade, Bill asked, "Either of you fellows work with the Slash Nine?"

"What the hell's it to you?" the older brother asked.

"I know this is Slash Nine country," Bill answered, in a voice far too cheerful to belong to a man with a gun pointed at him, "and I thought you boys might be with their outfit."

"We don't work for nobody," the younger man said hesitantly.

"Just thought I'd ask," Bill said. "My old man rides with the Slash Nine. You know him? Cal Sidey?"

"Never heard of him," the older man said, but it didn't matter. Bill's willingness to name himself had made him impossible to kill.

The brothers spat out a few more threats—"Don't ever wet a line along this stretch of the river or you'll find yourself facedown in the water"; "Any fish you caught you leave 'em on the stringer; they're ours now"—but their venom had lost its potency, and they soon sent Bill and his friends on their way.

Later, back in Gladstone, after Bill, Chuck, and Sleepy told others about their run-in, they learned about the Hanlon brothers, owners of a small ranch that shared some fence line with the Slash Nine. The Hanlons had a reputation for being not only maniacally territorial but also for black-hearted meanness. Rumor had it they had once cut the balls off an Indian and left him in a ditch, possibly to bleed to death. Chuck swore that he would return to that span of the river and have his revenge on the brothers. Maybe on his first furlough he'd load up a truck with Gladstone's toughest men, and they'd give the Hanlons the beatings they deserved. Chuck McMahon was not inclined to bluster or boast; that he never followed through on his vow had nothing to do with a lack of courage or resolve and everything to do with the fact that he left most of his right leg on an island in the South Pacific.

Bill never knew for certain if the mention of his father's name had anything to do with extricating him and his friends from their difficult situation. The Slash Nine was a huge outfit, and Bill's father was just one more hired hand, exactly what he had been since the day he left Bill and his sister when they were children. But Bill had invoked the Sidey name, and because he did, he has often wondered, did he save himself, or was it the father who saved the son? For that matter, back at his father's trailer, was the son asking the father for help, or was the son trying to help the father?

THE SUN HAS SET, and darkness is leaping forth from inside the grove of cottonwoods and the thickets of sagebrush, snowberry, and chokecherry. Nighthawks are swooping invisibly overhead, their presence revealed only by their *peenk, peenk* calls. The river itself still shines, its surface somehow able to find light that has all but vanished from the sky. Bill reels in his line again, this time for good. He hooks his lure through a rod guide and begins the long walk back to his car.

Why doesn't his father make his home in a spot like this? Near fresh water, shade, and shelter from the wind. With heavier woods right over there, with a supply of blown-down and deadfall trees and limbs that would offer winter fuel. This is a site that Bill would choose, and solitude aplenty if that's what a man wants. But this is just one more useless observation about the difference between him and his father.

IF HE KEEPS DRIVING, he can pull into his driveway in no more than ten minutes. Nevertheless, Bill decides to pull off the road on top of one of the bluffs that overhang the city of Gladstone. He climbs out of the car and walks closer to the edge of the butte, accidentally kicking an empty beer can. He's sure there are more in the vicinity.

He lights a cigarette. From this height Bill can see the conflu-
ences—the Elk River, Willow Creek, the Northern Pacific railroad
line, and mile after mile of rolling grassland—that led to the for-
mation of a community down there in the first place, and in the
middle of the panorama is the city itself with its glowing, winking
lights. He has a perfect view of the lights that, this year, spangle the
night sky over Gladstone for the second time inside of three weeks.
The exploding rockets, star bursts, and fountains leave a much different impression when a man looks down rather than up at them.
You'd think they'd look puny with the vastness of the night sky as
backdrop, but the opposite is true. It's all the land surrounding this
exhibition that makes it seem small and a little sad. Perhaps this is
why no other spectators are parked up here tonight.

The display won't last long. Gladstone celebrated its seventy-
fifth anniversary on June 16, and last winter the Rotary Club voted
in favor of an unequal division of the annual budget for fireworks:
seventy percent for the town's birthday and thirty percent for today,
July 4, 1963.

There—that probably represents the grand finale. The cottony
booms that reach him after those flashes are the loudest so far, and
nothing else has reached as high, glowed as brightly, or lingered
as long as those red, white, and blue sparks. His wife and son and
daughter are down there someplace, perhaps close enough to smell
the black powder and trace the pattern of smoke in the aftermath
of each explosion, and though Bill knows he belongs with them,
he still cannot make himself move. The car's cooling engine ticks
impatiently, the stars recapture the night sky, but Bill remains on
the top of the hill. As soon as he returns home, he'll have to tell his
family that Calvin is coming for a visit.

THREE

||||||||||||||||||||||||||||||||||||

In order to see to the back of the refrigerator, Bill pushes aside the wedge of watermelon, the bowl of creamed cucumbers, the tinfoil-covered tub of potato salad, and the half-eaten ham—all items he returned to the racks only moments before. "I could have sworn I had another beer in here," he says.

"One isn't enough?" Marjorie asks. She knows her husband's habits well; Bill drinks infrequently and seldom more than a single beer.

"I spent part of the day in Calvin Sidey's company," Bill says, "in his oven of a home. So no, one's not enough." He means the remark as a joke, but it elicits no laughter. He gives up on the idea of a second beer and returns to his place at the kitchen table.

Marjorie stands across the room from him, her arms crossed as if she feels a chill. That, of course, is impossible. Nightfall has not brought any relief from the day's heat. "I just don't understand." She speaks so slowly even the last word comes out as two. "I thought when we talked about this before, we decided it wasn't a good idea."

Only now does it register on Bill that his wife has dressed herself for the holiday. She's wearing a sleeveless red bandanna blouse knotted at her midriff, blue pedal pushers, and white sneakers that might have been Ann's. Her dark freshly curled hair has been combed out to frame her small, pretty heart-shaped face. Yes, her pretty face, even when it's darkened by a frown, as it is now.

"I've reconsidered," says Bill. "I think this will work. And to everyone's benefit."

Marjorie crosses the room, pulls out a chair, and sits down wearily across from him. She takes off her glasses, and she rubs her eyes. When Bill told her of the arrangements he made for his father's visit, she said nothing. But now she's had time to worry over all the implications of her father-in-law's visit.

"You *think* it will work? You want to trust the care of our children to a man they barely know, who barely knows them, a man who abandoned his own children . . ."

Bill lights a cigarette, even though each one he's smoked in the last few hours has left a bitter, dusty taste in his mouth. "Why is it, Marjorie, that I've been able to forgive my father and you haven't? I was the one he left."

"Maybe because there are some things people shouldn't be forgiven for."

"Is that," Bill asks, "for us to decide?"

For the moment, Bill holds the advantage. Marjorie's religion teaches that it falls only to God to judge, and it's a lesson she tries to obey. In consternation, she rubs her hand across the tabletop as though there are wrinkles in the Formica that could be smoothed out like a tablecloth.

"Besides, it's not just for the kids," Bill says. "I think we'd both feel more comfortable knowing a man is in the house. But he knows the business too and probably better than Don or Tom. After all, Dad used to be in real estate."

"But he's not in the business anymore," Marjorie quickly points out. "He's a cowboy, an old cowboy who's never shown the slightest interest in his grandchildren. Why would we leave Ann and Will in the care of a man who might walk off?"

"That happened once and under special circumstances, Marjorie. He deserves a second chance."

"A *chance*—do you hear what you're saying? You want to take a chance with Ann and Will? And he's had plenty of chances, hasn't he? He didn't have to leave, but he didn't have to stay away either. He could have come back to you and Jeanette at any time."

"You know as well as I do," Bill says sternly, "what kept him away."

"Even grief has its limits."

"And I'm not talking about grief alone."

"You're so quick to make excuses for him."

"Look, he's out there in the middle of the prairie in that little trailer. I'm concerned about him. It's no use telling me I shouldn't be, that I owe him nothing. I can't help it. If something happened to him, he could lie there for days, for weeks, and never be discovered. I'd like to see if I can't get him to come back to town."

That remark instantly erases the weariness from Marjorie's face, and just as quickly Bill realizes he's made a mistake.

"To live *here?*" she says.

"No, no—"

"Because if that's what you mean—"

"That's not what I have in mind. Not at all. Just . . . someplace a little closer, so I wouldn't have to drive for hours just to check up on him."

"Is that what he wants?"

"Well, he said yes to coming here so maybe he's changing his mind about some things."

Marjorie shakes her head. "This sounds like some kind of plan for redemption."

Bill smiles. "I can't think of anything that would matter less to Calvin Sidey. Redemption isn't in his vocabulary."

"I didn't say *he* wanted it. But I certainly believe it's something you want for him."

My God, her aim could be unerring at times! Bill has no choice but to skate around her remark.

"Besides," Bill says, "once he spends some time with the kids . . ."

"Yes?"

"You don't think our kids are lovable enough to melt any heart?" Bill says and laughs. He adds, "You could still have the operation here."

"You know I want that doctor Carole had. And I want to be free of this."

Bill thinks but doesn't say, Yes, but Carole only had to drive across town for her operation while you have to travel close to four hundred miles for yours.

As if she can hear his thoughts, Marjorie says, "Carole tried everything, and if she wouldn't have found him she'd still be in misery."

Like I am. She doesn't have to say the words. The insinuation is clear, and no matter how skeptical Bill might be about the necessity for Marjorie's operation, much less having it in Missoula, he does not want to be the kind of husband who stands in the way of his wife's hope for good health.

"I'm already on the surgery schedule," says Marjorie, her voice trembling and her eyes brimming with tears.

Bill reaches across the table to lay his hand on top of his wife's. Her flesh is surprisingly cool. "We'll stay with the original plan."

And just as quickly the advantage is back to Marjorie. "Your father wasn't part of the original plan."

"You know I was never real comfortable with the idea of leaving the kids alone. I know Ann's not the sort to be throwing wild parties, but putting her in charge would mean giving her a lot of responsibility. Think of what you were like at that age."

He immediately wishes he could take his words back. Marjorie hates being reminded how at sixteen, her father and mother sent her to live for the summer with an elderly aunt in Billings. The old woman had been ill, and Marjorie was supposed to help with the cooking and cleaning. Anyway, that was the reason Mr. and Mrs. Randolph gave to family and friends for sending their daughter away, although the truth was they were desperate to break up Marjorie's relationship with that twenty-year-old cowboy. They had tried forbidding their daughter to see him—he was too old for her, too wild, the two of them were too serious—but Marjorie and Tully could not be kept apart. The Randolphs hoped that miles would accomplish what all their prohibitions, all their punishments, and all their pleas could not. But Tully had followed Marjorie to Billings, and by the time he moved on—or was chased off by Marjorie's aunt—he and Marjorie had decided that they would never return to Gladstone. At the end of August, once Tully could collect a good portion of his summer wages, he would come for Marjorie and together they would leave Billings for a destination where they could make their own new life. Young people always make such promises and plans, but maybe that one would have worked out had Tully not gone back to a job that required him to fix a stretch of fence during a thunderstorm. You would have thought that a nearby stand of lodgepole pines presented an easier target for that lightning bolt.

When Marjorie returned to high school that fall, like everyone else, Bill noticed the change in her. She was no longer that bright-eyed, laughing, lovely girl who used to dash out of the building in winter months with her coat unbuttoned because she couldn't wait to meet her boyfriend. Instead, she trudged listlessly through the halls and through her classes as if she had been awakened from a drugged sleep.

Rumors about the altered Marjorie Randolph raced around Gladstone. One version had her running off to Billings the previous summer to have Tully Heckaman's baby, which she then gave up for adoption. Another whispered story said that she tried to poison herself after Tully's death. Then about the time of graduation Bill saw another change come over her. Suddenly it seemed as though Marjorie was trying to make Tully's untamed spirit her own. She drank, she smoked, she went out with men and boys who were willing to tell their friends what Marjorie Randolph would let them get away with. When Bill finally stirred up the courage to ask Marjorie to go out with him and later to marry him, he believed she said yes not only because he offered her security but also because he understood a thing or two about loss and abandonment.

But if Bill's remark takes Marjorie back to her own past, she doesn't acknowledge it. Coolly she says, "Beverly is right next door. It's not exactly like the kids would be without adult supervision."

"And she'll still be here," Bill replies. "I'll tell her about Dad staying at the house and ask her if she'll keep an eye on him and the kids."

Marjorie puts her glasses back on and looks squarely at her husband. "Suppose he starts drinking again."

"It's not going to happen, honey. Not after all this time. He hasn't had a drink in over ten years."

"That you know of."

Rather than concede that point, as he must, Bill says nothing.

Up and down the block, firecrackers still snap, singly or serially, and bottle rockets still hiss, but more and more time passes between these small explosions. Soon Gladstone will finish its celebrating, and once again it will be heat and not noise that stands between the townspeople and their easy sleep. Marjorie looks off expectantly, as though she's counting off the minutes between detonations.

"They could come with us," Bill suggests cautiously. "And I could tell Dad he isn't needed."

Marjorie shakes her head. "It would be too hard for them. They couldn't come to the hospital."

"Ann's old enough."

"But they'd never let her take off work for God knows how many days. She'd come back and find she's out of a job, and Penney's is just too good an opportunity. This is something she can keep working at right through the school year—"

Bill holds his hands up in surrender. "You're right. I know. We talked about that."

Marjorie sniffs as if the odor of black powder has drifted into her kitchen. "He'll be here Saturday?"

"Right. Saturday afternoon or evening."

"Maybe I'll fix fried chicken. That's something we can have cold if he doesn't get here until late."

"Fried chicken sounds good."

"Maybe," says Marjorie, "a ham for Sunday."

"Which they could have for leftovers on Monday."

Marjorie nods, as if settling on those menu items has resolved every difference between them. "Well, I'm going up," she says. "When you come, leave the stove light on for Ann." Then Marjorie stands up, walks around to Bill, and kisses him lightly on the lips. But she doesn't leave the room. "I guess I still don't understand," she says, "why he agreed to come . . ."

"Give him some credit, Marjorie. He's an old man. He might want to make amends."

Not that Bill believes this for a moment.

FOUR

||||||||||||||||||||||||||||||||

Ann Sidey does not look back when she turns the corner and starts to walk up Fourth Street. She doesn't have to. She hears the car make the same turn, lugging along in second gear, its headlights off. She knows it's following her, yet so far not trying to overtake her. The car radio is playing—Lesley Gore singing "It's My Party"—so Ann decides to concentrate on the song. She'll walk faster only if the radio gets louder, and she won't break into a run unless the car pulls to the curb alongside her. Then she'll take off across the lawns. The Halls live halfway up the block, and if she can make it to their house, she'll bang on their door until they let her in.

"Cry if I want to, cry if I want to . . ."

The car is a black 1952 Ford Tudor, and Ann is familiar with many of the ways its owner has customized the car. He has done things to the engine she doesn't entirely understand, things with valves and carburetors and plugs and points, and he's changed the exhaust system so it growls a warning even when the car is standing still. He moved the gearshift from the steering column to the floor, and the top of the shifter is an oval of wood crudely carved to look like the head of a ferocious Indian warrior. The seat covers are rough wool and can scratch the backs of your bare arms and legs, and the knob on the window crank and the door handle can gouge into your back if you're pushed up against the passenger door. Ann knows that if you push the first button on the radio, the station will jump to Miles City; the second will bring in Billings; the third Dickinson, North Dakota; and the fourth and best, KOMA in Oklahoma City. Ann knows the sound the cigarette lighter makes when it pops out, and she knows the look of it close-up as it glows red-orange.

The sidewalk climbs and curves, and Ann moves to the edge of the cement, almost stepping into the weeds of the vacant lot. Here, without a house staring down at her, Ann has to be ready to run. The air feels slightly cooler as she walks past the open field, and the sound of the car's engine throbs all the way over to the next block. But she passes safely, and the next house not only has its porch light on but its curtains open as well.

Off to her left a Roman candle fizzles into flight—did it come from McDonoughs' backyard? It must have been a dud because it didn't attain any height but instead sparked and spiraled erratically into the lower branches of a curbside tree.

That sudden flare is enough to distract Ann and prevent her from noticing the cherry bomb that rolls into the gutter only a few paces behind her. By the time she registers the hiss of the fuse, the detonation is only a half second away.

She has walked unperturbed through a day of explosions, but this *blam!*—a sound she feels in her chest—frightens a shriek from her, and she starts to run as if a shell from an enemy's artillery has burst at her feet.

Between two houses she runs, and once she's away from the streetlights and into the backyards, she can no longer see where her feet will fall, but she does not slow. In the hour past midnight, dew has begun to form, and she slips and sinks on the wet turf. She crosses into another yard, and when she does, she alerts a dog back by the alley—a big dog by the sound of its bark. Its chain rattles and snaps taut, and Ann veers in another direction. She needs to stay away from the alley anyway in case he circles around and drives behind the houses.

What trips her she isn't sure—a croquet hoop? a sprinkler? a wire fence around a flower bed?—but she goes sprawling and skids forward on her hands and knees. The odor of wet grass fills her nostrils, and for a moment she's tempted just to lie still and hope she won't be seen. But her white slacks will probably glow against the black-green lawn, and she'd rather be chased down than to have him come up behind her, grab her ankles, and drag her off to God knows where.

When Ann rises and begins to run again, she takes it a bit slower and lifts her feet higher, and soon she comes to the end of the block and a familiar sight—the white shed in the Rhinebohns' backyard, and she's sure of the landmark because before Mr. Rhinebohn began to store his garden tools in there that little building had been Mary Rhinebohn's playhouse, and all through grade school, Ann, Mary, Karen Kemper, and Judy Falk used it for their clubhouse. Then, in the summer before seventh grade, Mary drowned in the Elk River, and the following year Mr. Rhinebohn moved out the toys and the play dishes and old dresses and moved in his shovels, rakes, hoe, and mower. Ann has not been inside since Mary was alive, but she's sure she can still work the latch on the bottom half of the double door, and if she crawls inside she can probably make her way to the back wall and find the spot where she, Mary, Karen, and Judy wrote their initials in purple crayon.

But she doesn't have to hide. Not yet. Not now. The sense of being pursued is gradually leaving her, and if she stands still for just another minute or two, she might be ready to step back into the light. She's only a block from home, close enough to feel not only that safety is reachable but also to feel a little power flowing back in her direction. Seventeen years of living in this rectangle of rectangles—the right angle geometry of intersections and streets, of sidewalks and alleys, of lawns and houses—now counts for something. Sometimes she can feel her heart quicken with fear when she thinks about her little town's isolation, how frail and temporary it seems in comparison to the hundreds—thousands!—of miles of shapeless prairie that surround Gladstone. How comforting it must be, she thinks at those times, to live in a huge city, block after block of sheltering bricks and boards. But right now she's close enough to being inside that she dares to step into the open.

Through the space between the Rhinebohns' and the Winters', Ann walks calmly, but when she reaches the sidewalk, even though there's no sign of the car or its driver, she breaks into a run again, and she does not slow until she turns into her own driveway.

The light is on over the side door, and she stands in that circle of luminescence and waits for her heart rate to return to normal. If her parents are still up, she doesn't want to have to answer their questions about why she's breathing so hard.

Overhead, moths and insects whirr, flutter, and crawl around the porch light, and Ann retreats into the darkness to get away from them, especially the thick-bodied, clicking June bugs. She steps back into a sulfurous smell, and it takes her a moment to locate its source: Her little brother Will has been lighting snakes in the driveway again, those long tubes of black ash that writhe mysteriously forth from a tiny pill when set aflame. The odor is not merely unpleasant but disgusting—it reminds her of farts. And her mother hates the black smudges the snakes leave on the concrete. Poor Will. While his friends have moved on to firecrackers and bottle rockets, he's still lighting snakes and waving sparklers.

ANN DOES EXACTLY AS her mother taught her, filling the washtub first, then pouring in a cup of Oxydol and a half cup of bleach, the smell of which stings her nostrils. She takes off her slacks and drops them into the water. As they slowly sink they seem to turn gray, and Ann knows the stain won't come out. Maybe she can cut them off and make shorts out of them.

She looks down at her bare legs. She's been working thirty-five to forty hours a week in the Boy's Department at J. C. Penney's, so she doesn't have many opportunities to get out in the sun. Nevertheless, she still has a tan line, two, in fact, one in the middle of her thigh from her in shorts and another, much higher, from the fewer occasions when she's been out in her bathing suit down at the river. That was where he and his friends were drinking beer and eating fried chicken, when Ann and Kitty walked by. "I'd like to take a bite out of those thighs," he'd said. Ann knew he was talking about her, because he was looking right at her, and then he tossed a chicken bone that landed in the sand at her feet. That was before she started at Penney's, when she could spend as much time down at the river as she liked. Maybe she should have gotten angry at his remark, but she knew who Monte Hiatt was and what her friends had been saying about him. He came from Laramie, and he moved to Gladstone because his parents split up and his mother's cousin lived here and he gave Mrs. Hiatt a job in his furniture store. The new boy was going to be a junior, but right from the start he hung out with the seniors, especially the car guys. Was Monte Hiatt a hood? She couldn't say for sure. That hair . . . and he smoked. He had his own car, and from what the other boys said, it was impressive, but Ann understood little about cars or the worship of them. What she did understand was what the girls meant when they talked about him. Monte Hiatt was cute, and according to Laurie Dwyer who lived on his block, he was nice. Cute and nice. There were not two other words in the English language that could be applied to a new boy from Laramie that would make him more appealing.

And hers were the thighs he wanted to take a bite from. Ann had laughed over his comment. Not in front of him, of course. But she and Kitty both burst out laughing as soon as they had walked far enough along the sand that the boys couldn't hear them. Take a bite—it was exactly the kind of stupid thing a boy might think was clever or flirty or even romantic.

She doesn't know how it could have happened without tearing her slacks, but one of her knees is scraped raw. The first layer of skin has peeled back, exposing a wet, pink layer. A few years ago a neighbor cut his hand with a power saw, and her father had taken him to the hospital. "I was surprised," her father said, "there wasn't much blood, but that blade cut right through the meat to the bone."

Meat. Is that what's pinkly showing under that scraped-away first layer of skin? Is that what he wanted to bite his way down to? Ann knew he wanted to put his hands on her—in her—but maybe it was more . . . maybe it was worse. He wanted to rip her apart, to explode her into pieces. Isn't that what he was doing when he tossed that firecracker in her direction?

Oh, she has to stop! She's going too far, just being melodramatic as her mother says Ann can be.

Footsteps thump down the basement stairs, and Ann grabs a towel from the laundry basket and wraps it around her waist. Her father thrusts his head around the corner and peers into the laundry room.

"Hey, sunshine," he says. "Kind of late to be washing clothes, isn't it?"

"I got a grass stain on my new pants. I thought I'd better soak them before it sets."

He asks, "Enjoy the fireworks?"

"I guess." Ann doubts that her father has come down here to make small talk. In an attempt to hurry him to his real reason for being here, she stages an elaborate yawn that turns into the real thing.

Her father takes his cue. "Do you have to work tomorrow?"

"Not until noon, but I told Kitty I'd come over to her house early and help her paint her room."

"Smart—do that work before the day heats up." He clears his throat and pats his shirt pocket for the pack of cigarettes that isn't there. "Look," he says, "there's been a slight change of plans. Your mom and I are still going to Missoula as scheduled, but instead of you and Will being by yourselves, I've asked your grandfather to come and stay with you. Now, before you say a word—this isn't for you. God knows you're old enough to stay alone. But Will needs somebody close by, and with you at work so much of the time . . . Besides, it's not fair to ask you to give up your summer freedom to care for your little brother."

Her summer freedom—it's all Ann can do not to laugh out loud. She can't walk through her own neighborhood without looking worriedly over her shoulder. She says, "I don't mind."

"I know. You never said a word of complaint. But I just think this is a better arrangement. And again—it's for your brother. It's not because we don't trust you or think you can't handle things. You understand that, don't you?"

"Okay. Sure."

It's her father who doesn't understand. Ann isn't angry or offended that their grandfather is coming to stay with her and Will. She's *nervous*—wouldn't anyone be if a stranger was coming to live within your walls? For that's what her grandfather is to Ann. He lives alone out on the prairie in his little trailer, and he almost never comes to Gladstone, even though the town was once his home. Ann can't even be sure when she last saw him. Four years ago? Five? He came to Gladstone to attend a funeral, and before he drove back to his trailer he stopped at the Sidey home for supper. She remembers a tall white-haired man in a black suit striding up their front walk, a man who looked so stern as he approached the house that Ann wondered if the family was in some kind of trouble. Oh, it has to be at least five years, and when her father introduced her, he said, "You remember Grandpa Sidey, don't you?" and though Ann nodded yes, she couldn't be sure. And now that man will be staying in their house. What will she say to him?

Now it's Ann's father's turn to yawn. "You won't spend the whole night down here, will you?"

"I'm just going to soak my pants a little while longer."

"Okay. Good night, sweetheart."

He's almost out of the laundry room when Ann calls her father back. "Dad?"

Her father turns to her with such an innocently expectant look she immediately realizes she can't say what's on her mind. That's the face of a father who wants to hear his daughter say that she's glad he's home or that she doesn't think this year's fireworks were as good as last year's . . . How can she say to that face, Daddy, someone's after me—he wants to blow me up, rip me apart, eat me alive.

"What is it, honey?"

"It's been so long since Grandpa lived in town—does he even know how to do it?"

"He's out of practice, that's for sure, so he'll probably need some help. You'll get him over the rough parts, won't you?"

She nods.

"And you'll be patient with him?" He laughs when he says this, and while she isn't sure if he's serious, she nods at this too. But isn't that the kind of remark that her father should have been making to her grandfather about his grandchildren?

"Okay. Good night again." He starts to leave, and though Ann does not call him back, he returns to the laundry room.

He knows, she thinks. I don't have to find the words; *he knows*.

"You didn't happen to take a beer from the refrigerator, did you?"

"I didn't," Ann says.

"Of course you didn't. And I'm not going to wake your brother to ask him!" He laughs again as though that's the punch line to a joke everyone knows.

FIVE

In the alley behind his home, Will Sidey smooths a circle in the dirt. The sun has not yet reached mid-morning height, but the pebbles he picks out of his circle are warm to the touch.

He puts a firecracker—nothing more powerful than a ladyfinger—into the center of the circle and then places an empty, upside down Butter-Nut coffee can over the firecracker, making sure to leave as much of the fuse as possible sticking out from the can's rim.

Will touches the fuse with the smoldering punk he's stuck into the dirt, and then scurries back a good ten feet. There's a quick sizzling sound like spit, but no explosion—the can must have pinched off the fuse. Will is about to step forward to investigate when a voice stops him.

"Jesus. You think you're far enough away?"

Coming down the alley are three boys close to Will in age. Like Will, they all wear sneakers, jeans, and T-shirts. For reasons none of them can recall, they've decided to favor the Cincinnati Reds this year, so they've cut off the sleeves of their T-shirts in imitation of the uniform of their favorite team. Only Stuart Kinder, the tallest of the three, wears a Reds cap; the other two wear caps with ironed-on *B*'s because Boyd Insurance sponsors their little league team. Will is bareheaded, though he also plays for the Boyd Bulldogs.

Will has just turned away from his coffee can circle and is walking toward his friends when there's a tiny, pinging explosion behind him. He jumps, and Stuart points at him and laughs. "What the hell was that—a ladyfinger? One of those fuckers went off in my hand last year." He wiggles the fingers of his right hand. "You don't see nothing missing, do you?"

The coffee can still stands bottom up in the middle of the circle, but Will only stares at it. He jams his hands into the pockets of his jeans in case the trembling in his hands is visible. If his friends hadn't appeared at that moment, Will would have lifted the can to investigate why his firecracker hadn't gone off. He doesn't care what Stuart said; Will is sure that firecrackers—even ladyfingers—can do real damage. What if he would have put his face down there because he thought the firecracker was a dud—he could have lost an eye!

"You should light a whole pack under there," Bobby Mueller says. "I bet that can would jump around like it was dancing."

"I blew a chunk out of a soup can with a Silver Salute," says Glen Spiese.

"Where'd you get Silver Salutes?" asks Stuart.

"My cousin goes up to Canada every summer. He brings back a whole shitload of stuff you can't get here."

"Lemme know the next time he goes. I'll put in my own order."

Will finally lifts his Butter-Nut can but slowly, as if he fears another explosive might still be under there, its fuse burning at its own willed speed.

"Hey, Will," Bobby says, "you still got that can of beer?"

Under the can is nothing but paper, shredded into scraps tinier than any hand could tear. "It's hidden in my closet," Will says.

"So it ain't cold," Glen says.

"No, my closet is refrigerated, shit-for-brains."

"My old man says drinking warm beer is like drinking piss."

"He'd know, I guess."

"Fuck you."

Stuart loops a finger through a belt loop of Will's jeans and tugs him to his feet. "It don't matter. Go get it. We can stick it in the river, and it'll get cold in no time."

"The river? I thought we were going to play ball."

"We ain't got enough guys," Bobby says.

"Not even for workup?"

"Gotta have at least five, and even then it ain't that great."

"Did you try the Lucas twins?"

"The Lucases—shit." Stuart spits in the dust. "We ain't that hard up."

"Besides," Glen says, "I heard my brother say there's maybe going to be a party down at the sandbar."

"My mom doesn't really let me go down to the river," Will says.

"So don't tell her. Get your fishing rod and say you're going to Willow Creek."

As if to close off the discussion, Stuart kicks the coffee can across the alley where it comes to rest against a stalk of rhubarb in Mr. Neaves's garden. "Yeah, don't tell her nothin'. But get that beer."

Will walks across his yard, taking it slow in order to give himself time to think up a reason he has to stay close to home today. It's not his parents who don't want Will going to the river but Will himself, although he's sure his mother and father would forbid him from going if they had any knowledge of what went on there.

For one thing, it's a dangerous place. The river's currents twist like snakes, and a channel where the slow water was no higher than your waist last week might now be up to your neck and trying hard to pull you under. Just a few years ago a friend of Ann's drowned, and she had been wading out to a sandbar where her father was waiting for her.

Will and his friends have taken to hanging around the edges of the beer parties the town's teenagers hold on the river's sandbars and in the cottonwood groves. As the parties have grown wilder, he and his friends have ventured closer, hoping to steal beers or cigarettes. On a few occasions, Stuart has even flirted with the high school girls, using at first his freckled innocence to amuse them and then catching them off guard with requests for everything from cigarettes to peeks down their swimsuits. Most of the time, however, Will and his friends remain on the fringe and watch, which is both exciting and frustrating.

Just a few weeks ago, the river's level dropped sufficiently to create a new sandbar south of town, a location perfect for parties since it not only allowed cars to drive across a shallow channel, but it also afforded a perfect view of the road by which the sheriff might approach. Will, Stuart, and Glen found their own grandstand, a newly carved bank where they could sit among the cottonwoods and look down at the teenagers as they splashed their way out to the sandbar. Two bluffs upriver, Blackfeet were supposed to have cornered a group of settlers a hundred years ago, some of whom tried to escape by leaping into the river. Will had just been imagining what it was like, to have to choose between drowning and being scalped, when Glen punched his arm.

"Lookit, lookit!"

Wading through water that didn't quite come to their knees were three girls in bathing suits. The sun glinting and reflecting off the water showed all three girls to their best advantage, but the girl in the lead—taller than the other two and statuesque in a white bathing suit—looked regal as she crossed the water.

"Jesus Christ, Sidey," Stuart said, "is that your fucking sister?"

Will's first impulse was to deny it, not only because he didn't want Stuart and Glen looking at Ann that way but also because he didn't immediately recognize his sister—not with her hair bunched up on top of her head like that, not with that gait—the way she lifted her knees reminded him of a prancing horse caught in slow motion. And not in that swimsuit—did Mom and Dad know how she looked in it?

"That's her all right," Glen said. "And the one with the fat ass is Janice Grand, and I'm pretty sure the other one is Kitty McGregor." Glen pulled himself closer to the edge of the bank as though he needed those few extra inches to be sure of his identification. "Yeah. That's her. My brother said Ronnie Dillard finger-fucked Janice Grand."

"Shit, Sidey," Stuart said, "where's your sister been hiding herself?"

"She's working at Penney's this summer."

Stuart clapped Will on the top of the head. "Numb nuts. I mean why ain't she ever around when I come over? Like just coming out of the shower or something?"

"You ever spy on her when she's in the can?" Glen asked.

"Hey, hey, where's her room?" Stuart said. "Is she on the first floor?"

Will shook his head. "She's upstairs."

"We ought to rig up something so we can spy on her," Stuart said.

"Fix her curtains maybe, so they don't close all the way," Glen suggested.

"Or Sidey can call us when she's taking a bath and we can peek through the keyhole."

"You guys. She's my sister . . ."

"And how did an ugly little fucker like you get a sister who looks like that?" Stuart asked.

Glen said, "Her hair looks sort of reddish. Is her pussy hairs that color?"

"Who cares? I'd just like to stick my face in her snatch."

Though vaguely troubling, most of this Will understood only dimly. Stuart and Glen both had older brothers, and as a result, Will's friends were far better educated in sexual matters than Will. He acted as though he knew what they were talking about, but most of the time he felt as if he had been absent or asleep when all this essential information was given out. He was determined not to ask, however. He hadn't understood long division at first either, and now arithmetic was one of his best subjects.

On that day at the river, he didn't quite get what Stuart meant, but he was reasonably certain the reference was not to Ann's breasts—and at that moment they were the part of his sister's anatomy he couldn't stop staring at. They looked like—he couldn't think of any other comparison—a movie star's!

Will reaches the back door, and he still hasn't thought up an excuse not to accompany his friends to the river. He enters the kitchen where his mother is shaking scouring powder into the sink.

"Your friends were here," she says. "I told them you were out in the alley. Did they find you?"

Will wishes he could arrange something with his mother whereby, unless he tells her otherwise, she will not tell his friends where he is.

"Yeah. We're going fishing, I guess."

"Your father said you were going to play baseball."

"We don't have enough guys."

"You can't just play catch?"

"All day? No."

"I was just asking. I don't know what your rules are."

Even though his mother does not look up from her scrubbing, Will can tell his response wounds her. As the time for her operation draws closer, she's quicker to register both irritation and pain.

"We're going to Willow Creek," Will volunteers.

"Well, I hope you catch lots of fish."

Will is almost out of the kitchen when he turns to ask, "Is Ann working today?" He tries to make it sound as though his question is simply an afterthought.

"Until five thirty. Why?"

"I just wanted to ask her about something."

"Anything I can answer for you?"

"It isn't that important."

He climbs the stairs to his room, closes the door behind him, and goes into his closet where the can of Schlitz is hidden inside a shoe box and under layers of green plastic army men. He transfers the beer to his tackle box, but before he leaves the house, Will checks the bathroom door. Just as he thought: The house has been remodeled over the years, and the lock is no longer the type that has a keyhole.

SIX

|||||||||||||||||||||

The day that Calvin Sidey knew would eventually come has finally arrived: When he drives into Gladstone, there are more places and faces unfamiliar to him than familiar. That Chevrolet dealership with its snapping banner and rows of sun-glinting windshields occupies the space where a feedlot used to be. Joe Tidwell had a little saw mill right where Meissner Appliances is now perched. C. C. Hurley used to have his blacksmith shop there. And that office building over there occupies a space that used to be a vacant lot, and it was where the Haskells would stretch out the hides of the coyotes they killed. By God, the youngest Haskell boy—what the hell was his name?—had a nose for sniffing out coyote dens. That gathering of young people in front of the Range Rider Cafe—would they be the grandchildren or the great-grandchildren of men and women Calvin Sidey used to know? Chances are just as good that they all have last names unfamiliar to him. And that quartet of men standing in the shade of the Farm and Ranch National Bank, all of them in shirt-sleeves and ties and two of them with pearl-gray Stetsons and two with straw fedoras? These are probably Gladstone's current shakers and makers, and Calvin doesn't recognize a single one of them, nor any other man, woman, or child on the sidewalk. There was a time when anyone he drove past would likely raise a hand in greeting.

Not only did he once know every street, store front, and build-ing, he could feel as though he had something to do with this town becoming what it was. Hell, they're practically the same age. He sold the lot that the Nash Finch is built on. He helped Clarence Beall swing the financing for that apartment complex on the cor-ner of Third and Front. Calvin Sidey helped get the bridge built that now connects Gladstone's north and south sides. And maybe there's still a family or two living in a house that Sam Dellum's construction company built in partnership with Sidey Real Estate. Calvin gave the Olivet Lutheran Church's board of directors a good price on a lot when they wanted to expand and add on a Sunday school wing. He was on the school board when Oscar Kershaw was hired as superintendent. And Calvin was still on the board when that high school history teacher was fired after having an affair with the school secretary. He can still remember the year—1927—because the teacher's name was Lindberg, the name that was on every American's lips that year. Although the teacher spelled his name without the *h*, he still believed he might be a cousin to Charles, and when it was announced that the famous aviator would visit Boise, the teacher went there in hopes of introducing himself to the most famous man in the world. It was while Phil Lindberg was in Idaho that the secretary confessed their affair to another teacher, and by the time Lindberg returned to Gladstone, the school board had already convened, and the teacher was out of a job. In the years since, Calvin has sometimes wondered why he didn't defend the teacher's right to fuck whom he pleased.

Now it almost feels to Calvin Sidey as though he navigates the streets of Gladstone not by sight but by memory, since he recognizes so little but remembers so much. Just last week he was picking up supplies in the general store in Gable, and as the storekeeper, Henry Foss, brought items down from the shelves, he asked Calvin, "Have you run into old Ben Murrow lately?"

"Not lately."

"Well, Ben's gone senile. He doesn't remember his goddamn name. Thinks his son's his father and his wife's his baby sister."

"Jesus."

"Can you imagine? Trying to call up a memory and get no answer? My God."

Calvin had heard such remarks before, and he never argued, much less suggested, that for some people life would never offer any peace as long as their memories were in working order.

And now Calvin gives his memory a little test: How many times has he taken his leave of this town, each time believing it would be for good? The first when he was barely eighteen and just out of high school, and rather than join his father in the real estate business Calvin ran off and hired on with Brierly Marker's Diamond B outfit. For the first few months he didn't do much more than shovel shit and buck hay, but that was work preferable to selling off town lots so little cracker-box houses could be built on them. Calvin had every expectation that he'd live the life of a ranch hand forever, but the war brought him back to Gladstone. He remembers well the day he walked through the door of the army recruiters—the office was down on Main Street where Woolworth's is now. He brought Pauline back after the war, but you could as easily say she brought him back. If he didn't have the responsibility of a wife, he would never have returned to the family business. And it was responsibility of a different kind that drove him away again. In his grief, his crazy-drunk grief, he didn't think he could be responsible for his own life, much less his children's. He wasn't the first man to walk away from his family and he wouldn't be the last, but most men leave with a wife in the house to curse him or make excuses for him when he walks out the door.

Well, hell, since he's done such a piss-poor job of going and staying gone, maybe he ought to give up and come back here for good. Get himself a little shack, down in Dogtown perhaps, and live out his years here. Buy his groceries in a supermarket. See a dentist about that tooth that's been troubling him. Have the truck's transmission fixed. Look for a new edition of Catullus in the library. Find a few other old mossbacks to play penny ante poker with. Sit down for Sunday dinner with Bill and Marjorie and their children. Die in a hospital.

Calvin turns onto the street that ought to be more familiar to him than any other. How much has changed here? The trees are taller. The electric wires, the telephone wires. No more outhouses. No more stables or chicken coops. More fresh paint. More flower gardens. More fences. If he could fly above this street instead of drive down it, he'd see nothing but the leafy tops of trees, and there was a time when he could see all the way out to Sentry Butte from an upstairs window. Hell, maybe Calvin should be glad of all that's changed. Fewer reminders this way.

• • •

BEVERLY LODGE WATERED HER garden for two hours this morning, hoping that by the time she came out in the afternoon pulling weeds would be easier. It isn't. She still has to dig the roots out with a pronged instrument. When she stands to give her aching back a break, she notices that her knees are as muddy as a child's. She could bring out a towel to kneel on, the way Alice Westrum does, but Beverly figures it's easier to launder her skin than a towel. For similar wash-day reasons, when she works outside she wears one of Burt's old T-shirts so she won't have to soak grass and dirt stains.

While she is massaging the small of her back, a truck drives up the alley, leaving a dust cloud in its wake. Traffic in the alley has become a familiar sight. For weeks, someone in a black Ford has been circling the block, and sometimes he shortens his circuit by cutting through the alley, always driving too fast. She assumes the driver of the Ford is Ann Sidey's boyfriend, though Beverly isn't sure how she arrived at that conclusion; she can't recall ever seeing Ann in the car. The truck parks by the Sidey garage.

It's no teenager who steps out of the truck but an older man. He's tall, and his posture brings him up even taller; there's not a trace of slouch or slump in his back or shoulders. He's dressed in boots, faded Levi's, a western shirt, and a battered, sweat-stained cowboy hat. He needs a haircut; his white hair curls and tufts over his collar and behind his ears.

Beverly watches while he lifts an old leather suitcase from the back of the truck. He begins to walk toward the Sidey home, and something in his stride—rapid, purposeful—makes Beverly feel for an instant that the Sideys should be warned, that on this hot, dry Saturday afternoon a man who portends danger to the family is coming their way. Then she sees his face, and she almost laughs out loud in relief and embarrassment.

Yes, his expression is stern and maybe even a little menacing—he has a large jaw and a wide mouth and both seem locked tight with determination. Even with his hat pulled low he squints against the light and that puts even more wrinkles in his leathery skin. But the truth is, Beverly Lodge knows him: Calvin Sidey, father to Bill, grandfather to Ann and Will, and who once lived in that very house.

Like Bill Sidey, Beverly lives on the same block on which she grew up, although, unlike Bill, not in the same house. Beverly's parents lived at the bottom of Fourth Street's hill in a small frame house that is currently painted a mustardy yellow so ghastly that Beverly often goes out of her way so she doesn't have to drive past it. She certainly grew up with the awareness that her family—her three older sisters, their mother, and postal-clerk father—were on the lower end of Fourth Street, both literally and figuratively. And one of the families living at the top of the block was the Sideys, able to afford a house of stone rather than sticks because the senior Mr. Sidey—did Beverly ever know his name or had he been only initials, G. W., to her as to everyone in Gladstone?—bought land cheaply when he came to Montana.

The Sideys had a son, Calvin, and two daughters, Wilma and another who died in infancy. Calvin was at least ten years older than Beverly, but her aunt Doris was Calvin's age, and for many years of their youth Doris had a desperate crush on Calvin, though Beverly now has trouble reconciling these twin facts with the image of her aunt, crippled with a stroke in a Seattle old people's home, and this fierce old man walking across the grass.

From her aunt's descriptions of Calvin back then, Beverly was not surprised that her aunt, or any female, was in love with him. He was a top-notch student and athlete, the broad-shouldered, blue-eyed handsome boy who was always chosen as captain or president.

He wore lightly his mantle as son of a rich man, his aloofness excused as shyness. Then, when he graduated from high school, rather than go away to college or begin the gradual but inevitable process of taking over his father's real estate business, Calvin Sidey left Gladstone and hired on as a ranch hand.

The cowboy life Calvin signed on for was rawhide rough, yet many young people regarded him with even more envy than before. As they saw it, they were buckling themselves into stultifying jobs that would constrict them all their lives, while Calvin was galloping free across the prairie. When war broke out in Europe, Calvin was one of the first to enlist, and after the war, Calvin came home with ribbons on his chest and a beautiful French wife at his side.

Soon, however, Calvin was no longer the embodiment of a free, rebellious life; he moved into his parents' home, and he began to sell real estate with his father.

And that was the Calvin Sidey whom Beverly knew best from her own memory, simply one more of Gladstone's businessmen, preoccupied with making deals during the week and cutting grass and scolding his children on the weekend. His wife was another story. Gladstone had its share of residents who had come from another country—Beverly's own grandmother had emigrated from Germany as a teenager—but none who spoke with a French accent or who possessed Pauline Sidey's exotic beauty. Beverly remembers her as a cheerful if somewhat bewildered woman who seemed more comfortable in the company of the town's children than with other housewives.

Then, sometime in the 1930s, Pauline returned to France to visit her own family. She hadn't been home since she and Calvin were married, and though another war seemed imminent and more people were leaving Europe than visiting, Pauline's mother was ill, and Pauline worried that she might not see her mother again.

Her father had already died during her absence. So she traveled to France for what was to be a visit of no more than a week, the longest period of time she could bear to be away from her husband and children, Bill and Jeanette. Yet back in the village in which she was born, Pauline Sidey was killed in an automobile accident, dead before her dying mother. It was one of those ironies about which people talked for years.

Calvin Sidey was inconsolable, and his grief, its intensity and its dimension, was frightening to behold. His drinking was soon out of control and his moods turned darker and his temper hotter. Beverly remembered being in Soward's Butcher Shop when Calvin stormed in and began to berate and threaten Mr. Soward for selling an inferior cut of meat. Beverly had her son, Adam, with her, and since she couldn't cover Adam's ears in time to keep him from hearing Calvin Sidey's curses, she turned to leave the store.

Even in his drunken rage, Calvin Sidey must have realized how inappropriate his actions were, and he fell suddenly silent and stumbled backward as if he had been blocking Beverly and Adam's path to the door. But oddly, Mr. Soward suddenly stopped defending his product and told Calvin Sidey that perhaps he was right; perhaps that meat had been unusually gristly. He offered to replace the roast free of charge, a bit of charity as remarkable as Calvin Sidey's outburst.

Beverly had often wondered about that day and the alteration of both men's behavior. What had caused it? The presence of a woman? A child? Those were plausible explanations, yet she couldn't shake the thought that the change that transpired in that room with its raw reek of butchered flesh and fresh blood had more to do with Calvin Sidey than her, that he had somehow been able to inspire—simultaneously?—courtesy and terror in others and himself. And then she mocked herself for such thoughts, telling herself that she was letting her image of a grief-stricken drunk be affected by her recollection of Aunt Doris's moony talk about the man.

Within a year or two of the incident in the butcher shop, Beverly had moved into the house next to Calvin Sidey's. Her husband, Burt, through a willingness to work eighty-hour weeks and to accept the case of any client who walked through his door, was finally able to afford a home on Fourth Street, though by then those residences no longer had the prestige of Burt's boyhood. They were simply nice houses, which suited Beverly just fine; she never expected to live in a home finer than her mother and father's. And poor Burt. He got so little enjoyment out of the house that meant so much to him. His hard-charging years caught up to him, and he was dead of a heart attack before he turned fifty.

And that meant neither of the houses at the top of Fourth Street had a man as the head of the household. Around the time of Burt's death, Calvin Sidey left Gladstone. Beverly still remembered the day Calvin's mother and sister came to the house, two black-clad women looking like bobbing magpies as they came up the front walk. They had been living together in a small apartment above the Gladstone Memorial Clinic, but when they entered the Sidey house, it was to stay. And their arrival coincided with Calvin's departure— for good. Jeanette must have been fifteen or sixteen, and her brother Bill two or three years younger. If their father ever returned for his children's birthdays, for their high school graduations, or for holidays, Beverly never knew about it. She wondered if he even knew, at the time, that his son enlisted in the armor that his daughter ran off with a Louisiana oilman.

When Calvin left Gladstone, the word around town was that he had returned to the cowboy life, hiring himself out to any rancher who'd have him. Then Beverly heard that he was living like a hermit on land that a family member had homesteaded in the previous century.

By then, Beverly knew a thing or two about grief herself. She knew its agony didn't grow worse over time. Day by day, week by week, its pain lessened, although sometimes so imperceptibly that it seemed a wound that couldn't heal. And grief didn't drive you away from your family and civilization. Beverly had clung so tightly to her son after Burt's death that she sometimes wondered if Adam's problems had their origin in that period when he lost his father, when his mother asked of him something he could not give.

As if she were among the last to catch a flu that had been making the rounds, Beverly heard a rumor that offered up another reason for Calvin Sidey's departure. The story had obviously been in circulation for a while because when it was brought up in Beverly's presence, it was with the assumption that she would know it as well as anyone in town.

Del Murdock, a rancher, was found dead in his own driveway. The cause of death was clear—his skull was fractured—but the cause behind the cause was not. He was lying by his truck's open door, so it was possible that he got out, slipped, fell backward, and split his head open on the running board. That was certainly a plausible explanation; on many nights he staggered out of one or another of Gladstone's bars, climbed into his truck, and negotiated the long drive back to the house where he lived alone most of the year. His wife spent more and more of her time down in Casper, Wyoming, where, or so Mrs. Murdock said, she had a sick mother who needed looking after. Most of Gladstone figured she grabbed onto any excuse she could find to put distance between herself and the foul-mouthed drunk she was married to.

But many people claimed that Del's skull had fractured from something other than a fall and a truck's running board. A pipe or a gun barrel or a two-by-four could also have done the damage, and that version had someone waiting for Del when he drove up that night, someone who clubbed Del in the back of the head. That someone was rumored to be Calvin Sidey, and in that narrative he left Gladstone to avoid arrest and prosecution.

The story had never made sense to Beverly. What did Calvin Sidey have against Del Murdock? And why would Sidey believe that living far from town put him out of the reach of the law?

She finally asked her husband, though reluctantly. Burt, whether through the fault of his lawyer's training or his own contrary nature, did not like to respond to any question put directly to him, and on that occasion he behaved as he so often did. He worked his tongue inside his cheek and lip, tsked softly, and then said, cryptically, "The French, they are a funny race . . ."

"What on earth does that mean?" Beverly had demanded, thereby guaranteeing that she would get no more from Burt than a nod of the head and a raised eyebrow.

Beverly sat on her curiosity for a long time before she had the nerve to inquire again into the death of Del Murdock and Calvin Sidey's alleged role. Finally, she asked May Swearingen, who not only knew most of the town's gossip but much of Gladstone's official history as well. And if May had any pertinent information, she was not to offer it with enigmatic phrasing.

" 'The French are a funny race—what's that supposed to mean?' " Beverly asked. "And what could it possibly have to do with Calvin Sidey and Del Murdock's death?"

"You never heard that saying?" May Swearingen was hugely overweight, and she paused to pinch two more of the gingersnaps

Beverly set out. "I guess your hubby wants to spare you the vulgarities. 'The French, they are a funny race—they fight with their feet and fuck with their face.' The story going round had Del Murdock in the Pioneer Bar reciting this little ditty one night shortly after Mrs. Sidey died overseas. Del speculated out loud that maybe Mrs. Sidey had gone back over there to get some of that French fucking. Folks think news of this little incident found its way back to Calvin Sidey, and that's why he was waiting for Del when he pulled up to his house that night."

"That's a ghastly explanation! Do you believe it?"

"I don't believe it," said May. "But I don't *not* believe it."

"According to that story, Calvin Sidey left Gladstone so he couldn't be arrested . . ."

May took two more cookies and put them both in her mouth. "Yep. Though it seems to me if they had any kind of case at all they could arrest him out on the prairie as easy as on Fourth Street. Of course, they'd have to catch him first and out there that might not be so easy. But gone he is, that's sure, and I don't think he plans to come back."

But now Calvin Sidey has returned to Fourth Street and with suitcase in hand. Beverly supposes she should wave and call out, Remember your old neighbor? Then she might ask him if he's coming back for good. Or for ill . . . But the July sun supplies all the heat Beverly Lodge can handle. She doesn't need the blue flame of that old man's gaze turned on her as well.

SEVEN

||||||||||||||||||||||||||||||||||||||||||||

Bill Sidey slaps on the light that illuminates the basement stairs and calls out over his shoulder, "Dad? I'll show you what I've set up for you down here."

Toting his father's suitcase, Bill starts down the stairs, the hollow thump of his father's boots following him. With each step the men take, the temperature drops a few degrees until, at bottom, they've escaped the day's heat entirely.

Nightfall is hours away, but the unfinished basement, with its gray concrete walls and floor, its untreated studs and joists, its encroaching clutter, is so dark Bill has to turn on another light, this one an old floor lamp he has placed next to the bed. The lamp shade has yellowed with age and gives the bulb a dim, autumnal cast. There's enough illumination, however, for Bill to see again how dismal are the surroundings in which he's housing his father.

Bill sets the suitcase on the bed, and as he does, he notices how many tufts are missing from the old chenille bedspread. He points to a dresser he has positioned in the middle of the room in an attempt to partition off a sleeping area from the rest of the basement. "The top two drawers are empty, and if those aren't enough, I'll clear out others. And I know that's not much of a closet," he says, indicating the wire hangers hung on nails pounded into two-by-four studs, "but you can hang a few things over there."

Calvin looks around the basement. "Where did the bed come from? You bring it down from upstairs? I told you, I didn't want to turn anyone out of their bed."

Bill shakes his head. "It came from a rental. A house we're trying to rent furnished, but since no one has looked at the place since January, I don't believe it'll matter that the bed isn't in there."

"So you didn't just lug it down the stairs," Calvin says. "You hauled it across town and *then* down the stairs."

Bill sits down heavily on the bed. He'd like to stretch out and close his eyes. His father has been in the house less than an hour, and Bill already feels a kind of exhaustion coming on, the kind that comes from being in the company of this man who is so difficult to satisfy. And why should it be Bill who tries to please? Shouldn't it be the other way around?

"You said you wanted to stay down here, Dad," Bill says, spreading his hands in a gesture that takes in the entire basement. "And here we are."

"This place you can't rent—have you come down on the price?"

"Have I . . . Of course. Twice."

"Maybe try it unfurnished? Someone looking for a whole house has probably got some furniture."

Bill sighs. "Maybe."

Calvin nods, then walks toward the basement alcove where a bathroom has been roughed in—a toilet, a sink, and a galvanized steel shower stall. He peers in, then moves on to the laundry room where he makes a quick circuit that seems to have as its purpose nothing more than the confirmation of something hoped for or suspected. He returns to where his son is sitting on the bed. "How much are you asking?"

For a moment Bill thinks his father has lost his mind and is wondering how much it will cost him to rent this basement space. Then Bill realizes that his father is still referring to the unrented house.

"One twenty. That's what we're asking now."

"Seems steep to me," Calvin says. "But hell. What do I know. Get what you can get."

Then Calvin reaches past his son to spring the latches on his suitcase. Bill stands and steps aside so his father can proceed with his unpacking.

"This will do," Calvin says.

Bill supposes that his father is referring to the basement and the way it's been arranged for him. And that expression of approval should be enough for Bill. It should be. He knows that. To expect, hope, or push for more from this man is almost certainly an exercise in futility. Yet Bill can't help himself.

"Jesus, Dad. You don't have to stay down here. Let us put you in our room."

"Not necessary," says Calvin.

"You said you wanted it cool. We've got a window air conditioner up there." As Bill says this, however, he recalls his father's trailer and its suffocating heat.

Calvin reaches up and with the tip of his index finger touches one of the rough wood joists as if he's confirming the solidity of what's overhead. "This is fine," he says.

"In Will's room then. Or Ann's. This makes no sense. You down here and an empty bedroom upstairs."

"This will do fine," he says again.

"You know, Dad, this is your house. No matter how long it's been since you lived here, it's still in your name."

"Should we take care of that while I'm in town? Sign the papers and make it official? You know I've got a will drawn up, and this will all be yours when I'm gone. But if you want to get that out of the way now, it's fine by me."

"No, no, that's not . . . I don't care about the paperwork. I want you to feel comfortable. To feel at home here. For Christ's sake, you haven't even taken off your hat."

Calvin swiftly, angrily, removes his hat. For a second, it looks as though he's going to sail it onto the bed, but then, as if recalling ancient superstition, he stops himself. He pinches the hat's crown and runs his fingers around the brim as if reshaping it were the reason he took it off in the first place. He drops the hat on top of the dresser. He tugs on the pulls for the top drawer, and the drawer sticks, the wood probably warped by the basement's damp. When the drawer pops open, Calvin feels around the drawer's interior, touching the bottom and sides as if he's searching for a secret compartment.

"This was your mother's," Calvin says without looking at his son. "Hers and her idea. I remember the day we bought it. At a furniture store in Bozeman. Had a little quarrel over it. We've got a dresser, I told her. But hell, we both knew she'd have her way . . ." He takes his hand out of the drawer and rubs the top. "Bird's-eye maple. We had a hell of a time hauling it back here. What were we driving then? That big DeSoto maybe . . . And what the hell were we doing in Bozeman?"

Bill could pretend as though the conversation really is about furniture, but he's disinclined to do so. "I missed her too, you know. We all did."

"I'm sure you did." Calvin slowly pushes the drawer shut, and once it's closed, he flips the drawer pull up and down, making a clacking sound like a door knocker. "But the hell of it is, I never stopped." Then he turns away from the dresser and back to his son. "Marjorie doesn't look sick to me. She looks damn good."

Bill can't say to his father, I've noticed the same thing. But the truth is, as the time for their trip draws closer, Marjorie has become more energetic and animated.

"She's not sick, Dad. She has a condition."

"If this operation's a success, how's she going to be different?"

Bill knows what he wants the answer to be, though it's not an answer he could ever give to his father. He secretly hopes that once his wife's uterus is removed, she'll regress and he'll no longer find himself married to the cautious, modest, anxious Marjorie but to the wild, uninhibited Marjorie of her teenaged years, her Tully Heckaman years, as he has come to think of them. In marriage, Bill has provided her with stability and respectability, and she's thanked him by being a faithful, proper wife. How could he ever convey to her, much less to his father, his desire that Marjorie be for her husband what she once was for a young cowboy?

"She won't have such bad periods for one thing," Bill says, hoping that his candor will push his father away from the subject.

"They won't go on forever, you know. How old is Marjorie?"

"Thirty-nine."

"She can't put up with this problem a few more years?"

"You know what, Dad? She's not one of your goddamn ranch wives who has a kid during the night and is up fixing breakfast for all the hands the next morning and then castrating calves in the afternoon. Those women don't exist anymore. I doubt they ever did."

"Don't be too sure—"

"This isn't up to me, Dad. Or you. A doctor says Marjorie needs this operation. That's good enough for me."

"A *Missoula* doctor," Calvin says scornfully. "What about insurance? Have you talked to Jess Stabler? Will they pay for an operation on the other side of the state?"

"Jess isn't with Blue Cross any longer. He retired more than ten years ago. But to answer your question: Yes, insurance will cover the operation and the hospital stay. Most of it, anyway. And we can take care of the rest."

"Good for you." Calvin turns his back to his son and reopens the dresser's top drawer. Then he crosses to the bed and from the suitcase takes out a small stack of T-shirts and briefs and a few pair of socks folded into a ball, the whiteness of all these startling amid the basement's gray. Bill knows he's being dismissed, but he doesn't care.

"Could you hold off on that, Dad? I'll help you unpack in a minute, but first I've got something I have to say."

Calvin puts his underwear on top of the dresser and pushes the drawer closed.

"After Mom died," Bill says, "Jeanette and I needed you. All right, since then I've learned enough about human nature to know that maybe you just couldn't give us what we needed. But hell, you probably needed something from us too. It doesn't matter. Not now. It's all water under the bridge. No reason to go back to that time. But now it's my kids who will be in your care, and I'm putting you on notice: You will *not* abandon them."

His father smiles faintly. "You *are* coming back, aren't you?"

"You know what I'm talking about. I didn't ask you to stay here just to make sure the house doesn't blow away while we're gone. These kids are going to worry about their mom. They need to know they're with someone who cares about them. And while we're gone, you'll be that someone."

"You want me to tuck them in at night?"

"Ann and Will don't need that kind of treatment," Bill says brusquely. "But if there's anything else, you damn well better provide it."

His father's smile widens, but not one extra ounce of mirth enters the room. "What are you trying to do, son—threaten me into loving those children?"

"If I thought I could, that's exactly what I'd do."

His father says nothing but turns back to the contents of his suitcase.

"But we both know it doesn't work that way, don't we, Dad?"

Calvin Sidey looks up as if he hasn't heard any of the words whose saying required so much of his son's courage. "You have packing of your own to do, don't you?"

The smell of mildew hangs in the air. Since both father and son have made their home here, it's an odor familiar to both men, and as it enters their nostrils, it evokes memory, as smells almost invariably do. But neither Calvin nor Bill Sidey can find the other often enough in remembrance, and they stand in this concrete room with a suitcase yawning open between them, a distance that might as well be as wide as a canyon.

ONCE HE CAN BE certain that his son has reached the top of the stairs and won't be coming back with another warning or piece of advice, Calvin proceeds with his unpacking.

Into the dresser's deep second drawer, Calvin stacks his four shirts and two pair of Levi's. He hangs his black suit from a nail. And why the hell, he wonders, did he bother bringing a suit? Maybe he packed it simply because a funeral occasioned his last trip to Gladstone, so that's what the town has turned into—the place where his few remaining friends are likely to drop dead and Calvin might be called upon to tote another coffin. His toilet kit and his copy of Catullus he sets on top of the dresser. Into the top drawer he puts his kerchiefs and his pocket watch. Only a few items remain in the suitcase, and he takes them out and tucks them under the T-shirts in the top drawer, where he expects them to remain, un-used, strictly in case of emergency: an unopened pint of Canadian Club whiskey, a box of ammunition, and a Colt .45 semiautomatic, the sidearm issued to soldiers in the First World War.

Calvin closes the empty suitcase, clasps the latches, and slides it under the bed. He smooths the bedspread, his index finger catching on a loose tuft . . . He'd had pneumonia as a child, stricken with the disease during a particularly frigid winter. His parents' bedroom, now the room with the air-conditioning unit that cools his son and daughter-in-law, was the warmest in the house, and young Calvin was put to bed in there. His parents had a chenille bedcovering, like this one, and when Calvin's recovery was almost complete, he relieved his boredom by plucking out one tuft after another. When his mother caught him in the midst of this activity, she asked him an unanswerable question: "Does destruction give you pleasure?"

Calvin's son has placed a wooden chair next to the bed to serve as a nightstand, and on the chair seat is a tin ashtray and a wind-up alarm clock. Next to them Calvin puts his tin of Sir Walter Raleigh, a packet of rolling papers, and a box of matches.

He walks over to the stairs but without the intention of ascending. Linoleum covers the basement floor, and Calvin lifts the linoleum and rolls it back to reveal the cement underneath.

Paulette asked him to come down into the basement. That too was during the winter, but if Calvin recalls correctly, it was one of the mild years, an open winter. He'd been busy with something, real estate paperwork probably, since so many evenings seemed filled with it, and he resented being called away from his desk. But Paulette told him that Bill asked for them, so Calvin followed her down the stairs.

Bill couldn't have been more than five or six, and he was astride the stick horse that seemed to accompany him everywhere but to school and church.

"See how fast I go," Bill said, and began to gallop around the circumference of the room.

After four circuits, Bill stopped in front of his parents and breathlessly asked, "How fast?"

Paulette clapped her hands enthusiastically and said, "Oh fast! Very, very fast!"

"But *how* fast?" Bill insisted on knowing.

Calvin caught on before his wife did. The previous summer the family had attended the Florence County Fair, which featured horse races. The Sideys had seats in the grandstand right next to old Doc Vincent, an area veterinarian, who had a stop watch he was using to time the winning horses. What Bill was asking for when he galloped around the basement was an official time.

Calvin took out his pocket watch and commanded his son, "Around the track again." Only then did Calvin notice that there really was a track. With chalk Bill had drawn a wavering, lopsided oval on the basement floor. And around it he raced again, slapping his own haunches as he ran, his shoes clap-clapping on the cement.

There's not a trace of that chalk line under the linoleum now, but Calvin has a troubling suspicion that his son still wastes his time running in circles.

EIGHT

||||||||||||||||||||||||||||||||||||

Because of the long drive ahead of them, Bill and Marjorie Sidey attend the first service instead of the second at Gladstone's Olivet Lutheran Church. Their presence, along with their children's, causes a minor disruption in the church. The Sideys sit in their usual pew, failing to realize that in doing so they're taking the place of the Hurds, the family that always occupies that space at eight o'clock on Sunday morning. The Hurds, unwilling to say anything but mildly flustered, slide into the pew where the Froelichs usually sit. Fortunately, this ripple of confusion and displacement goes no further. Diane Froelich simply smiles and waves at the Sideys and the Hurds, then leads her husband and three daughters to a pew at the back of the church, a space generally reserved for irregular attendees, late arrivals, or wives who have not been able to persuade spouses or children to accompany them.

EARLIER IN THE SUMMER, Will Sidey got into trouble for fidgeting and kicking the pew in front of him during the service. In the midst of his father's lecture on piety and respect, Will blurted out, "Dad, I didn't even know I was doing it!" At that, his father's heart seemed to soften, and he told Will that he realized sitting still for an hour could be difficult. When the boredom gets to be too much for you, Bill Sidey told his son, "Go ahead and tune Pastor Sodegard out for a while. Let your mind roam a bit." He leaned forward and confided to his son, "I've often planned out my whole week during one of his sermons."

This Sunday, Will Sidey plans out a good deal more than a week. Sometime during his grandfather's visit, Will is going to ask him what it will take for Will to become a cowboy. Maybe he'll ask his grandfather if, when Will's parents return from Missoula, he can go live with his grandfather for the rest of the summer. After the latest trip down to the river with his friends, Will feels he has to get out of Gladstone.

The beer that Will stole never got very cold, and when Will took his turn sipping from the can, the warm, bitter foam bubbled astringently back into his throat and he began to cough.

"For Christ's sake," Stuart said, "whiskey's supposed to do that to you, not beer!"

When they lit fat, cigar-sized chunks of driftwood and attempted to smoke them, Will had to puff while trying—impossibly—not to breathe through his nose. If dog shit could be set on fire, it would smell, Will was certain, like burning driftwood. They waded through a waist-high channel—shrieking when the icy water hit their genitals—hoping to get to the very edge of a sandbar where they could cast their lures into the river's main current. Before they reached their destination, however, they came upon a pothole teeming with frogs.

The hole, shallow and not much bigger around than a kitchen table, must have been created when the river shrugged and left a tiny pond behind. A good rain upriver would probably allow its warm, stagnant water to join the rest of the river, but for now it—and its frogs—had nothing to do but steam under the summer sun.

Will wasn't sure whose idea it was or if it even began with an idea, but soon they were picking up lengths of driftwood and killing frogs. Someone flipped a frog in the air with a stick, someone else took a baseball swing at a flying or leaping frog, and soon dead or dying amphibians were everywhere, the pink loops of their intestines littering the sand and their blood swirling in the water. Will didn't actually kill any frogs himself; when he pretended to spear them with the forked end of his stick, he was actually prodding them toward the water, the sanctuary most of them seemed to seek. But this ruse didn't work for long. Bobby Mueller started beating the pond's surface, yelling, "Frog soup! Frog soup!" as he flailed away. At that point, Will simply backed away from the boys. They didn't even notice he was no longer with them.

And yet it was not until after all this—the taste of warm beer, the stench of burning driftwood, the sight of the blood-slaughter of frogs—not until they were walking their bikes through the soft sand on the way back up to River Road, that Will's disgust with those boys, boys he couldn't find a way not to call his friends, became so great that he determined there was no other solution for him but to leave the place where he had lived all his life.

Stuart turned his bike around from the head of the line and

came back to Will. "Hey, Sidey," Stuart said, "have you come up with some kind of deal so's we can spy on your sister?"

"Deal . . . ?"

"You know. So's we can watch her naked in her bedroom or in the biffy even."

"Biffy?"

"I got to tell you, the bathroom would be cool because when I was jerking off last night that's what I was thinking about. I was in your bathroom with the shower curtain closed almost all the way, but when your sister came in and started to strip I was watching her the whole time. Then she opened the curtain and seen me there, and she wanted it bad as me, so I fucked her right there, the both of us slipping around like . . . like . . ."

"Like frogs?"

"Frogs! Shit, Sidey, what's with you? Frogs . . . Hell no, not frogs. Do you even know what people look like when they screw?"

"We don't have a shower curtain," Will said. "We have a sliding door."

"A sliding door? A *sliding door*? Jesus Christ, I was just saying that because . . . Fuck it. Forget the bathroom. It doesn't have to be the bathroom. How about her bedroom? You know Billy Doyne, don't you? His sister? With the big knockers? She was a basketball cheerleader last year. My brother said they used to spy on her all the time. They stood on a box outside her bedroom window. He said they used to watch her squeeze her pimples. She'd be naked and turning all around trying to squeeze pimples on her back. Jesus! What I'd give to see that!"

"Billy too? Was he watching?"

"Shit yes, Billy too!"

"My sister doesn't have pimples . . ."

Although they had come to the black-topped road, Stuart did not get on his bicycle and start to pedal off with the other boys. Instead, he stared at Will so long that Will began to contemplate the empty spaces between the freckles dotting Stuart's face. And then Stuart began to laugh.

"You're a nut, Sidey. You know that—a fucking nut! No pimples. No shower curtain!" When his laughter subsided, Stuart swung onto his bike.

Will couldn't bear the thought of remaining in Stuart Kinder's company any longer. He slapped dramatically at the back of his jeans. "Oh no! Oh shit!" Will said.

"What?"

"I lost my billfold. I bet it came out when we took our pants off to cross the deep water. Damn it! I gotta go back."

Stuart looked questioningly at him.

"That's okay. You go ahead. I'll go back and find it. I'm pretty sure I know where it fell out."

"What the hell were you doing with a billfold?"

"I thought maybe we were going to stop at Holt's Confectionary."

"Yeah, maybe we should've." Stuart stood up on his pedals and began to pump, but within twenty yards he jammed on his brakes. Over his shoulder he shouted another question. "How do you know your sister ain't got pimples?"

And then Stuart was off, the cackle of his laughter mingling with the rattle of his bicycle chain.

When he returned home, Will had to answer to his mother's interrogation. Where were you, she wanted to know; she had seen Glen go by on his bike over an hour before. Only recently Will had discovered that his ability to lie to his parents had become so well honed that it was no longer necessary to prepare a fabrication in advance; he could concoct a serviceable lie when the moment demanded. He didn't come back with the other boys because his favorite fishing lure got caught in a bush, and it took Will some time to untangle his line and retrieve his spinner. His friends were jerks sometimes; they wouldn't help him or wait for him.

And that addendum to his lie Will was able to deliver with absolute conviction. On the long, solitary bicycle ride back from the river, Will made a decision: He had to get away from his friends, and he had to do it soon before they started skulking outside his house to get a look at Ann.

It seems to Will that he has no alternative but to run away from home, yet as he becomes less and less interested in the world his friends inhabit, home is increasingly where he wants to be. Going off to live with his grandfather is hardly the ideal solution, but Will can't think of a better one.

MRS. BISHOP PASSES THEIR pew, and Ann lowers her head. Penney's has installed new cash registers, and some of the employees, including Mrs. Bishop, who has worked at the store since it opened twenty years ago, have been having trouble learning how to operate the new machines. The store's solution has been to team the slow learners with the employees who quickly got the knack of the new system. Ann and Mrs. Bishop both work in the Boys' Department, and Ann was assigned to oversee the older woman to make certain she rang up her sales correctly.

For reasons Ann can't imagine, Mrs. Bishop dislikes her— perhaps the older woman thinks that Ann wants to take over Mrs. Bishop's basement domain—and the business with the new registers has smelted that dislike into white hot hate. And Ann has discovered what an obstacle to learning hate can be. The more Mrs. Bishop fumed, the more frequent were her mistakes on the machines. Transaction after transaction had to be voided, and at times Mrs. Bishop seemed to have totally lost the ability to make change. And though the older woman would not look at or speak to Ann unless absolutely necessary, Ann found Mrs. Bishop merely pitiful. And then two days ago, Mr. Van Vliet, the store manager, came through the basement just as Mrs. Bishop was attempting to ring up a sale with Ann watching over her shoulder.

"How are we doing here?" Mr. Van Vliet asked. He seldom left his office, and most of the day-to-day operations of the store were handled by two assistant managers.

Mrs. Bishop stepped aside and motioned for Ann to take over on the register.

"She had a little trouble at first," Mrs. Bishop said, "but she's getting the hang of it."

Ann certainly couldn't contradict Mrs. Bishop in front of a customer, a woman who already seemed embarrassed by the packs of Towncraft briefs she was buying for her son.

"There's always a period of adjustment learning a new system," Mr. Van Vliet said to the little assemblage of women. To Ann, he added confidentially, "You couldn't have a better teacher."

Ann expected Mrs. Bishop to scurry off when Mr. Van Vliet and the woman with the underwear left, but the old woman held her ground. Not only that, she glared at Ann, daring her to say the first word.

Ann wished she could have thought of something better than "Ring up your own sales."

Two pews ahead of Ann, Mrs. Bishop slides into place. Ann stares at the back of the woman's head and imagines that the ornate pattern of curls and waves represents a maze, and if Ann can find the right whorl to enter with a wish, it might weave its way to the old woman's brain. *I wish Mrs. Bishop would quit Penney's . . .*

Ann stops herself. Church is the place for prayers, not selfish wishes, and Ann has already started petitioning God to watch over her mother during her upcoming operation. Not that Ann truly believes in the power of prayer. Too many have gone unanswered over the course of her life—especially during that night in March—for Ann to think that God intercedes in human affairs. Prayers make about as much sense as trying to push a wish through another person's skull.

FOR ALL THE WRONG reasons, Bill is eager to leave Gladstone. On Friday afternoon, he mailed a notice to a renter that she would have to be out of the house by August 1. She's three months behind in rent, she seldom mows the lawn, and the last time Bill drove by, it looked as though someone kicked through the front screen door. There are frequently so many cars parked in the driveway or in the side yard that Bill is certain that it's not only Brenda Cady and her two children who are living in the house.

Evictions are always unpleasant, but in this instance Bill would have to hear I-told-you-sos from Tom Gates and Don Luckshaw, the two agents who work for Bill. Tom and Don had warned him not to rent to Brenda.

"You know who the father of one of her kids is, don't you?"

"She didn't say anything about a man, just her and the two boys," Bill said.

Don leaned across Bill's desk and said, "Lonnie Black Pipe." Then he stood and crossed his arms, as though that name summed up everything to be said on the matter.

"You'll have half the goddamn reservation living in that house," Tom added.

"Lon's not from the reservation," Bill said. It was the best argument he could muster.

Lon Black Pipe is, in the phrase that Tom and Don and many of the citizens of Gladstone would use, a bad Indian, which not only means that he's not meek and deferential but that he's downright difficult. Lon has served at least two terms in Deer Lodge State Prison, one for assault (he beat up a young cowboy so severely in a bar fight that there was serious doubt whether the cowboy would live), and one for grand theft auto. And those are only the crimes he's been convicted of; he's been suspected of committing many others in Gladstone and the surrounding region.

Although Bill knew all along about the connection between Brenda and Lon, he was trying to demonstrate that he did not share the prejudices of his co-workers and many of his fellow citizens. Most Indians are decent, hardworking people who deserve far better than they receive in this part of the world, and Bill long ago resolved to treat them fairly and respectfully, exactly the way he would behave toward white people and just how he would like to be treated.

Besides, ever since that Christmas when Bill was ten, they've looked out for each other. On a cold, snowy Saturday just before the holiday, elementary school children were invited to the skating rink outside the high school for a gift giveaway from the Gladstone merchants. A big pile of wrapped presents sat on the ice, a sight that would have excited children at any time, but this especially in the depth of the Depression, when a good many children faced the prospect of a holiday without any presents. It soon became clear, however, that these gifts would not simply be handed out. The children had to line up at the opposite end of the rink from the presents, and at a signal they were to race across the ice and grab whatever they could. Bill Sidey was not a big, fast, or athletic child, yet for some reason—perhaps the galoshes he wore gave him extra traction, perhaps he had a special sense of balance that before that day he had not discovered—he and another boy were the first ones to reach the pile. The other boy was Lonnie Black Pipe.

For a brief moment, while the other children were slipping, sliding, falling, and shrieking across the ice, and while the business-men who sponsored the event were laughing uproariously at the spectacle, Bill and Lonnie tried, by feeling the packages and guess-ing at the shapes, to find and grab the best gifts for themselves. Maybe because the boys had tied in their race across the ice, maybe because there were obviously more than enough gifts for the two of them, maybe because they felt united against the mockery of the adults—whatever the reason—Bill and Lonnie cooperated in their scavenging. "Don't take that one," Bill advised. "That's a book." In turn, Lonnie said, "That's just a goddamn stick of candy." Both boys eventually took small, wrapped discs, objects they couldn't identify but whose compact heft made them seem possibly more valuable than the lighter, flimsier packages, the obvious mittens or pencils. Once they were off the ice, they eagerly unwrapped their presents and found that they had claimed hockey pucks. And in spite of Gladstone's long, cold winters that kept ice in steady sup-ply, no one in the community played hockey. Bill wasn't even sure how he knew what the black disc was, but he shared his knowledge with Lonnie.

Rather than reveal their disappointment to anyone, they made a joke of the incident, a joke that continued for years. Bill Sidey and Lonnie Black Pipe had no classes together in elementary or junior high school (and Lonnie, like most of the Indians with whom Bill went to school, dropped out before high school), but when they saw each other, on a playground or a city street, one of them would invariably ask the other, "How are you fixed for hockey pucks?" And that would be prelude to a conversation. *What's going on with you? Not much. How about you?* They'd talk about local sports teams, or about some of the town's fast cars and their owners. Lonnie would ask if a certain girl had a boyfriend, though Bill seldom had the answer.

Later, in high school Bill had a morning newspaper route, delivering the *Gladstone Gazette*. He was trudging down Fourth Street on a gusty cold dark morning in late October, and he must have been half asleep as he walked because he didn't notice the car pulling to the curb alongside him. "Hey," the driver said, "if you're on your way to buy some hockey pucks, I can give you a lift." It was Lonnie, of course, and he was not up early but out late.

Lonnie said, "Guess what? My old man kicked me out of the house."

"No shit?" Bill responded. "I can go that one better: My old man kicked *himself* out."

"At least you still got a bed to sleep in," Lonnie said.

Bill had considered inviting Lonnie to spend a night at the Sidey house, but he told himself that one night wouldn't make a difference in Lonnie's life. Besides, Lonnie said, "At least I can come and go as I please without putting up with anyone's bullshit."

A couple years ago at the Florence County Fair, Bill and Will were walking toward the grandstand for the rodeo competition, when someone called out, "Hey, hockey pucks."

Bill turned around, knowing who it had to be, and there was Lonnie, sitting on a stool next to a horse trailer. Yet if not for the hockey puck reference, Bill might not have recognized his old friend. Lonnie had been a restless skinny kid, but was now a fat man, bloated and slow. A massive gut hung down between his spread legs, and even though Lonnie wore a big black hat with its brim pulled low, Bill could see the scars that had turned half of Lonnie's face into a horror. He had heard that Lonnie had been in a serious auto accident and had to be pulled from the burning wreck. Lonnie's left eye and the left side of his mouth were pulled down tight in a kind of grimace, and on that same side of his face the skin from his forehead down to his neck was reddish purple and looked like wrinkled cellophane. His nose had flattened to little more than a smear, and Bill wondered if Lonnie could breathe through it.

"How's it going, Lonnie?" Bill said, extending his hand. The hand that Bill shook had the same wrinkled cellophane quality as Lonnie's face, but the grip was strong. Even sitting quietly on his stool, Lonnie Black Pipe's bulk had the look of power in reserve.

"I been better," Lonnie said. "But I been worse too."

"I heard about the accident," said Bill. "I'm sorry."

Lonnie shrugged. "The women ain't scared away. That's all I care about." He pointed to Will. "This your boy?"

Bill said, "Yes, this is Will."

"You ride, boy?" asked Lonnie.

Will looked up to his father, and Bill said, "He's a city boy. Bicycles and baseball."

Lonnie raised his thumb in the direction of the horse trailer. "My nephew's roping today."

"Good luck to him," said Bill. "We better get to our seats. Take it easy, Lon."

"Hell, I'll take it any way I can get it."

And will that eviction notice now turn Lon Black Pipe out of a home? Bill's best hope is that Brenda and her children, and anyone else sheltering under that roof, will simply leave. It's just as likely, however, that she'll ignore this letter too, and Bill will be a part of one more entanglement involving Lon Black Pipe and the law.

So the prospect of being in Missoula when Brenda Cady makes her wheedling phone calls and whining excuses suits Bill fine. And really, she's only a part of his desire to leave. The Kiwanis meetings about the Labor Day picnic, the pressure from that Billings developer who wants to partner up and build a four-unit apartment building on Gladstone's east side, the demands of the recently widowed Mrs. Glocklin who wants to sell her house but doesn't want anyone "traipsing through her house just to gawk," the fund drive to build lights for the high school football field, the church board's struggle to decide if a new minister is needed—Bill won't mind being free of these obligations and spending some time in a city where no one knows him or wants anything from him.

GOD FORGIVE HER, BUT the pages of the Bibles in the pews of Olivet Lutheran Church always remind Marjorie Sidey of cigarettes and the month of May.

Tully Heckman used to roll his own cigarettes, and he preferred pipe tobacco—she couldn't remember the brand, but it was something expensive that smelled of licorice—to the tobaccos like Drum and Bull Durham that were made for cigarettes.

On a Sunday morning in May, Tully picked Marjorie up after church, and they drove out to Willow Creek. It was the first hot day of spring, and their plan had been to spread a blanket under a tall cottonwood and make love to the applause of its leaves. But the creek had overrun its banks, and the ground was too muddy for them to walk close to the tree. Instead, they climbed into the back of the truck, and because Marjorie could not take a chance on wrinkling or soiling the dress she wore that morning to church, she undressed completely before she lay down on the blanket Tully spread for her.

If Marjorie had ever been naked outside before, she could not remember the occasion, nor could she recall a time when she had ever seen anyone completely unclothed in the open air, and since Tully kept his clothes on, she felt that day as though she was the only person who was free enough, bold enough, young and lovely enough, to walk the earth as naked as she came from the womb. Tully often brought along beer or a bottle of sweet wine when they were going to park somewhere and although on that day they had none, laughter kept bubbling out of Marjorie as if she were drunk. It felt so strange—so wonderful and sexy and strange—to be touched by the heat of the sun on her body where the sun had never shone before!

But when she lay back on the truck bed the blanket's wool was as itchy on her naked back as the truck's bits of hay and straw would have been. Furthermore, the blanket was not cushion enough to keep the bed's uneven boards from hurting her back. Tully rolled them over, and that was the first time she ever went on top—and her first orgasm, a sensation that was like an explosion occurring simultaneously in air, water, and fire—a gasp, a flood, a sudden suffusion of heat. She couldn't help thinking that the cause was not only the new position but the hot sun on her back as well.

After, they both wanted to smoke, and it was then they discovered that Tully had tobacco but no papers. Neither did they have tailor-mades, as Tully called them. But in their search for a substitute of some kind, they came across Marjorie's Bible lying in the front seat under her clothes. White leather with her name stamped in gold on the cover, the Bible had been a confirmation gift from her parents, but that day Tully Heckman showed her a new use for it. Its paper was of a size and weight just right for rolling cigarettes. "It don't work with most books," Tully said, "and not most Bibles either. Usually the paper just starts on fire. But this thin paper works fine, if you don't mind takin' in the word of the Lord with a mouth-ful of smoke." Marjorie didn't mind. It was one more occasion for laughter on a day when laughter was as abundant as sunshine.

Those days seem to belong not only to another time—and not even her youth but someone else's, someone Marjorie once heard talked about in whispers—but also to another place, a countryside so foreign to her present life that she finds it next to impossible to believe that she can actually climb into a car and drive to the spot on Willow Creek where a giant cottonwood tree's branches hang out over the rushing water. Far away, it's all so far away, until she picks up one of the Bibles from the racks in Olivet Lutheran Church.

NINE

⁜⁜⁜⁜⁜⁜⁜⁜⁜⁜⁜⁜⁜⁜⁜⁜⁜⁜⁜⁜⁜

On the day after Bill and Marjorie Sidey have left for Missoula, their garbage is strewn all over the alley behind their home, a discovery Beverly Lodge makes when she carries a sack of trash out to her own garbage cans.

She isn't sure what to do. Knock on the Sideys' door and tell whoever answers about the mess? Should she pick up the garbage herself? She has to do something. Campbell's soup cans, a Post Toasties box, watermelon rinds, apple cores, crumpled balls of tinfoil, and meat wrappers lie in the gravel and dust. Beverly can't help it; she worries that somebody might think the trash is hers.

After debating this dilemma for a moment, Beverly finally decides just to go back in the house for another paper bag. Before she can move, however, Calvin Sidey comes striding toward the tipped-over can.

Her first impulse is to run back to the house, afraid that he might consider her responsible. But before Beverly can retreat, Calvin has her fixed with his gaze as surely as if she's been staked to her own lawn.

And maybe he *does* think she's to blame because he pointedly asks her, "What the hell is the meaning of that?"

It's all Beverly can do not to shout her innocence like a child. "It's . . . I believe the Neaveses' dog is to blame."

"Neaves?"

Beverly points toward the light green house across the alley. The Neaveses have been her neighbors for over ten years, but she feels now as if she has betrayed them with nothing more than her raised index finger.

She hastens to explain, to excuse the family she has just condemned. "They have a dog, an Irish setter, who's always getting into garbage cans up and down the alley."

"You've seen this?"

Beverly nods. "It's something of a joke in the neighborhood. I think one year the dog was blamed for something trick-or-treaters did—"

"Has anybody talked to them about keeping the dog tied up?"

She shrugs helplessly. In Calvin Sidey's presence, she feels reduced to tongue-tied girlhood, a sensation that both flatters and humiliates her.

"You're sure it's the dog? How come he hasn't knocked over anyone else's garbage?"

"She. Her name is Queenie. I don't know. Maybe she found what she was looking for right away."

Calvin Sidey walks toward the alley, leaving Beverly to wonder whether it's her yammering or Queenie's behavior that has him shaking his head in disgust. After a moment, she runs after him.

"Mr. Sidey! If you wait a minute, I'll go get a sack and help you clean this up."

Beverly Lodge is a tall woman, but when Calvin Sidey stops and pivots, he seems to look down at her from a height far greater than inches. "Who are you?" he asks.

There's no reason he should know who Beverly is, no reason at all, yet she feels diminished by his question. "I didn't think you'd remember me. I'm your neighbor. Beverly Lodge? From next door?"

"I don't live here," he says, bending to pick up the dented garbage can.

Beverly takes pride in being able to bring if not a smile, then at least a measure of pleasantness from anybody, from those surly ranch boys who glower at her in the classroom to the grouchy attendant who pumps her gas to the dyspeptic checker at the Red Owl. And Beverly is not about to give up on Calvin Sidey. He'll simply require a bit more . . . what is it? She won't call it charm. She's too artless, too straightforward, to think of herself as charming. And she certainly won't win anyone over with her beauty. She's always been gawky, long-jawed, and toothy, though in her younger days she turned a few heads with her thick dark hair, slim hips, and long legs. Now, however, most of her hair has gone gray and those legs and hips just make her look bony and underfed. But Beverly has something—optimism, good cheer, a belief in human goodness—whatever it is, it burns bright enough in her to shine forth when she smiles. And when radiance and straight teeth are not enough Beverly still has persistence.

She raises her voice slightly as if she's trying to reach an inattentive student in the back row. "Maybe I should have said we *used* to be neighbors." She increases the wattage of her smile and asks, "Do you remember Burt Lodge? Burt was my husband. When you used to live here."

Beverly isn't sure how she can tell, but she knows he's trying not to remember.

"No," he says, "I don't recall. That was a long time ago."

"But I remember you."

Calvin Sidey subjects her to a moment of head-to-foot scrutiny, as though he's trying to decide if she's worth the effort. It isn't easy, but Beverly holds her ground. She doesn't fidget, she doesn't speak, and she doesn't take her hands from her hips. When Calvin Sidey finishes his inspection, his expression doesn't reveal whether she's passed or failed the test.

"Do you need to see the teeth?" she asks. "They're all mine." She lifts each foot in turn, then says, "The hooves probably need to be reshod."

In the next instant, Beverly sees something she wouldn't have thought possible: His face, as dark as saddle leather, takes on another shade—a blush of red.

"Who owns the dog again?" he asks.

"The Neaveses. In the green house. Let me go get that bag now."

"Don't bother."

"I don't mind helping. It could just as easily be my garbage that Queenie got into."

Calvin kicks a Kleenex box. "You didn't make the mess," he says, "and neither did I. So we're not cleaning it up." With that, he strides off toward the Neaveses' home.

Beverly considers staying right there in order to watch the

fireworks, but she knows she has to return to her own home. She doesn't have the time of day for her neighbors across the alley—not loud, vulgar Dalton Neaves nor his shrill, whiny wife June—yet they'll still be living in that pea-green house and she in hers long after Calvin Sidey has once again ridden off into the sunset.

"I FIND IT HARD to believe anything out there can be that amusing."

Adam, Beverly's son, has caught her staring out the kitchen window at exactly the scene she came inside to avoid. Calvin has brought both Mr. and Mrs. Neaves outside, and although Beverly doubts that her son could appreciate the little drama that's playing in the alley, she doesn't care. She's simply happy she has someone with whom she can share the sight.

"Look," she says, making room for her son at her side.

Adam pulls his bathrobe tight and steps to the window. Beverly isn't surprised that he's not dressed; she is surprised he's out of bed. Adam has been living with her since the first of June, when the school year ended in Dickinson, North Dakota, where he was teaching high school English. He wasn't offered a contract for the following year, and around that time, Adam and his wife decided to end their marriage. Beverly isn't quite sure if, when those knots were untied, her son deliberately made for Gladstone and his childhood home or if he simply drifted back to his mother's house.

And what does it matter, finally? He's here, and Beverly worries it might be for good. She shed a few tears when he went away to college, but having him back within these walls is sadder.

He's made no effort to find work. Instead, he worked out a deal with Beverly. If she'd support him for six months, thereby freeing him to write the novel he's been plotting for years, come January 1,

1964, he'll take the first job that comes along, even if that's bagging groceries at Red Owl.

Adam has never been much of a worker, so he must have high hopes for that novel. Beverly hasn't read any of it; she only knows it's supposed to be a western. She can't feature her son carrying bags of groceries out to people's cars, but neither can she imagine him completing a project the size of a book. Well, she supposes she's raised him to be who and what he is. Hard work killed her husband, so as long as she's able, she'll make life easier for Adam. If the result of that philosophy is a son returning home when he's almost thirty years old, she'll have to live with it.

"What am I looking at?" Adam asks as he peers out in the direction of the alley.

"Our neighbors are resolving a dispute," she says. "Watch."

Without that explanation, Adam might not be able to tell much about what's going on, but he can certainly see what Beverly sees. Calvin Sidey standing tall and still with his arms crossed while Mr. and Mrs. Neaves shuffle around in the dust, pointing both north and south to deflect the blame, mouthing their denials and counter-arguments. Dalton Neaves is the first to walk away, but his wife lingers a moment, and her expression leads Beverly to believe that June Neaves might be issuing a qualified apology.

Adam says, "I guess it just doesn't hold the fascination for me that it holds for you." Her son turns to walk away.

Mildly disappointed herself, Beverly is about to leave as well when she sees something that makes her stay. While Mrs. Neaves is trying—futilely, it appears—to engage stone-faced Calvin Sidey in conversation, her husband returns to the alley. He carries two paper bags, and he shakes one out and hands it to his wife. She immediately begins to fill it with the garbage scattered at her feet.

Dalton Neaves watches his wife for a moment. He seems, along with Calvin, to be supervising her work, but finally Mr. Neaves opens his bag also and begins to pick up garbage, albeit much more gingerly than his wife. Only when both Mr. and Mrs. Neaves are engaged in the cleanup does Calvin Sidey walk back to his son's house.

Beverly can't help herself. She claps her hands at what has occurred in the alley. The sound of applause brings Adam back, but he only sees Mr. and Mrs. Neaves cleaning up the alley, not an uncommon sight in a neighborhood dedicated to neatness.

"I guess I missed the best part," Adam says.

"These dramas are best viewed in their entirety," Beverly says. "If you come late or leave early, they don't make much sense."

"Just give me a capsule review. What was it about?"

"Power," she says.

TEN

||||||||||||||||||||||

The doctor scheduled to perform Marjorie's hysterectomy has been called away for his own family emergency, and he isn't sure when he'll return to Missoula. Because Marjorie has already checked into Good Samaritan Hospital and been assigned a room, and because the doctor might still return on short notice, she has to remain in the hospital. But there's no reason for Bill to stay, and Marjorie shoos him out.

"Go out and see the sights," she says. "I'll be fine."

"I'll be back for evening visiting hours," he assures her.

Then he's not sure if he should go. Is it only his imagination, or when he kisses her good-bye does that little tug on his shirtsleeve have an urgency that's usually not there? He looks down at her with a questioning look.

"Go," Marjorie says. "I'll be fine."

When Bill exits the hospital, he feels, as he's sure many people must when they walk through those doors, lighter, liberated, as though he's been given a gift greater than a few hours of freedom. Marjorie didn't specify what sights he might take in, but Bill knows exactly where he'll go.

Bill Sidey loves neighborhoods, especially those with architecturally interesting houses and carefully landscaped lawns, and though his business is buying and selling houses, this interest is more than professional. For him, houses and their grounds offer aesthetic pleasures; what the sight of a mountain range or a woodland meadow is for many people, a stretch of well-kept homes is for Bill Sidey, yet he's never seen a picture of a block of Craftsman bungalows hanging over anyone's sofa. He climbs into his car and heads for his favorite section of Missoula.

He parks his car on a residential street near the University of Montana. Oaks, elms, and maples, all taller and older than the tallest and oldest trees in Gladstone, arch over the street. The houses are a mix of styles—Queen Anne, Greek Revival, Dutch Colonial, Tudor, and Victorian. Most of them sit back comfortably on hedged, evenly trimmed lawns. On and around the houses are weather vanes, cupolas, gingerbread trim, paneled doors, leaded windows, wrought-iron fences—decoration found on very few houses in Bill's own town or, for that matter, in the part of the city where Marjorie's sister and husband live in a single story ranch house on a treeless cul-de-sac. July has been hot here—as in Gladstone—and this day is no exception, but because this neighborhood has not only the shade of its mature trees but also the cooling shadow of nearby Mount Jumbo, the heat doesn't feel as punishing.

The first time Bill visited this neighborhood—that time in flight from his sister-in-law's incessant chatter—he thought, looking at these many grand houses, life has to go well in there. How could any unhappiness find its way inside walls that were so plumb, true, and well tended on the outside? He recognized immediately the foolishness of that thinking, yet some of its prettiness remained, as stubborn in its place as rows of brickwork.

He sets out walking on a sun-dappled sidewalk. When she was younger, really, not that many years ago, his daughter, Ann, liked to walk with him through Gladstone's neighborhoods. She'd hold his hand and listen attentively when he told her about who lived in this house or that house back when he was her age. If these recitations bored her, she didn't show it. Ann doesn't walk very often now; one friend or another is always cruising up to the house to pick her up and take her somewhere, often to a destination close enough for anyone to walk, and certainly for young people with their strong, healthy legs. But Bill is guilty of the same. He drives distances he could easily walk. And both he and Marjorie have wondered why Ann hasn't shown any interest in driving herself, though she passed legal driving age a few years ago.

Up ahead a barrel-chested bald man is watering his flower garden. He's an older man and wearing wingtips, dress slacks, a white shirt and tie, and most of the tie's length is tucked inside his shirt. Perhaps he's left his office just to come home and give his garden a drink. Bill slows in hopes of eliciting a greeting. It doesn't come, and Bill walks past, but then decides he gave up too easily. He turns around, and this time he stops on the sidewalk near the man with the hose.

When the man finally looks Bill's way, Bill says, "It's hard to keep up, isn't it?"

The man cocks his head quizzically.

"When it's so dry, I mean." Bill points to the flower bed. "It seems like they're always thirsty."

The man nods and adjusts the nozzle so the spray of water changes from a stream to a diffuse mist to shower gently on his nasturtiums.

Had the man turned the hose on Bill, he could not have made it plainer that he has no interest in conversation, but Bill won't be deterred. "Or maybe you've had rain here?" Bill asks, looking up and down the block. "It sure looks green."

"No, we're waiting on a good rain. It's been a while. And we're coming off a dry winter and a dry spring."

A good rain. Now Bill knows they can converse. They're two Montanans who draw distinctions between good and bad rains.

"I'm from the eastern part of the state. Gladstone? We're not officially in a drought, but we're not far off."

"Then I guess you don't want to trade water bills, do you?"

"On my block," says Bill, "we've got folks running their sprinklers all night."

The man shakes his head, but whether in pity or disgust it's unclear.

"How are prices for houses running around here?"

The man stiffens, and Bill knows immediately that he's erred, bringing up a subject so closely related to money and how much this man might earn. Bill tries quickly to make up for his mistake.

"I've got a couple reasons for asking. One's professional. I'm in real estate, and I know what a place like this"—he deliberately points to the house next door—"would go for in Gladstone, but I'm always curious about housing costs in other communities."

Perhaps the man moves away from Bill because he simply wants to keep his watering pattern even, but move away he does, though only a few paces. Bill follows and keeps talking. "The other reason I ask is that my wife and I are thinking of relocating to Missoula. And a street like this, houses like these—well, this is just the kind of neighborhood we've always wanted to live in. Anything for sale around here?"

The man looks warily at Bill. "Here in Missoula?"

"I was hoping to see something for sale on this street."

The man sniffs. "We've got nothing for sale around here," he says curtly. "And I doubt anything will be available in the near future. People on this block tend to stay put."

Ah, there it is! Bill has bumped right up against it! If Bill already had a home on this block, this man might be the most neighborly of neighbors, ready to help Bill shovel out his driveway, to bring in the mail when the Sideys leave town, to jump start Bill's car if it doesn't turn over on a frigid winter morning, to rake the oak and elm leaves that fall on both lawns. But for an outsider, the man and his block have no room. This behavior toward strangers is probably basic human nature, something Bill could encounter anywhere on the planet. But he's sure to find it in Montana.

"Well," says Bill. "Thank you for your time."

The man twists his nozzle again, now shutting off the flow of water entirely, and without another word he walks off toward his house.

Bill contrasts this neighborhood and its stately houses with his father's sunbaked, wind-buffeted dwelling out on the prairie. Yet the house where Bill lives now—and its size, construction, and style—would fit in nicely on this block. He wonders if he'll ever think of it as anything but his father's house, whether Calvin Sidey is sleeping in the basement or roaming free on every floor. When Bill was a child and adolescent, he used to wonder why the house itself wasn't enough to bring his father back. As children do, Bill was willing to blame himself—he simply wasn't good enough to make his father stay in the first place or later to return—but even then Bill had sufficient appreciation of the house, its bricks, mortar, boards, and nails, to wonder, Why wouldn't he want to live here?

Bill looks at his watch, and the position of the hands tells him nothing of what he needs to do or where he should go, but he's walked far enough. There's no point in returning to the hospital; evening visiting hours are hours away.

He returns to his car and heads to downtown Missoula, and there he parks on Higgins Avenue and walks a block to the Wagonmaster Cafe, a diner that's been in business for decades. Bill sits on a stool at the counter. It's early for supper and there's only one other customer, an old man sitting at a table by the window, drinking coffee and reading a newspaper. From the waitress, a heavyset woman wearing a red apron and a hairnet, Bill orders liver, bacon, and onions with mashed potatoes on the side, a meal he'd never eat at home—Marjorie not only dislikes liver, she can't stand the smell of it frying. For dessert he has apple pie à la mode.

Bill eats his meal slowly, savoring every bite. When he's finished, and enjoying his after dinner coffee and a cigarette, a few more customers filter into the Wagonmaster. All of them are men and all of them are alone. At a table, at a booth, at the counter, they seat themselves, and though they appear to be regulars in the Wagonmaster, they don't offer anything more than a silent greeting to the other diners. The satisfaction that Bill Sidey felt eating his solitary, forbidden meal suddenly vanishes. He stubs out his cigarette and signals for the check.

While paying his bill, he says to the waitress, "I'm on the way to Good Samaritan. My wife's a patient there."

It's not exactly what Bill wants to say, but he wants to explain that he's not like these other men in the diner. He has a wife, a family, somewhere he has to be, and someone there waiting for him. He has obligations.

"Do tell," the waitress says, but she doesn't look up as she counts out Bill's change.

WHEN BILL RETURNS TO Marjorie's room, he finds her sitting on the edge of the bed nervously smoking a cigarette. Her gown is up around her knees, and her bare legs look pale, as if two days in the hospital have already been enough to fade her summer tan. Carole and her husband, Milo, are there too, hovering near the bed and wearing expressions of concern.

"Where have you been?" Marjorie asks, blowing smoke toward the ceiling.

"Just wandering. Why—what's going on?"

"The surgery's back on. For seven o'clock tomorrow morning."

Bill can't say so, but he's relieved; from their expressions he feared that something was wrong back in Gladstone. "What happened? The doctor—"

"He doesn't want to make me wait. He'll perform the operation, *then* he'll leave town."

Although Bill doesn't like the idea of the doctor not being available for postsurgical care, he doesn't give voice to his concern. He says, "That's great . . . having the surgery right on schedule. So why am I seeing these glum faces?"

Marjorie crushes out her cigarette and lies back on the elevated head of the bed. "I don't know. I thought I was ready, but now . . ."

"It's major surgery," Carole says. The fact that she's already undergone the operation obviously makes Carole feel as though she's entitled to that observation, but the remark irritates Bill. As so much about his sister-in-law does. She likes to flaunt her knowledge of doctors, drugs, and medical procedures, and Bill wouldn't be surprised to learn that she's been frightening Marjorie with tales of all that can go wrong during the operation or in its aftermath. And she'd do it all under the guise of merely wanting Marjorie to be well informed about what to expect.

Bill has never been sure whether Marjorie is aware of the extent to which her older sister is jealous of her, and that jealousy probably goes back to a time when it first became apparent that slender, dark-haired, vivacious Marjorie would not resemble the other members of the Randolph family—father, mother, and daughter Carole all snub-featured, dull-eyed, and with hair the color of cardboard. Marjorie's easy popularity in school doubtless only exacerbated Carole's envy. Nevertheless, the sisters have always gotten along and in fact, since their parents died, have become even closer. For that reason alone, Bill is careful never to speak against Carole.

Milo is another matter. If he had all day to think about it, Bill could not come up with an unkind word to say about his brother-in-law. Shy, silent Milo, tall and crew-cut and sun-tanned from all the hours he spends on his lawn and garden. Milo is a junior high school math teacher and one of the gentlest men Bill has ever met.

And, true to his character, Milo now sees something going on in the room to which his wife is blind. "I think," Milo says, holding out his hand for his wife, "we better leave these two alone."

Before she leaves, Carole kisses her sister on the cheek and hugs her tightly. "I'll see you tomorrow," Carole says. "If I'm not here before you go in, I'll for sure be here when you come out."

Once they're alone, Bill walks from the foot of the bed to Marjorie's side. "If you sit up," he says, "I'll rub your back."

By way of assent, she pushes herself to a sitting position and hangs her head. Her hospital gown ties in back, but only the top strings are knotted. She leans forward, and in the process allows Bill to look all the way down the ridge of her spine to her underpants. He begins his massage near her shoulder blades, slowly ranging outward until he reaches the softer flesh near her armpits, then he moves back toward her spine. He repeats this pattern, each time moving closer to her sides and closer also to her breasts, free inside the loose gown. He can feel her relax under his touch.

In recent years, Marjorie has shrunk from his embraces and caresses more and more often, but she'll allow him to knead the knotted muscles of her back until his own fingers cramp from the effort. In fact, the first time they made love the experience grew from a back rub. He can still remember how his touch altered—or was the alteration only in his mind?—until its purpose was not relaxation but arousal, hers and his.

And his touch is changing now in just that way. Soon he's brushing the sides of her breasts, and in a few moments he'll work all the way around to the front and gently tease her nipples. Unless she stops him, and Bill doesn't believe she will. She knows what he's doing, and she shifts her body slightly to accommodate his touch. She even leans forward to press her breast into his hand, and Bill gives up the pretense of massage and lets his fingers slide slowly down her abdomen.

He has to stop, he knows this, he has to, but against that inevitable moment, he goes on. He has two fingers inside the elastic of her underpants when she leans away from him. But she doesn't seem to have stopped him because he has angered her or offended her sense of decorum. Through her gown, she puts both hands on Bill's and for a moment simply holds his in place. Then, in a voice that hints of frustration and sadness equal to his, she says, "We can't."

With a sigh that sounds like a prelude to tears, Marjorie lies back on the bed. She turns her face away from Bill. "I'm scared," she says.

What Bill wants to answer is, Then let's get the hell out of here. Right now. And let's not go back to your sister's or head for home. Let's find a motel right here in Missoula and finish what we started. This operation isn't something you *have* to do, goddamn it; it's something you *want* to do. Instead, he remains silent. He strokes the back of Marjorie's hand, careful to convey that his touch now is intended to comfort rather than excite.

"I know this operation worked for Carole," Marjorie says. "But sometimes things go wrong. Or they find something they didn't expect . . ."

"Shhh. Don't even think like that."

"It's not even for me I worry. Will needs a mother. Ann too. She might act grown up, but she's still got a lot of little girl in her. I know what it could do to the kids." She smiles sadly at Bill. "I know what it did to you, losing your mom."

"I survived." He smiles back at her. "But you can cut out that kind of talk. Ann and Will have a mother now, and they'll have one for a good long time. You'll be Grandma Sidey someday."

"I know it's wrong, but I tried to make a deal with God. Let me live until Ann and Will graduate. Just that long, and then I won't care."

Bill feels too much pity for his wife to argue with her, but a dissenting thought certainly comes to mind: Then what the hell is this operation for if you don't even care if you live more than a few years? To fight his own thoughts as much as to console his wife, Bill kisses her on the forehead.

Marjorie pulls her hand out from under Bill's, sits up straighter, and clears her throat. "So I've been thinking, if something should happen to me, maybe it would be best if Carole and Milo took the kids."

"Took?"

"Ann could go to college here, and Will . . . Will would have Danny, someone his own age to play with, to go to school with . . ."

Bill steps to the window. Marjorie's room is on the third floor, and Bill looks out, over rooftops to where the setting sun has left the foothills to the east half in light and half in shadow. With as much calm as he can summon, he asks, "Did you talk about this with Carole and Milo?"

"I brought it up. They said they were willing."

He grips the window sill tightly, trying to hold back his anger until he can be certain it won't explode and wound his wife—and perhaps himself—in ways that will never heal.

"And if they weren't willing," he says, his voice vibrating with held-back emotion, "then I suppose you wouldn't have mentioned anything to me about how you don't feel that our children belong with their father or in the town they've lived in all their lives. Maybe if Carole and Milo didn't want our kids, then you'd just as soon they be made wards of the state."

"Please, Bill. Don't get mad. I didn't mean it like that . . ."

She doesn't finish her sentence, but she doesn't have to. He knows what she believes: that under certain circumstances he will behave just as his father did. If Bill hadn't brought his father back into their lives, would Marjorie have entertained such thoughts?

"I'm not my father, Marj. I'm not going to cut and run. No matter what. Will and Ann are as precious to me as my own life. Or yours." The words are as tender as any he owns, yet they come out sounding as hard as an eviction notice.

He comes back to Marjorie's bedside, and though he can't bring himself to touch her again, he tries a little joke to convince her he isn't angry. "Besides, where would I go? I don't think either one of us can feature me hiring on as a ranch hand, can we?"

Marjorie pinches her lips tight and shakes her head.

"But the important thing here," Bill continues, "is that you push these gloomy thoughts out of your mind. You're in a good hospital. You've got a good doctor. You'll come through this just fine. Tomorrow when you come out of surgery, we'll call the kids."

She tries to smile, but the mention of her children only brings the glisten back to her eyes.

"Buck up now," he says. "You've been looking forward to this operation for a long time. You can't let your spirits slide now, not at the last minute." His words are costumed as a pep talk, but even a stranger can probably detect the scolding underneath. He tries again. "And once you're back on your feet and we're on our way out of town, I'll find that street I was walking today. With its fancy old houses and iron fences and tall trees. I want you to see it. You won't believe you're in Montana."

ELEVEN

‖‖

Is this the same rocking chair that's always been in the parlor? Calvin isn't sure. Back when this house was his, he wasn't much for rocking chairs. But now, with the way his back tightens up on him, if he doesn't sit up straight, he'll pay for it. So this high-backed rocker suits him fine. Old men and their rocking chairs—now he understands.

And this is where he liked to sit in the hot weather, right between the bay windows to take advantage of any cross-ventilation.

Why, in the heart of this hot day, is Calvin being overpowered by the memory of a winter night? And why, since Pauline is at the heart of the memory, does it come wrapped in rage?

They were going to attend an elaborate dinner that night, a banquet sponsored by the chamber of commerce, and local construction company owners, bankers, and realtors would be present. Were awards going to be handed out? Speeches made? Is that why Calvin Sidey was angry? Because they needed to be there on time, and Pauline was, as usual, running late? Was it snowing that night? Yes . . . and coming down so heavily that even driving the few blocks to the Gladstone Hotel would take longer than usual. And most aggravating of all, Pauline would be unable to understand his impatience. And then there she was, coming down the stairs at last and looking lovely—didn't he appreciate the time she took to make herself beautiful for him? Was he doubly angry because he knew he couldn't hold on to his anger in her presence?

Now something enters the memory that acts as a corrective, as if he's been tuned to the wrong frequency, and now the signal comes clear. It wasn't the night of the banquet. It was the night Pauline told him she wanted to return to France. Just for a visit. Her mother was ill, and Pauline was worried that she might not see her again. That had already happened with her father, the news of his death arriving a full week after the fact. What was so troubling to Pauline, as she told it, was that she had gone about her day-to-day life thinking of her father as alive . . . Calvin hadn't spoken his thought: What difference was there in how you thought of him? And it was a good thing he held his tongue because it wasn't long before he experienced something similar to what Pauline went through; Calvin believed his wife was still alive. Somehow that made him feel not only bereft but foolish, as if he had been walking blithely through a world that had changed, changed utterly, but he'd been insensible to its fundamental alteration.

But then the memory undergoes another transformation. God *damn*, is he turning into one of those old men who holds on to his memory but can't keep one day, one year, one decade from sliding into another? It wasn't a winter night when she told him she needed to go back to France for a visit. It *was* spring. It was a mild night in May, and that wasn't snow falling outside the windows but blossoms from their crab apple tree. "Calveen," she said, "I must go away for a short while."

His mind, however, has not misgiven him entirely. He did sit here in this very room and watch the stairs for Pauline to descend. And his memory of rage is not wrong. Calvin Sidey raged and grieved, grieved and raged, winter and spring, snowfall and petal fall, over the woman who never came back to him.

WILL ISN'T SURE IF he should ask his question just now. Grandpa isn't doing anything but staring out the window, but he does that so intently—has he moved at all in the last five minutes?— that Will wonders if his grandfather has seen something dangerous out there.

Will cautiously steps to his grandfather's side. No gophers are visibly digging in the yard. No crows bounce in the branches of the crab apple tree. No bums are loitering in the alley. No thunderheads are building in the summer sky.

"Grandpa?" His grandfather gives no sign that he knows Will is in the room, much less that he's heard the boy's voice.

Will tries again. "Can I ask you something?"

The rocking chair suddenly lurches into motion, and with that his grandfather comes to attention. "Ask away."

"Would you teach me to be a cowboy? Please, I mean."

"Be a cowboy—what does that mean?"

"You know. Like you."

"Like me. Now that's a howler." His grandfather finally looks at Will. "Tell me. Do you like to dig?"

"Dig?"

"That's right. With a shovel. Dig."

Will shrugs. "I don't know. Not really."

His grandfather reaches out a long leg and with his boot hooks the little footstool and pulls it close to his rocking chair. "Sit if you like," he says.

Will lowers himself to the footstool.

"You make the mistake a lot of folks make," his grandfather says. "You think a cowboy *is* something when the fact is a cowboy *does* something. And the something he does is likely to be about as far from what most people think of as the cowboy life as pigs from horses. That's why I asked you about digging. Believe me when I say I've sunk a hell of a lot more fence posts than I've roped cattle. I've never busted a bronc, but I've broke my collarbone and my arm and a few ribs because I couldn't stay on a horse or two. And now I've got a saddle but no horse, but that's all right because I've chased more cattle on foot or in a truck than I have on horseback. Now you tell me—does that sound like the kind of life you're looking for?"

"I don't know."

"You don't? Pah!" His grandfather waves his hand at Will as if his grandson could not have uttered a response more disgusting. "Trust me: You don't. Study hard. Go to college. Get a good job behind a desk where the sun won't fry your hide and the cold won't freeze your ass. Be like your father. Then you can sell land instead of roam all over it."

His grandfather has probably said all he has to say on the subject, but it's so far from what Will needs to hear that he can't get up from the footstool. It has taken too much of his courage to speak to his grandfather; he isn't about to simply walk away.

He takes a deep breath and then lets it go. "Okay, then will you teach me to do what a cowboy does? What you do, I mean."

His grandfather chuckles, but it's not the kind of laugh that an adult humors a child with; this is the laugh one man uses to humiliate another. "You think you might have to ride into a neighbor's hedge and jump a steer or string barbed wire up and down the alley? Or maybe you saw a horse hobbling up Fourth Street that needs shoeing? Jesus Christ, boy, you live in the middle of town. Why in hell would you need to learn any of that?"

"So I can get a job. I don't want to live in town."

His grandfather tilts back in his chair. "Oh, you don't, eh? Looks like a damn good life to me."

Will knows he's being mocked, but he likes that his grandfather is willing to swear in his presence. "Maybe I could live with you," Will says. "I could sort of be your helper."

His grandfather reaches out and with the tip of his finger he swivels Will's face toward the window. "See that garage out there? I live in a place smaller than that. Most of my meals I don't bother sitting down to eat. And I eat them out of a can. I've barely got room for myself, much less a growing boy."

Before Will can tell him that he has a tent he's perfectly willing to live in if he can pitch it on his grandfather's land—there's a knock at the back door. He follows his grandfather through the kitchen.

Through the screen Will sees Mrs. Lodge, and she's holding a covered plate. He hopes peanut butter cookies are under the napkin—Mrs. Lodge chops up peanuts and puts them in the cookie dough.

Will's mother or father would simply shout for Mrs. Lodge to come in, but his grandfather talks to her through the screen. "Yes?" You would think the discussion he and Will were having was so important he resents this interruption.

But if Mrs. Lodge is offended, she doesn't show it. She keeps smiling that pretty smile. "I brought the family a little something." She raises the plate a little higher.

Will's grandfather opens the door cautiously, and that's all the invitation Mrs. Lodge needs. She's in the kitchen and has her plate on the counter while his grandfather is still standing by the screen door.

She lifts the napkin. "Date bars," she announces. Will can't help making a face, and keen-eyed Mrs. Lodge notices. "Not your favorite, eh Will?"

He shakes his head.

"Suit yourself." She turns back to Will's grandfather. "I brought these as a little thank-you."

Calvin Sidey raises his eyebrows quizzically.

"For speaking to the Neaveses about that dog of theirs. Maybe you solved the neighborhood's problem. I notice that any time Queenie's outside now she's chained up. What did you say to them?"

Will's grandfather stands by the door as if he's waiting to escort Mrs. Lodge out.

"If you don't mind my asking," she says.

"I told them," he says, then clears his throat. "I told them I'd shoot the dog if she came near the garbage again."

Mrs. Lodge lets out a low whistle that slides down the scale. "Did you now? And I imagine you said it in such a way that they had no problem believing you'd do exactly that. I wish I could have seen June Neaves's expression."

"She didn't have much to say on the subject."

Will has always thought Mrs. Lodge is about as comfortable with herself as a person can be, but now her fingers fly to her blouse and fidget there as if she thinks a button might have come undone. "I almost forgot my other reason for coming over," she says. "How would the Sideys like to come for supper tomorrow evening?"

His grandfather glances down at him, and Will has the strange feeling that his grandfather wants Will to accept or decline the invitation. He gives his grandfather a quick nod.

"I'll have to check with the girl," his grandfather says.

"Ann doesn't have to work tomorrow night," Mrs. Lodge says, "if that's what you're wondering. But I'll understand if she's got better things to do. How about you, Will? Feel like sitting down to supper with a couple old fogies? Steak and baked potatoes are on the menu. Rhubarb pie for dessert."

Will doesn't care for baked potatoes or rhubarb pie, but he nods in assent.

"All right then. Supper will be at six, but come on over earlier if you want to tell me how you like your steak done." Mrs. Lodge is halfway out the door when she pauses. "Oh, and if he decides to come out of the basement and grace us with his presence, my son, Adam, will join us."

Mrs. Lodge departs, but his grandfather remains by the door, watching her walk back to her own home. "I didn't know I said yes to her," Will's grandfather says.

"Dad says Mrs. Lodge is like a car with no reverse. She can only go in one direction."

"Well, I guess we're going out for supper."

Will follows his grandfather back to the living room where he walks to a window with a view of Mrs. Lodge's home. For a long moment he gazes intently at her house, as if there's a message in those gray-painted boards that he'll be able to decipher if he just stares long enough. Will looks out too, but once again he can't understand what's outside the walls of this house that's so deserving of his grandfather's attention.

Will gives up. "Can I turn on the TV?"

"What would your mother say?"

"She'd probably say okay."

"Go ahead then."

Will squats on the floor in front of the television but doesn't turn it on. "Can I ask you something else?"

"As long as it's not about coming to live with me."

"Would you really shoot Queenie?"

"Queenie?"

"The dog? The Neaveses' dog?"

"I don't say I'll do a thing if I'm not willing to follow through. Which is the way everyone should live, even ten-year-old boys—"

"Eleven," Will says. "I'm eleven."

"Eleven. Fine. My point is, if you say you'll do something, then by God you better be ready to do it. Otherwise, you're just making empty threats. And no one's going to respect that kind of man."

"But Queenie? You'd shoot *Queenie*?"

His grandfather turns back to the window. A hot wind has risen, and the town is so dry that blowing grit and sand scratch at the glass and screen. "I don't believe it will come to that. If you're not going to watch the television, why don't you scoot. Go play with your friends."

"I don't like my friends."

"Then they're not your friends. You run along anyhow."

WILL DOESN'T GO FAR. He enters the bathroom and locks the door behind him. He stands before the mirror and tries to put on one of his grandfather's expressions. He draws as tight and straight a line with his lips as he can; he narrows and deadens his gaze and scowls a vertical crease between his eyes.

"Look, Stuart," he says to the mirror. He'll have to speak louder if he wants the words to rumble out like his grandfather's. So his rehearsal cannot be heard, Will turns the water on full force before he continues. "Look, Stuart, I know you and Bobby and Glen are fixing to spy on my sister, and I'm here to tell you I'm not going to allow that. The first one of you I catch even looking in the direction of Ann's window will have to answer to me. And if you thinking I'm making"—Will has to search for that phrase, how did he put it?—"an empty threat, you're mistaken."

And there Will stops, not only because he can tell he's no longer imitating his grandfather but instead a character in a western movie or television show, but also because he remembers the fight Stuart was in last fall. Stuart, Gary, and Will had been downtown on a Saturday afternoon, and on their way to Gary's house, they cut across the playground of Horace Mann Elementary School. Four boys their age stopped them and said Lincoln kids weren't allowed on Horace Mann property. Without a word of argument, Stuart flew at the biggest boy and in an instant Stuart had him down, straddled and held by the back of his shirt collar as if he were a miniature horse. "We go where we fucking want to go," Stuart said, bending down to hit the boy in the back of the head with his fist, producing a sound like a door being knocked on with a rubber mallet. Stuart released the boy, and all the Horace Mann kids ran off. As Stuart, Gary, and Will continued on their way, Stuart shook out his hand. "That bastard's head was hard as cinder block." Will is smaller than the Horace Mann boy, and Will knows he'd fare no better in a fight with Stuart.

The running water reminds Will that he has to pee. He shuts

off the faucets, unzips his jeans, and steps to the toilet. He's next
to the window, and he glances in the direction of the Neaveses' and
the yard where Queenie is chained. How would his grandfather do
it? Will can no more imagine himself doing such a thing than he can
imagine Stuart Kinder beaten and bloodied at Will's feet.

CALVIN LIFTS THE NAPKIN from the plate of date bars. They
look appetizing enough, but he's never much cared for dates, figs,
raisins, or currants. For that matter, he seldom eats sweets or baked
goods. After dinner on Saturday night, Marjorie brought a chocolate cake to the table and asked him how big a piece he'd like. He
demurred, and Bill said, "Come on, Dad. You used to have a sweet
tooth, didn't you? How long has it been since you've had some
pastry?"

Calvin knew exactly how long it had been. Two summers ago,
he and Shorty Oak, who was neither short nor sturdy, took on the
job of painting the barn and a few outbuildings at Ed Vernon's
place. It had been hot, tedious work, and when the job was finally
done, and Calvin and Shorty were cleaning their brushes, folding up the drop cloths, and putting away the ladders, Shorty said,
"Don't go anywhere. I'm going into town to get us a reward."
Calvin didn't need any reward, though he would have appreciated
help with the cleanup.

Shorty returned with a six-pack of Pabst Blue Ribbon and a
cherry pie, purchased from Harley's Bakery, a shop where Calvin
occasionally bought his bread.

Calvin refused Shorty's offer of a beer.

"What's the matter? Not your brand? Hell, after all these days
of working in the heat, I'd drink it warm and flat if that was all I
could get."

"I don't drink, Shorty. I thought you knew that."

"Not even beer?"

"Not today."

"Maybe tomorrow then, hey?"

"Ask me tomorrow."

"Well, hell," Shorty said, "you ain't got nothing against pie, do you?"

So Shorty got out his jackknife and cut into the pie, lifting out big, dripping wedges, and the two men sat on the lift gate of Shorty's truck and ate pie right out of the tin. In between bites, Shorty drained a Pabst and opened another. When he wiped his mouth with the back of his hand, he smeared a streak of red across his face that looked like blood. Calvin couldn't see his own face, but he imagined he didn't look much different. Pie filling dripped from his fingers. And though Calvin didn't think of himself as particularly delicate or refined, he wondered when he had become a man willing to eat pie with his fingers from the back of truck. What was left of his slice of pie he let drop into the dust.

"God damn," said Shorty. "I'd of eaten that."

As Calvin walked away, he called over his shoulder, "Tell Ed he can mail my check to me."

Calvin places the napkin carefully back over the date bars.

He hears the toilet flush upstairs, and for a minute—for less than a minute, for seconds—Calvin imagines what life would be like at his place shared with a ten- —*eleven*- —year-old boy . . . To hear a child's soft chuffy breathing as he sleeps at night. To wake in the morning and move slowly and quietly so he doesn't disturb the boy. And why are his first thoughts of a sleeping child? To allow himself to contemplate for a little while the sweeter thoughts of a child living with him before he lets in the reality of the nagging, restless commotion that a boy's presence would inevitably mean? My God, what would Bill say if Calvin told him that he'd decided to take Will off to live in his little tin box on the prairie and to teach the boy the cowboy life? Bill would bust a gasket and Calvin couldn't blame him. Calvin barely knows his grandson, and he surely doesn't know what kind of life he wants for the boy beyond knowing that it isn't Calvin's own. He wouldn't wish that on anyone, much less his own grandson.

The reality is, of course, that the boy could probably educate the man. How much Calvin doesn't understand of contemporary life. Rockets fired into space and cars taking their shapes from those same rockets. Crowds of Negroes marching and loudly insisting on their rights, as if that kind of demand ever did any good. Men and women—like his own daughter-in-law—whining and wanting a pill or a procedure so they don't have to put up with any discomfort or unpleasantness. And television, television, television everywhere— so every family lives like their home is a damn movie theater. No, Calvin Sidey might know how to bridle a horse that fights the bit, but little Will doubtless comprehends this world better than his grandfather ever will.

TWELVE

ıı

A nn wonders if she should give up and go out to him.

He drives through their alley almost every night, sometimes several times, but tonight he's just parked there, not even bothering to idle the engine for a quick getaway. She first noticed the car around midnight, and now it's after one. Will he stay there all night?

That Monte might do just that is not however what makes her consider walking out of the house and getting in his car. What she really fears is that he might come in. Like every other family up and down the block, the Sideys leave their doors unlocked night and day, and during the summer, her father insists that the inner doors be kept open so the cooler air can flow through the screens. Not that any of the house's locks or latches could prevent or discourage anyone who wants to force his way in. Nor could anyone in the house stop him.

She remembers when, shortly after he and Ann began to date, they were together with friends in Pioneer Park. In the park on that same day the local Kiwanis club was hosting a cookout and picnic to raise money for the eye operation that the Methodist minister's son needed. Ann's father was grilling the hamburgers and hot dogs, and he wore an apron as he served the children and their parents lining up for food. When he saw Ann and her friends sitting on a picnic table fifty yards away, he smiled and twirled his spatula and tongs in the air like a pair of Fourth of July sparklers.

"That your old man?" Monte asked Ann.

There were many fathers gathered near hers, but Ann simply nodded in assent.

"He's a cook?" Monte asked.

"No, he's just helping . . . Oh, never mind." She felt he was being deliberately thickheaded about her father. Monte knew Mr. Sidey had his own real estate company, didn't he?

"Must be good eating at your house. Your old man being a professional cook and all."

"And what does your father do?" It was a cruel thing to ask because Monte's father and mother were divorced, and his father lived in Laramie, Wyoming, where he was a dentist. But Monte had annoyed her with those remarks about her father, and sometimes Ann couldn't stop her tongue in time.

"You know damn good and well what he does. He looks in people's mouths. All damn day long."

"Then I guess there's no cavities in your family if your dad's a dentist."

Instead of answering her silly question, he looked long and hard at Mr. Sidey. Finally, he said, "He ain't much, is he."

She already regretted saying something about Monte's father, so she didn't offer a defense of her father but simply shrugged and said, "He's pretty much like all the other fathers."

"Yeah. That's what I mean."

So if Monte decided to get out of his car and march into the house after her, her parents would probably be no more deterrent than the flimsy screen door. Would he hurt them? Ann believes he might. Just as she believes that if he knew now that an old man was the only adult in the house he would certainly come crashing through the door.

But if she walks out of the house of her own volition, if she simply walks out and wordlessly climbs into his car, then no one will get hurt.

No one but her? Isn't that what she really means? But perhaps that isn't a certainty. Maybe if she doesn't resist him he'll revert to that gentler being he had been in the beginning.

She knows now that he had been following a schedule: Wait two weeks before putting his arm around her in the back row of the Rialto; three weeks before asking for a kiss good-night; four weeks before suggesting that she sit close to him as they drove up and down Gladstone's Main Avenue; two full months before he drove her to the top of cemetery hill after the high school's Winterfest Dance and parked with the rest of the herd of lightless, window-fogged cars and attempted to make out with her. Which she allowed because at every one of those other steps he had been courtly and tender, as if not only would he stop if she seemed the least bit hesitant but he would also be embarrassed and ashamed. And it gave Ann a special pleasure that his solicitous, gentlemanly behavior was completely at odds with how others saw him. To them, he was a hood, a hell-raiser, one of the dangerous crowd that hung out in the lot behind Scanlon's Truck and Auto Body Repair, smoking, looking for someone to buy them beer, shoving and punching each other in the arm in preparation for the fights they would get into if any of the ranch boys, the good student athletes, or the Indians from the nearby reservation looked at them crossways. The report she had been given when he first came to town—that he was cute and nice—had been modified considerably, yet to Ann he kept both those qualities.

And Ann liked that he was something to her that he was to no one else. When anyone said anything in the least disparaging about him (like Janice: "He lives in the nice part of town; why does he have to be such a hood!"), Ann wouldn't argue; she simply smiled to herself and thought, You don't know him like I do. Perhaps it was true that in her thinking of him as her secret love (had she really gone around humming the Doris Day song?—yes, she supposed she had) she had failed to see some of what others saw.

Nevertheless, her months with him had gone so well she was content to lean into his arms that night on cemetery hill and count their kisses—twenty-seven during that session. And oh my, what a good kisser he was! He didn't scrape his teeth against hers like Donnie Gustafson. He didn't drool like Jim Tetzloff. His lips weren't tight and cracked like Morris Moer's.

The next time there were forty-two kisses. She knew exactly because she made coded entries on her calendar. Supplementing the kisses were the compliments and the gifts: a necklace with a pearl pendant, stationery, a box of Russell Stover chocolates, Shalimar perfume. He had been not only patient but thoughtful and kind.

And Ann had been naïve enough to believe that he was as

satisfied with their relationship as she was. He gave her no indication that he was anything but content, though he never said much one way or another. She must have believed that he, like so many other Montanans, thought that if he spent too many words on any subject he'd end up impoverished in some way, in debt to his listeners.

The weather turned warm, and they parked near Willow Creek. The waters had recently thawed, and with their newfound speed, they made a sound that caused Ann to think someone was coming toward them, splashing his way across the stream from the other side. She kept looking out, and perhaps that distraction on her part was what set him off.

She had been with boys before who had put their hands where they shouldn't, but she never needed to discourage them more than twice—twisting away or pushing their hand away had always been enough. And usually the embarrassment of rejection ended the matter right there. Only Morris Moers tried a pleading negotiation. "Please," he said, "if you'll just let me put my hand there, I won't try anything else. And I won't even move my hand."

But that night by Willow Creek was different. He came at her as if there were no possibility he could be deterred. Soon Ann was the one tempted to bargain: *Please, if I let you put your hand there, will you stop?*

Four kisses in—*she could not believe she had still been counting*— he grabbed her breast. He did not try, as some boys had, to slide his hand there surreptitiously; he simply grabbed. And squeezed. And when she pushed his hand away, he shoved it in her crotch so hard it hurt. Thank God she had been wearing slacks! She got hold of his wrist and managed to twist him out from between her legs. But he just moved back to her breast, this time forcing his way inside her blouse and popping off a button in the process. When she got him out of there, he dove down again below her waist. He was still following a schedule!

Everything he rammed and pushed at her—tongue, fingers, knees—came with such force that if she weren't braced for the onslaught he might tear right through her flesh. "Don't," she said, "don't. *Don't!* I mean it!" But even to her own ears her voice sounded weak, with no more power to affect him than the splashing water had on the creek stones.

Just as she was resigning herself—*I'm going to be raped*—and she was trying to find a place in her mind that would be far away from the moment she was trapped in, he stopped. He shoved her shoulders and said, "Ah, this is bullshit!"

He got out of the car, slamming the door behind him, and walked toward the creek. Ann considered jumping out of the car herself, running away as fast as she could. She still wasn't sure why she hadn't. Because she was so relieved not to have him pawing and poking her that she felt safer than she should have? Because she felt it was better to see him and know where he was than to turn her back on him as she would have to if she ran?

The moon was not quite full, but from its station behind them, high in the eastern sky, it cast enough light for her to watch him.

He stopped less than thirty feet away, near the creek's rushing water, its rippled surface glinting in the moonlight. He was . . . was he going to urinate in the stream?

And then she knew, knew without doubt, though what she saw she had never seen before. He was playing with himself—that was the phrase she had heard others use, but she had to wonder—what could *play* possibly have to do with this life or death night?

He was dressed, as he almost always was, in dark colors, tight jeans and a long-sleeved denim shirt, so when he turned it was his face, his hands, his cock—jutting from his jeans—that caught the moonlight, each inch of flesh the color of pale stone.

But he was not made of stone. He began to walk toward the car, his steps slow compared to the speed with which his hand pumped up and down on himself. Ann believed he was looking right at her, but she couldn't be sure. Perhaps there was too little light available to allow him to see inside the car. And it occurred to her that maybe she should lie down or crouch under the dashboard— anyplace where he couldn't see her, and she couldn't see him. She didn't want to watch, but she was afraid that if she turned away, he'd become further enraged, that he was trying to prove some- thing to her, that he was performing for her—whatever it was, he would not take it well if she covered her eyes. So she didn't look away, and just at that moment when she would have thought there was nothing else pale or white out there to catch the moonlight, there was more. He stopped, spread his legs as if he were bracing himself, and bared his teeth—a mouthful of gray pebbles—and then something—a string? a plume?—arced out of him, his hand, his cock, white as milk or smoke.

They both shuddered. He zipped himself back up, walked to the driver's side, and got into the car.

Ann wedged herself as tightly as she could into the space be- tween the seat and the passenger door. Monte took a fresh pack of Pall Malls from the overhead visor and proceeded to tap the bottom of the pack hard on the dashboard. In the confines of the car, the cigarette pack made a sound like the slap of a rolled-up magazine, and Ann flinched at every *whap*. His window was open, and he craned his head out in order to look up into the night sky. Was he trying to determine whether the moon or stars beamed down suf- ficient light for her to see what he had done?

He pulled his head back in. "You don't know a goddamn thing about me, do you?"

"I thought I did."

He shook his head. "Did you hear what happened out at Del-Ray Lanes?"

"I heard something." What she heard was that he got into a fight with Ron Engen, a senior football player, in the parking lot outside the bowling alley. In the most detailed version that came Ann's way, he knocked Ron to the blacktop and then kicked him in the head. Rhonda Sikorski was sure she saw one of Ron Engen's teeth fly out and bounce under his own car.

"Did you hear what that was about? No? Well the sonofabitch said something about you, and believe me when I say you don't want to know what it was."

Ann had known Ron Engen since elementary school, and it was hard for her to believe that that red-haired serious boy could say anything that would give offense. It was even harder to believe he could be knocked down—he was tall and had a tree's thick sturdiness about him.

Monte tore open the cellophane, slit the foil with his thumbnail, and tapped out a cigarette. With his lips he pulled it from the pack but then took it out again, unlit. "When he was shooting his big mouth off, he didn't know you belong to me."

Ron Engen had sat across from her in Miss Shepard's sixth grade class, and he used to tease her by pulling on his fingers and making the knuckles pop, knowing she hated the sound.

"Would you take me home now? Please."

"You want to go home? Yeah, I bet you do." He put the cigarette between his lips again and spoke around it. "You know what else you don't know anything about? You don't know shit about what a man needs."

She was tempted to say, but you're not a man; you're a boy. However, she didn't want to do or say anything that might antagonize him. Besides, he had started the car now, and maybe if she kept quiet he'd drive back to town. Even if he wouldn't take her home, once he was in Gladstone she could jump out of the car at an intersection.

But instead of putting the car into gear, he pushed in the cigarette lighter, and Ann allowed herself to breathe for a moment. He was spent now and relaxed.

The lighter popped out, and just as it did, she thought, That's funny; he never uses the car lighter. He always clanks open that heavy chrome Zippo.

And as quick as that thought, he was on her, bringing the red-hot lighter so close to her face she could feel its heat and count the glowing coils.

"Did you hear what I said? Did you? You belong to me! Do I have to put a goddamn brand on you?"

Ann thrust her hand up between the lighter and her face, and she remembered thinking, too clearly and too calmly, that her palm would be seared but perhaps the lighter would cool itself sufficiently on her hand's flesh that when he pressed it to her face it would not be hot enough to burn her as badly.

But he pulled the lighter away and put it back in its socket on the dashboard, leaving Ann to wonder how a chill could course through her a second after that intense heat. He arranged himself behind the steering wheel once again, and now he did put the car into gear. He lay his arm across the top of the seat, and Ann flinched, but only so he could look back while he backed up. While he was turned toward the rear window, he spoke placidly to Ann.

"You'll come around. I know you will. You're just not ready yet. But you will be."

Ann wasn't sure if he smiled when he said these words, but every time he spoke them or some abbreviated version of them over the coming weeks—when he passed her in the hall, when he drove past her and her friends on the corner outside Finley's Drugstore, when he saw her at the river, at the movie theater, at the Rim Rock Cafe—"Are you ready now?"—he smiled, and sometimes he winked too or put his finger to his forehead as if he were tipping his hat. *Are you? Are you ready?*

If readiness is kin to fear, desperation, and resignation, Ann supposes she's ready now. She peeks out the corner of her window. He's still there all right, just the front bumper and part of the Ford's hood nosing out from behind the Lodge's garage where he's parked. Ann listens hard, trying to hear the engine under the higher notes of chirping crickets, whistling nighthawks, and hissing lawn sprinklers. Yes, there it is—that steady rumble.

Ann takes a look around her room, and the affection she feels for all its odd and mismatched parts—the rocking chair with the missing dowel, the bookcase that she painted with the same white paint her father used in the hallway, the worn gray carpet, the sagging bed—makes it seem as though she's gazing at them for the last time. Good-bye to the photograph of Grace Kelly she clipped from *Life* magazine, good-bye to the newspaper headline taped to her mirror announcing that the Gladstone boys came in second in the Class B high school basketball tournament, good-bye to the record player with its snug little stack of 45s, good-bye to the cane with the kewpie doll attached that she won at the Shrine circus, good-bye to the floral print bedspread that she bought for herself with her Penney's discount—farewell, farewell! Good-bye, good-bye!

She closes the bedroom door tightly, something she never does if she's planning to return soon, and begins slowly to descend the stairs, careful to step to the sides to make as little noise as possible.

Just as she reaches the bottom of the stairs, a voice says, "Going somewhere?"

Startled, she clutches the banister and barely suppresses the impulse to turn and run back up. In the next instant, she realizes that the voice came from her grandfather, sitting in the rocking chair. Nothing but moonlight and light from the street lamp illuminates the room.

"I was . . . it's so hot upstairs. I thought I'd sit down here. Just for a while."

Her grandfather stands. "You're welcome to this chair. There's a little air coming through the window." Her mother's lace curtains flutter uncertainly into the room.

She crosses the room and sits down, and as soon as she does, it's not coolness that comes to her but warmth. In its cane webbing, the rocking chair holds a remnant of heat from her grandfather's body, and though the chair's wood is unyielding, she still feels enfolded. She knows her grandfather is not about to take her in his arms and hold her tight in a protecting embrace, but for the moment, the rocking chair's cage is comfort enough.

"You want the television on?" he asks. "I'm not in the habit of the thing, but I'll switch it on, if you like."

"No, that's all right." Only then does she realize that her grandfather has been sitting in the dark with nothing—no book or magazine, no radio or television—but what Ann guesses are his dark thoughts.

"Feel any breeze?"

"It's nice."

"Tomorrow a working day for you?"

"I don't have to go in until eleven."

Her grandfather nods as if this is a fact he's forgotten. "No one's going to hold it against you if you decide to excuse yourself from supper at the neighbor's tomorrow night."

"That's okay. I want to go."

Calvin Sidey glances over his shoulder toward the back of the house, and Ann's heart seizes with the thought that perhaps he has heard something.

"You wouldn't know anything about that car out there in the alley, would you?"

"No."

"Same car that's driven past the house a few times."

Ann shakes her head.

"There's not someone in that car you were planning to go out and meet?"

She feels her face flush and hot tears spring to her eyes. "No." She knows he doesn't believe her, and if he asks her one more question, she might not be able to help herself; she'll tell him who's driving that car and what he's doing out there.

But he doesn't say anything. He stands near the window and stares down at her. Ann doesn't know where the feeling comes from, but she senses that Monte is no longer waiting out in the alley. This will not be the night she'll leave her home.

"You know," her grandfather says, "when you were coming down those stairs I looked up and damned if I didn't think I saw your grandmother."

"Me? Do I look that much like her? I wish I could have known her. In Dad's photo albums, she looks so . . . nice." Pauline Sidey looks more than nice; she looks beautiful, but since Ann's grandfather has compared her in appearance to her grandmother, it would be immodest for Ann to make that connection.

He gazes at her for a long moment. "You're considerable taller," he says, and with that he steps away from her and the open window and walks from the room.

He goes into the kitchen, and Ann hears the sound of a chair being scraped away from the table and then the scratch of a match as her grandfather lights one of his hand-rolled cigarettes. Although she can't feel any cool air coming in, she remains by the window. She feels something better than a breeze. She feels safe.

THIRTEEN

||||||||||||||||||||||||||||||||||||||||||||||||||||||||||

Beverly wishes she'd never invited the Sideys for dinner.

The meal went all right—even skinny-as-a-stick Will asked for seconds, and when she cleared the dishes, she could damn near have put them right back in the cupboard, so thoroughly had all the diners cleaned their plates.

But what's supposed to happen next? They've finished their dessert (instead of rhubarb pie, pineapple upside-down cake with whipped cream), and now they're just sitting around the dining room table wearing their own personal shade of miserable.

No doubt the heat is a big part of the problem. The thermometer on the front porch topped a hundred that afternoon, and even making allowances for the fact that the house faces west and so is bound to be hotter, there's no getting around it—this has to be the summer's hottest day so far.

To make matters worse, Beverly changed the menu from the steak and baked potatoes she'd planned, but instead of going with something like cold chicken and potato salad, something she could have prepared the evening before (when she made the cake), and had sitting in the refrigerator, she decided to fix roast beef, mashed potatoes and gravy, and corn on the cob. She had chosen this meal for the timing—she could serve everyone at once, and if she would have gone with steaks, she could have prepared no more than two at a time. But roast beef meant she had to turn on the oven, and the corn and mashed potatoes added two burners, and almost two hours after the completion of the meal the kitchen still radiated heat.

But she had managed to put all the food out at once, though now she wishes she could excuse the guests so they could all run off to the somewhere else they plainly wanted to be.

Only Adam seems to be enjoying himself and that's because he can't get enough of Ann Sidey and her teenaged beauty. In fact, the way he stared at her throughout the meal, and now tries to charm her with tales about what Gladstone High was like during his student years, makes Beverly wonder if something other than a budget cut was behind Adam's not being offered a teaching contract.

Ann doesn't seem particularly comfortable with adoration. Her posture is probably an attempt at prim good manners, but she looks as though she has a touch of indigestion.

"And is Mr. Reed still there?" Adam asks her. "Teaching history?"

Ann nods. "He teaches sophomore English too."

"My God! I would have guessed he was in his seventies when I had him. So that must mean he's—what? —pushing ninety?"

Ann's laughter is merely polite and doesn't match Adam's in volume or duration.

"That face of his," Adam says. "It always reminded me of a bloodstained sock. Is it still a mystery how it got that way?"

"Someone said it was from being gassed in the First World War," Ann suggests tentatively.

Adam's laugh is skeptical. "Gas doesn't do that to your skin. It attacks your lungs."

Calvin Sidey has been sitting as straight and silent as his grand-daughter, but now he clears his throat and speaks up, a little too loudly. "If you're talking about mustard gas, it sure as hell could burn your skin. Burn and blister. And I'll tell you something else about it: Those gas masks couldn't do a damn thing to keep it out."

Adam throws a jokey little salute in Calvin Sidey's direction. "I stand corrected."

Because she feels older folks have to stick together, Beverly puts in her two cents' worth. "And in the case of Henry Reed, he looks like that because he pulled a pot of boiling water over on himself when he was a boy."

"Huh," Adam says. "I wonder why we never heard that."

"Maybe," Beverly says, "it's not something he cared to advertise."

"Or he figured it was nobody's business," Calvin says.

And then another silence descends, this one more uncomfortable than any brought on by the heat or full stomachs.

After another moment, Ann speaks again, brightly and looking around the table as if she feels it's her duty to get the conversation started again.

"Darlene Holton's cousin is one of those college kids who's going down south this summer to help the Negroes vote and—"

"Where's he from?" interrupted Adam. "Not around here."

"She," Ann corrects him without looking at him. "She's from Minneapolis. Anyway. Some of us were talking and we're thinking maybe we should do something like that here. Only for the Indians. We could help—"

"Which Indians?" asks Calvin.

"Which?"

"The reservation Indians? The town Indians? The Indians who don't look like Indians?"

Ann's smile fades, and she looks at her grandfather as though she's not exactly sure who this man is.

"Because," Calvin continues, "the reservation Indians are pretty well taken care of by the government—"

Adam interrupts again, this time to ask, "Can a reservation Indian vote? Legally, I mean?"

"They can," Calvin says. "They've got to travel a hell of a ways to do it, but they can. Most, I'm guessing, don't bother."

Ann begins to ask a question, "Why should—" but her grandfather cuts her off again, his voice rising as though he's addressing a room larger than Beverly's kitchen.

"Your town Indians, the sober ones, a good many of them have learned to make do. And the Indians who don't look like Indians? Well, good luck getting them to step forward and say who they are."

Beverly feels sorry for Ann, who is still sitting up as straight as ever, but the color that's risen to her cheeks says that she is probably now confused, angry, and humiliated. Beverly reaches out her hand toward Ann, pats the table, and says, "I think it's good that you and your friends want to do something."

For a long time Ann stares at the tabletop. When she finally speaks, in a tone as formal as if she were addressing strangers, she looks to both Beverly and Calvin, as if she's not quite sure whose permission is required. "Some friends of mine are going to the Legion baseball game tonight. May I go with them, please? I'll still clean up."

Beverly guesses that the young woman is simply concocting an excuse to get away from these adults and their pettiness and condescension. And Beverly doesn't blame her a bit. "I appreciate the offer, honey, but I'm not doing anything but stacking the dishes. I won't do another blessed thing to heat up this room, and that includes running hot water. Maybe I'll set the alarm for four a.m. and wash dishes then."

"I have no objection," Calvin says.

Ann stands, and in a display of manners Beverly has never seen before, Adam gets up too, his face wearing an expression of obvious disappointment.

Ann says to Will, "Would you like to come along?"

Will has been sitting quietly, so bored he's been concentrating on fitting the edge of his dessert plate between the tines of his fork. He almost jumps out of his chair at his sister's proposal. "To the game? With you? Is anybody else going?"

"Kitty and Janice." She must understand her brother's dilemma because she smiles and adds, "But you wouldn't have to sit with us."

The boy looks to his grandfather for permission.

"If your sister will have you, it's all right with me."

They're almost out the door when Ann turns back. "If Dad or Mom calls—"

Calvin waves them on their way. "If there's any news, I'll track you down."

As soon as they're gone, Beverly's son excuses himself as well. "I'm going downstairs," Adam says, "to see if I can't pound out a few more pages." He takes his coffee with him, but he also stops off at the refrigerator and takes out a bottle of Schlitz. Beverly cringes, knowing that Calvin has seen the beer. Certainly a summer day like this one calls for a cold beer, but knowing Calvin Sidey's history with drink, she never offered any.

The basement door closes behind her son. "Adam's writing a book," Beverly explains. "He has a little office set up down there, and I have to say he's been pretty diligent about putting in the hours."

"What's his book about?"

"He hasn't shown me any of it, but from what I understand, it's a western."

"That something he knows a good deal about, is it?"

"Gladstone born and bred—does that qualify?"

"About as much as the rest of the scribblers filling up the racks at the drugstore. What the hell. No reason he shouldn't get in on it."

"How about you? Are you still doing ranch work?"

"When I can find someone willing to hire me. That's not as regular as it used to be."

"You could always come back to town." It's an innocuous re-mark, yet Beverly winces to herself after making it. Will he think she's trying to trap him into saying something about the circum-stances of his leaving?

He flicks a crumb from the table. "I've been away too long. I'm afraid I'm not much suited for civilized society anymore."

If you ever were, Beverly says to herself and shivers inwardly again. "So—your daughter-in-law's surgery is scheduled for tomorrow?"

"That's what I'm told."

"I imagine Marjorie's eager to have done with it."

"I'm sure she is." With the edge of his thumb, Calvin wipes sweat from above his eyebrow.

"Sorry about the heat," Beverly says.

"So you're responsible."

Even when he says something like this, something that could be a joke, Beverly feels as though she's being reprimanded. "I just meant . . . I couldn't come up with a damn thing to offer any relief. I considered hauling all the food outside, but it's no cooler out there. In here we don't have to contend with the mosquitoes and the flies." Just as she says this, she notices a fly twitching in the shade of Adam's plate. She reaches over and nudges the plate, sending the fly into sideways flight. With a laugh, she adds, "Mosquitoes anyway!"

Earlier, the room's silence was that of relative strangers forced into close company, but now it seems to come from a man and woman alone together, and one of them is staring so hard at the other that Beverly feels herself flush with the attention. The sensation reminds her, simultaneously and paradoxically, of a schoolgirl blush and a middle-aged hot flash. She would have thought both were behind her by now. Well, this heat can do strange things.

"If you're really looking to beat the heat," Calvin says, "I've got the answer."

"Anything short of sticking my head in a bucket of ice water," she replies, "I'm game."

THE BASEMENT OF THE Sidey home is at least twenty degrees cooler than her kitchen, and once Beverly gets past the smell of mildew and the fact that somewhere in the room a cricket is chirping—she hates crickets—she has to admit, she feels more comfortable than she has in days. But she'd never spend a night in her own basement, and it has linoleum floors, paneled walls, and an acoustic ceiling. This is nothing but concrete, studs, joists, and discarded furniture and trunks from the rooms upstairs.

"This is where your son put you up?"

"My choice," Calvin says. "I had my years aboveground here."

His shirts hang from nails, and the narrow bed is neatly made. On the straight back chair next to the bed is a book, and Beverly can't resist picking it up to read the gilt letters on the spine.

"Catullus. My goodness."

"Helps me fall asleep."

Beverly opens the book. She had two years of high school Latin, but she can't understand a word. "Yes, I believe I'm feeling drowsy already."

He takes the book from her hands. "Go ahead and lie down."

"It was a joke, Mr. Sidey. A joke."

For answer, he sticks his finger inside the armhole of her sleeveless blouse. He knows what he's doing because he gets inside the strap of her brassiere and runs his finger down to where the strap attaches to the cup. She knows she should twist away from him and slap his face, but forces—as overpowering as the heat that pressed in on her only moments before—freeze her in place.

This man is, after all, in spite of his age and years of absence from Gladstone, a Sidey, a name that connoted power and influence in their town, and to be looked on with favor by one of them still means something to people who grew up in the family's shadow. And yet Beverly Lodge has never had a problem telling any boy or man—she would have said it to President Kennedy himself—to put his hands back in his pockets. Is she letting this moment go on so she'll have something to tell her aunt Doris the next time Beverly visits Spokane? *You'll never guess who made a pass at me. Calvin Sidey! That's right! Who'd have thought he'd turn out to be nothing but a lecher in his old age.* But most days her aunt doesn't remember Beverly; why would she remember someone from half a century past?

All of these thoughts, however, are an attempt to locate outside herself a reason for why she doesn't bat his hand away, and if she stops scrambling for just a moment from another thought—this one more frightening and inexplicable than any other—she'll admit: Yes, she likes the feel of this man's finger on her skin, and yes, she wants more.

FOURTEEN

||||||||||||||||||||||||||||||||||||||||||||||||||||||||||

The family and friends of surgical patients are provided a special waiting area on the third floor, a long windowless room furnished with mismatched chairs and couches pushed back against the walls. In the middle of the room, there's nothing but dark green carpeting, a blank space so large it seems as though it's waiting for a performance of some kind. At one end of the room is a console television that commands the attention of most people in the room. Bill doubts that anyone is truly interested in *Queen for a Day* or *Guiding Light* but that they, like him, look at the snowy black-and-white images to keep from staring rudely across the room at the grim, drawn faces waiting to receive the news that their loved one will live or die.

That news is never delivered in the room. Instead, an elderly nun knocks on the door, peers in, and calls out the last name of the patient who has been operated on. The family then steps out in the hall in order to learn whether they have drawn the joy or grief card on that day.

As noon approaches and passes, Carole repeatedly suggests to Bill that he go down to the hospital coffee shop for something to eat; she knows he hasn't eaten since breakfast, and even then he had nothing but a slice of toast and coffee. No, Bill insists on waiting right where he is. He says he's not hungry, but that isn't quite true. He has found a way not to notice hunger, just as he learned early on to ignore the uncomfortably hard curve of his chair's back. Carole lights cigarette after cigarette, but Bill has let go of that craving as well. He knows that only by numbing himself—paying as little attention as possible to the passage of time or the requests of his body and mind—will he be able to endure the hours of waiting.

This skill, and Bill thinks of it as a skill, the ability to fold his hands and wait without agitation or expectation, is not something he developed or discovered for the first time that morning. Marriage to Marjorie has been one long training session in patience. He waited for Marjorie's dark moods to brighten. For her brooding silences to break. He waited—is still waiting—for her to explain how she had replaced the abandon of her youth with the fearful caution of adulthood. And this patience he believes, he has always believed, will one day be rewarded, though he has no real idea of what the precise nature of that reward will be.

He permits himself a quick glance around the room. The obese woman with her clicking crochet needles. The old farmer whose pale forehead tops a face burned to leather by years in the fields. The young couple who never look at each other but never let go of the other's hand. They all wait without any expression or sign of impatience, unless you count the cigarettes. Perhaps Bill Sidey isn't unique. Perhaps they all have their own anesthesia to get them through the hours of surgery.

Finally, however, Bill and Carole are the only ones left in the waiting room. It's midafternoon, hours past the time when Marjorie was scheduled to come out of surgery.

"This isn't right," Carole finally says. "I'm going to find someone who can tell us what the hell's going on."

Just as Carole reaches for the door, however, the elderly nun comes through from the other side. Carole stops abruptly, and when the nun says, "Sidey?" Carole steps back so clumsily Bill thinks she's about to reel. He rises and moves toward her, ready to rescue the wrong sister.

"You can sit back down," the nun says. "The doctor will talk to you in here."

Carole sits down again next to Bill. "How's that for service?" she says.

Although Bill expects the doctor, when he comes through the door it's with such haste that Bill startles at the sight of him. Underneath his white coat Dr. Carlson wears a white shirt, a blue-and-green-striped tie, and dark trousers.

"Don't get up," the doctor says, a useless remark since neither Carole nor Bill make a move to rise.

Dr. Carlson is a tall, ruddy-complexioned man who adds to the effect of his height with his erect bearing. His reddish-blond hair is close-cropped, but he has a luxuriant waxed, curled mustache, an improbable affectation in a man so rigid and conservative in other respects. The tips of his mustache point upward now, and since Bill doubts they could have held that shape when they were pressed under a surgical mask, that means the doctor has taken the time to freshly wax his mustache as well as change his clothes after surgery. Bill wishes the doctor would sit down so he and Carole won't have to keep staring upward, but Dr. Carlson stands before them with his hands behind his back as if he's about to scold two wayward children.

"The operation went fine, just fine," he says in his too-loud voice. "You know what was involved, don't you? Do you want me to run through the procedure again?"

Carole relaxes visibly, but Bill thinks something in the doctor's manner indicates more is coming.

"No? So I don't have to give the anatomy lesson?" He probably believes his smile puts people at ease, but he flashes it too quickly and doesn't allow it to linger on his lips. "Was it without complications? It was not. The human anatomy always has a few surprises for us. But what we set out to do, we did."

Bill is aware that his hands are poised on the arm of the chair as if he's about to push himself to his feet. "How's Marjorie doing now? Is she ready for visitors?"

"Where Marjorie is now visitors are generally not allowed."

Something in the carefully worded phrase makes Bill think the doctor isn't talking about an actual physical location but a psychic state. He can sense Carole staring at him—it's still Bill's place to ask the questions, but he has no idea which one is supposed to be next in the sequence.

But since the doctor used the word *where*, Bill decides he will too. "Where is she?"

"She's in recovery. As I said, she came through the surgery just fine. And came out of the anesthetic without a problem. But her body must have needed a bit more rest, because she went right back to sleep."

"Sleep . . . And is she still sleeping now?"

Grudgingly, the doctor nods.

"When do you expect her to wake up?"

"When?" Dr. Carlson permits himself another tight smile, although Bill didn't think there was any humor in his question. "We don't have any particular schedule that says 'when.' She'll wake up when she wakes up."

Bill looks questioningly at Carole. Since she had this operation perhaps she wants to make a comment or raise an issue that corresponded to her own experience. She's staring at the floor, however, and when Bill follows her gaze, he sees something that angers him. The doctor wears white shoes, like all medical personnel, though his look to have once been another color and material—tan suede perhaps—but they are now painted over with white shoe polish. On the toes of both shoes are small red spots—blood, without question, and it could certainly be Marjorie's. This man has the effrontery to stand before Bill, to evade his questions, with Bill's wife's blood on his shoes.

"Have you tried waking her?" Bill asks.

"As I said, she came out of the anesthetic fine."

Bill pushes himself to his feet, and the doctor pivots slightly as if he expects Bill to walk past him and out of the room. Bill, however, simply wants to stand so that the dark dots he concentrates on will be the doctor's glistening pupils and not the circles of blood on those white shoes.

"Other patients, patients who have this surgery—when do they wake up?" His tone of voice, Bill realizes, makes this question sound more aggressive than he intends, but he doesn't care.

Dr. Carlson glances down at Carole as if he expects her to answer.

Bill pushes a little harder. "Patients are supposed to be awake by now—isn't that so?"

The doctor keeps looking in Carole's direction.

"Don't look at her," Bill says. "I don't give a damn what happened with her. Is Marjorie supposed to be awake now and she's not? Is that what you came in here to tell us?"

"I'd prefer that Marjorie had come around by now. Yes."

To the floor Carole says breathlessly, "Oh, God. She's in a coma." Like her mother, Carole runs to greet bad news as soon as it comes into view, and though Marjorie has a similar tendency, her pessimism isn't her sister's or mother's eager variety. Yet even knowing this about Carole, Bill can't keep from having the sudden urge to drop into a crouch when he hears the word *coma*. Instead, he gropes backward for his chair and as soon as his hand touches the hard wood he sits down hard.

Carole's remark seems to restore Dr. Carlson's authority. "Coma! My God!" he says. "Where in hell did that come from? She's barely out of surgery!" He shakes his head in disgust. "Television? Women's magazines? Is that where you people get such ideas? You don't hear any of the medical personnel mentioning anything about a coma, so I sure as hell don't want to hear talk of it from either of you. I'm going back up to check on Marjorie right now, and I won't be a bit surprised if I find her sitting up in bed asking for a steak dinner. And if that's the case, I'll come right back down here and escort you to her room."

As soon as the doctor leaves, Carole begins to sniffle. "I knew it. I had a bad feeling about Marjorie's surgery. I just had a bad feeling."

Bill grits his teeth at this remark, but he says nothing. He leans toward his sister-in-law, thinking that if he does nothing more than place his hand on her shoulder the gesture might bring some comfort to both of them. But something in her attitude stops him. She seems to draw inward, clenching her entire being like a fist.

"Are we supposed to keep waiting here?" Bill asks. "Was that your understanding?"

"Get up and leave this place, I almost said to her last night. Something just didn't feel right to me. But I bit my tongue, and look where we are now . . ." Carole lowers her head as if to sob, but no sound comes forth.

Now Bill finds himself in the uncomfortable position of having to defend a surgical procedure that he had doubts about. "You can't let yourself think those thoughts, Carole. Marjorie needed this operation. And now we need to have faith that everything will be all right. We have to believe that."

With her red-rimmed, slitted eyes, Carole glances up at him, a look so feral he almost expects it to be accompanied by a low growl.

"What I mean is," he says, "we shouldn't automatically expect the worse."

For much of the day Carole has kept a tissue balled in her hand, and now she wipes her eyes with it. Then, apparently deciding it's too frayed to stand up to the sorrow that likely lies ahead, she rises and crosses the room to the box of Kleenex next to an African violet. She pulls two fresh tissues out of the box. "Do you want to call the kids now," she asks Bill, "or wait until tonight?"

"No sense calling before I have something definite to tell them."

"Would your father bring them out here?"

"Bring them . . . here?" Is Carole referring to the arrangement that she and Marjorie had discussed—Ann and Will moving to Missoula if Marjorie doesn't survive the surgery?

Carole says calmly, "If there's a crisis. If it looks like they won't have another chance to see their mother."

Bill would not have been able to utter such a sentence, but the new Kleenex seems not only to have dried Carole's tears but also to have dammed the source.

"I can't hear that kind of talk, Carole."

"You don't want to listen now, but your next chance might be too late. They should be standing by."

"Jesus Christ, Carole! You heard what the doctor said—the operation went fine. He expects her to be all right!"

She simply arches her eyebrows, and Bill knows Carole and her expressions well enough to interpret this one: Believe what you like.

Carole sits down heavily in a chair across from Bill, crosses her ankles, and stares away from him and toward the television where a program called *Up and Down Missoula* plays. The show is apparently devoted to informing viewers of the notable events upcoming in the community. "The host of this show?" Carole says. "He goes to our church."

After this remark, they fall silent. If someone were to enter the room now, they would never guess that Bill and Carole are together, a judgment that Bill thinks might not be far from wrong. Between Carole's bleak outlook and his more hopeful view lies a distance as great as any that separates strangers.

TULLY HECKAMAN LIVED FOR a time with a cousin who had taken up residence in a rundown farmhouse ten miles outside of Gladstone, and one night Tully took Marjorie to the farm for what was supposed to be a family gathering.

Marjorie soon discovered that the gathering was really a drinking party, and the house was so packed with people there to drink the cousin's homemade beer and moonshine—Marjorie believed he sold both out of the house—that she never knew for sure who Tully's actual family members were.

In order to put herself at ease—and to enter into the party's spirit—Marjorie drank too much too fast, and by the time Tully led her down into the basement, she was drunk and needed help negotiating the open stairs.

The cellar was dirt-floored; musty-smelling; and cluttered with boxes, barrels, empty burlap bags, and broken furniture. They both knew why Tully had brought her down there, but even in her drunken condition, Marjorie would not consent to lie down on the damp dirt. Tully spread out a few of the burlap bags, and once Marjorie was lying on the coarse fabric, she could smell that the bags had once held potatoes. When Tully turned out the light, the basement was totally lightless, and the earth's chill rose up through her. Marjorie was grateful then for that odor of potatoes; without it, the sensation of lying in a grave might have been too much for her. As it was, she tried to hurry Tully to a conclusion, but he mistook her efforts. Believing she was intent on her own pleasure, he slowed down, and by the time they finished, she was exhausted and had to reach out and press her hands and arms down on the dirt to halt the sensation that she was spinning through a lightless void.

She soon fell asleep—or passed out. When she came around, Tully was gone, or at least he was not near enough for Marjorie to hear his breathing or to reach out and touch him. The blackness she opened her eyes to was so complete she couldn't see if he—if anyone—was also in the cellar. Or had she opened her eyes? Since there was no discernible difference between opening her eyes or closing them, she wondered if her waking was only a dream of waking. She was still drunk enough that the state didn't panic her. She gave in to it, and toward morning when a blade of light was finally able to slice its way through a crack in the farmhouse's foundation, when she could open her eyes and know with certainty that they were open and know with certainty that her waking was real, Marjorie laughed at herself. Potatoes! Why hadn't she relied on her nose to tell her the difference between dreaming and waking? Dreams had no smell . . . or did they?

The experience was unlike anything Marjorie ever lived through again . . . until she struggled free of the anesthetic after her surgery only to find herself in a blackness like that cellar's.

And she finally relaxes into that state too when she determines that it doesn't matter whether she wants to be awake or asleep: Neither condition is susceptible to her will.

FIFTEEN

"I *think* I know what's going on here," Beverly says, "although it's taxing my memory a bit. But isn't it more than a little strange—we don't even call each other by our first names."

"Beverly," Calvin says, and tries to tug her a little closer.

"At least you know the name." She takes a small step forward, easing the strain on her undergarment. She notices now the spicy sweet smell of his after shave. She has to ask, "Did you have this in mind all along or are you just making it up on the moment?"

He brings up his left hand and curves that index finger around her brassiere strap also. When he does, Beverly has a new thought that won't be kept away: He has his hands on the reins.

"This moment or any other," Calvin says, "I'm looking to take some pleasure out of this life."

"Well, I asked. I appreciate your honesty. Though I don't believe that answers my question."

"You must feel the same. Or else you wouldn't be here."

"To tell you the truth, I'm not sure where I am . . ." Or what I'm feeling, Beverly might have added. But one emotion she's quite sure of: She's relieved, and relief, in Beverly Lodge's view, is a much underrated emotion. For years she has worried that she no longer possesses any of the attributes, qualities, or features necessary to excite a man's desire, and although the attention of Calvin Sidey, considering his age and remove from polite society, is hardly enough to qualify her as one of the world's most desirable women, it's something.

Calvin pokes his fingers deeper inside her brassiere, and when he does, another feeling overtakes her. Beverly's breath quickens and a sudden heat travels through her torso from high in her throat to between her legs. She moves so close to him the tuft of white hair curling out of his shirt's open collar tickles her forehead. Now she catches another odor, this one hiding under his after shave and sweat. It's very faint, but there's no mistaking it. She associates it with the homes of older people she entered in childhood. Later in life she assumed its source was the food the elderly ate—boiled, overcooked, reheated—but with her nose this close to Calvin Sidey's chest she realizes it's the smell of age itself, yet not an overripe rotting as of vegetation or flesh but of something dry, wood or bone perhaps, turning to dust. She has not worn any perfume for this occasion—she had not known there would *be* an occasion—so she imagines she gives off a similar odor, only fainter by the years that separate them in age.

"Do you know if your son has a drink of whiskey or something on the premises?" she asks. "If we're about to do what I think, my nerves could use a little firming up."

Calvin releases the reins and walks over to the chest of drawers. He brings out a pint of Canadian Club, and although it's difficult to tell in the dim basement, it looks to Beverly as if it hasn't been opened. He unscrews the cap and holds the bottle out to her. "I won't be joining you," he says.

"You just keep it around for your basement guests?"

"I quit drinking a number of years back, but I want it to be my choice, and not because I can't get my hands on a drink."

"So you make it easy to take a drink and hard not to . . . Mr. Sidey, you do like a challenge, don't you?"

"I suppose."

She still doesn't take the bottle. "I'm afraid I'm not made of stuff as stern as you think. Could you water it down a bit? Maybe an ice cube?"

"A little sugar too?"

"I don't need that much help."

Calvin climbs the stairs, and as soon as Beverly hears him reach the top, she begins to undress. If she hurries, she'll be naked and under the covers before Calvin returns. She's ready to go along with just about anything he has in mind, but she doesn't want her body naked and available for his cold eye to scrutinize. She doesn't bother folding anything but tosses all her clothes and undergarments on the chair. The sheets feel not only cool but damp, and she pulls the chenille spread to her chin.

How long has it been? This is 1963. Burt died in 1938, and not long after, Ed Emshier from the First National Bank began his pursuit of her. Poor Ed. She put him off for a few years, and then out of a combination of pity and exhaustion, she relented. If Ed would have had his way, they would have married, and maybe Beverly would have eventually given in there as well, if the sex hadn't been so god-awful. And perhaps she could have gotten past that if Ed would have been able to enliven her life in other ways. But the truth was, the man was as bland as baby food.

Since then—nothing.

Beverly thinks of herself as a practical woman who understands—and has always understood—that life frequently means settling for less. And though she's never let it stand in the way of getting through a day, she has sometimes imagined someone—a stranger, she guesses it would have to be—driving into town and carrying her away.

None of her fantasies, of course, have her lying on sheets smelling of mildew, staring up at bare ceiling joists, waiting to spread her legs for an old man who has never even bothered touching his lips to hers. An old man who might have murder in his past. If she isn't going to jump up, grab her clothes, and run away—and she isn't about to—well, she might as well smile about where she finds herself.

She hears his footsteps on the stairs, and she hastily rearranges the bed coverings so her body isn't outlined quite so obviously. Not that she'll be able to fool him much longer.

He carries a water glass more than half full, and from its dark color she guesses he hasn't diluted the whiskey much. Two ice cubes, melting rapidly, swirl on the surface.

"Better sit up," Calvin says, "and take your medicine."

A joke? Has he just made a joke?

She sits up, bringing the covers with her, and takes the glass from his hand. "I don't think I'll need quite this much courage."

"I had no way of knowing."

She swallows as much as she dares and feels the whiskey scorch a path that ends just below her breastbone.

"Whew!" She fans her face to cool the sweat that has popped out at her hairline. "While I'm priming myself here, you could go turn out that light."

He walks over and throws the switch, but even with the bulb dark at the bottom of the stairs, the basement dims only to gray. Through two of the tiny underground windows the setting sun has found its way, sending angled shafts of dusty light across the room.

Calvin sits down on the chair beside the bed and pulls off his boots, an action that relieves Beverly. She had a vision of him climbing shod under the covers. He opens the snaps on his shirt and tugs its tails out of his jeans, but he leaves the shirt on.

Beverly takes another sip of whiskey. "You're not going to take out your teeth, are you?"

He unrolls his socks and tucks them inside his boots. "That's the second remark you've made about teeth. No"—he clacks his teeth noisily—"they're all mine."

"I guess I'm just trying to gauge the amount of romance I'm in for."

Does this man never laugh? Beverly tries again. "You looked like you were getting ready to bed down for the night is all I meant."

He reaches down and lifts the bedspread and sheet. The air is not moving in the basement, yet it feels as though a cool breeze blows over her when he exposes her body. Parts of her chill and shrivel—is it only the cool air?—and she covers her chest with her arm.

"I could say the same about you." He points to her glass of whiskey. "You drunk up enough courage yet to let me between those sheets?"

Beverly takes one more swallow and sets the glass down on the concrete floor. She lies down and pats the bed. "Come on then. I never could resist that kind of sweet talk."

CALVIN CAN STILL REMEMBER the first day when he didn't think of his dead wife. Pauline had been gone maybe four or five years, and though he was working for the Slash Nine then, on this particular day he and a few other fellows were loaned out to Willis Ritter's Rocking 3 to help with the branding. For some reason, Willis had been caught short-handed, and Tom Arndt, the owner of the Slash Nine, sent some of his men over to the Ritter place.

The Rocking 3 wasn't a big outfit, but Willis still had upward of two hundred head that had to be branded. They ran fifty or so calves into the catching corral at a time, and Calvin and Ray Kellogg alternated their work. For an hour or so, one of them would tend the fire and keep the irons hot while the other would rope and drag a calf to the fire. Then they'd switch. Willis and one of his boys would throw and hold down the calves, and another of Willis's sons would slap on that big Rocking 3 brand. The smoke and the smell of the burned hide, the dust and the cow shit in the corral, the calves bawling inside the fence, and their mothers bellering outside—it was work that filled up all of a man's senses and most of his mind.

It was not until Calvin was back at the Slash Nine, in the bunk-house, and smoking a last cigarette before he collapsed onto his bed, not until then did he realize that he had not thought of Pauline once that day, and then the thought he did have was so minor and so swift, like a bat hunting in the night sky, it hardly seemed there at all. He recalled how annoyed she'd get when he smoked in their bedroom. The smell and the smoke, she said, lingered and became part of the darkness; she'd wake and worry that something in the house was burning. Calvin grumbled something about the odor of her "woman things" in the room, but he acceded to her wishes. If he needed a smoke, he left the room. But when the memory of her came back to him in his exhaustion—and hadn't he taken on the cowboy life so its long days and man-killing work would keep him from dwelling on grief and loss?—it came with renewed force, as if his grief had hidden from him all day in order to gather its power and devastate him all over again. Better, Calvin realized, and he has lived by this principle ever since, to keep some thought of Pauline Sidey always near at hand and thus prevent the familiar daily sorrow from gathering its strength and growing into ruinous pain.

Even now, as he enters this woman—and my God it feels good, so good, to use his muscles, his entire body, for pleasure, to press down hard on her until it seems as though his flesh and hers, his bones and hers, his blood and hers, fuse—Calvin keeps a part of himself out of the moment, noticing that Beverly Lodge's legs are considerably longer than Pauline's were and that Beverly can bring her heels high up on the backs of his legs. But even the sensation of the calluses on her heels scraping against him turns into the pleasure that's ready to do battle with sorrow.

BEVERLY LODGE LIVES MUCH of her life in the company of others. Friends, neighbors, colleagues. Her son. And this is the way she wants it. But she hadn't realized the solitude that she's been living in, not having wrapped her legs around a man in so long. She hadn't known that unrequited lust or desire—heat with nothing to burn—could bring on its own brand of loneliness. This closeness, her skin rubbing against his, her heart beating against his, is so unlike all the other moments in her life that she might have been living alone on a desert island until now. She was sure she'd never have this in her life again. And oh God, to be touched there again, and there, and there, and like that, and like that. She can't help it; she thinks of Ed Emshier. Maybe she should have been more patient with him.

And here's another surprise. A ramming, slamming affair was what Beverly expected this to be, not only because all the love-making in her life has been a variation on that theme—hard and quick with her husband, who had no more time to spare in bed than in any other place away from his job, and soft and quick with Ed Emshier—but also because she guessed that would be Calvin Sidey's style, going greedily for his pleasure.

But he takes his time, and though Beverly thought at first, oh hell, of course—a seventy-year-old man has accumulated a lot of rust, to say nothing of the inevitable worry over his heart—once she catches his rhythm she realizes this is how an old man takes his pleasure: making last as long as he can what he cannot be sure he'll experience ever again. Sexual urgency belongs to the young; they can rush through the act because they can be sure so many more opportunities lie ahead.

How strange, that on a day when Beverly had been deviled by the heat, the wonderful feeling that suffuses her from head to toe, as Calvin rocks both their bodies on the narrow bed, is heat—a sensation very like lowering herself into a hot bath.

But then the feeling is suddenly not heat but electricity—a current that runs vaguely through her, settles between her legs, and from there—doubled, tripled in power—emanates out through her torso and clamps her tight to Calvin Sidey.

SIXTEEN

||||||||||||||||||||||||||||||||||||||||||||||||||||||||||

Beverly stays in bed while Calvin sits on the chair. He's pulled on his Levi's, but that's as far as he's gotten. He's smoking a hand-rolled cigarette, the sweet scent of its tobacco pushing aside the basement's smell of mildew. She considers picking up her whiskey but decides against it. She wouldn't have to drink much more to fall asleep in this bed. Besides, the liquor has already done what it was supposed to do.

"I don't want to disturb your brown study," she says to Calvin, "but I have a question I'd like to put to you."

"All right."

"I probably shouldn't say anything because this just opens the door for you to make your own observations about someone's body and its features, but I couldn't help noticing"—she points to his bare torso—"that's an impressive scar on your right side." In truth, he had plenty of smaller scars, including a nasty one across his cheek, but they were the nicks that a man in his line of work naturally accumulates. The one on his side was different, however, and she hadn't seen it so much as felt it, a rough raised surface that felt like a length of cord just under the skin.

"This?" He points to his ribs. "A souvenir from my time in the military."

"I bet there's a story there." She's heard enough tales told by ex-GIs over the years to know they're seldom the stories that a woman would be interested in hearing, but she has to ask. Even another anecdote about a drunken soldier falling off a truck would be preferable to Calvin Sidey's silence.

"This came my way courtesy of a German soldier with a bayonet. But he only got the one chance and he didn't take sufficient advantage. My aim was better than his."

"Yes? Tell me more."

He begins to speak but seems uncertain about the decision, as if speech's victory over silence has been won by the narrowest of margins. "I've always felt sort of strange about this scar. Or what put it there. Can't say I'm fond of it exactly. But it brought me my wife and most of the good in my life."

Beverly sits up, keeping herself covered with the sheet as she does. "Come now—you can't say something like that and then not explain yourself."

He bends over and taps the ash from his cigarette into the ashtray at his feet. "We were in France, fighting one of those battles that was too small to have a name. We kept going back and forth, scrapping with the Krauts over a hill and a few acres of hardwoods.

We were finally hand to hand among the trees. That's when I got this." He points again to his side. "And as I said, he got paid back for his trouble . . . Anyway, of the seven of us doughboys who walked into the woods, four of us came out, and I wasn't the only one who was a might worse for wear. None of us was too sure about how to join back up with the regiment, so we decided to head off in different directions. Not the wisest course of action, but what can you expect from boys, green as grass every one of us. Maybe we all felt the way I did, that I'd do better on my own than roped in with the other three.

"I headed north, sticking to the hedgerows when I could. Caught sight of a German patrol, so I figured I was headed the wrong way. I backtracked and maybe I would've ended up in those goddamn woods where we had our skirmish, but I got so thirsty I ventured out to find some water. So though I said it was a bayonet wound that brought my wife and me together, could be it was simple thirst.

"I wasn't far from a French village—I'd been circling it for a while—but then I saw a farmhouse on the outskirts of town. And it had a well. I didn't give a damn—I set out across the field to draw myself a drink of water or get shot trying. Before either happened, a couple women came scurrying out, squawking away in French. They saw my uniform, and while the older one was trying to shoo me away, the other was motioning me to come closer.

"This was the Costallat farm, and while Monsieur Costallat and his son were off to war, his mother, wife, and daughters were working the place. They had geese, I remember, and they put up a bigger fuss than any barking dog would. Then the daughters came out to see what the commotion was about, and I reckon together they outvoted the grandmother because they were soon hustling me inside before I could make them understand all I wanted was a little water. But they kept better track of the Germans than I did—the roads were crawling with them.

"They put me down in the root cellar, and when they discovered I'd gotten myself sliced open, they insisted on trying to patch me up. The old woman seemed to have some knowledge of wounds. She might have had a husband who fought his war with a saber. Anyway she said I had to be stitched up. But she couldn't do the job, not because she didn't have the stomach for it but because her fingers were stiff and gnarly as twigs. The older daughter—that was Pauline—said she'd give it a try.

"She was the one who spoke the best English too, so there she was, trying to work the needle and thread in and out of my skin and apologizing to me every other second. I was trying to help. I was pinching the wound shut and telling her she was doing a good job, just get on with it. The mother and sister hung back, but that old grandma had her nose right in there, telling Pauline to pull the stitches tighter and get them closer together.

"But they got it done, and I thought I'd say good-bye and thank you and hit the road. When I look back, I have to shake my head over how damn cocky I was. I was in France, but beyond that fact, I didn't have much idea of where I was. I didn't have a map. I didn't know where the Krauts were except nearby, and that I had to be told. I didn't know which direction to head in to rejoin my own army. In the end, it didn't matter. Those women wouldn't hear of me leaving, not in daylight and not without feeding me a hot meal.

"Well, the next morning there was no question of me leaving. I woke up sicker than a dog. To this day I don't know if I came down with the influenza that was cutting down as many soldiers as the bombs and bullets, or if I had an infection from that bayonet wound, or if it was both. By nightfall I was rattling with fever and chills and out of my head. The woman who went on to be my wife later told me they were so sure I was going to die they started discussing whether they would bury me there on the farm or wrap me up in a shroud and try to lug my body back to the army so I could be shipped home.

"But I was probably too young and dumb to die. I recovered, but I wasn't too quick about it. For days just climbing those cellar steps was all I could handle. I sort of lost track of time for a while there, and I'm still not sure how long I stayed at the farm. Maybe a couple weeks. I guess I don't have to tell you I had a reason for staying beyond getting my strength back."

Here's a man for you, Beverly thinks. The sheets haven't even cooled, and he's yakking about his dead wife. Maybe his silence wasn't so bad. Yet she wants him to go on. She's seen more softness in him telling the tale of his scars than when he was braced above her in bed.

"That's when it happened?" Beverly asks. "You and Pauline?"

Calvin casts a baleful eye in her direction, and Beverly thinks, Oh God, now I've done it; I've broken the spell. I'm allowed to moan in his ear, but I'm not worthy of speaking her name.

In another moment, however, he continues with his story, though Beverly thinks she detects a slight alteration in his tone: His voice had dropped dangerously close to his heart, and now he lifts it back up again.

"When it came time for me to try to rejoin the troops, a good portion of the Allied army was waiting just over the hill, and the German forces were hightailing it back to their own territory. The war was petering out and soldiers on both sides were running around in every direction. My unit welcomed me back, and it wasn't long before I was back on the lines, back in the trenches. When officers on each side remembered we were still supposed to be fighting a war, bullets would commence flying and bombs would start falling again.

"When they stopped for good, and when we were told we were no longer soldiers but free men lucky to be alive, I didn't get on one of the boats headed back to America. Instead, I headed for the village of Nonsard and the Costallat farm.

"By the time I arrived, Pauline's father and brother had returned as well—the brother with only half the arm he left with—and the two of them welcomed me like they'd known me for years. *Le cow-boy, le cowboy, oui, le cowboy* who lived in the cellar . . . They were a pair, I tell you. Two Frenchmen who liked their wine but wouldn't turn down a drink of whiskey if the bottle was going around.

"Anyway. The plan was Pauline and I would get married, and we'd stay and help out on the farm until we could find a place of our own. But it was Pauline's family who spoke against that idea. Stay in France where the best we could hope for was a few acres already plowed up by bombs when we could go to America where I had a brick house and the family business waiting for me? Hell, I had to come around to their reasoning myself. We were in a country that wouldn't get back on its feet for a while. So back we came. I guess you know the rest."

Beverly gives out a low whistle. "I know some of it. I remember when the two of you came back to town. That was quite the occasion. Calvin Sidey and his French wife . . . Didn't the town put together a parade for the two of you?"

He crushes out his cigarette and glowers in her direction, but it has no effect. There must be something about lying naked in the man's bed that renders her immune to his dark looks.

"I'm not mocking you," she says. "You must have known you

were the closest thing this town had to a celebrity, and with Pauline on your arm—my goodness! What a pair the two of you made."

"If I'd had my way," Calvin says, "we would never have come back here."

"You wanted to stay in France for good?"

"I did. Why—is that so hard to believe?"

"I don't know. Look at yourself. You belong here."

Calvin's laugh reminds her of the sound of her spatula scraping at the frost buildup in her freezer. "Belong here?" he says. "I don't even live here."

"But you did."

He kicks at something invisible on the floor in front of him. "Well, I don't now."

Beverly Lodge is not the sort to hold back or bite her tongue just because her inquiries might offend someone. And she doubts she'll ever have a better opportunity to ask of Calvin Sidey, Was it sorrow or murder that drove you from this town? Yet when she opens her mouth she says, "I've never been to France. What was its appeal?"

"Green fields. Trees. Hundreds of years of history everywhere you looked."

"In other words, it wasn't Montana."

He shrugs. "There's a hell of a lot of world out there that isn't Montana."

"So go back to France now. What's stopping you?"

He doesn't hesitate before answering. "I don't belong there either."

She leans toward him, still clutching the sheet to her body, although not as tightly as before. "Is it permitted for me to say I for one am glad you're here?"

At this he says nothing but grunts softly. He picks up his tobacco and papers as though he's about to roll himself another cigarette, but then he seems to think better of it. "Can I get your opinion on something that happened last night?"

Asking that question probably cost him more than taking off his pants in front of her, she knows. "Fire away," she says.

"I don't sleep so good as I once did and last night was one of those nights. So I was sitting up late when Miss Ann came sneaking down the stairs. She sure as hell didn't expect to see me, and I suspect I fouled up some plans she might have had. There was a car parked in the alley and likely she was going out to meet someone. This seem possible to you?"

Beverly shrugs. "She's a teenager. So certainly it's possible. But I'll tell you something about that girl, if you haven't noticed already. As pretty as she is? She's got a character every bit as good."

Calvin nods in agreement. "She didn't make much fuss."

"Of course, if she's in love—"

"And then while I'm staring out the window I remember another summer night when something just like that happened. Back then I likely had a glass of whiskey in my hand and it was Bill I saw sneaking across the backyard. I had a pretty good idea where he was going. He'd been keeping company with those no-good Ballard boys and he was probably going out to raise some kind of hell with them. I could have stopped him; I didn't. Instead, I told myself he was old enough to take care of himself. Now I look at Will. Not much younger than Bill was then. A boy that age—take care of himself? About the only thing they *can* manage on their own is getting into trouble. But I had my hands full with being a widower, or so I thought. Took that on as my full time occupation. And I let my boy go. Take care of himself? Jesus. I might as well have let the coyotes raise my kids."

"It was a different world back then," Beverly says. "We could let the rope out a little because the whole town looked out for our children. Any adult could tell any child to mind his p's and q's."

Calvin shakes his head as if to reject any attempt to absolve him. "Well, there must have been a hell of a lot of them telling my son how to behave. He turned out fine, no thanks to me."

He stands, takes his shirt off the chair, and something in the way he thrusts his arm into a sleeve says their conversation, and probably their time together, has come to a close.

"My, my, Mr. Sidey. Is that a cotton shirt you're wearing? Or a hair shirt?" Beverly sticks a bare leg out from under the covers and puts a foot on the cool floor. "You might as well hand me my clothes. And turn your back or cover your eyes."

He lifts her clothes from the chair and hands them to her. "I've seen all there is to see," he says.

"But you're looking at me with different eyes now."

SEVENTEEN

‖‖‖

No matter what the condition of your family member or friend, you are not allowed to stay beyond visiting hours at Missoula's Good Samaritan Hospital. Bill Sidey, however, has found a way to work around this regulation. The surgical waiting room, where he and Carole spent so many hours earlier, is empty at night, and this is where Bill is hiding out, although he's not sure why he's here. If there's any change in Marjorie's condition, the call will go to Carole and Milo's home. But Bill has the hopeful, irrational belief that if Marjorie wakes up, he'll somehow know it, or she'll know that he's nearby and . . . and what? Call out for him? Oh, none of it makes any sense. But Bill feels as though he's doing *something* by sitting here, rather than doing nothing at Carole and Milo's.

Shortly after ten o'clock, an elderly nun enters the room. The room is dark but for one small lamp on the table next to the over-stuffed chair where Bill is sitting, and when the nun notices him, Bill stands and says, "I'm sorry. I was just—"

"Oh, pssht," she says, waving him back down. "Sit. I'm not the night watchman."

Bill guesses she must be at least eighty, her large-jawed masculine face creased with wrinkles that, in the dim light, seem carved by shadows.

"If I turn on the television, will I disturb you?" Her accent is faintly Germanic.

"Not at all." He drops back into his chair.

She switches on the set, fiddles with the rabbit ears to sharpen the picture, and sits down one chair away from Bill. "I sneak in here every night for the sports. Just to see what the Red Sox have done."

"I'm afraid," Bill says, "I've lost track of the standings. How are they doing?"

She shrugs. "Not well. It will be the Yankees again. As usual."

Bill crushed out a cigarette just a few minutes before the nun walked in, but since he feels that he shouldn't light up in front of her, he suddenly craves another.

"Are you a baseball fan?" she asks.

"Halfhearted. Not like when I was a boy. Then I could name every team's lineup. The Tigers were my team, and Charlie Gehringer was my favorite player."

"The Mechanical Man," the nun says with a smile.

The sports announcer appears on the screen, and they both watch until the baseball scores are concluded. Both the Red Sox and the Twins, the team that Bill tries to follow, have lost. The nun rises stiffly and goes back to the television. "Or should I leave it on?" she asks Bill.

"You can turn it off," he answers.

They both watch the picture dwindle to a tiny silver dot, and once that too is pinched into darkness, the nun speaks.

"Your wife? Am I remembering right?"

"My wife," Bill said. "That's correct."

"She is not doing well?" Bill wonders if it's nothing more than his late-night presence that allows the nun to guess this truth, or if there is something in his face, his voice, his posture, that reveals how worried he is.

"She's in a coma."

"A coma. My. I hadn't heard we had a patient in such a condition."

"They won't use the word, but that's what it is. A coma." Bill's remark sounds as though it could have come from his sister-in-law's mouth.

"This is an excellent hospital," the nun says. "Everything will be done for your wife that can be. You mustn't lose hope."

This is very similar to the counsel Bill gave Carole in this very room. Now that he is in the presence of a person of faith he finally feels free to express his own pessimism. He wishes she could talk him out of his despair.

"I'm a hopeful man, Sister. But it can be a struggle."

"Prayer helps us in that," she says. "But when that doesn't seem quite enough, it doesn't hurt to remind oneself that strong young women such as your wife generally don't die before their time."

But when they do, Bill thinks but doesn't say, they do it in places like this. Instead, he says, "I've never prayed so much in my life as I have today."

She nods in approval. "Do you have children?"

"A boy and a girl."

"They must be worried about their mother. Your strength will be necessary to help them."

Is this why he has not yet informed Ann and Will about their mother's condition—so he won't have to be strong for them?

"They're such good kids." As he says this, Bill feels his eyes sting as they do when tears are close. "I wish there was a way to make life easier for them."

The nun nods knowingly again. "For the good, life is sometimes harder."

The nun is moving toward the door, but Bill doesn't want her to go, not yet. He finds her company quietly comforting—this old woman spends her days and nights amid illness, calamity, and heartache, yet she seems unperturbed in the presence of it all. A heart attack or a gallbladder surgery is as commonplace to her as a Red Sox loss. Bill gropes desperately for another reason to make her stay. "Before you go, Sister"—is he entitled to refer to her this way, or is this a term reserved for Catholics?—"can I get your opinion on another matter?"

She inclines her head slightly as if to say, of course.

"If a person . . . if someone has a bad deed in his past, something he did long ago, does that automatically mean his soul is in jeopardy?" Then, to make sure there's no misunderstanding, Bill adds, "*His* soul. His. I'm not talking about my wife. She's a good woman. I'm worried about her fate in this life, not the next."

The nun looks down at her hands and taps her fingertips together, but she doesn't say anything. "And it's not me either," he further adds.

The nun nods. "This is a good man we're talking about?"

"More or less. But as I said, with something bad in his past."

"The bad deed is—?"

Bill doesn't answer right away, and the nun raises her hand. "You don't have to say. He has or has not repented for what he did?"

The nun has misunderstood Bill's hesitation. It's not that he's reluctant to speak of his father's deed but that suddenly Bill is unsure himself what he's been referring to—murder or abandonment? A crime that requires God's forgiveness or a son's?

It doesn't matter. Either way, Bill can speak with confidence of his father's attitude. "Has not."

"Repentance is necessary. He's not a Catholic?"

"No. And I'm not either. I'm a Lutheran." Bill has never asked, but he doubts that his father has any religious convictions.

She shakes her head as if to say that this confession is of no consequence. "But you should speak to your minister about this matter."

"I have a pretty good idea what he'd say. I just thought I'd get your opinion."

The nun raises her hands helplessly. "We can still pray for them . . ." She says this as though she knows prayer can do no more for an unrepentant soul than Bill believes it can for a wife who will not wake up.

EIGHTEEN

||||||||||||||||||||||||||||||||||||||||||||||||||||||

Beverly has a recipe for a hot dish that everyone seems to like. She browns ground beef and chopped onion in her big cast-iron skillet, pours in tomato soup and canned corn, dumps the mixture into a deep Pyrex dish, spreads mashed potatoes over the top, and then bakes it at 350 degrees. That morning, before the day got too hot, she doubled the ingredients and fixed two casseroles, one for her and Adam and the other for the Sideys.

The dish is cooling on her cupboard and it's almost midday, yet Beverly is still waiting for the right moment to carry it next door. Will Sidey pedaled off around eleven o'clock with a baseball glove looped on his handlebars, and he won't return until midafternoon. Ann will soon walk down Fourth Street for her afternoon shift at Penney's, and then after she departs Beverly will knock on the Sideys' door with the reasonable expectation that Calvin will be alone in the house.

The casserole is not the only preparation she has made. Last night when Calvin led her down to his basement lair Beverly wasn't sure what might happen, but today she's ready. She shaved her legs and under her arms, and she searched through her underwear drawer for a bra whose once-white straps didn't look gray and a pair of underpants where the tendrils of elastic hadn't sprung loose. She put on a sleeveless floral-print dress that she'd worn in the classroom on the warmest days of spring and fall, and for the first time she pulled the stopper on the bottle of Prince Matchabelli perfume that Adam gave her the previous Christmas. She dabbed a little scent on her wrists and between her breasts, in imitation of a woman she once read about in a novel. After all this primping, she looked at herself in the mirror and laughed: To think she was going through all this for an old man who probably hadn't been with a woman for so long the last thing he cared about was how she smelled! With a washcloth she scrubbed between her breasts until the scent was entirely gone.

Beverly watches Ann Sidey walk past the house, then picks up the casserole and heads out the door.

After there's no answer to her second knock, Beverly opens the screen door and steps into the Sidey kitchen. "Hello! Anyone home?" She sets the warm dish on the counter. "It's your neighbor!" Her hearing isn't what it once was, and she has to cock her head to the side to listen for a response that might be coming from another corner of the house, the basement perhaps. She has just stepped toward the dining room when someone bangs on the screen door.

Beverly, startled, turns quickly and sees a dark form filling the frame. It's a wide-bodied, big-hatted man with his fist raised. He must have seen her at the same time, and the sight of her keeps him from striking the door again.

Yes, he sees her all right, but he misidentifies her because he shouts, "You tell that goddamn husband of yours he sends another fucking letter like this he's going to be sorry!"

Because the light is coming from behind the man and she's looking at him through the screen, Beverly thinks, but can't be sure, that he's an Indian. His rage, however, she recognizes immediately. Burt dealt with more than a few men like this one—deadbeats and abusive husbands, for example—and they sometimes came to the house—drunk, usually—to demand that he stop threatening garnishment or an injunction against them. Beverly quells the impulse to explain, My husband's dead, and instead stammers, "I'm not—"

But before she can finish, he pulls open the door and hurls a crumpled ball of paper in Beverly's direction, which falls to the floor. She flinches nonetheless. She immediately wants to retrieve the paper—perhaps it can solve the mystery of this confrontation— yet she knows not to take her eyes from this man.

Yes, she's right—he is an Indian. But neither his race nor his size is his most distinctive feature. One side of his face is hideously scarred—both his eye and mouth twist downward and his skin shines as if it's wet. His nose is flattened against his cheek.

"He's going to kick *her* out of her house?" he shouts. "He's the one who'll be out of a house! I'll burn this fucker to the ground!"

As he backs out, he tries to slam the screen door, but its spring prevents it from slamming. He settles for a kick that makes the door jump and rattle in its frame. Then he's gone, and the rectangle that he darkened is once again flooded with the sunlight of high noon.

Beverly's hands are trembling, and her legs feel as though they might give out.

While she's watching the door, another voice startles her, and for the second time inside of a minute, her heart lurches with fear. When she turns, she sees Calvin Sidey.

"What's going on here?" he says. "I heard someone shouting."

"A man . . . he . . . I think he was looking for Bill."

"Who was it? What did he want?"

"He said . . ." She isn't sure why, but she doesn't want to repeat what the man said about burning the house down. As frightening as that was, Calvin Sidey's likely reaction to the threat is even more terrifying to imagine. "Apparently he was angry about getting that letter." She points to the ball of paper on the floor.

Calvin bends over stiffly and scoops it up. He spreads it open, reads it, and then walks hurriedly to the door. "Did you see him leave?" he asks Beverly. "Was he on foot?" He opens the screen door and looks down the driveway.

"I think I heard a car. I'm not sure."

"He came inside?"

She nods.

"With your permission?"

She shakes her head.

"Did he lay his hands on you?"

"No, no, he wasn't after me."

He looks carefully at her, as though he believes she might not have answered his last question truthfully. "You're sure?"

She nods again. "I'm all right." But now Beverly fears that she has gone too far the other way and is minimizing the threat the man posed. "He said he'd burn the house down," she whispers.

Calvin's eyes flare at her remark, and she quickly adds. "Just big talk, I'm sure."

But Calvin is already on the move. He crosses the room, opens a cupboard drawer, and brings out a set of keys. "Let's go."

Not until they're out of the house and heading for Calvin's truck does she ask, "Where are we going?"

He still has the paper in his hand, and he waves it in the air. "This is an eviction notice. And we're going to the address on the notice."

He unlocks his truck and gets in, then reaches across and unlocks the passenger door. Beverly pulls it open and the hinges groan. She climbs into a cab that smells of tobacco and motor oil. She tries to settle into her seat but finds she has to move toward the middle to keep from being poked in the backside by a broken spring. "I'm not sure why you need me on this expedition."

Calvin rams the truck into gear and backs up fast into the alley. When he brakes, gravel pings against the garbage cans. "You're going to tell me how to get to that address," he says, pointing to the letter on the dashboard. "And when we get there, you can tell me if I've got the right man before I have words with him. Now, which way?"

The address is on the south side of town, and Beverly directs him to drive straight down Third Street. She composes herself slightly. "When you say 'have words'—is that what you had with the Neaveses? Words?"

"This will be a bit more forceful."

"You threatened to kill their dog. What could be more forceful than that?"

He turns and looks directly at her. "Someone came barging into my son's house. You know that can't be allowed. It *can't*."

"Maybe we should notify the police."

"Maybe." He has to work the shift lever hard before he finds the right gear and the truck bucks into motion.

"Or the sheriff. Isn't the sheriff supposed to handle eviction notices?"

"Who's the sheriff now?"

"Neal Garner. He's in his second term, I believe."

"Is he any relation to Louie Garner?"

"It's his son. Did you know Louie?"

Third is not a through street, but Calvin Sidey doesn't slow down at any intersection. "Louie was sheriff years ago. Not that he was much good at the job."

And if he were better at it, Beverly wonders, would he have arrested you for murder? "Louie served a couple terms as mayor too. A lot of people believe he was good for this town."

"Do they."

"I always thought he was a decent man."

Beverly isn't sure why she's defending Louie Garner. She was never impressed with his intelligence or his leadership, but perhaps she wants to let Calvin know that since he left this town he has forfeited his right to criticize the people who stayed.

"Louie died of a heart attack winter before last," Beverly says. "He was shoveling snow and he dropped dead in front of his own house."

"You don't say. Do I just keep going straight here?"

They're in Gladstone's business district now, six square blocks of stores and office buildings, and while they're stopped at a red light, a friend of Beverly's, Lois Parvin, exits Woolworth's and crosses the street in front of them. Lois's mouth opens as if she's going to speak and her hand starts to rise, but then she looks away and hurries across the intersection. What happened? Did Lois take in that battered, rusted, coughing old truck, then catch a glimpse of Calvin Sidey behind the wheel, and conclude that the woman in the sundress sitting closer to the driver than the passenger door couldn't possibly be Beverly Lodge? As for Beverly, she feels she should do something—lower her head, put her hand over her face—anything to keep from being recognized should Lois turn around and look again. But that feeling passes in an instant. Why should she cover her face in the town she has lived in almost all her life? She doesn't care who sees her cruising around in Calvin's truck! Beverly sits up straighter and even considers pulling her dress off her shoulders to give Lois, or anyone else—there's Jack McCumber coming out of the Rim Rock Cafe and Janet Burwell is digging into her purse before she enters Powers Department Store and Otto Heinrich is climbing into his big Oldsmobile—an eyeful if they glance in her direction.

But then the light turns green, and as they continue their tour through the center of town, Beverly begins to question that brief surge of boldness. Was it nothing more than a determination not to feel ashamed, or is she actually proud that Calvin Sidey finally returned to Gladstone and chose her to ride beside him?

She immediately chides herself for even that brief flirtation with pride. Anyone who sees her might wonder who Beverly is riding with, but they're unlikely to see anything scandalous in the sight. After all, there aren't that many people in Gladstone who would recognize Calvin Sidey. He's just another old man in a truck, a stranger in town.

SILENTLY CALVIN CURSES HIS son. Why did Bill leave town with this matter of the eviction left unresolved? He knows who his tenants are, and he must know who has this capacity for trouble. For that matter, what the hell is he doing renting a place to a single woman? And while he's at it, Calvin lavishes a few of these unspoken curses on his daughter-in-law as well; if she weren't intent on in-dulging herself with this so-called special operation—and in a city hundreds of miles away—Bill wouldn't have felt he had to accom-pany her. Finally, however, Calvin spends his most damning oaths on himself. He didn't have to say yes to his son's request, but once Calvin did, he was the worst kind of goddamn fool if he let himself believe that the job wouldn't ask any more of him than to sit in a rocking chair for a few days.

And now he's brought this woman in on this. Calvin didn't need her to accompany him, not really. He has the letter and the address; he could have found his way there eventually. Is he trying to repay her somehow for getting into bed with him? *In gratitude for fucking me, I'd like to invite you on this expedition to track down a deadbeat.* What woman wouldn't be flattered by that invitation?

But here she is, at his side. Is she the first woman inside this truck? Is that possible? If she thinks there's any danger in this ven-ture, she sure as hell isn't showing any fear. She's sitting up as if on alert, his keen-eyed sentinel. Business, just plain business, he supposes this might be called, and among the many entanglements he's tried to keep his life free of, business is high on the list. Jesus, how he resented the time he had to spend on contracts, on negotia-tions, on procuring buyers and sellers and then, once the deal was done and hands were shaken all around, on extricating himself from them. Sell a man a house and he thought your friendship should be thrown in as part of the bargain.

Now, in front of the Farm and Ranch National Bank, are the men who conduct as much of a town's business on its sidewalks and in its saloons as in its offices. By God, that could be the same group Calvin drove past on his way into Gladstone! Calvin complained to his grandson about the labor involved in the cowboy life, but he'd rather spend a day sinking fence posts than waste an hour yakking outside the bank.

He has to hand it to his son, however. Bill seems to understand that success in commerce has as much to do with those conversations on the street as in drawing up a contract. As much? Hell, *more*. Sidey Real Estate is in the right hands, that's for sure, which is one more reason, God damn it, why Bill should be here handling an eviction that has his signature on it.

Calvin turns to Beverly. "Did he have a weapon?"

"Did he what? No. None that I could see, anyway. Unless you count his face. Which would likely scare more people than a shotgun."

"So there's no doubt: You'll know him again if you see him."

"That's not the problem. The problem is forgetting him now that I've seen him."

"I can take you back home," says Calvin. "I'll find the address on my own. And from what you say, I'll recognize him."

Without hesitation, Beverly points down the street. "You need to turn left at the next intersection. We're almost there."

At that announcement, Calvin Sidey's heart hammers a little harder and a little quicker. He pictures his .45 back in the dresser drawer. If he hadn't left the house so abruptly, if he'd given himself a few minutes to think through what he was about to do, would he have gone downstairs, retrieved the pistol, and brought it with him? But opening that drawer means bringing that bottle of whiskey into view, and he spends far more time thinking about that and the use he could put it to than he could a gun.

NINETEEN

||||||||||||||||||||||||||||||||||||||||||||||||||||||||

Once they cross the narrow bridge spanning the Elk River, they are in a section of town that Beverly seldom has reason to visit. The houses here are small and often dilapidated. Lawns are sparse and yellow-brown or nonexistent, yet grass sprouts freely in cracks in the concrete or asphalt. Driveways aren't paved and sidewalks gap and tilt. Beverly never uses the term herself, but she knows that this area is frequently called Dogtown. And though she was born and raised in Gladstone, she had never known how the section got its name. So she finally asked Burt. As usual, he waited a long time before answering, a maddening tactic that was calculated to make Beverly withdraw her comment or question. When she demanded to know, he answered her question with one of his own: "Who lives there?" She had to concede that the area had a large Indian population.

Burt hesitated even longer, but finally said, "And what do Indians eat?" "Oh my God," she said. "That's absolutely ridiculous! That's *hateful*!" Her response, however, did nothing to prevent him from continuing to use the term.

As they turn onto a narrow unpaved street that has neither curb nor gutter, Calvin says, "Right around here I drove my first motor car. It belonged to George Ellingsen, one of my father's business partners. Of course there weren't houses or streets around here then. Just an old wagon road and a couple of hardpan fields and he didn't give me a damn bit of instruction. Put me behind the wheel and told me to go to it."

"How old were you?"

"Twelve? Thirteen maybe? Too young to be doing what I was doing. Of course there was nothing around here for me to run into or run over. Later I found out the expedition was my father's idea. He had a notion that cars were going to be the way of things and he thought if I was going to take over the business someday it would be good for me to know what to do behind the wheel. He was too old to learn, he said, but I wasn't going to get left behind."

"Your father must have been a wise man."

"Only where it came to turning a dollar."

"A few years ago," Beverly says, "some developers were interested in this area for a supermarket. They wanted to buy up all the land and houses around here and tear them down. Put in a parking lot and a big new Red Owl. Or SuperValu, I forget which. Your son opposed the plan."

"Not a good idea to stand in the way of progress."

"I can't believe you're saying that."

"I can't either." He leans forward and looks for a house number. "Are we getting close?"

"Take a left up ahead."

They turn onto a paved street. Beverly peers out, trying to see a house number. "Okay," she says. "The third house on the right. That must be it."

Calvin Sidey pulls to the curb in front of a tiny house with peeling white paint and torn screens. An old once-black Hudson with a flat tire slumps into the tall grass of the side yard, and a cardboard box outside the front door overflows with beer cans.

Calvin reaches past Beverly and opens the glove compartment. Inside are a box of safety matches, a crumpled bandanna, a Sir Walter Raleigh tobacco tin, and a stag-handled hunting knife in a leather sheath. Once she sees the knife, Beverly knows that's what he's searching for, but she still lets out a little groan when he brings it out.

"Take it easy," he says, opening his door. "Whether I need this or not won't be up to me." He slips the knife and sheath into the back pocket of his jeans.

"Won't you reconsider? I really think this is something for the sheriff to handle."

"We're here. No sense turning back now."

"Should I come with you? To make the identification?"

"I'll signal if I need you."

He hasn't quite finished arming himself. As Beverly watches him through the back window, he walks to the back of the truck, unfurls a canvas tarp, and lifts out a tire iron. He holds it close to his leg as he crosses the grass and steps onto the foot-high concrete slab that passes for a porch.

He pulls open the screen, holds it with his boot, and knocks on the door. Beverly takes it as a good sign that the inside door is closed. If people were in there, surely they'd keep that door open to try to get some air moving through the house.

She looks again at the eviction letter. It's addressed to a woman, Brenda Cady, so Beverly has to wonder who came banging on the Sidey's door. A husband? No, his name would have been on the lease. A boyfriend? A brother? A son?

Calvin has stepped off the porch and is peering inside the front window. Beverly cringes. If someone were inside with a rifle, this is when he'd open fire. But there's no gunshot, and soon Calvin is out of sight, having walked around to the back of the house.

Early in her marriage, before Adam was born, Beverly sometimes accompanied Burt on business trips. There was nothing glamorous or exciting about these excursions; the two of them usually did nothing more than travel to a county seat to look up deeds or other documents in the courthouse. They seldom even stayed overnight, but Beverly enjoyed getting out of Gladstone, even for a day, and she liked riding with Burt, seeing new parts of the state, and helping him search through dusty county records.

Late one summer night they were coming back from Bentrock, where they'd spent the day in the basement of the courthouse, when they came upon an accident. A car had flipped over into the ditch. Broken glass and twisted chrome glittered in the gravel along the shoulder of the road, and the beam of one headlight stared off crazily into the night sky.

Burt grabbed a flashlight to investigate and told Beverly to stay in the car. She understood that he didn't want her to see what gruesome sight might be waiting in the wreck, and his concern touched her, even through her fear for the car's occupants.

She did as her husband instructed, but it was difficult; curiosity and a desire to be of some use kept trying to propel her from the car.

She was startled by someone who suddenly appeared in the ditch, stepping high over the tall grass and coming her way.

It was a young man, and when he saw Beverly he said, smiling, "Can you give me a hand? I ran into some trouble here."

She called for Burt, and he came running. They soon got the young man's story. He had been in a baseball tournament in North Dakota, and he was on his way to his home in Livingston, Montana. He must have dozed off, he said, and missed the curve. When the car rolled, he was thrown clear, and he came to in the weeds. He wasn't injured seriously, he insisted, nothing more than a few scratches on his hands and face and "a hell of a bellyache." He reeked of beer, and though his speech was slurred, he made no effort to stop talking. "If my mama hears me complaining of a bellyache I'll get a dose of castor oil. I hate that castor oil!" They took him back to Bentrock, delivering him to the sheriff who assured Burt and Beverly that the young man would receive medical attention—whether he wanted it or not.

Weeks later, over breakfast, Beverly said to Burt, "I wonder whatever happened to that young fellow who rolled his car." It was nothing more than an idle comment.

Burt barely looked up from his eggs. "He died."

"Died? When—how do you know?"

"He died the very next day. Internal injuries, the sheriff said. Not a damn thing they could do. He gave me a call at the office."

"And you didn't think—what?—that I should know? Why didn't you tell me?"

"I'm telling you now."

Perhaps most people would have taken from that incident a lesson about the danger of driving Montana's highways at night or the fragility of the body's organs, but what Beverly learned was that what might seem to be gallantry could be just another way for a man to control what a woman sees and knows. She climbs out of Calvin's truck.

BEVERLY FINDS CALVIN IN the backyard, crouched over a couple of sagging cardboard boxes filled with hunks of greasy iron and steel. Nearby another disabled car—this one with at least two flat tires—crushes what little is left of the grass. This automobile—Beverly believes it's a Studebaker—looks to have once been maroon, but its paint has oxidized and the finish is fading in places to a shade that isn't far from the color of lilacs.

Calvin startles at her approach, but he doesn't get up, not immediately. "I told you I'd let you know if I needed you." It takes some effort for him to push himself to his feet.

"You said you'd signal me. But you never told me what the signal was. For all I knew, you being gone for more than ten minutes might have been it."

He points down at the boxes. "Damn near all the parts I'd need to rebuild my carburetor."

"Well, maybe after you bend that tire iron over his head you could work out a deal to buy some spare parts."

He gives her a long stern look. "Go wait in the truck. I'll be right along."

Beverly is aware that the smile she gives him is the same one she would shine on Ivan Kuntz just before she pinched a sizable hunk of skin on his arm and led him off to the principal's office. "We might as well walk together."

Back in the truck, Calvin rolls a cigarette, but before he puts it to his lips, he offers it to her.

What a strange set of manners this man has, thinks Beverly. "Thanks," she says, "but I don't smoke."

He licks its seam once more before lighting it. "And if you did, you wouldn't smoke these."

"I like the smell. My father smoked a pipe, and his tobacco had a similar aroma."

He scratches a match into flame, lights the cigarette, and inhales deeply. "On the job I smoke tailor-mades. No foreman wants to see someone stepping off to roll himself a smoke."

"The foreman . . . that's not you? Ever?"

"I've never been anything but a hired hand."

"And that's the way you want it?"

"It is."

Beverly isn't trying to send Calvin a message, but once again the springs poking her butt make her move closer to him. "If you don't mind my saying so," she says, "I have trouble imagining you taking orders."

"Those of us who take orders don't have to take on the order-givers' responsibilities."

"You told me you're looking to take as much pleasure out of life as you can. Do you also mean to avoid as much responsibility as you can?"

"I'd just as soon keep the weight off my shoulders, if that's what you're asking."

"For a man who doesn't want responsibilities, you sure took on a few when you came back to town this time."

There hasn't been a car driving this street for at least five minutes, but Calvin still leans out his window to look up and down the street for any sign of activity. Fine, Beverly thinks, don't answer me.

"Do you mind telling me what we're doing right now?" she asks. "And I'm not talking about responsibilities. I mean, why are we parked on Lanier Avenue staring at a house with nobody in it?"

"We're waiting."

"For how long? What if I have to be somewhere?"

"Like where?"

"I'm on the school library board. We usually meet today."

The skirt of Beverly's sundress is partially spread across the seat, and Calvin pinches a bit of the fabric between his thumb and index finger. "Is that why you're all dressed up today? For the library board?"

"We usually meet at the Harmon House. They provide a lunch for us."

He doesn't let go of her dress. Instead, he tugs gently on it. "That's the second time you've used the word 'usually.' *Does* your board meet today?"

"You are paying uncommonly close attention to my choice of words, sir."

"I sometimes go a week or more without hearing a human voice. That's good training for listening close." Now he rubs her dress between his fingers as though he's assessing the strength and quality of the material. "And you still haven't answered my question: Do you have a board meeting today?"

Merely considering a lie is enough to make her flush. "No. But I could still have something planned for today. Something that doesn't include staring at—" she looks again at the letter—"Brenda Cady's house."

He lets go of her dress. "It's not her house."

"I know whose house it is. And you know what I meant. Do you have a length of time in mind for staying here? An hour? Two? Twenty-four?"

"If you need to be somewhere, I'll take you. I can find my way back."

Beverly twists up a handful of hair at the back of her neck and lifts it to let any trace of a breeze cool her sweat. She lets out a sigh of resignation. "Mr. Sidey. The dress was for you. And the casserole that's sitting on your cupboard right now was nothing but an excuse to come over to see you. So I guess I got what I wanted out of the day: Time alone with you. Although I was hoping the circumstances would be a little different."

He flips his cigarette into the street. "I appreciate your attentions."

"My attentions? You appreciate my *attentions*? Oh my, I'll float on those words for a week!" She leans toward Calvin Sidey in an attempt to make him look at her. "Tell me: Have there been other women in your life recently?"

"White women, do you mean?"

The broken spring be damned—Beverly has to slide away from the man who makes such a remark. "A woman, Mr. Sidey. Any kind, any size. Any living, breathing woman. Have you had relations with another woman in the last, oh, ten years?"

He turns his intent gaze on her. "There's a woman who cooks and cleans on the Jarman ranch, not far from me. We've occasionally found ourselves in each other's company. She's a Blackfoot. That's a distinction that matters to some folks."

"But not to you?"

He shrugs. "I saw fit to mention it, so maybe it does."

Beverly is responsible for the silence that now fills the truck's cab. She can't give voice to her next thought both because she's ashamed of herself for thinking it and because she's afraid of how he might answer. She doesn't ask, And am I more to you than she is?

For the next half hour Calvin slouches down with his eyes closed, and Beverly might believe that he's dozing while she does sentry duty, yet at every sound of a car approaching—or of a child's bicycle rattling closer—he comes alert.

Finally, just when she's convinced he really is sleeping, he asks, with his eyes still closed, "You probably don't spend much time in this part of town, do you?"

"I've lived in Gladstone most of my life. I'm all right on either side of the river." Beverly sits up straighter. "In fact, there was a time when I thought I could turn my knowledge of this town to my advantage. I seriously considered selling real estate."

Calvin smiles. "Did you now? It's a job that takes more than a pretty smile and a nice pair of legs, you know. You have to pass a test."

"I don't know how you do it, Mr. Sidey, but you can be insulting even when you hand out a compliment. Yes, I know there's a test. I've managed to pass a few over the years."

"I'm sure you have," Calvin says. "But it's generally men who make the property-buying decisions. And they'd rather shake another man's hand over the deal. That's true on both sides of the river. Up on your side of town or here in Dogtown."

"I know where that term comes from. And I don't much care for it."

Calvin says, "I didn't make it up."

"But it sure came ready to your lips."

He tilts his hat back on his head, and looks up and down the block. "I'm surprised my son has properties in this part of town."

Beverly says, "They need places to live too."

"They? Who are they?"

"Well, Indians, I suppose."

Calvin smiles again. "Now you're doing it too."

"Speaking of which," says Beverly, "you were a little hard on Miss Ann last night when she brought up the idea of trying to help out the Indian population. She wasn't doing anything more than displaying some youthful idealism. But I don't suppose you ever had a case of that, did you?"

"If I did," he says, "I had a war to wring it out of me."

"And you don't think the Indians have had a rough go of it in Montana?"

"Does it matter what I think?"

"I'm interested in your opinion, Mr. Sidey."

He continues to survey the street in both directions. "We won," he says. "They lost."

"Simple as that?"

"Simple as that."

Beverly well remembers Burt saying, on the occasion of yet another injustice involving an Indian, "They bring it on themselves." Is Calvin's attitude any improvement over Burt's? They're Montana men cut from the same cloth, that's sure, and Beverly feels the familiar old frustration and hopelessness in the face of their hardhearted social philosophy. She's about to say—and this time she really will say it—I've had enough, take me home. But then a car comes down the street and pulls into the driveway. The woman who's driving and the little boy with her barely have time to climb out of their car before Calvin is out of the truck and striding over to meet them.

"Brenda Cady!" The way Calvin shouts the name it is not a question, and her fearful expression when she sees the man coming toward her convinces Beverly once again to get out of the truck and follow Calvin.

Beverly catches up to him just as he reaches the woman's car. "Do I know you?" Brenda Cady asks, glancing briefly at Beverly but trying to keep her attention focused on Calvin.

"You don't need to know me," he says. "You just have to listen to what I'm about to tell you."

Brenda Cady is plump, probably in her early thirties. She's dressed in a sleeveless white blouse and bright blue pedal pushers.

She's almost pretty, but there's something slightly lopsided about her pushed-in features that give her a look that's both sullen and submissive. The skinny little boy clinging to her leg is four or five years old, dark-haired, and dark-complected.

"You've been given notice to vacate these premises," Calvin says, and at first Beverly is surprised at his phrasing, but then she remembers that Sidey Real Estate had once been in his hands. "And I expect you to comply with that order."

Brenda Cady has driven up in a pastel-green Chevrolet, and now she reaches over and slams its heavy door. Beverly sees in the backseat two grocery bags.

"I'm workin' on it," she says, hugging the boy closer to her.

"You'll do more than work on it. And I'll tell you what else you'll do: You'll tell your husband or your boyfriend or whoever the hell that was that if he comes around my place making noise again he'll have trouble the likes of which he won't believe."

"Lonnie? What did he—?" Brenda Cady stops herself and leans toward Calvin Sidey. "Lonnie's not scared of you." Brenda Cady's mouth twists down and her eyebrows arch. In all her years of teaching, Beverly has never struck a student, but every time she comes across an expression like Brenda Cady's in the classroom or the schoolyard Beverly has to fight an impulse to slap the wearer across the face.

"Isn't he?" Calvin steps forward and places his hand on top of the Chevrolet. "Well, now, Lonnie doesn't know me." He runs his hand lightly over the roof as if he's a prospective buyer come to inspect the merchandise. When he gets to the back window, he stops stroking the car and taps on the glass lightly with his fist. "So it's up to you to educate him. You teach him he damn well better be afraid." Then he looks down at the child, a stare so steady and thorough he could be trying to see into the boy's ancestry. Brenda Cady's son ducks behind his mother.

Calvin turns then and begins to walk back to his truck, leaving Beverly to stand with Brenda Cady and the boy. Beverly feels she should say something, but what? Everything that comes to mind immediately cancels itself because she can't be sure of its truth. *Don't mind him; his bark is worse than his bite.* That wouldn't do—she suspects Calvin Sidey's bite could go very deep indeed. *He didn't mean to frighten your little boy?* No, he probably intended to throw the fear of God into anyone who crossed his path. Perhaps Beverly should get right to the heart of the matter: *You might think that was nothing but a crotchety old man, but that's only because you're new to Gladstone—that was Calvin Sidey, and many people believe he once caved in a man's head because the man made a vulgar remark about Sidey's wife. What do you think he'd do to someone who actually burst into the Sidey home and made a threat?*

But Beverly says not a word to Brenda Cady and her scared little boy. Instead, she runs across the street to join the man about whom she might have issued such dire warnings, the man with whom, for better or worse, she has thrown in her lot.

TWENTY

|||||||||||||||||||||||||||||||||||||||||||||||||||

Will leans his bike against the garage and heads toward the house. He's thirsty after baseball and he plans to make a pitcher of lime Kool-Aid. Will's almost to the door when he hears Adam Lodge calling out from the Lodge's yard.

"Hey, kid. Come here for a second."

Adam Lodge has been mowing the lawn, but he hasn't progressed beyond cutting one or two strips around the perimeter. He shuts off the mower and crosses to meet the boy.

"Come here," Adam repeats. "I've got a business deal for you."

Because Adam Lodge is tall and slender, Will has always thought of him as kind of a sissy. But when he sees the man without a shirt—Adam is wearing only a pair of grass-stained high top basketball shoes and plaid Bermuda shorts—Will is surprised at how muscled Adam is. Yes, he's skinny—his ribs show—but his shoulders are broad, his pectorals are hard plates, and his long arms are knotted with muscle.

"What's the matter?" Adam says. "Didn't you hear me? How'd you like to make a couple bucks?"

"I guess."

"If you finish mowing the lawn, I'll give you two dollars."

Will knows exactly what he'd like to spend the money on. That afternoon at Little League he borrowed Mike Florence's thick-handled bat, and he got two hits. With two dollars and a little from his savings, Will could buy his own Richie Ashburn model Louisville Slugger. Nevertheless, he says to Adam Lodge, "I better check with my grandpa."

"Your grandfather isn't here. He and my mother drove off together over an hour ago. So what do you say?"

Will's father often complains about the lack of attention Mrs. Lodge pays to her lawn, and there's the evidence—grass so tall it's started to tassel and so many dandelions their gray puffy heads look like fog rising out of the lawn. Will imagines he'll have to lean hard on the mower to get it through this pasture. But maybe when he finishes he'll still have time today to buy that bat.

THE MOWING IS TOUGH going all right, but Will puts the slow circuits around the yard to good use. He tries to think of how he can discourage Stuart and Glen and Bobby—Stuart especially—who won't rest until they can spy on Ann when she's naked. Yet for all his concentration on the dilemma, Will can come up with no reasonable solution. He *has* to persuade them that they must leave his sister alone, but how could he possibly persuade someone like Stuart Kinder? No *reasonable* solution . . . Suddenly Will feels as though he understands how a murderer might think—it's someone so powerless he resorts to his crime because it seems no other option is available.

The most dangerous places in and around Gladstone, at least those that Will is familiar with, are the river with its shifting channels and unpredictable currents, and an old coal chute, a steep galvanized steel slide that starts at the railroad tracks on a bluff above the river and finally empties onto jagged boulders far below. The problem is, how can Will lure or direct Stuart to either site? And how can he then position Stuart at the top of the chute in just such a way that Will can push him to his death? Or how can he get Stuart to step into the river right where the river is waiting to pull someone under and hold them down all the way to Wyoming? Maybe Will can use Ann as part of the trap. *Stuart, Ann's sunbathing naked over on that sandbar—no, you can't see her from here; you have to cross that part of the river.*

By the time he pushes the mower through a few more circuits, his face is hot not only from exertion but embarrassment. He's a kid, and he can no more put these plans into action than he could have imagined into life his plastic cowboys and Indians. Now, if Will's father were like almost all the other fathers he would have guns, and Will could simply wait inside the house with a Winchester or a Colt .45 at his side, and if Stuart Kinder entered the Sidey home, Will could be ready and waiting to blast them away. The mower snarls and coughs its way through the thick grass, and its fumes fill the air, but it's not the smell of exhaust that's sickening Will. His own fantasies make him feel like throwing up.

ALL THE GRASS IS cut except a bed-sized rectangle in the middle of the yard when the mower quits. Over and over Will winds the starter rope around the housing and yanks, but the engine just gasps. Will unscrews the cap on the gas tank, holds his breath, and peers in. He hates the sharp smell of gasoline even though for him it has become the smell of summer. The tank looks empty, and when he taps on it with his fingernail the way he's seen his father do, the tank echoes hollowly.

Some lawn mowers need gas *and* oil, and Will isn't sure he can come up with the right mixture, so instead of checking for gas in the Lodges' garage, he'll get the can from his family's garage, where his father has already mixed them.

Will is just exiting the yard when a voice stops him. "Hey, you quitting on me?"

Adam Lodge is standing on the back patio. He's smoking and holding a Budweiser beer bottle at his side, his index finger looped around the bottle's neck.

"The mower quit," Will says.

"There? With only that little patch left?"

Will nods. "It's out of gas, I'm pretty sure."

"I filled it up before I started." Adam drops his cigarette and crushes it out with his foot. "That's usually enough to do the front *and* back."

Will doesn't know what to say. Is Adam Lodge saying Will lied about the mower stopping? "I went kind of slow," Will replies.

"The deal was two dollars for the whole backyard. Not most of the yard."

Will wants to explain that he wasn't quitting, that he was only going for gasoline, but Adam Lodge has turned to the side in order to take a long swallow of beer, and Will thinks he should wait until

Adam finishes drinking. But when Adam brings the bottle down it's apparent that he's no longer paying attention to Will. He's focused on something next door.

Ann has come out the back door and is walking toward Will, and with a startling swiftness, Adam Lodge leaps over the row of scrubby spirea bushes lining the patio and then he too is heading toward the part of the lawn where Will is standing.

But, of course, it's not Will that Adam wants to get close to. "Hello there," Adam says to Ann.

Ann ignores him and asks Will, "Do you know where Grandpa is?" She has walked home from work on this hot day, and sweat has glued strands of hair to her temples and colored half-moons under her pink blouse's arms and scoop neck.

"Your brother here is trying to wriggle out of a job," says Adam. "Maybe you can tell him how important it is to finish what he starts."

Ann acts as though she hasn't even heard what Adam said. "There's a casserole on the counter. Are we supposed to have that for supper?" she asks Will.

"Maybe you'd like to finish the job? What do you say?" Adam asks her. "I'll pay you what I was going to pay him for the whole yard." Adam runs his fingers lazily up and down his side, tilting his head as if he expects his ribs to make music like the keys of a xylophone.

Ann glances at Adam only fleetingly. "I'm finished with work for the day." Turning back to Will, she says, "Do you know if Grandpa wants me to heat that up?"

When his father corrects Will's behavior or appearance, he often includes a reference to the family as part of the scolding. "You're a Sidey. Act like one." Will usually does as he's told, but he's never understood what his last name has to do with whether his shirt is in or out. He still doesn't know what "Sidey" means to most people, but he realizes that Ann must have an understanding of ancestry that Will lacks. She *is* standing straight and tall, and her haughty expression seems to have as its purpose informing Adam Lodge that she—that they, she and Will—are Sideys and that Adam Lodge would be well advised to remember that.

And perhaps Adam knows now that he'll get nowhere with Ann by criticizing her brother. "Why don't we all just say the hell with work for the day? Let's forget about the lawn."

Only now is Will able to explain why he quit mowing, and he offers his explanation not to Adam Lodge but to Ann. "I wasn't quitting! It ran out of gas, and I was going to fill it up from our can!"

Ann moves closer to Will. "My brother's a good worker. He doesn't shirk," she says coldly to Adam Lodge.

"Okay, okay," Adam says, leaning back and laughing. "I'm sorry I said anything. Can't we forget about work?" He holds up his beer bottle. "Can I get you a beer?"

"I'm seventeen," snaps Ann. "I don't drink."

Adam Lodge looks Ann over from head to foot as though he has to reassess her in light of her statement about her age. "I won't tell if you won't."

Ann turns back to Will. "How much was he going to pay you?"

"Two dollars."

She steps to the side so she can see around Adam Lodge and gauge how much grass remains to be cut. "You owe my brother one dollar and eighty cents."

Will looks up at his sister with something very close to awe. Where did she find the anger and the courage to speak to Adam Lodge this way?

"Whoa!" Adam holds up a halting hand. "What's this—you two ganging up on me? Who are you—the business manager?"

Ann brings Will back into the argument. "Did you mow all the rest of the yard?"

Will nods. "Almost all of it."

Ann slides closer to her brother. Will can smell her now, the floral scent of her perfume mingling with her sweat.

"Jesus, you two. I was just joking around and—oh boy, here comes the cavalry."

Will glances over his shoulder in time to see his grandfather and Beverly Lodge climbing out of the truck, and his grandfather obviously sees them because he immediately heads their way, his strides so long and rapid that Beverly Lodge has to break into a jog to keep up. Is Will's grandfather's haste occasioned by nothing more than the way the three of them are arrayed, Will and Ann squared off against the bare-chested Adam Lodge?

"What's going on here?" Calvin Sidey demands.

Ann is the first to speak. "He hired Will to mow his lawn, and now he won't pay."

Adam Lodge rolls his eyes. "That's not exactly . . . I was just trying to teach the kid a lesson about doing the job right. And now I've got the whole damn Sidey clan on my back."

"You, Adam, were lecturing someone on work habits?" Beverly Lodge says. "I'm trying not to laugh."

Ann must have believed that Will no longer needs her help now that Grandpa and Mrs. Lodge are on the scene. She walks off toward the house with her arms folded as though the day has suddenly turned cold.

And with Ann absent, Adam Lodge has no choice but to return to the issue underfoot. "You say you have gasoline?" he asks Will.

"In the garage."

With an exaggerated courtesy, Adam asks Will's grandfather, "May I use some of your gas? Please?"

"If you replace what you borrow."

"Show me the way," Adam says to Will.

"And Adam," Beverly Lodge says, "pay the boy what you owe him."

When Will notices that Adam is not right behind him, Will turns around and sees Adam still standing in the spot where he watched Ann walk away. Now, however, his head is thrown back and he is staring into the cloudless blue as if he's waiting for the sky above to betray him just as the grass below has.

TWENTY-ONE

||||||||||||||||||||||||||||||||||||||||||||||||||||||||||||||||||||||||||

After Bill Sidey has told Will about the nun who sneaks off every night to find out whether the Red Sox have won or lost, and after Bill has described to Ann how the University of Montana is beautifully snugged up against the side of a mountain and he has suggested again what a wonderful place it would be for her to study, and after he has assured both his children that their mother's operation went well and that she's a little weak but resting comfortably, after ten minutes of those evasions and awkward half-truths, Bill asks to speak to his father.

When Bill hears his father's familiar raspy voice, a voice that always sounds as though it's about to scratch itself into little more than a whisper, Bill suddenly discovers that he's lost his own voice.

"Hello?" his father says again. "Bill? You still there? Hello?"

Bill clears his throat and that's enough to get started. "Hello, Dad. Are Ann and Will still there?"

"Not right here. Nearby. Did you want to talk to one of them again?"

"No, no. I just wanted to make sure they weren't close enough to be in on this part of the conversation."

"They're out of earshot," Calvin says.

"What I told the kids about Marjorie's condition? It wasn't exactly true." He pauses to make certain he still has full possession of his voice. "She's not doing well, Dad."

The accident that claimed Bill's mother's life occurred in the afternoon in France, but Pauline's French family took hours to adjust to the fact of her death and to figure out how they could notify her husband. That phone call didn't ring in the Sidey residence until well after midnight, and after the news came, Calvin Sidey stayed up alone with his grief throughout the next night. When Bill and his sister woke, they found their father in the kitchen with a coffee cup and a full ashtray in front of him. The whiskey glass wasn't present then, but it would be in nights to come.

Their father told Bill and Jeanette to sit down. On the table there was also a sheet of paper that their father unfolded and glanced down at before he began to speak to his children.

"Your mother won't be returning to us," Calvin said. "She was struck by a car in her native village and killed."

The news was so stunning—would it have been any less so had it not been delivered in the language that a stranger might have used?—that neither Bill nor his sister could think of a thing to say. The silence soon compounded itself, and when it became unbearable, Jeanette, weeping, scraped back her chair and lurched from the room.

Ordinarily, Bill would have followed his sister—he relied on her example in most unfamiliar situations—but there was his father, motionless, staring unblinking at the floor.

But after moments passed—moments and nothing else, not words or touch or even a look—his father stood up and walked away, taking with him the sheet of paper, which he balled up and deposited in the garbage.

Bill fished the crumpled paper out of the trash, believing not only that he might read additional information about his mother but also that he might be able to discover a mistake—France was so far away, so different in language, customs, values—wasn't it possible that an accident there wasn't what an accident was here, that dead didn't mean dead.

Written in his father's hand the note read: *Your mother won't be returning to us. She was struck by a car in her native village and killed.* Their father had read to Bill and Jeanette the news about their mother . . .

And that Bill could not forgive. When their father left them—abandoned them—Bill felt as though that act was the natural conclusion to a process that began with his father not immediately sharing with his children the news of their mother's death, deciding instead to write a script from which he could read. For years, Bill kept that crumpled piece of paper in a dresser drawer, holding on to it for the day when he would hurl it in his father's face.

Yet now, as Bill buckles pronouncing that simple, bland sentence regarding his wife's condition—"She's not doing well, Dad"—he feels he understands his father as never before. How much easier it would be to read those words than to build them out of thought and then bid them make that precipitous, dreadful drop from brain to tongue.

"Not doing well *how*?" Bill's father asks.

"Well, it's tough getting a straight answer out of them. They said the operation was a success, but she just hasn't come around."

"Hasn't come around. What does that mean?"

In their Montana home, where Bill is now, Carole and Milo have installed a pale green carpet sculpted with a pattern resembling ocean waves, and though Missoula is almost as far from any sea as any point on the continent, when Bill stares down at the rug he feels something like the pull of undertow. "She's out," he says. "Unconscious. She never came around after the surgery."

"So what are they doing for her?"

"Doing? Not much. Giving her IVs. Watching her. The doctor keeps saying he expects her to wake up any minute."

"You're there—what do you think?"

On most days, Bill has the knowledge or the instinct to move safely, correctly, productively through the hours. In his business, he can calculate accurately and fairly the needs of Gladstone's citizens or of people new to the area. He can talk companionably with other businessmen, and together they can anticipate what's needed to sustain the town and its traditions. All the duties of fatherhood suit him, and none of the small ways his children might irritate him are anything compared to the overwhelming joy they bring him. He counts himself among the luckiest men on the planet because he climbs into bed every night to lie beside the woman he loves and desires more than any other on the planet. And yet, on the margins of his life are shadows, hints of a darkness that could, without warning, blot out the light that shines on most of his days.

This uneasiness—this dread—Bill has always supposed originated in his childhood when first his mother and then his father left him, and forever after he felt that at any time life might offer up something that he has neither the skill, courage, nor character to handle. *Things could get out of hand* is how this fear insinuates itself into his thoughts. His father is a man about whom it has been said *took matters into his own hands.* Bill has always known what that is a reference to. Calvin Sidey is supposed to have killed a man who insulted Bill's mother, and though Bill doesn't believe it himself it's enough that many others do. And since Bill is a man aware of his own limitations, it stands to reason that when things get out of hand, as they are almost certain to, in a manner great or small, it will help, won't it, to have nearby someone who can take matters into his own hands?

Bill understands how contradictory this longing is. Being abandoned by his father has created most of the anxiety in Bill's life, yet at exactly when he feels most anxious, he wants his father's reassurance.

"I'm afraid she's going to die, Dad, and I don't know what to do."

"I'll tell you what to do," his father says. "You go sit by her bedside and you stay there. Stay even if they try to drag you away."

Although his father hasn't commanded him to do anything different from what Bill would have done on his own, he follows the order as if someone has just shown him the single narrow path to salvation. It's for the comfort of my soul I asked him back, Bill realizes, mine, not his.

CALVIN HANGS UP THE phone gently. He didn't mean to speak so gruffly to his son, but God damn it, he wants Bill to understand—*you might not have another chance.*

When Pauline left Gladstone, she and Calvin were barely on speaking terms, so angry was he over her decision to return to France. They hadn't quarreled over the matter, not exactly, but he'd said, repeatedly, You don't have to go. And Pauline would reply, I do, Cal-veen. I do. She seldom stopped smiling, his wife, and in their first years together Calvin thought that smile was simply to help her get through the moments when something in the language or the culture bewildered her. And that was true enough. But over time Calvin also came to understand that there could be as much steel in a smile as in a tightly clamped jaw. Pauline Sidey was not a stubborn woman, except in the matters she was stubborn about, and then she was as set on her track as a locomotive. She gave up much to match her life to his in Montana—her religion, her language, her family, her farm girl ways—but she wasn't about to forgo this trip just because her husband sulked about the house like a child who's been denied a toy.

On their last night together, Pauline took off her nightgown in bed. That was something he often asked her to do, but she had a shyness that usually got in the way. Isn't it enough, she would say, that we . . . that you can touch? No, he'd say, it isn't enough. I want to *see*. So Calvin knew. He knew what it meant that she was naked in bed. His back was turned to her, and she pressed herself against him. She reached inside his pajamas, something else she was generally reluctant to do. But he wouldn't turn toward her. We have to get an early start tomorrow, he said, if you want to catch that train.

Put her on the train he did, without an embrace. And when the train carrying his wife on the first leg of her journey back to her homeland pulled out of the station, his heart thudded so hard in his chest it was all he could do to draw a breath. If he left right at that moment, he wondered, and if he drove like hell could he beat the train to its first stop? Could he be there when it pulled into the station? He could climb aboard and go from car to car until he found her. Of course he didn't do that. He drove like hell, but straight to the Pitchfork Saloon, the only bar open that early in the morning. By the time the train made its first stop, Calvin Sidey was drunk.

How many times over the years did Calvin ask himself, could he have come right out and forbidden her to go? Would she have obeyed? Most wives back then believed they had no choice but to follow their husbands' command. Wasn't it part of the vows? But Calvin wanted Pauline to stay because it was her decision. Hell, he should have chained her to the bathtub.

Then as now, Calvin would have given anything to have what his son has. His wife lying in bed, home or hospital, asleep or comatose, it wouldn't matter, as long as she was alive, and he could hold her warm hand, whether she knew it or not.

TWENTY-TWO

〰〰〰〰〰〰〰〰〰〰〰〰〰〰〰〰〰〰〰〰〰〰〰〰〰〰〰〰〰〰〰〰〰〰

Will has skipped Little League. His team was scheduled to play the Heidt Paint and Glass Bengals, and Dickie Mahlberg pitches for the Bengals. No one throws harder than Dickie, and he's wild. Just last week he beaned Owen Cullen, and Owen's parents took their son to the emergency room that night when Owen fainted at the supper table. Owen only had a concussion, but that was enough for Will. He's always nervous up at the plate anyway, and he sure isn't going to take any chances by standing in against Dickie Mahlberg and his fastball. Instead, Will goes out to the backyard and bounces a tennis ball off the back porch, pretending that he's pitching for his team and he's striking out more batters than Dickie.

The day is cloudy, and Will wonders if it might rain, in which case Little League would be canceled anyway. But it never rains, not this summer. He winds up and fires another strike—*pock*—the ball hits the cement and comes bounding back at him, and he fields it cleanly.

When Gary and Stuart amble into the yard, Will wishes he would have stayed inside and read his Joe DiMaggio book, *Lucky to be a Yankee*.

Neither Stuart nor Gary have any thoughts about today's Little League games. "Hey," Stuart says, "did you see what we rigged up."

"See where?" Will jams the tennis ball into the pocket of his glove and turns the glove over on the grass so Stuart and Gary can't see that he's been playing with a tennis ball.

"Come on," says Stuart, nodding in the direction of the alley.

Will follows them, but they don't go far. Stuart stops behind the Sidey's garage.

"Well, what do you think?" Stuart asks.

"About what?"

Stuart smiles slyly at Gary. "See? I told you he wouldn't notice a fucking thing."

"What?" Will says impatiently.

Gary walks over to the steel rack holding the Sideys' two garbage cans. He just stands next to the rack, but when Will continues to look on uncomprehendingly, Gary grabs one of the rack's steel rails and shakes it hard, rattling the cans. Only then does Will realize that the rack isn't in its usual position. It hasn't been moved far, but now it stands closer to the oak tree whose branches shade the roof of the garage. For a couple years now, Will's father has said that he means to cut down a few of the tree's branches since they scrape the roof of the garage.

"Okay," Will says, still mystified.

Stuart climbs onto the rack and then steps onto a garbage can, clanging and denting a lid in the process. From there he jumps up and grabs an oak branch—unreachable from where the cans originally stood—pulls himself up, and then scoots himself along the limb until he can drop down onto the garage roof. To Will and Gary standing below he smiles widely and gives a thumbs-up sign. Then he scrambles down by the same route, and when he lands in the alley's dirt and gravel he looks about surreptitiously to make sure that no one but his friends have observed his climbing routine.

"If you wanted to get up on our garage," says Will, "why didn't you just tell me and I could've got our ladder for you."

Stuart grabs Will in a loose headlock and pretends he's about to throw an uppercut at his captive's head. "Hey, numb nuts—we don't want to advertise what we're doin'."

Once Stuart releases him, Will shakes his head to free himself of the stink from Stuart's sweaty armpit, darkly furred where Will's are still as bare as a doll's.

"My folks are gone," Will says. "Nobody cares if you climb up on the garage."

"They would if they knew what we were doing up there," Gary says.

"We moved the garbage cans last night and climbed up there about eleven," Stuart says. "Gary figured out that there's your sister's bedroom"—he points toward the second story of the Sidey home—"so we was watching for her to undress."

"But we couldn't see anything," Gary adds. "What you got to do is get in her room and open her curtains. We could see the shadow of her moving around in there—"

"So if the curtains was open," Stuart says, "we could see *everything*."

"Especially with these." Gary walks over to his bicycle and

removes the binoculars looped over the handlebar. "My dad's. He got 'em in the war. Took 'em off a dead German."

Every addition to their basic plan is another weight on Will's heart.

"Now here's all you gotta do," Stuart says. "You're gonna go in there and open her fuckin' curtains."

At last—Will sees a flaw in their strategy! "She'll just close them. She always does."

"Yeah, we thought of that. So you can't just open them—you got to *break* 'em open. You know, like so they won't close. Get it?" Stuart is practically rubbing his hands together in diabolical glee, so pleased is he with how well they've worked out all the details of their plan.

"Break her curtains?"

Gary has the binoculars to his eyes, and he is systematically scanning the overcast sky as if he's watching for enemy aircraft. "You could maybe cut the cord," he says. "Or jam something inside the curtain rod."

"You know, the part that goes over the window," Stuart says.

"I'm not sure we have that kind," Will weakly offers.

"Well, whichever." Stuart's voice and expression both harden. "No matter what kind you got you just make sure they're open and stay open."

"And figure out for sure when she's going to be home, so we can all get up there."

"We?" Will asks. "Are you talking about just the two of you?"

"What the hell," says Stuart. "You can join us."

Gary swings the binoculars down and around until they're trained on Will. "Unless you don't want to."

Will steps back, worried that from that distance the binocular's powers might magnify the tiniest trace of a frown, the smallest downturn of his lips—anything that might reveal the loathing he feels for his friends and their scheme.

"He probably don't need to," says Stuart. "He sees her all the goddamn time, I bet."

Will can do nothing but meekly shake his head. He's afraid to tell them he doesn't want to spy on his sister because they might think he doesn't have a boy's normal interests. Why not, they would surely, incredulously ask. And Will doesn't know what he'd tell them.

Doesn't he know his sister is pretty? More than pretty, beautiful perhaps? Doesn't he know she has a good figure? Isn't he curious about what girls look like—you know, their tits and down there? Yes. For sure, yes, he wants to see a girl without her clothes on, but.

But what?

When his grandfather told Will that cowboys spend more time building fences than roping calves, something in Will shrank and withered, and he's afraid that something like that might happen when he sees a naked woman for the first time. What if Will looked at Ann and didn't feel what a boy is supposed to feel because she was his sister? And what if he does feel it—she's his sister!

These thoughts and more swirl in Will's mind, and he becomes angry and angrier still because he shouldn't have to explain himself for not wanting to spy on his sister.

The thunder that's been grumbling in the distance all morning suddenly booms almost overhead. A few heavy drops of rain splat into the alley's dust. If only a bolt of lightning would have struck the tree and the garage when Stuart and Gary were up there, Will's problems would be solved.

"Hey, what was your grandpa up to last night?" asks Gary.

"My grandpa?"

"He came out of your house last night to have a smoke, and we wondered if maybe he was going to do some window peeking himself."

Will's heart catches on Stuart's words.

"Yeah, he walked over toward Mrs. Lodge's, but all he did was stare at the house."

ANN STOPPED BRINGING HER lunch to work on the day when she found herself sharing space in Penney's break room with Mrs. Bishop and Ethel Cutter, Mrs. Bishop's friend. Throughout the lunch break, the two women huddled together and whispered quietly, all the while glancing furtively in Ann's direction. Since then, Ann either skips lunch altogether or goes next door to the counter at Finley's Drugstore.

Today she has just ordered her usual, a tuna fish salad sandwich and a glass of milk, when a man sits down one stool away from her. Just like in the song, she sees by his outfit that he is a cowboy. A real one. His boots have riding heels, and the brim of his hat has that slope that comes from it being tugged down to keep it on tight or to shield his face from the sun and the wind. There's dirt caked on his boots and sweat stains on his hat.

Ann hates cowboys. Oh, not this young man specifically. When he leans toward her and asks if she's going to be using the ashtray, she sees that his eyes, squinty and weather-wrinkled, have a sad, shy look. And her favorable impression of him continues when he simply lights his cigarette and turns back to his coffee, allowing her to eat her sandwich in peace. She even feels a little sorry for him; if he's sitting at Finley's lunch counter in the middle of the day, that probably means he's out of work.

But Ann wishes she lived someplace where cowboys, whether

on horses, in trucks, or on lunch counter stools, aren't the region's most important people. And again, that doesn't apply to this—or any other—specific cowboy. A young man who works on the Hilltop ranch is certainly not a more respected member of the community than Dr. Clay, and no cowpoke has as much influence as the lawyers who work across the street in the offices of Hart, Bergin, and Kraus. Yet if it were the only way they could keep their cowboys, the citizens of Montana would cast all the doctors, lawyers, druggists, teachers, and real estate agents—especially the real estate agents—out of the state. Of that Ann is certain.

What do cowboys even stand for? They're a rowdy, restless bunch who make the world a better place for no one but the boss they work for. Schools or museums or art or music—none of these will ever be valued very highly in a region that has the cowboy as its patron saint. Ann knows that this attitude means her grandfather as well. But she hasn't seen much from him that exempts him from her judgment. Besides, she suspects that after all these years he thinks of himself as a cowboy more than a Sidey.

This is why Ann intends to leave Gladstone as soon as she graduates—if not before—and she's determined to head east, not west to Bozeman and Montana State or Missoula and the U, where her dad hopes she'll go.

Ann's friend Jane Folger visited her older sister in Grand Forks, North Dakota, last spring where her sister was a junior at the university, and Jane came back to Gladstone not only determined to attend the University of North Dakota but to take Ann with her. They would pledge the same sorority (Sigma Nu, to which Jane's sister also belonged) and share a room in the sorority house. The campus, Jane said, was like nothing in Montana. Enormous trees shaded the sidewalks, and ivy crawled up the bricks of the buildings.

Jane told Ann about the concerts and plays they would attend, the tea parties and formal dances they would be invited to, and Ann found Jane's enthusiasm so compelling that Ann might very well apply to the University of North Dakota too.

Kitty McGregor hops onto the stool next to Ann.

"Thought I'd find you here," Kitty says, spinning back and forth in half circles.

"But I thought you didn't come within a mile of the place on your day off," Ann says. Kitty works at Finley's, and she complains often about how men stand at the magazine rack paging through *Cavalier* and *Stag* and then practically lick their chops when they look over at her behind the register.

"I'm delivering party invitations," Kitty says. "And I have to do this in person, so it stays a secret." She leans toward Ann and whispers, "Gwen's having a party tonight. Her parents are out of town, and Gwen's home alone."

Gwen's parents trust her to stay home without supervision, yet Ann's father insisted on having Grandfather Sidey there with Ann and Will. And now Gwen is demonstrating that her parents' faith in her is wrong.

"I don't know," Ann says. On the other side of the counter the waitress, Mrs. Tawny, who has been working at Finley's soda fountain for as long as anyone can remember, frowns in their direction and pokes at her hairnet where a few coils of steel-gray hair have sprung loose. Mrs. Tawny probably resents Kitty and Ann because their jobs are easier and higher paying than hers.

Kitty raises her voice back to its normal level. "He's not going to be there, if that's what you're worried about." Kitty, like everyone else in their circle, knows only that Ann no longer has a boyfriend; she has no idea what precipitated the breakup.

"How do you know?"

"Joan said. He left town with her brother, Rick, and a couple other guys. They were driving up to Kalispell to bring back a car Rick's buying from his cousin."

"You're sure?"

"Joan said they left yesterday when Rick got off work." Kitty shakes a finger in Ann's face. "You're going to this party. I mean it. I'll drive. I'll pick you up and we'll go to the Corral and eat first." The Corral is a new drive-in on the east side of town. The log fence enclosing the parking lot gives the place its theme and its name.

"All right," Ann says, and then by tugging closed her own blouse tries to signal to Kitty that the top two buttons of her blouse are open and that her brassiere is visible through the gap.

Kitty waves away Ann's concern. "Maybe somebody else will notice!" With her eyes and a subtle nod of her head, she indicates the cowboy seated behind her. Kitty mouths the words *He's cute.*

Throughout the elementary school years, Kitty was always one of the smallest girls in her class. In the past year, however, she has acquired a woman's full body, all the more obvious because she's still barely five feet tall. If it's true that Finley's customers leer at her, Kitty probably welcomes it.

"Seven o'clock," Kitty says as she spins off her stool.

Kitty's departure is so abrupt, Ann is left staring at the cowboy. Yes, she supposes he does qualify as cute, even if she isn't interested in him. At least not as a boyfriend.

What if she hired this out-of-work cowboy to be her escort, her protector? He needn't come any closer than he is right now, but that would be near enough to discourage anyone who might want to bother her. Wouldn't he be perfect for such a role? Aren't cowboys supposed to be both gallant and tough, quick to pull out a lady's chair and quick with their fists? Ann allows herself a peek at the width of the young man's shoulders and the bands of muscles twining up and down his forearms. Yes, he would no doubt be capable of defending her. But though a cowboy is willing to work for low wages, he still expects to be paid, and Ann is fairly certain what payment he would expect from her. She'll just have to continue to take care of herself—don't Montanans believe in that as well?

TWENTY-THREE

|||||||||||||||||||||||||||||||||||||||||||||||||||||||||||||||||||||||||||||||||||||

EVERYONE HAS BEEN WAITING for the dry spell to break, and
when it finally does Beverly Lodge is probably the only person in
town over the age of twelve who's not pleased about it. But the
downpour catches her out in the open, blocks from home and without a raincoat, umbrella, or even a hat. Within minutes she's soaked
to the skin, and she has to bend over her bag of groceries so the
paper won't get wet and tear from the weight of two cans of cream
of mushroom soup, a cantaloupe, a box of Post Toasties, and a box
of Cheer.

It's the Cheer that put her in this situation. She went downstairs
that morning to wash clothes, and only when the washer was already
filling did she realize she was out of detergent. Adam wasn't home;

he had risen early and driven out of town in order to do "research" for his novel. He was going to look for a site where an Indian battle was supposed to have taken place. And he had taken her car because his was almost out of gas. Yes, yes, she could have driven Adam's car and hoped there was enough fuel to reach the Mobil station, but then she would have been not only paying for his gas but also getting the gas for him. She's willing to do the former; she draws the line at the latter.

Yet Beverly didn't have to walk to the store. The laundry could have waited. Or she could have borrowed detergent from a neighbor. But she was angry at her son for taking her car and—why not admit it?—she was angry at Calvin. She had cooked for him the day before, dressed up for him, accompanied him on his expedition to Brenda Cady's, and then once they returned to their neighborhood, he went off to his house without a word to her. He might have thanked her or talked to her about what had happened during the day—to say nothing of the night before—or he might have asked to see her later in the evening. Instead, she got nothing but his back as he walked away.

So it had been anger at those two men that sent her out of her home on a day when the skies looked dark enough to keep most people indoors, but by the time she returned from the store, she was mostly angry at herself. She—not Calvin or Adam—was the one she had punished with her impulsive behavior. And now to make matters worse, she has to slow her gait—every time she takes too long a stride her drenched canvas shoes threaten to slip from her feet. Oh well, she can't get any wetter.

She's still berating herself when she turns up her walkway and sees Calvin standing under the shelter of her front porch, smoking a cigarette and squinting through the rain at her as she approaches.

With the hand that's been holding the bottom of the grocery bag, Beverly, in a little gesture of vanity, pulls her wet hair from her face. But without her hand's support, the bag tears open, and its contents tumble at her feet. The soup cans roll down the sidewalk, and Beverly runs to retrieve them. One can makes it almost to the street, and by the time she catches up to it and makes it back to her porch steps, the spilled detergent—a corner of the Cheer box has split open—has had time to bubble up a little puddle of suds. She picks up the box carefully so more powder doesn't spill out, kicks what's left of the grocery bag toward the window well, and looks around for her cantaloupe.

Calvin has picked it up from where it rolled into the grass, and he holds it out to her.

"Could you hold on to it for a moment?" she says. "As you can see, I'm a little short of hands."

"I've been waiting for you," he announces solemnly. "I'd like a word with you, if I may."

"Help me get these inside, and I'll listen to more than one word, if you like."

In the kitchen, Beverly dumps everything on the cupboard and then shakes rain from her hands and hair. "I'll tell you what. If you should ever find yourself waiting for me in the rain again, why don't you search somewhere other than my porch. If you would've headed out in your truck to find me, maybe I might have been spared dragging home looking like a drenched dog."

She turns around, and there's Calvin, staring at her as if he has never seen her or her species before. And perhaps he hasn't. Her wet slacks cling to her as if they've been painted on, and her white blouse has turned transparent. He can see not only the lace pattern of her brassiere but the pale pink of her flesh. She starts to pull the fabric away from her skin so it isn't quite so revealing, but he steps forward and brushes her hand away just to replace it with his own, though his hand pushes the cloth against her once again. In his attempts to put his lips to her neck, he has to fight through a tangle of wet hair.

He yanks her blouse out of her slacks, but when jamming his hand up her blouse creates too tight a fit, he tries a different approach. He brings his hand out and tries the buttons.

A neighbor coming to the back door might peer through the veil of rain and see Beverly and Calvin plastered to each other. Adam might walk in at any moment. She has to tell Calvin to stop, she *has to*, yet she lets her lips scrape across the stubble of his beard until she finds his mouth and there she fastens herself so that even if she could resolve the struggle between what she wants to say and what she should say speech would not be possible.

Let this be passion. Let this be her own long-suppressed lust. Let this be love. But please God, Beverly silently prays, whatever force is swiftly sweeping her past any capacity she might have to say no or wait, please let it not be mere vanity!

He has trouble with her buttons because the wet fabric keeps twisting and slipping in his fingers, so she opens up just enough space between them so she can unbutton herself. She has barely let the blouse land on the floor when he's trying to pull up the cups of her brassiere. The wet fabric sticks to her, and his urgent efforts to get at her skin cause her bra to twist and bind, and once again she has to push his hands away. She shrugs out of the bra and can't help but critique her own dark and shriveled nipples, but his hands cover her so quickly she doesn't have to contemplate her appearance for long. He wants her out of her slacks as well, so she tugs down her zipper and wriggles out of her pants, pulling the underpants down with them.

Could the rain have penetrated her completely, found its way not only through her clothes but through all her body's membranes? How else to explain her wetness in a woman of her age? When Calvin, having lifted her onto the cupboard, enters her, he slides in with an ease that's almost frightening. When he pushes so hard he seems to have struck bone, she lets out a gasping cry unlike any sound she has made in her life. *Who is this woman?*

IF SOMEONE CAME TO the door or peered through Beverly's window, he or she would witness a scene so typically domestic that there would be nothing remarkable—much less scandalous—in it. At the kitchen table a man and woman sit across from each other, and the steam rising from their cups probably means the coffee was just poured. He smokes, careful not to exhale in her direction. She wears a bathrobe and a towel turban. Although they seem pleased to be in each other's company, neither can resist glancing out the window at the steady rain that parched Montana needs so badly. And with that thought a strange competition suggests itself to Beverly: Both needs have now been met, but which was greater—Montana's for precipitation or a widow's for touch?

"You said you wanted to speak to me," she says to Calvin. "Or was that a euphemism? You've barely said a word."

He crushes out his cigarette. "I talked to Bill last night. Marjorie's not doing well."

"Oh no! What's wrong?"

"She had the surgery, but she never came out of the anesthetic. Sounds to me like she's in a coma."

"My God. How are the kids taking it?"

He shakes his head. "They don't know. Bill didn't say anything to them, and neither did I."

"What's the point of that? They have a right to know what's going on with their mother."

Calvin rises from the table but continues to stare out the window. "Do they? They'll be happier without that knowledge. As far as they're concerned, their mother is doing fine, and they'll be seeing her soon. Why not let them believe that as long as they can?"

"I can't agree—"

"When Pauline died I stayed up all night trying to think of the right words to break the news to Jeanette and Bill. And just about the time I realized there were no right words, it occurred to me that I didn't have to tell them at all. I could just say their mother decided not to return from France. They might have hated her for that but she would have remained alive for them. In the end, I decided the truth is always the right course. So I gave it to them straight. And I watched them crumble under that news like I'd just put a thousand pounds on their shoulders."

The mother in Beverly thinks but does not say, But you might have stayed around and helped them carry that weight. "It's never easy," she says instead.

He scowls in her direction at her little platitude.

And for all this talk of withholding information, Beverly thinks, you came here to share the news with me—what should I make of that?

She asks, "How's Bill doing?"

"He's pretty shook up."

"Next to the death of a child, having your spouse die is about as bad as it gets. As we both know." He doesn't move from the window, but Beverly has already had sufficient experience with Calvin to know that her last remark was the sort to send him out of the room.

She stands and walks over next to him. "You don't have anything to say to that?" He doesn't turn to her, so she studies his profile. His jaw clenches, relaxes, and then clenches again. Pulling tighter the knot, Beverly thinks, that ties back the words.

"I didn't think it called for a response," he finally says.

"I just meant the memory of our own sorrow makes us feel especially bad for Bill and what he's going through."

"I know what you meant."

"Sometimes I wonder if you believe you've got the market on grief cornered."

"I've never said that."

What is it about this man that seems to alter the climate around him? Not long ago it was heat, but now the air has acquired a chill. She wraps her robe tighter around herself. "Not in so many words you haven't."

"There's no way to say a thing but in words."

Was there a time in Beverly's life when she had too much pride to do what she's about to do? Probably. She grew up like other girls—like other women—wary of any hurt, accidental or intended, and Beverly slammed her share of doors, shed her portion of tears, and wore down the heels on more than a few shoes by spinning and walking away. But if the years have taught her anything, it's that pride of that sort is a luxury no one can afford, not if they expect to find any happiness in the company of others. She wedges her way into the narrow space between Calvin and the window, and when he doesn't back away but puts an arm around her, she doesn't care if he does it grudgingly or not.

"You don't think I'm saying something now?" she asks.

"*Sed mulier cupido quod dicit amanti, in vento et rapida scriber oportet aqua.*"

"Mr. Sidey, maybe you're trying to impress me, but I don't know if that's an insult or sweet talk."

"'What a woman says to her man ought to be written in wind and running water.' Something like that."

"And I still don't know." She shakes her head and lets the furled towel fall to the floor. "Does it strike you as odd that while Bill and Marjorie are going through their miseries you and I are—well, what are you and I doing? Shall I be crude about it—going at it like a couple of rutting rabbits?" Although she doubts it will happen, Beverly hopes he'll correct her and apply a more romantic term to their activities.

"You can call it what you like," Calvin says. "I haven't let it get in the way of what Bill asked me to come here to do."

"Did Bill want you to come to town and threaten to shoot your neighbor's dog and scare the wits out of a little boy?" And, she thinks but does not say, fuck the woman next door.

In response to her question, his arm drops from her shoulder, and he steps back from her embrace. As suddenly as the space opens between them comes Beverly's insight: Calvin Sidey is always ready to run, and it doesn't take much to set him in motion. As a young man, he ran from this block, from Gladstone, from Montana, from this country. From his family and the family business. He ran from sadness, and he ran from responsibility. If the gossip was true, he ran from the law. And if Beverly doesn't set up an obstacle or a reason for him to stay now, Calvin Sidey will go, and anytime he goes it could be for good.

"Wait—I'm sorry!" As she grabs for his hand, her robe falls

open. Her desperation, however, quickens her mind, and she makes it seem as though her sudden exposure is planned. She catches his hand in hers, brings it to her breast, and holds it there. And he doesn't pull it away.

"I've spent too many years in the company of children," she says. "I can't seem to break the habit of thinking anyone can be teased out of any mood."

"Teasing," he says. "Is that what you call it? And what do you think I need to be jollied out of?"

The calluses on his palm are rough, and Beverly feels as though her breast is being caressed by a hand made of splintered wood.

"You know—that trying-to-see-past-the-rain mood."

The door between the kitchen and the garage creaks. Adam— why didn't she hear him drive in! Why didn't she consider that the rain would bring him home early! Then Beverly does exactly what she does not want Calvin Sidey to do to her—she pushes away from him and tries to cover herself before her son enters the house.

Adam startles when he walks into the kitchen, suddenly confronted by his mother and Calvin Sidey staring at him as if he's a teenager sneaking in past his curfew. But Adam recovers quickly. "Hello!" he says in a too-loud voice. "Am I interrupting something?"

"I was caught in the rain," Beverly says. "Mr. Sidey was kind enough to help me with my groceries. How was your expedition? Did you find what you were looking for?"

"Not exactly. Kind of hard to get a feel for things just by looking at sagebrush and a few hills."

"You got a bank robbery in this book of yours?" Calvin asks.

The question surprises Beverly. Calvin sounds as though he's truly interested in Adam and his project.

"Because I was thinking," Calvin continues, "you could track down old Horace Hagerman and talk to him. I believe he's still alive. When Horace was a boy, he saw the James gang rob a bank in Northfield, Minnesota."

"Minnesota?" Adam says skeptically.

"Horace's uncle even fired off a few shots at Jesse himself. Missed, of course."

Before Calvin has finished speaking, Adam is shaking his head. "My novel takes place in Montana."

"I believe what Mr. Sidey is saying," Beverly says, "is that you could talk to someone who actually—"

"Never mind," Calvin says.

Adam shrugs and says to Calvin. "Hey, I'm sorry about that little misunderstanding with your grandson yesterday. I tend to forget that I don't have to turn every dealing with a kid into a lesson."

"Did you pay the boy?" Calvin asks.

"He walked off before I got around to it."

"You can pay me. I'll see he gets his money."

"Now?"

"Now."

But Adam doesn't reach for his billfold, and the silence and stillness in the kitchen takes on a charge, as if the air itself is first to sense the sudden antagonism between the two men.

"Oh, for God's sake," Beverly says, grabbing up her purse from the countertop. "Two dollars? Was that the amount?" Without waiting for confirmation, she thrusts the bills in Calvin's direction.

He stuffs them into the front pocket of his jeans. "Looks like the rain's let up," he says. "I'll head on home."

Beverly doesn't follow him to the door. She's frozen in place, trying to figure out if by paying Adam's debt she has taken her place with the Lodges or the Sideys.

TWENTY-FOUR

Will measures off a length of string that will reach from the back of the garage down the alley and into the lilac bushes behind Mrs. Lodge's house. He dips the length of string into the gasoline can in the garage. After pulling out the saturated string, he stretches it along the garage wall, careful to keep it close to the foundation and twining it in and out of the rakes, shovels, strips of lath, paint cans, and snow tires so it looks as though the string belongs there, just more crap lying about until the day comes when Will's father or mother summons the energy to clean out the garage.

Will trails the string out into the alley, snaking through the gravel and dust until he comes to the lilac bushes, its flowers long since fallen and their perfume just a vanished memory. With the string still in hand, Will crawls under the shade of the heart-shaped leaves. He finds a stone the size and shape of a hamburger bun, and he weights the string down so it'll stay put.

With the string's other end still in the gasoline can, Will has a fuse long enough to allow him to light it from a distance and be out of danger before it goes off, no matter how fast it burns or how powerful the explosion might be.

He has no intention of helping Stuart and Gary spy on Ann, but he also knows there's nothing he can do or say to stop them. So he'll let them go ahead with their scheme. When he's certain they're on top of the garage, he'll circle around the house so he can sneak undetected into the lilac bushes and light the fuse.

The gasoline, he's pretty sure, will explode, maybe blowing out the garage walls and collapsing the roof. But if the gas only wants to burn, Will has prepared for that too. He's taken a couple of old torn-up towels that his father uses for washing the car, poured a little gasoline on them, and left them, under crumpled balls of the *Gladstone Gazette*, next to the gasoline can.

Will's primary objective is getting Stuart and Gary off the garage roof and keeping them off, but beyond that, he thinks it likely that he can escape blame for the fiery event. First of all, aren't most garages, with their oily rags and containers of various flammable materials, fire traps? And if spontaneous combustion isn't cited as the cause, certainly fingers will be pointed toward the Gitners, the Sideys' neighbors to the north.

Mr. Gitner still burns his family's trash in the alley in his "incinerator," a fire-blackened oil drum, and he often leaves his fire unattended. When the sparks and feathery bits of burning papers rise with the smoke and heat, the wind could very likely send them right onto the Sidey property. Worse still, Mr. Gitner doesn't seem to care what he tosses into the barrel, and both Will's father and mother have heard the distinctive *pops* that come from doing something not only foolish but dangerous—tossing aerosol cans into the fire, for example. After the fire department tries to save the Sidey garage, won't they notice the Gitner family incinerator and believe they've found the cause of the blaze?

But again, the important thing is that the garage will be gone, either its walls blown away by an explosion or the building burned to the ground, and once it's gone, Stuart and Gary will be unable to climb onto its roof to spy on Ann Sidey. Will's father will rebuild the garage, of course, but the new one will be closer to the house, exactly where his father wishes the garage were every winter when he has to walk through the cold and the snow to get to his car.

And does Will care about what might happen to his friends when the garage goes up in flames? Not really. As his grandfather said, they're not really his friends, are they?

ANN SIDEY DOESN'T EVEN like the taste of beer, yet she's already drinking her second cup. She hoped that if she got a little tipsy she'd be able to lift herself into a party mood.

But so far she can't, and she knows the fault is in her. There's nothing wrong or unusual about this party. Beer, whiskey, vodka . . . cigarettes . . . dark bedrooms and basement rec rooms for making out and more. And the Jensens' home is in Western Meadows, the new subdivision where the houses are larger and spaced more widely apart, so that means the music can be louder. Because the night is warm and mild more kids gather out on the patio and in the backyard.

Ann stands alone at the edge of the sloping lawn, right where the grass runs out and a steep ravine begins. The night has taken its time coming on—it's close to ten o'clock and the horizon has only now lost its last blush of light, allowing the darkness that began down in the ravine, among its boulders and its bent and broken trees, to rise and finally overtake the land.

Since the day her parents left town, Ann has been reasonably successful at not worrying about her mother. Both her mother and father assured her that the operation was safe and routine, and Ann took them at their word. Besides, she had other matters to worry about.

But earlier tonight, when she was preparing for tonight's party, Ann looked at herself in the mirror and wondered why her mother seldom wore makeup. She looked so pretty when she did. Two years ago, for example, when her parents went to the Christmas party at the country club, Ann's mother not only put on rouge, eye shadow, and mascara, but she also wore lipstick that seemed to match perfectly the deep red of her dress. And oh, that dress! She had been with her mother when she bought it at Dalton's in Billings, but Ann never saw it on her mother until that December night. A simple wool jersey, it clung to her mother like no other article of clothing she owned. It was low-cut too, and Ann could tell her mother was self-conscious about the décolletage because she kept tugging at the shoulders and neckline. But she did it in a good-humored, almost giggling way, and it occurred to Ann, perhaps for the first time, that her mother might be as excited about going to a party as Ann and her friends could be. But her mother hadn't worn the dress since that night.

Didn't her mother want to be beautiful, Ann wondered, as she put on her lipstick? Her mother was losing her looks already—the sad pouches under her eyes, the deepening lines framing her mouth. Didn't she realize . . .

Ann had a vision of her mother dead, her face painted for eternity by a stranger, her beauty sealed in the grave. Ann's hand began to tremble, and soon she could not follow the outline of her own lips, and in another moment, muddy rivers ran down her cheeks from her freshly applied mascara.

After she stopped crying, Ann washed her face and started over. This time, however, she skipped the eye shadow and mascara, and when Kitty picked Ann up for the party, she asked Ann, "Are you sick or something?" "Just tired," Ann replied. Although only the two of them were in the car, Kitty leaned across the seat and asked confidentially, "Is Aunt Flo visiting?" At that moment, a false admission seemed easier than any attempt at explanation, and Ann nodded her head.

Kitty must have spread the word about Ann and her mood throughout the party because no one even comes near Ann out here at the edge of the yard. Earlier Cam MacLeod stepped off the patio, and Ann thought he might be coming her way—she had heard that Cam wanted to ask her out—but a few paces onto the grass he ran out of interest or nerve and turned back to the party.

If she stayed home, she could be there if her father or mother call, or Ann might have phoned Aunt Carole's. Just hearing someone's voice, someone who has seen her mom and can testify that she's all right, would be enough to blow away those morbid thoughts that are taking a firmer hold in her mind by the minute. But it's already too late to call, and by the time she gets home, Ann's grandfather will probably be asleep, and it won't do to wake him and ask if there's any word from her parents.

The last time Ann spoke to her father, he had intended to put her mind at ease about her mother, but he had not entirely succeeded. Her father had sounded cheerful and optimistic, but since he believes that a hopeful outlook and a ready smile are always the keys to happiness, Ann placed a little asterisk of qualification beside much of what her father said. If she could hear her mother's voice, Ann would know whether her worries are warranted or not.

While she's thinking of her mother's voice, how she so often keeps it low no matter how circumstance might demand another tone, Ann hears another voice, almost as familiar as her mother's, but this voice sends a chill through her and stops her breath. *Monte.* She's sure, yet her fear talks her into doubt. It can't be. He's in Kalispell. Still holding her breath, she listens, and when she hears that laugh like three grunts—*huh, huh, huh*—she doesn't wait a second longer. She puts her cup of beer down in the tall grass and looks for a direction she can run in.

He returned early. Or perhaps he never left. Maybe he lied and let it be known that he was leaving town in order to lure Ann out into the open. Maybe he was working with someone—Kitty? Would Kitty do such a thing?—who tricked Ann into coming to the party with the promise that he wouldn't be there.

There's only one way for her to go. If she goes back toward the house, even if she tries to circle wide around either side, she runs the risk of him seeing her, or worse, of him believing that she's coming toward him.

So she walks straight ahead, and within a few paces, she no longer feels the Jensens' spongy grass underfoot, but the stony steep slope of the ravine. She descends sideways, trying simultaneously to do contradictory things—hurry, so she can put as much distance between her and him as possible, and slow down, so she doesn't trip on a rock or a clump of sagebrush.

The night is clear but moonless, and the deeper into the ravine she goes the darker it becomes. She makes her way by sense as much as sight, and when the darkness seems to thicken and gain texture, Ann slows and gropes with her hands until she can be sure what—a boulder, a tree, a waist-high tangle of tumbleweeds—blocks her path.

For the second time this month, Ann is on the run, allowing herself to be chased through what is supposed to be her town, her *world*, the place on the planet that she knows better than any other and where she should feel safer than anywhere else. Yet lately she has been making a point of stopping and looking up and down the street before she pushes open the doors and exits Penney's. Only days ago she ran through the backyards of her own neighborhood.

Years ago, when she was five or six and there were no houses out here, when it was nothing but hills and sloughs and gullies, her family had driven out here, bumping across the prairie—there wasn't even a gravel road—to set off their fireworks a safe distance from town. Maybe they had even arced their bottle rockets out over this very ravine. And now she's feeling her way along in the dark, hoping that the rattlesnakes have slithered under their rocks for the night.

If the branches and trunk of the fallen tree weren't bleached near white, Ann probably would have walked right into it, poking out an eye on one of those twigs that stick out like accusing fingers in every direction. But Ann does see it and feels down the tree's length, toward its roots, trying to find a place low enough and free enough of branches that she can climb over and continue on her way.

She hikes up her skirt and throws one leg over the trunk, a motion that reminds her of climbing on a horse. Is Jensens' house near where those stables used to be? Hadn't they been west of Gladstone? Ann was eight or nine when she and her friends were in love with horses, when they all begged their fathers and mothers to take them horseback riding as often as possible.

If thoughts of horses and her past had not taken Ann's attention, perhaps she might have noticed, even in the darkness, that when the tree fell it dragged down with it a sizable branch from another tree nearby and it's on *this* branch, as thick and round as a man's leg, that Ann lands when she dismounts the trunk.

Her feet slip out from under her, and she topples backward. She gets her hands back under her to break her fall, and she thinks at first that the *snap* comes from a dry twig she lands on, until she registers the sharp pain in her forearm.

The darkness and the fallen tree also conceal the steepness of the slope that increases sharply just on the other side of the trunk, and she begins to slide down the hill. A rock scrapes the side of her head. She doesn't know how to slow or stop her descent. If she sticks out an arm or leg it might snag on a rock or stump, and she knows by now that one arm is already injured, though how badly she can't be sure. Finally, the earth, as if it can feel pity for its inhabitants, comes to Ann's aid. She slides into a depression the size of a car's trunk, created perhaps when a boulder rolled away. In this bowl, Ann first puts her hand to her head. Her fingers do not come away wet with blood, but when she tries to push herself to her knees, the pain in her right arm is so intense she cries out.

Cradling her arm, she scrambles to her feet. The span between her elbow and wrist curves, a shape that might be graceful if a substance other than human bone were involved. But the actuality is grotesque, and Ann has to look away to keep from becoming sick to her stomach at the sight of a part of her own body.

She's close to the bottom of the ravine, but she doesn't hurry. She can't. Not only is she terrified of falling again, but each step sends a jolt of pain directly to her arm.

The cloudburst early in the day brought no more than a quarter of an inch to Gladstone, yet it was enough to form pools of runoff at the bottom of the gully. Ann's foot sinks up to her ankle in the mud. She tries to pull free, but that causes the wet earth to suck harder, and she frees herself by letting the mud keep her tennis shoe.

The slope leading out of the ravine is not as steep or rugged as the path down, and Ann begins to climb a diagonal course up toward the road that leads back to town. Weeds scratch at her ankles and small stones jab at the sole of her bare foot, yet she's grateful for the easier ascent. Her arm feels as though someone is squeezing it, the pain increasing as the grip tightens.

When Ann finally reaches the road, her relief is so great she stops for a moment to catch her breath. But with her first hard sigh, she suddenly feels lightheaded, and she bends over, just as her father taught her when Ann felt faint during the rehearsals for her seventh grade Christmas program. Lowering her head, however, is not enough. Her vision dims as if the darkness at the bottom of the ravine has followed her up the hill and is now wrapping itself around her. She sits down on the shoulder of the road, the gravel rough but warm under her.

In another moment, she sees the headlights of a car in the distance, and though she knows she should get back on her feet and flee back down the ravine—or at least to go far enough so she isn't visible from the road—she can't make herself stand up. She hears the steady roar of the car's engine grow louder and then feels its vibration through the heel of her bare foot where it touches the asphalt, but she stays put. The rumble of the car's muffler—that could be the sound of Monte's Ford—but still Ann stays where she is. The driver obviously sees her, slows, then stops right in the road alongside Ann. The passenger door opens, but Ann does not alter her position, seated cross-legged in the dirt and cradling her bent arm like one of the dolls she stopped playing with half a decade ago.

TWENTY-FIVE

||||||||||||||||||||||||||||||||||||||||||||||||||||||||||||||||||||||||

Beverly is in bed reading, only two chapters left in her Erle Stanley Gardner mystery, when the doorbell rings again and again. Her first thought is of Adam—he's gone out for the evening and forgotten his keys. Which only shows how absorbed she is in the novel. Adam is home. Of course. She doesn't even have to listen very carefully before she hears the sporadic clacking of his typewriter in the basement, a sound that even after all these weeks that her son has been home still reminds her of the furnace and its ductwork clicking and ticking with heat.

She puts her book down, grabs her robe, and runs toward the front door.

She flips on the porch light, and when it illuminates Calvin Sidey's form, she sighs with relief, believing that the same need she struggled with earlier has finally gotten the better of him too.

But he does not pull open the screen door and try to get under her nightgown's thin cotton. Instead, he speaks, and with the same urgency with which he has been leaning on her doorbell.

"My granddaughter's in the hospital, and I've got to get over there right away. Can you come over so if Will wakes up it won't be to an empty house?"

"Ann? Ann's in the hospital? My God, Cal, what happened?" She steps back and Calvin follows her into the house.

"I'm not sure. I've got this second or third hand. Apparently she fell somewhere. She was being chased . . . ? I don't know."

"How bad?"

He rubs his jaw with the backs of his fingers the way men do to check if they need to shave. Beverly recognizes the gesture for what it truly is—the action of a man trying to hold down his panic.

"They told me her life's not in danger, but she's banged up."

She hears the urgency in his voice. "I'll throw on some clothes and be right with you."

Back in the bedroom she tosses her robe on the bed, pulls her nightgown over her head and lets it fall to the floor, and from the closet grabs the sundress she took off only an hour or so earlier. She's buttoning herself up and hurrying back to the living room when Calvin's words catch up to her. Chasing her—someone was *chasing* Ann?

Calvin is standing at the door, staring out at the night and eager to be on his way. Beverly puts a restraining hand on his shoulder and leans tenderly against him.

"I should go with you," she says. "If someone's after Ann, that's something she might feel more comfortable talking to a woman about."

"Will—"

She cuts off his concern. "Adam's here. I'll ask him to stay with your grandson."

"Fine. Maybe we can take your car then. My truck's low on gas."

"I'll get Adam."

She hasn't been able to shake free of the image of Calvin striding across the street toward Brenda Cady's house with a tire iron in his hand. If he armed himself for a confrontation with a man who only made a threat, what is Calvin likely to do to someone who has actually brought harm to a member of his family? And what if the years-old gossip is true—that Calvin once caved in a man's skull for a rumored insult to his wife? No, Beverly better stay close to Calvin. If for no other reason than to try to prevent him from doing something that will land him in Deer Lodge State Prison for the rest of his days.

BILL AND MARJORIE HONEYMOONED down at the Chico Hot Springs Resort, and when they returned to Gladstone, Bill did not carry her across the threshold of his—*their*—house on Fourth Street. He held the door open for her, bowed low, and said, "Enter, Mrs. Sidey." It was, of course, not the first time she had been in the house; Bill had lived there all his life, except for his years in the service, and during the time they dated, Bill and Marjorie were more likely to spend an evening at his home rather than at her tiny apartment above Woolworth's. But she had never been inside as "Mrs. Sidey," and that slight difference was enough to discomfort her and to trouble her sleep for nights to come.

She was, first of all, not entirely certain how she felt about being a Sidey. In Gladstone it had always been a name to be reckoned with, tied up as it was with the town's history, its prosperity and property. But not long after Bill's mother's death—the previous Mrs. Sidey—the family's reputation changed. When grief and drink and a possible murder drove Calvin Sidey out of his mind and out of his home, suddenly the Sidey name was one people whispered about and muttered over, a name associated with tragedy, scandal, and strangeness. Marjorie knew Gladstone had been talking behind her back ever since she began keeping company with Tully Heckaman, but she could live with that. To be a Sidey, however, was another matter.

Marjorie also worried that she wouldn't be able to adjust to her new name, that something in her would so resist being a Sidey that she would fail to acknowledge any "Mrs. Sidey" directed at her. And she certainly didn't want Bill to believe she was ashamed of taking his name. So she practiced. She wrote the name over and over, filling sheets of paper with "Mrs. Bill Sidey," and "Marjorie Sidey." All the while she did this, she could not shake the worry that somewhere was a notebook that might turn up also filled with her handwriting, but with the name Heckaman rather than Sidey. She had whiled away many classroom hours practicing *that* name as well.

Yet in spite of the rehearsals, the Sidey name seldom seemed a part of who she was. And there were times when she didn't *want* to answer to the name, when, for example, men with whom she'd had some history called her "Mrs. Sidey," and they used a tone—how did they manage it, those men who were usually so inexpressive and inarticulate?—that had a leer tucked inside it. Perhaps worst of all were the nightmares: She would be someplace where she was in danger, but the danger was invisible to her. She might be in a building, for example, that was on fire, but she was in a room where the flames had not yet reached. People outside tried to warn her by calling her name, *Mrs. Sidey, Mrs. Sidey, Mrs. Sidey*, but inside her dream Marjorie could not comprehend that they were calling her.

Or as in this dream. She is in a hospital, and a name is being called, *Mrs. Sidey! Mrs. Sidey!* Gradually, it dawns on her that the hospital authorities are looking for someone to come forward because there's a baby in the nursery whom no parent has claimed. *Mrs. Sidey!* Can that possibly be Marjorie? She's a mother, she knows that, even if she's uncertain about any of her other roles. No, she can't take a chance, not if a child is in distress. She struggles toward waking, a destination that suddenly recedes exactly at the instant that Marjorie decides to make for it. *Mrs. Sidey! Mrs. Sidey!*

But make it she does, and she opens her eyes to a lantern-jawed elderly nun who smiles down at Marjorie as if she's the child who has been missing a mother.

BEVERLY CLOSES HER EYES, leans back in her chair, and rests her head on the waiting room's cinder-block wall. She hasn't seen Ann yet, and the only injury for certain is a broken arm. She hopes it's not a compound fracture. Beverly shudders at the thought not only because of the pain it would cause Ann but also because of the grotesque image of bone tearing through skin, through that lovely skin. Beverly opens her eyes to banish that picture.

Adam, bless him, for once did not disappoint her. When she went down to the basement to tell him what happened to Ann and to ask him if he would go over to the Sidey home, Adam immediately picked up his typewriter and a stack of paper and hurried up the stairs.

Beverly's fond thoughts of her son are interrupted by the sound of a woman clearing her throat. When Beverly looks up, she sees Mrs. Teed cautiously approaching. It was Mrs. Teed who brought Ann to the hospital.

"I'm sorry," Mrs. Teed says, "I didn't mean to startle you."

"No, no, not at all. But I thought you went home."

"I couldn't. Not until I know I how she's doing."

Beverly shrugs helplessly, and at that Mrs. Teed sits down in the green chair next to Beverly. The vinyl squeaks and the cushion sighs under Mrs. Teed's weight. She's a stout woman, but attractive nonetheless. She has a quick, bright smile, high cheekbones, and long-lashed dark eyes that any woman would envy. Like Beverly, Mrs. Teed is a widow, and to much of Gladstone that means the women should automatically be as close as sisters, but Beverly can't remember an occasion when they've done anything more than exchange a word or two about the weather. Beverly is also aware that Gloria Teed has a reputation as a gossip, and this knowledge makes Beverly wary.

"To tell you the truth," Mrs. Teed says, "I wondered if I made a mistake, just bringing her to the hospital." She lowers her voice to a whisper. "I wondered if I should have called the police or the sheriff. I mean, if someone was after her, my God, I can't believe that could happen here. Not in Gladstone."

"If he thinks the authorities should be notified, I'm sure Mr. Sidey will take care of that."

"So that's her grandfather? Calvin Sidey is her grandfather?"

Beverly nods.

Mrs. Teed makes a low hissing sound as she draws air past her teeth. "I heard he was dead."

"No, alive and well."

"I used to hear Jim and my folks talk about him. But I guess

I never put it all together—Bill and Marjorie, their kids. So that's Calvin Sidey . . . my goodness!"

Even without knowing what Mrs. Teed has heard about Calvin, Beverly feels she has to defend him. "He's been doing ranch work for years, but he came back to Gladstone to watch the kids while their parents are out of town." Beverly cringes inwardly. Since they're in a hospital where one of the children lies injured, this isn't much of a defense, so she quickly tries to undo the damage with a lie. "He's devoted to those grandkids."

She can't tell whether Mrs. Teed's head nod signifies skepticism or acceptance.

"So," Mrs. Teed says tentatively, "you came here with him?"

"I live right next door to the Sideys," Beverly adds quickly. "I've known those kids since they were toddlers."

Mrs. Teed nods as if, though she accepts everything Beverly says, she's still curious about something. Finally, after a long moment during which both women stare at the speckled floor tiles, Mrs. Teed leans close to Beverly and whispers, "What I remember hearing is that after his wife died he went to France and killed the driver who ran over his wife. And then he had to go into hiding so he couldn't be found and extradited."

"Oh, no, no! Nothing like that ever happened. As I said, he's been working on a ranch for years. He's just one of those men who's not well suited for town living."

Although Beverly doesn't think her correction of Mrs. Teed has been forceful enough to give offense, the woman stands abruptly. "I'd better get going," Mrs. Teed says. "I'd sure appreciate if you give me a call and let me know how she's doing." She smiles politely down at Beverly. "Tomorrow's early enough."

Of course it's possible, Beverly thinks, that Mrs. Teed enjoyed believing that story about Calvin Sidey and didn't much care whether it was true or false. And then Beverly Lodge has to come along and puncture one of Mrs. Teed's cherished beliefs. Oh, well. Beverly can't be responsible for preserving every cockamamie myth that people want to subscribe to.

A nurse appears at the nurse's station. Beverly rises and approaches the desk.

"Ann Sidey?" Beverly says. "Can you tell me anything about her condition?"

"In regards to Miss Sidey—you're related to her how?"

"I'm not a relative," Beverly confesses. "I'm Ann's next-door neighbor."

The nurse, a young woman with lacquered straw-blond hair, subjects Beverly to a long, impassive stare, a look that probably causes most people to mutter an apology and step back. Then the nurse quite deliberately looks down at the forms on the desk. "Dr. McKee will be out shortly."

Beverly knows Leo McKee. He's the doctor who delivered the news to Beverly that Burt was dead. She can't remember a word the doctor said on that occasion, but she can still recall that he had a mustard stain at the corner of his mouth, a faint smear of yellow for which Beverly was grateful. It provided her with a way to gain a little distance from shock and grief—what had the doctor been eating—potato salad? a frankfurter?—but perhaps that thinking was wrong. Perhaps only someone who has already taken a step back from grief can notice such a detail.

"I'm just trying," Beverly says with a smile, "to get some word on how she's doing."

The nurse doesn't look up. "Doctor prefers to speak to family members. Only family members."

Beverly is about to deliver one of her standard stern lectures on the importance of good manners and respect when Calvin comes around the corner. He could not have looked more drained if he had just donated half of his blood.

Beverly rushes to his side. "How is she?"

"Not bad. They're taking her up to an operating room to set her arm. The doctor wanted to check her over for other injuries before sending her on." He takes a deep breath, then exhales. "Let's step outside," Calvin says. "I want to breathe something other than hospital air."

To the nurse Calvin says, "You'll come for me if I'm needed?"

"Of course," she replies.

Calvin and Beverly stand under the portico where the ambulance usually parks to unload.

"So it was just her arm?" she asks Calvin.

"She's got a helluva bump on her head and some scraped skin, but the arm's the thing the doctor said was most serious."

"A compound fracture?"

Calvin shakes his head and digs a flattened pack of Camels from the front pocket of his jeans. "The doctor said it looked like a fairly clean break. Both bones, though, so he's not sure how well it will set."

He gets his cigarette lit and inhales.

"What did she say about being chased?"

"Not much. She's backing off that story a bit. Could be she's embarrassed."

"Backing off? How?"

Calvin shrugs. "Says maybe she let her imagination run away with her. She might have heard something and got spooked."

"Oh, Calvin, that just doesn't sound like her. Another teenaged girl perhaps, but not Ann."

"No? Well, you'd know better than I would."

Coming from the mouth of another man, that remark might be tinged with regret or self-pity, even self-accusation, but from Calvin Sidey it's nothing more than a statement of fact.

Beverly says, "Maybe I shouldn't say anything . . . it's probably not remotely connected to this business of someone chasing her, but over the past few weeks I've noticed a car—"

"A Ford? A black Ford?"

"I'm not very good on makes, but yes, black. Definitely black. Circling our block. Parked in the alley."

"I saw that car. A black Ford—'fifty-one or 'fifty-two. It was parked in the alley a few nights ago, and I thought Ann might be looking to sneak out and meet someone."

"That doesn't sound like Ann either."

He walks a few steps away from the hospital doors, then stops and gazes up at the building. Is he counting lighted windows, trying to calculate the floor Ann is on? Or is he looking for the nighthawks whose whistles he can hear overhead? Beverly walks out to him and loops her arm in his.

"I'm not saying I'm right," she says.

"But if someone was after her, why wouldn't she say something?"

"Maybe she was afraid no one would believe her, that they'd say she was being silly or worse. Hysterical. Girls have to contend with such things. Or maybe she's trying to protect someone."

His laugh is quiet but hard-edged. "Who would she be protecting?"

Beverly takes a deep breath and draws herself closer to him. She can feel his heat through the damp cotton of his T-shirt.

"You," she says.

He doesn't pull away, as she feared he might. "I can take care of myself."

"That's not what I meant. Maybe Ann thinks you need to be kept *from* yourself."

"She doesn't know me that well."

"She shares your name. That could be enough to make her feel she knows you. Maybe you've been living like a hermit out on the prairie, but you've got a reputation that's still living in this town. She might have heard talk."

Beverly holds her breath again, waiting for him to ask *What talk?* But the question doesn't come, and in its absence she lets go a sigh and plunges ahead. "Can I confess something? That's why I was willing to go with you to Brenda Cady's house. Because I was afraid of what you might do. I wasn't going along to help you so much as to get in your way, if it came to that."

"I figured as much."

"But I *am* trying to help, to help you understand. You can't just act the way you do, not without knowing certain things." She presses herself tighter to him, hoping to soften him with the softness of her body. In all her years of marriage, she probably never spoke to Burt the way she has just spoken to this man, of whom she knows little but his capacity for ferocity.

Yet he doesn't explode in anger. He speaks as softly, in fact, as he would if he were still in the hospital's corridors. "It's been a long time since anyone expected me to think or know much of anything. I've drawn wages for most of my years for simple doing."

"And do you think your son asked you to come here to *do* something?"

"If need be." He flicks away his cigarette, and together they watch its sparks pinwheel down the drive. "If need be."

"Have you called Bill?"

This is the question that moves him to extricate his arm from hers. "Not yet. I'll wait until morning. At this hour a phone call wouldn't do a damn thing but worry him. I wouldn't want him racing home in the middle of the night."

Beverly thinks of that earlier conversation about Marjorie's condition and about Calvin's wife, a conversation that was, of course, about ignorance and knowledge.

"Should you be the one to decide that?" she asks. Why does she persist in asking him questions that are sure to challenge and probably irritate him as well? Is she trying to drive this man away? The best she can do for an answer is this: If they are to have a future together—a future beyond this night—it can only be with full awareness of who the other is. Beverly has decided, without even knowing when or how, that she'll live alone—without love, a man, a mate—if companionship requires her to clamp her jaw or bite back a single word.

"Since I'm the one who made the decision," Calvin says, "I guess I am." He takes a couple steps toward the hospital, then stops and turns back to Beverly. "As long as we're making confessions, I've got one of my own. My truck's got damn near a full tank of gas. I wanted us to take your car, so I could get in your garage and put my hand on the hood. If it was hot, that would mean it had been driven recently."

"But it was cold?"

"As cold as metal is likely to be in this weather."

"So as a result of your detective work, you concluded—what?"

"Well, I already checked out your son's car, so I knew he hadn't been driving that one. And with your car cold, that meant he couldn't have been the one chasing Ann."

"That was your only reason for ringing my doorbell?"

"I needed someone to be there for Will. I was telling the truth on that score."

She steps close to him. "God *damn* you." She folds her arms tightly to make certain she doesn't give in to a temptation to strike him. "You say something like that? To me? About my son?"

But as Calvin Sidey has said about himself, he has been away from civilization for a long time, so long in fact that he perhaps doesn't know that there might be a reason other than the obvious one that will make a woman stand close to a man.

Calvin reaches out and tenderly but determinedly pulls her close to him. He performs this action with one arm, as if, like his grand-daughter, he has a partial disability. And because Beverly knows the incapacity is not in his arm but in his soul, she relents and allows herself to be held.

TWENTY-SIX

‖‖‖

Will wakes at three o'clock in the morning and knows instantly that Ann has not come home yet. He knows because he put a note on her bed: *Wake me up when you get home, it doesn't matter what time it is.* Will is certain she will because she'll believe he has news about their mother. In reality, he planned to sneak outside after Ann woke him. He'll go out the front door, creep through Mrs. Lodge's yard, and into the lilac bushes. From there he'll be able to see if Stuart and the others are up on the garage—they'll be silhouetted by the street lamp in the alley—and if he sees them, he'll light his fuse.

But the luminous hands of his Westclox say it's 3:00 a.m., and Ann has not wakened him. Is she taking advantage of Dad and

Mom being gone to stay out as late she likes? Wait—what's that click-clicking sound? Is it possible that Ann has come home but not yet gone to her room? Will throws off the sheet and heads for the source of the noise.

By the time he enters the kitchen where the only light in the house shines, he knows what he heard. It's the sound of a typewriter, and he's heard it in the house plenty of times before. Mom types up papers for Dad's business. This time however the herky-jerky clacking of a typewriter's keys comes from Adam Lodge, sitting at the kitchen table with his back to Will.

Will speaks up in a voice close to a shout: "Where's my grandpa?"

Adam jerks around in his chair, knocking his cigarettes to the floor. "Jesus! Clear your throat or something—you scared the hell out of me."

"Is my grandpa here?"

Adam pulls out a chair for Will. "Come on over. Have a seat."

Warily, reluctantly, Will follows Adam's suggestion. In the warm house, the chair's chrome tubes are cool on the backs of his legs.

Adam moves his own chair closer to Will. Adam Lodge was once a schoolteacher, and Will knows that this is exactly the way teachers sit—leaning forward, their elbows on their knees—when they want to have a "special" talk and you're supposed to be honest and they'll be understanding. Will wraps his legs tighter around the chair and grips the seat cushion with both hands.

"The first thing I want to say"—Adam pauses and clears his throat, just enough time for Will to think, So say it!"—is that your sister's okay. She's in the hospital, but she's okay."

"Ann . . . ?" This is why it's wrong for Adam Lodge to be here; he doesn't know what's going on with the Sidey family—it's Will's *mother* who's in the hospital, not his sister!

"She broke her arm. I'm not sure how it happened. She fell. But it's nothing serious, and she'll probably be home tomorrow."

"A broken arm?"

"That doesn't sound too bad, does it? And I bet she'll let you be the first one to sign her cast."

"I can sign . . . ?"

"Her cast. You know, plaster . . . Haven't you had any friends who broke an arm or a leg and had to wear a cast?"

Will wasn't there when it happened, but two summers ago Joel Bevan fell from a tree and broke his leg. That happened in early June, and he was still on crutches and in a cast when school started.

Will didn't write his name on Joel's cast, and he didn't care if he got to sign Ann's or not. Another idea has occurred to him, and Will has all he can do not to jump up and run around the kitchen, so excited is he that his dilemma has suddenly been solved.

Ann will have to wear a cast! Won't that fat white hard sleeve have the same effect as a disfiguring scar—only temporary? Won't she become, like Joel Bevan, an object of laughter? Won't Stuart and Gary—won't *any* boy—lose interest in seeing her without her clothes on now that she can't be naked, not really?

"How long are you going to be here?" Will asks Adam. He doesn't mean to sound rude, but Will is so excited he momentarily forgets his manners.

Adam sits up straight and looks carefully at Will as if he, Adam, has to recalibrate his judgment of the boy. "I'll be here until your grandfather returns. Or until my mother comes to relieve me."

"I'm old enough to stay by myself. I have lots of times."

"Sure you are. Sure. But I have to obey *my* mom. She told me to stay here, and I'll get in trouble if I leave, even if you gave me permission."

Will is fairly certain that Adam is humoring him, but that doesn't matter. Some of the antipathy he felt for Adam Lodge begins to dry up. "I'm hungry," he says finally. "Can I have something to eat?"

Adam glances at the clock. "Why don't you just go back to sleep? In a few hours, it'll be time for breakfast."

"I'm pretty hungry right now."

Subjected to Adam's prolonged stare, Will knows he's supposed to give up and return to his room, but Will holds fast. Finally, Adam rises and goes to the counter. "What are you hungry for? How about a bowl of cereal?"

Will shakes his head.

"I don't even know what you've got . . . Toast?"

"No."

Adam opens the refrigerator. "How about some of this hot dish?"

"I didn't really like it that much."

He pulls out the produce bin. "You want an apple?"

"Could I have a sandwich? My mom fixed a ham before she left, and she said we could have that for sandwiches."

"A ham sandwich . . . Yeah, okay. What do you want on it?"

"Mustard."

"And where do you keep the bread?"

Will points to the counter and the white metal bread box, its surface decorated with red bundles of wheat.

"What the hell," Adam mutters. "I might as well have one."

While Adam slices the ham and prepares the sandwiches, Will walks around to see what's printed on the paper rolled in the typewriter. At the top of the page in capital letters are "Showdown at Red Rock" and the number 121. Below that, is double-spaced typescript with many words and phrases x-ed out. Will reads:

In the mirror behind the bar, Matt Sloane watched the black-clad man across the room. That was Slade, the gun-fighter hired by the cattlemen, and Matt knew that Slade not only had a reputation for being fast, fast on the draw, but that he often was the first to go for his gun. Matt had not ridden that far to let Slade get the drop on him. Even as he raised his whiskey to his lips, Matt kept his eye on Slade's right hand, watching.

Adam brings the unsliced sandwiches, one stacked on top of the other, to the table.

"Like what you see?" he asks Will.

At first Will thinks that Adam is referring to the sandwich, but of course he means the story. "Is there going to be a gunfight?" asks Will.

Adam takes a large bite of sandwich, and when a strand of ham doesn't quite fit into his mouth, he pokes it in with a fingertip. "You'll have to buy the book to find out," he says.

"From you?"

"From me? No, not from me. From the . . . Oh, never mind. Eat your sandwich."

Will should have said that he likes *only* mustard on his sandwich. Adam has slathered on so much butter that some of it squishes out between the slices of bread. He isn't sure he'll be able to take a single bite.

He points to the typed page. "That's what Shane said."

"What?"

"In the movie. My dad and me went to it two summers ago. Shane said Wilson was fast, fast on the draw."

"Are you sure? How the hell could you remember that?"

Will shrugs and takes a tentative bite from the corner of the sandwich. "I saw it twice. Once with my dad and once with some friends."

"Shit," he says softly. "You're probably right."

"Have you seen it too?" asks Will.

Wearily, Adam Lodge holds up three fingers. "And read the book." He riffles through the typed pages as if he's searching for something, yet when he comes to the bottom of the pile, he pushes the manuscript away.

"I like the part where Shane teaches the little boy to shoot."

"Hurry up. You have to get back to bed."

His father, mother, and sister all know better than to prepare sandwiches with butter, and so do the mothers of his best friends. Or they ask. The point is, Will never has to eat a sandwich prepared with butter, and now he finds that he likes it! The butter makes the sandwich . . . juicier, as if the ham has been fried, which is the way Will's father makes ham sandwiches, and they're Will's favorite. For so many reasons, Will wishes his parents would return home, but now he has another—so he can tell them, Now I like butter on my sandwiches!

ANN WAKES TO DISCOVER that she has fallen asleep outside— she must have been sunbathing—and the sun is concentrating its rays on her side, no, its focus is even tighter: All the heat is baking into her shoulder and arm, and she must have slept so hard that she has cut off her circulation, for that limb is immovable, thick, and numb.

But then her second waking, following quickly the false first, reveals that she is lying in a hospital bed, and her right arm and its new plaster cast, extending from her knuckles to nearly her shoulder, is being baked by a heat lamp. She has to squint at the lamp's brightness, but when she turns her head she finds a light to which she could fully open her eyes. Sunlight shines through the row of windows at the far end of the ward, and from the sky's pink cast Ann knows it's early morning.

Nearby a child begins to cry, and it's the weak whimper of someone waking at midnight and wanting his mother near. Next comes a voice so rare to Ann's ears she doesn't know where in her life to locate it.

"That arm bothering you?" her grandfather asks.

"No." She answers without bothering to test it. In truth, her arm can't compete with her headache, a speeding, spiraling pain that seems as though it intends to lift her head right off the pillow. "Am I—?"

"In the children's ward. I told them this isn't where you belong, but they've got their rules."

He looms over her, and she remembers now that he had appeared at her side the night before in the emergency room. He reminded her then of a hawk perched on a tree branch or telephone pole, yet she never felt as though he was training his fierce eye on her as prey. Instead, he was watching for any sign of danger, a sentinel hawk. Now, however, his eye does not look so keen. Its blue is as washed out as the morning sky, and the white stubble on his neck and jaw seem a mark of old age's fatigue.

Ann asks, "When can I go home?"

"Maybe later today. The doctor thinks you had a concussion. That's why he wants to keep an eye on you. If you had to stay another night, that wouldn't be the worst thing, would it?"

The crying on the other side of the room intensifies, and Ann looks in that direction.

"Little boy fell out of a pickup truck," her grandfather explains. "He's going to be fine, the nurses say. Doesn't even have any broken bones. But he got skinned up pretty bad. If they want to keep you overnight, we'll see about moving you to a different room."

"Have you told my mom and dad that I'm here?"

Her grandfather shakes his head. "I thought I'd wait until you can make the call yourself. I can tell your father you're doing fine, but if he hears it from you, it'll mean more."

"Can you call work for me?" she asks. "I was supposed to go in at noon."

"I'll let them know." Her grandfather shifts from side to side and winces as if he wishes he could sit down and take the weight off his feet. "And now I'll ask you to do something for me."

"All right," Ann says, though she's immediately worried—what could her grandfather possibly need from her?

"Last night you were a little vague on this business of somebody chasing you. First it was maybe yes then maybe no. Now I want you to clear up the matter."

Ann hesitates.

Her grandfather doesn't give her a chance to make something up. "So I'm guessing the answer is yes. I think you know what's coming next. I need a name."

She turns her head, hoping that will make it easier to lie. But there's the heat lamp, and its glare is just like the bright lights that the police use on television shows when suspects are interrogated. Ann closes her eyes.

"I didn't want to say anything," she says. "It was my boyfriend. We had a fight—"

"Did he strike you?"

"No, no. It was just, you know, an argument."

"Did he put his hands on you? Twist your arm?"

"No, nothing like that. It was really all my fault. I was just mad at him because he was out of town and didn't come back in time to take me to a party. I finally sort of stomped off. I didn't want him to follow me, so I went down into this ravine. He wasn't chasing me, he wasn't even . . . I don't know why I said that he was. I was still mad, I guess."

"Uh-huh. But now you're not?"

Ann shakes her head and pays for her action—or is it for her lie?—with a fresh swirl of pain that concentrates itself at the back of her skull.

"I'd still like to know your boyfriend's name," her grandfather says.

"What for? I told you, it wasn't his fault."

Does no one ever refuse her grandfather? The clouds clear from his gaze, and its intensity blazes once more. "Let's just say I'd like to have it for personal reference." He offers a pained little smile, and even that sends the message, On this matter I'll have my way.

Reluctantly Ann says, "Monte Hiatt."

Her grandfather continues to look expectantly at her, and finally Ann understands: She said the name so softly that he needs to hear it again.

"Monte," she repeats. "Monte Hiatt."

Calvin Sidey nods. He has it. The name has been in Ann's possession, but now she has handed it to her grandfather. He has it now.

Suddenly Ann feels very, very tired, but it's an exhaustion mixed with relief, as if she can finally relax after carrying a heavy weight farther than she ever thought possible. She closes her eyes, and sleep, a white sleep that matches the room, the bright heat lamp, the bed, the blankets and sheets, enfolds her.

But Ann fights off sleep and struggles to open her eyes. Ah, that's why everything turned white—her grandfather had been standing between Ann and the window, and he has now stepped back, allowing sunlight to rush in and fill that open space. Ann can see that her grandfather, having gotten what he wanted, is ready to be on his way.

He nods in the direction of the boy who fell from the truck. "I'll ask about another room for one of you."

"It's okay," Ann says. "I don't mind." The truck itself could drive through the room, and she'd sleep right through it.

"I'll check back later," her grandfather says. He takes his leave then by reaching out and touching Ann tenderly on the arm, the arm that is, of course, encased in plaster.

MARJORIE HAS TO BE careful.

If she forgets to use her arms to raise herself from the mattress or twists too hard to one side, she receives a sharp pain at her surgical site that's like a hook's barb pulling at her flesh. And ever since she opened her eyes after the surgery, a headache has been waiting for her. If she so much as looks too quickly to the side, the constant quiet throb at the back of her head springs forth and pushes out every other thought.

So when the door opens and Bill peers in, Marjorie barely turns in his direction and even the smile she gives him is cautious and tentative.

"How are you doing?" he whispers. Visiting hours aren't until afternoon, but Bill has somehow found a way around hospital regulations.

"All right. Tired. I feel like I could sleep for a week."

"We were afraid you were going to do exactly that."

"That must be why someone's coming in every half hour to stare at me."

He starts to sit down on the edge of the bed, stops himself, and instead settles for gently patting and stroking her forearm. His caress seems less like what passes between a man and a woman and more like the way an adult would touch a child.

"A hospital's no place to catch up on sleep," Bill says. "We have to get you home where we can really baby you."

"Believe me, once I finally leave here, the last thing I want is someone doing things for me."

Bill clears his throat, and his hand stops moving on her arm. "I talked to Dad this morning."

Marjorie's abdomen clenches, bringing her a strengthened current of pain.

"Did he call you or did you call him?"

"He called me. Us."

"During the day?" Her hand drops to her abdomen as if she has to protect the surgical site from anything Bill might say.

"The kids are fine," he rushes to say, "but Ann had a little accident, and she had to spend the night in the hospital."

"An *accident*? What—?"

"A broken arm. Nothing serious. A broken arm and a bump on the head."

Marjorie hasn't moved her head, but the pain surges forward anyway, washing her vision with darkness. "But the *hospital*! Bill, what happened?"

"That's still a little murky. She fell. Someone was after her—or she *thought* someone was after her—and she took a tumble."

"Oh, my God, Bill! Someone was *after* her? Who—?"

"Easy. Take it easy. That's not for certain. Dad said Ann's going back and forth on that point."

Marjorie puts both hands on her abdomen. "You have to go, Bill. *Now*. You go there and see how she is and try to find out what happened."

"Dad's there, Marj. He's on top of the situation. And Dr.

McKee's the doctor who's looking after her, so you know you've got nothing to worry about on that score."

Not only does his statement fail to reassure her, she has to fight to keep from saying, This is why I didn't want to leave my children with that man!

"I'll call tonight," Bill says, "and talk to Ann myself. In the meantime"—he begins to caress her arm again—"I'm staying put. I'm not leaving Missoula. This is where I belong."

She knows he's worried too, and that's the reason for the awkward, unconvincing smile he's been wearing since he entered the room. But she has to make him understand. She closes her eyes, so she won't see her next words register on his face.

"No," she says as forcefully as she can. "This *isn't* where you belong. You need to be with our children."

Marjorie's command, however, has no effect. The touch of his hand on her arm tells her he's still there. She reaches across and pushes his hand away and then opens her eyes. His face is tormented with fear and bewilderment. And then it's she who understands.

"I won't die," she says. "Don't worry. I won't die while you're gone."

Relief spreads across his features. "Promise?"

"I promise. Now get going. And call me."

Once Bill is out the door, Marjorie closes her eyes again, hoping she can sleep. It would be the perfect way to hurry through the hours it will take Bill to drive to Gladstone. Like a child on a long car trip, she'll doze off and not wake until someone is carrying her into her home. But she knows sleep isn't likely to come, not with concern for her daughter pressing down on her.

• • •

CALVIN HANGS UP THE phone and crushes out his cigarette. He can't figure that son of his. Bill doesn't seem any more upset to learn that his daughter broke her arm than he would have been if Calvin told him she has a cold. But maybe having two of his girls in the hospital is just too damn much. Bill can only deal with one at a time, and Marjorie is first in line. And maybe Bill feels that Ann's trouble can wait. He might be right. Maybe it can. But Calvin doesn't have anyone ahead of her in line.

The ashtray is full. A few of the butts are Calvin's but most belonged to Adam's boy. My God, you wouldn't think he was here long enough to smoke that much. Especially since he finished off the ham in that time as well.

Calvin carries the ashtray to the garbage, but he stops before dumping the ashes. In the garbage sack is an unfamiliar ball of crumpled yellow paper. Calvin takes it out and smooths open the page on the counter. As soon as he sees what's on the page he realizes this must be from the novel Adam is writing.

Calvin reads a paragraph:

Matt Sloane held his .45 out at arm's length and aimed carefully at the mounted warrior. He pulled back the hammer and squeezed the trigger tenderly. In the next instant, the Indian fell from his horse, immortally wounded, at least two hundred yards away in the distance.

Calvin shakes his head in disgust. It's a good thing this page ended up in the garbage. And Adam believes that a .45 could be fired with accuracy at that distance? Maybe Calvin should take the young man out in the country and let him fire a pistol, let him feel it buck in his hand. You'd be damn lucky to hit a horse at twenty yards.

But Calvin never did that with his own son. Why would he do it with Beverly Lodge's boy?

LAST WINTER, REVEREND INGVALDSEN asked Bill and a few other men to come to his office after their monthly meeting, an early morning gathering called the Men's Breakfast for Lutheran Members of the Mission. The breakfast was an opportunity for men in the congregation to meet in the church basement, eat pancakes and sausage or bacon and eggs, drink coffee, smoke, and discuss upcoming projects, often having to do with raising funds or improving church attendance. Fifteen to twenty men could usually be counted on to attend the breakfast, but only five of them were invited to the minister's office.

"I'm a little concerned about some of the younger fellows," Reverend Ingvaldsen said to the group of men. "I know we've got them in the fold, so to speak. A few of them were at the breakfast this morning. But that doesn't necessarily mean we have them on the right path. I see them struggling, trying to do right by their jobs, their families, and their faith. It's too much for some of them. They feel overwhelmed, and when that happens, they start staying a little later at the office. Or they stop off at a bar when they should be on their way home for supper. And when they are home, they're short-tempered with the wife and kids."

Bill didn't know where Reverend Ingvaldsen was headed with those observations, but Bill agreed that yes, it sometimes took a while before a man found the right balance point for his life.

"So my notion," the minister said, "is that some of us older gentlemen might take the younger husbands and fathers under our wings, so to speak. Give them a little guidance. Help them learn from our experience. If you're agreeable, I'll assign each of you a couple of the younger men."

Upon hearing Reverend Ingvaldsen's plan, Bill's first reaction was that if someone had been available to counsel Bill's father after his wife died perhaps Calvin Sidey wouldn't have gone off the rails and abandoned his children, his job, and his home. But immediately following that thought was Bill's realization that if someone, if *anyone*, had tried to give his father advice on how he should live his life, that person might well have gotten knocked on his ass for his efforts. For his part, Bill had no desire to act as counselor or guide or what-have-you for anyone. He didn't have all the right answers for himself, much less for someone else.

Nevertheless, when Pastor Ingvaldsen looked at him, Bill readily agreed to participate in the program.

Another of the men asked what they might actually do with their young charges.

From his hesitation, it was apparent that Reverend Ingvaldsen hadn't given much thought to the practical application of his plan. "Well," he said with a smile that was supposed to be knowing yet came off as evasive and patronizing, "we never go wrong when we pray together."

Bill couldn't imagine himself asking another man to pray with him, but he said nothing. He had signed on to the minister's program, and he'd follow through the best he could.

Reverend Ingvaldsen gave each of the men in his office a name written on a folded slip of paper. On Bill's was Gary Graber's name. Gary was a twenty-five-year-old sales representative for Graber Dairy, a business that had been in the family for almost as long as Gladstone had been in existence. Gary worked for his father, and Bill had to wonder why the senior Graber wasn't a sufficient role model for his son. Bill knew Ralph Graber and thought highly of him. He was an astute businessman, a civic leader, and a good family man. Of course he didn't attend Olivet Lutheran Church, and perhaps that was the crucial point for Reverend Ingvaldsen. As it was, Gary belonged to the church because of his wife, the former Rose Hailey. Rose's family lived on Fourth Street not far from the Sideys, and when she was in high school, only a few years earlier, she babysat Ann and Will on a few occasions. Gary and Rose had two children, the son that Rose had been pregnant with when the couple married, and a baby girl.

Unfortunately, Bill did not hold Gary in the same high regard as he held Gary's father. Gary had always struck Bill as cocky, irresponsible, and selfish, a young man who'd done nothing to deserve his privileges yet was perfectly willing to take advantage of them. But perhaps Gary was trying to change. He was a regular at church services as well as at the Men's Breakfasts, though he never made any positive contribution to those meetings. Nevertheless, Bill was determined to try to do what Reverend Ingvaldsen asked of him.

The first opportunity Bill had to talk to Gary came about a week later. On a bitterly cold February day, Bill was exiting the courthouse when he saw Gary standing outside Ressler's Cafe. Bill called out Gary's name, raised a hand in greeting, and jogged across the street to meet the younger man.

In spite of the cold, Gary's overcoat was open, he was gloveless, and smoking a cigarette. "Want to sell me a house?" Gary said with a smile as Bill approached. "Or buy mine?"

Bill was oddly breathless, but he doubted it could be from merely running across the street. His nervousness about talking to Gary must have caused the condition.

"I'm wondering," Bill said, "if you'd have a little time for me. Maybe I could buy you a cup of coffee?"

Gary leaned back from Bill as if he'd just proposed something distasteful.

"Just a little friendly chat," Bill said, smiling awkwardly.

"What the hell. Sure. Maybe I'll even let you make it something stronger than coffee." Gary looked up and down the street. "But not today. Rosie's picking me up. She has the car today. She had to take the kid to the doctor."

A sick child. Here was a subject, with its accompanying worry and tension, that all fathers could relate to. Bill felt as though he'd discovered a way to talk to Gary. "Is it Jimmy?" Bill asked. "Or the baby?"

Gary shrugged. "She took the both of them in. But it's Jimmy who's sick. Or Rosie thinks he is. Nothing but a goddamn cold, if you ask me."

"Well. Women. They worry."

Gary continued to look up the street. "Huh? Oh yeah. No shit. One of them so much as sneezes, Rosie's ready to call the doctor." He glanced at his watch. "Where the hell is she?"

And just like that, she appeared, coming around the corner in their big brown Oldsmobile. She pulled into the diagonal parking place near Bill and Gary, and before he walked over to the car, Gary gave Bill a big grin, as if he believed that his impatience had been sufficient to make his wife materialize.

Rose opened the driver's-side door and started to get out, but Gary, with a brutally swift hand gesture, signaled for Rose to stay in the car and slide across the front seat. The baby must have been lying there, because Rose hesitated and fussed with a bundle. Jimmy wasn't visible, but he could have been lying across the backseat. If he were sick, that would make sense. Rose must not have moved fast enough for Gary's liking, and he shoved her with such force her head jerked to the side. But she finally moved to where her husband wanted her, and as Gary turned around in order to back the

Oldsmobile into the street, Rose looked right at Bill and gave him a tiny, tentative wave. On this day of low, leaden skies, Rose Graber was wearing sunglasses.

And in an instant Bill knew that Gary beat his wife. From time to time Bill heard men make remarks about having to "slap the wife around to keep her in line," and Bill knew that some of those men were serious. He also knew that some of them were nothing but tough talkers. But Gary, Bill was suddenly sure, did more than talk. That was why Reverend Ingvaldsen, that coward, wanted Bill to "counsel" Gary, to help him control his temper and to teach him that there were other ways, better ways, to handle a disagreement with his wife than to punch her.

What Reverend Ingvaldsen should have done with that gathering of men in the church office was to say, Gary Graber is beating his wife and tonight we're going to his house to teach him a lesson. Then the Lutheran Members of the Mission should have dragged Gary out into the street and pummeled the hell out of him, stopping only when they could be sure that Gary got the message: Lay a hand on your wife again and you'll get this and worse.

Bill couldn't recall anything about Rose's father, but he thought maybe he was the man who should be dealing with Gary. If Calvin were Rose's father, Calvin would have taken the matter into his own hands.

But marriage counseling and vigilante justice don't work together well. Even if Gary could be forcibly persuaded and threatened not to strike Rose, their relationship would almost certainly suffer. A marriage can't be held together by blood fear. And sooner or later Gary would take his anger and humiliation out on his wife.

Abruptly Gary stopped the Olds in the middle of the street. He rolled his window down, leaned his head out the window, and called out to Bill, "Hey, what the hell was it you wanted to talk about anyway?"

Bill could not bring himself to answer. He turned and walked away from Gary Graber, his wife, and their problems. A freshening of snow, as fine and dry as salt, had fallen the night before, and with a gust of wind, the snow swirled down the street like a cloud of summer insects. Bill wondered if, in walking away, he was acting according to a lesson his father had inadvertently taught him.

But he's not walking away now. He's driving away from Missoula and toward Gladstone as fast as he can. When he told Marjorie about Ann's injury, he hoped that she would urge him to go back to Gladstone right away. That was what Bill wanted to do, but he couldn't leave Marjorie without her consent or encouragement. He needn't have worried. Marjorie was, first and foremost, a mother, and nothing, not even her own health and well-being, could supplant her concern for her children and their welfare.

And if it turns out to be true that someone has been chasing Ann, if someone has been out to harm her, Bill will track him down and make sure he never does it again. No matter what kind of persuasion is necessary, Bill will make sure it *never happens again*. Maybe he's his father's son both in his willingness to walk away and in his willingness to rush toward. He keeps the speedometer's needle pegged at eighty-five.

TWENTY-SEVEN

Her grandfather is gone. The crying, whimpering little boy is silent. The rhomboid of sunlight on the wall is larger and lower. The heat lamp has been turned off. Ann doesn't know how long she's been asleep, but she's afraid it's been too long and she's too late.

She climbs out of bed, and almost loses her balance, which she blames on the heavy plaster cast encircling her arm from her knuckles almost to her shoulder.

Where could her clothes be? The only possibility seems to be one of the tall lockers across the room between an empty bed and a cart stacked with sheets and blankets. Although the lockers look exactly like those in the locker room at school—painted white, however, rather than gray—they have no locks, for which Ann is grateful. In the second locker she opens, she finds her clothes.

She looks around the ward. All the beds are empty but the one occupied by the boy who fell from the truck and he seems to be asleep. No one is there to watch her shrug off her hospital gown right out in the open. And privacy is not Ann's only problem. She has to find a way to dress herself with one arm, a process made doubly difficult because she must also fit her clothes over the bulky cast and with her arm bent at an unmoving right angle.

She dispenses with her brassiere. There's no way she'd be able to hook that. As it is, the sleeveless blouse she wore the night before buttons up the back, but Ann simply puts it on backward and fortunately she can manage all but the top two buttons. Her skirt she can zip up but not button. Close enough. She came in with only one shoe, and since that's gone, she walks out of the ward barefoot.

Ann hurries down the hall, feeling all the while like a criminal escaping from jail. She shares the elevator down to the first floor with a candy striper who looks familiar to Ann. Is she also a Gladstone High student? The girl takes in Ann at a glance—the bare feet, the clothes slightly askew, the bright white cast—and Ann instinctively brings a hand up to her hair, trying to pull her fingers through the tangle. She wishes she could say something to account for her appearance and why she's no longer in a hospital bed where she belongs, but she can't think of a thing. But the candy striper doesn't say anything either, and when the elevator doors open, she goes her own away, hurrying off with a stack of manila envelopes.

Never in her life has Ann Sidey called a boy, but now that's exactly what she must do.

On the wall just inside the hospital's main entrance is a pay telephone, but Ann doesn't have a dime. She uses the directory, however, to look up the Hiatts' number.

At the end of a corridor of offices is a waiting room, and there's a telephone. The phone rings and rings but no one answers. Ann can only pray that that means Monte and his mother aren't home and so are out of danger. No, that's not all she can do. She can't take any chances. She must go there, she *must*.

Last spring in Mr. Lynam's English class Ann Sidey learned, along with a host of other literary terms, the meaning of irony, and the lesson stuck with her well enough for her to know that her present situation qualifies. In fact, the hospital door has barely clicked shut behind her when Mr. Lynam's words come to her: "The actual contrasted with the expected." Last night she fell and lost her shoe and broke her arm rushing to get away from Monte. Now she's hurrying *toward* him, her arm in a cast, her bare feet blistering from the heat of Gladstone's sidewalks. The boy whom Ann feared and frequently felt she needed protection from she now must warn. Ann gave her grandfather a name only, but she knew he would soon match it with an address, and she has to get there before he does. She doesn't want to be responsible for what might happen to either her grandfather or the boy whose name she surrendered. Oh yes, Mr. Lynam would love to learn how well his lesson took!

As she hurries through town, Ann stays off the hot sidewalks when she can and walks on the grass, but even then some lawns are so sunbaked and dry that they offer little relief to her bare feet. The grass might be cooler underfoot, but it can also be as sharp as stubble. Inside her blouse, she feels rivulets of sweat running down her bare torso, and she has to stop occasionally to wait for her heart rate to slow. The harder and faster it beats the more her injured arm throbs, and sometimes she has to walk with the heavy cast held head high just to relieve the tightness and pressure. Now she understands why people with injured arms wear slings; the cast is heavy, and her arm aches with the strain of holding it close to her side. Occasionally, she has to reach across with her other arm for support. The bump on her head seems to be swelling in the hot sun, and it feels as though a band is tightening around her skull.

These physical discomforts, however, she can bear. Of far greater concern is what she might say when she finally confronts Monte. How can she convey the urgency of her message? How can she prevent him from misconstruing what her presence means? The mere fact that she has come to his home he will regard as a victory—he has said all along that she will eventually return to him. If she tells him that she's there to warn him, he'll want to know where the danger is supposed to be coming from, and when she says, "My grandfather," he'll only laugh. What if Ann says, "He'll kill you"? Would those words make an impression? Or would they only feed his bravado? *An old man—I'd like to see him try.* Maybe Ann shouldn't even attempt to talk to him. Maybe she should just hide near his home—the way he's been lurking around hers—and if her grandfather appears, only then would she reveal herself and step between them.

She crosses Pioneer Avenue, the street where the older residential districts give way to newer, larger homes. The houses flatten and spread out, and there are no trees that rise above sapling height. Nothing to shelter her from the noonday sun. Oh, this is a fool's errand! Why does she even believe he'll be home? Why is she so sure her grandfather is coming—or has come—this way? Monte's house is less than four blocks away now, and she still can't answer her own questions. Nevertheless, she doesn't slow her steps to give herself time to answer.

CALVIN SIDEY IS IN unknown territory. He's driving slowly through the curving streets of Western Meadows, block after block of so-called ranch houses, though Calvin can remember when the only dwellings around here were literal ranch houses and there weren't many and they weren't much. "Meadows," hell. These were rimrock hills and alkali flats and no good for planting or grazing. Maybe someone, a Russian immigrant Calvin seems to recall, tried running sheep in this area. And he hadn't any success either.

So Calvin is willing to tip his hat to the developer who turned this into prime residential properties. Whoever it was, he must have made a bundle. And then, probably as his own little private joke, he named the streets after precious gems. Calvin has passed or driven down Emerald Lane, Amethyst Circle, Ruby Boulevard, and Diamond Way. Well, maybe Calvin's son sold some properties out here. Calvin can only hope that's been the case.

And is it the fact of Calvin's mission that makes him wonder what on any other day he wouldn't question at all? Is the world better by even the smallest measure for there being houses here rather than sagebrush and scoria? Humans, of course, must have their shelter, and this valley is not so different from the one where Calvin makes his home. But time and weather will have their way, and the day will come when the houses will be gone, and the patient coyotes will return to rule this land. Time, the less he has of it, the more he respects its power and authority, qualities he's not willing to concede to any human.

Finally, after all his searching for street names and numbers, it's a car in a driveway that tells Calvin Sidey he's at the right address. It's a Ford all right, and probably a Tudor and a 'fifty-one or 'fifty-two—Calvin has never been real good at identifying cars by age and model. But there's no question that the color is right. It's black, a spotless, gleaming black, and the reason for its shine is immediately apparent. The car has just been washed, and its caretaker is finishing up the job now, rubbing down the car's snout with a chamois. The car has been backed into the driveway, and when Calvin parks his truck, he makes sure it blocks the Ford's path.

Calvin climbs out of the truck and starts up the driveway. The ascent isn't steep, but water has run down the entire cement slope and into the gutter, where a few soap suds still bubble. The kid has his bucket out there and a garden hose, its nozzle releasing a little trickle of water down the driveway.

The driveway runs up to a garage, which is attached to a house somewhat smaller than most in this part of Gladstone. Half brick and half stained redwood, the dwelling looks like a new construction, like many of the houses in this neighborhood.

Calvin is almost at the car before Monte Hiatt notices that someone is there; he must have seen Calvin's reflection in the chrome of the bumper. He doesn't startle at Calvin's presence. He simply stands and turns to face him.

"Yeah? What're you selling?"

He's a good-looking kid, Calvin has to admit. Wide dark eyes, dark complexion, thick lips that look as though they want to pout or curl into a sneer. And wavy black hair. His looks remind Calvin of a young cowboy he rode with many years ago. Billy McGinn, with the Slash Nine. Billy was Irish on his father's side and Crow on his mother's. A good kid, Billy, and a hardworking hand, right up to the day when he tried to ride one of Harry Carpenter's horses straight down a ravine and got the horse's leg broke in the bargain. Before he had to face Harry's wrath, Billy ran off, never to be heard from again. But Billy had a compact, muscular build and this kid is tall and rangy, built more along Calvin's lines. Billy McGinn. Jesus, it's been twenty years if it's been a day, but Calvin can still remember Billy and his name, whereas Calvin can't recall this young fellow's name. And Calvin's been looking at it for the better part of an hour. Soon after Ann gave it to her grandfather, he wrote it down, and then he matched the name to an address, and he got directions to the address from a gas station attendant. But now the name has slipped away. He can't take out the paper and read it, not right in front of the kid. Pieces of paper, is this what his life is coming to? An address on a letter to tell him where Brenda Cady lives, a name scrawled on note paper to tell him who's been scaring the hell out of his granddaughter, another address to tell him where the kid lives. God *damn* it. For the rest of his years, will he need a crib note to tell him where he's going or whom he's facing?

The hell with it. Calvin doesn't need to remember a name to do what he came here to do.

"This is more in the way of a delivery," says Calvin. "I'm delivering a message."

TWENTY-EIGHT

Perhaps it's her preoccupation with what might happen in the future that makes Ann Sidey oblivious to the present. Twice before in recent days a car has pulled alongside her, once to harm and once to help, and now it's happening again. By the time she startles into awareness, however, a door has already flung open to her and a voice commands her to get inside.

By way of argument, Ann helplessly, silently, points in the direction in which she's been walking.

"I know where you're headed," he says. "But you're getting into this vehicle and coming with me."

There are so many questions Ann wants to ask of the driver, but she says nothing and climbs obediently into her grandfather's truck.

BEVERLY CAN'T SIT STILL. She keeps walking back and forth from one window to another, first to her living room to see if Calvin's truck is parked at the curb in front of the Sidey house, then to the kitchen to check the alley in case he drove up that way. When the telephone rings, she runs to it, certain the voice on the other end will stop her wondering.

"Well, is there a police car next door yet?" a woman asks.

The voice is familiar, but the remark itself is so unnerving that Beverly can't concentrate on the identity of the person on the other end of the line. *How could she know I was watching the street?* "Who is this? What is this about?"

"It's Mary, Mary Betts. Maybe you should go look out your window and see if a police car is parked in front of Sideys'."

Mary Betts and Beverly Lodge are the same age and attended Gladstone schools together. In fact, Mary and her husband, a lawyer like Burt, once lived on Fourth Street and only recently bought a house in the new Western Meadows subdivision. Since the move, Beverly and Mary, friends who once saw and spoke to each other almost daily, now only exchange words on chance meetings at the grocery store.

"Are you looking?" Mary asks.

"I'm looking, Mary," Beverly lies. "What am I supposed to see?"

"If the police aren't paying your neighbor a visit yet, I expect they will before the day is out."

"My neighbor?" Beverly has a clutch of fear, a thought she immediately banishes as preposterous—that Ann Sidey lied about the circumstances of her accident and is in trouble far more serious than Beverly and Calvin had been led to believe.

"Calvin? Isn't that his name? The elder Sidey? Hasn't he come back to town?"

"Temporarily. He's watching the house and kids while Bill and Marjorie are in Missoula."

"Well, his stay might not be all that temporary. He might be spending thirty days in one of our local facilities."

"Mary, will you *please* tell me what you're talking about?"

"All right, but I have to tell you—I didn't see all of this myself. I had to confer with Nell Sleigh. She was out in her yard, and she saw and heard everything. You know who lives across the street from us, don't you? That divorced woman who came here from Wyoming? She and her teenaged son—"

"Yes, yes, I know." Beverly has no idea who those people are, but she wants Mary to get on with the story.

"Nell says the boy is polite enough, but he's never so much as said hello to me. And judging from the way he drives and the way he's out half the night—"

"Mary . . ."

"Anyway. He was out in the driveway today washing his car. I swear, I've never seen him do a lick of work around the place—they hire somebody to mow and shovel the driveway—but he spends hours working on that car—"

"What kind? What kind of car does he drive?"

Mary sighs in exasperation. "Bev, you know I can't tell a Ford from a Chevy. It's black, that's all I know. It's black and it's loud. I don't know how many times I've been awakened at two or three o'clock in the morning—"

"He was in the driveway?"

"Washing his car. That's right. And Calvin Sidey came driving up the street. He got out of his truck and Nell said pretty soon the two of them are having words. Something about the boy staying away from Ann Sidey. And apparently a few profanities were exchanged at this time, but of course Nell couldn't bring herself to report what those might be."

"You say you didn't hear or see any of this?"

"I saw some of it. Right about this time is probably when I looked out. I suppose I heard yelling or something. I peeked out the front window and saw the young man slap Mr. Sidey's hand away—I don't know what it is, but teenagers can't stand to be pointed at. I remember my Bonnie would just have a fit if I so much as wagged a finger in her direction. Nell says Mr. Sidey said to the boy, 'You don't need to know who I am. Just make sure you stay away from her or you'll wish you never heard the Sidey name.' Or did that maybe happen before? Anyway. After this exchange, Mr. Sidey turned and walked away. I guess he'd said what he wanted to say. And to his back the boy made what I assume is some kind of curse in sign language. Do you know what that means, by the way? I see the kids holding up that one finger, and I assume it's something dirty but really, I have no idea."

"It's obscene, Mary. That's all I know. What happened next?"

"Obscene—well, I know that. It still strikes me as a little like sticking your tongue out at somebody. Anyway. It must not have been sufficiently satisfying, because what he did next was a good deal worse. He picked up the hose he'd been using to wash his precious car, twisted the nozzle, and sprayed that old man while he walked to his truck."

Beverly winces in anticipation of what is to come. She has seen Calvin's anger in action and knows how sudden and terrifying, as if lightning might flash and then unleash a torrent of ice instead of rain.

"At first I wondered if he had missed Mr. Sidey," Mary continues, "because he just kept walking toward his truck. He didn't hurry and he didn't cover up, even when that kid got up a little closer and adjusted the spray so the stream was blasting Mr. Sidey right in the back. Nell said the boy was laughing through all of this, but I didn't hear that.

"Mr. Sidey climbed into the truck, and I thought, well, that's the end of that. I was about to turn away, and you have to believe me—I was going to call you then and there to see if you knew how the Sidey girl was involved in all this.

"Then Mr. Sidey got back out of his vehicle, and I think I probably let out a little moan. I thought, Oh, don't do it; don't make it worse. You lost—just drive away, even if it means going off with your tail tucked between your legs.

"But then I saw that he had something in his hand, and for the first time, I was tempted to do more than just watch the proceedings. He brought a hunting knife out of the truck with him, and even though it was still in its sheath, I thought maybe I should holler over at them or something. I mean, a garden hose is one thing but a *knife*? And like everybody else in town I heard those stories years ago about what Calvin Sidey was supposed to have done to a man who made some kind of remark about his wife. So I was wondering if someone—if *I*—should call the police. But while I was trying to make up my mind things started happening, and they happened so quickly . . ."

Beverly reaches out and when her hand touches wood, she pulls a chair toward her and sits down heavily. She performs all those actions blindly because she has closed her eyes. She's able to see all too clearly Calvin with a knife in his hand; what she wishes to blot from view is this room where he took her in his arms—there in front of her humming refrigerator, her cold stove, her unyielding countertop.

"Then I breathed a little easier for a moment, because Mr. Sidey didn't seem to be going toward the boy. He was heading for the lawn, but that boy just wouldn't leave well enough alone—he kept spraying the old man. Then that old man picked up a loop of the hose and crimped it—you know how you do, to shut off the flow? And that left the boy holding a nozzle that wasn't doing any more than dripping. But then Mr. Sidey threw the sheath off the knife and began to cut through the hose.

"Now I don't know about you, but I don't believe I have a knife in my house sharp enough to work through a garden hose without sawing away at it for a while, but that old man sliced it like it was string. And then while water was bubbling out of one end, he grabbed the other end and started hauling on it. I suppose he might have reeled that boy in like a fish if the boy hadn't let go of the hose. And *that* wasn't such a good idea. Old Mr. Sidey started twirling that length of hose overhead like . . . like I don't know what. A lariat maybe? No, a whip is what I mean. Because that's exactly how he used it. He started whipping that boy with the cut-off garden hose! If he would've been using the end with the nozzle he could've put out an eye or done some other serious damage. As it is, I'm sure he raised a few welts. The boy just cowered and tried to cover up. Nell said she's sure it's the first whipping that boy's ever got, spoiled as he is. Not that he deserved a beating like that—"

"You said police before, Mary. Did the police come there? To the boy's house?" Beverly opens her eyes. Her kitchen is still her kitchen—the dishes stacked in the drainer, the towel hung on the refrigerator door's handle.

"Wait—he wasn't done. After your neighbor was finished with the shorter length of hose he tossed that aside and went over and picked up the other end, still bubbling water, and he brought that over to the boy's car. He opened the door and stuck the hose inside—can you imagine? Then he pointed his finger again, and I could tell he was probably saying something to the boy, but neither Nell nor I could make out a word."

"The police, Mary?"

"Well, I don't know for sure. But I just assume . . . I mean, wouldn't you? Somebody gets a whipping like that, don't the police get involved?"

Beverly knows, of course, that it was never Mary Betts's intention to torment her with this phone call. Mary simply had a story to tell—perhaps the most exciting one of her life. She had been witness to an event as dramatic as Gladstone is likely to host for quite some time, an incident that will be talked about in bars, cafes, kitchens, and offices all over town. It will be another Calvin Sidey tale. And Mary will have special status for the rest of her life because she was there; she saw it with her own two eyes. No, Mary didn't want to torture Beverly with this phone call. Beverly certainly won't hold a grudge against an old friend who didn't know—who *couldn't* know—that Beverly is in love with the old man who figures so prominently in the narrative. After all, Beverly only realized it herself when Mary was barely halfway into her story.

"I'm sorry, Mary, but I'll have to hang up. You have me stretching the phone cord all over the kitchen trying to see if there's a police car outside."

"If they show up, you have to call me."

"Oh, I will, Mary. I will."

In truth, Beverly doubts that she'll ever speak to Mary Betts again.

As THEY RIDE BACK into town Ann keeps waiting for her grandfather to say something. But he doesn't explain how he knew she left the hospital, and he doesn't ask her what she hoped to accomplish once she got to where she was going. He says nothing about how his clothes came to be wet. And he makes no reference to the hunting knife that lies between them on the seat.

Ann picks up the knife, though she fails in her efforts to take it out of its sheath. Because of the gauze and plaster encircling her hand, she can't grip the leather sleeve tightly enough to work the snap with her other trembling hand.

Without taking his eyes from the street in front of them, her grandfather reaches across and takes the knife from her hand. "What do you need with that?"

"I wanted to look at the blade," Ann answers. "I wanted to see if there was blood on it."

He tucks the knife under his seat. "Where would you get an idea like that?"

"I know where you went. When you left the hospital."

"Do you."

"When I told you his name, I thought—"

"If he comes near you again, you tell me. That's all you need to know."

"What did you—?"

"Promise me. If he comes within so much as a hundred yards, you let me know."

"Okay."

"I'll take that as a promise." He turns the truck onto Fourth Street. "What the hell were you ever doing in the company of somebody like that."

Ann says nothing. If anyone can understand silence, surely her grandfather can.

Not until the truck is in the garage, its darkness startling after the glare of the midday sun, does anyone speak again. "Well," her grandfather says after turning off the ignition, "I reckon it's a good thing no one ever asked your grandmother that question."

TWENTY-NINE

Oh!" Beverly can't help it—she cries out when she sees a tired, bedraggled Ann limping barefoot across the lawn toward the Sidey back door. That lovely, lovely girl with her arm encased in a chunk of plaster, her hair matted and tangled, and her eyes downcast—she looks as though she's lost twenty pounds and put on twenty years since she was home last. The mother in Beverly wants to run out and put her arms around the girl. But Beverly stays by her kitchen window, waiting and watching for Calvin to follow his granddaughter.

Minutes pass before he appears, and then he too walks toward the house, but slowly, hesitantly, and he keeps looking back toward the garage. Beverly watches him until he passes from sight. She

turns away from the window and goes into the living room, determined not to call or go over. He'll need a few minutes to get Ann
settled, and then she'll allow him an opportunity to call her or come
over on his own. Her resolve lasts for less than three minutes, and
then she jumps up from her chair.

Beverly bursts through the Sidey's back door and immediately
begins to search for him in room after room. When she can't find
him, she has to decide between the basement and the upper floor.
Ann is probably upstairs, but Beverly runs toward the basement
steps. A light is on at the bottom of the stairs, and she grabs the
handrail and goes down as quickly as she dares.

It hardly seems possible that all the emotion that has sprung up
in Beverly Lodge, sprung up and swirled around in her until she
feels it not as emotion alone but as physical sensation, as if she's
ready at every moment to be touched and something in her is yearn-
ing and rushing out to meet that touch, that all this change in her
began when she first descended these steps.

She sees his bare legs first, pale, thatched with dark hair. He
must know it's her because he doesn't startle or cover up at her approach. She steps down onto the concrete and finds him standing
next to a chest of drawers. He brings a pair of Levi's out of an open
drawer and steps into them.

"I didn't hear your knock," he says.

"I didn't knock. Or ring the bell."

"You must be here on a matter of some urgency then."

"Not anymore."

Beverly can't see clearly into the shadows where Calvin's discarded clothes lie, but she has no doubt why he's taken them off. A
teenager soaked them with a garden hose.

"I heard about what happened with that boy."

He jams the hem of his T-shirt into the waistband of his jeans. "News always did travel fast in this town."

"That doesn't worry you?" Beverly asks. "That the police will be involved?"

"It's hard for most folks to reconcile themselves to a beating. Instead of letting it go, they say they're going to call the sheriff. Or the police. They're going to press charges, they say." He cinches his belt tight. "But they seldom do."

"Is this something you've had experience with?"

"Anyone lives to my age they're bound to see and hear a few things."

"So you're not worried."

He scrapes a handful of coins from the top of the dresser and puts them into his front pocket. Into his back pocket he wedges a wallet. "I'm not worried."

"So what my friend told me is true. You beat up a boy."

They're not far from the bed where they lay naked together, yet the gaze he turns on her now is as blank as the bulb burning overhead.

"If he'd been the one left standing, someone would've said to him, 'So you beat up an old man.' I didn't go over there with the intention that it would come to blows. That was his call."

"But you were ready?"

If he shrugs again, Beverly believes she'll begin to beat on him herself. So before he can offer another response that will frustrate or anger her, she rushes to ask another question. "Did that incident have to do with Ann? With what happened to her last night? I assume it did."

"She didn't want to talk much about it."

Beverly has a sudden memory of Ann's presence at Beverly's table, stretching forth her plate to receive a helping of roast beef, the plate at the end of a long, graceful, tanned arm. Yes, Beverly might well want to punish anyone who would cause harm to that girl. She would want to, but she wouldn't.

"But what *did* she say?" Beverly asks. "Did he hurt her in some way?"

"She didn't come right out and say."

"Then what—how do you know—?"

"I made a guess. And once I got a look at him I didn't see a goddamn thing that made me think I guessed wrong."

"A *guess?* Did you ever consider—"

From the top drawer of the dresser Calvin lifts out a pistol, an automatic she believes, an ominous oily dark steel rectangle. Next he brings out a smaller rectangle, and this he jams into the gun's handle.

"Oh, no," Beverly says. "No, no. Please. What are you doing with that?"

He jerks back on the pistol's action, making a clacking sound that in the basement's smothered quiet is loud enough to make Beverly flinch. Calvin tucks it into the waistband of his jeans.

"I have to go," he says, and tries to step past her.

Beverly grabs his wrist, and though it's done impulsively, something in her mind pulls her back and reminds her that she's clinging to a man with a gun. It might have been a comical observation were she not trembling with fear. Her feelings for him have carried her so far from what has been her life that she might as well have descended into this basement to be entombed.

"Haven't you done enough?" she says. "You've beaten him, you said so yourself."

He hasn't shaken off her hand, but neither did he stop when she took hold of his arm. She fears he might simply drag her along until the weakness of her grip causes her to drop away.

He stops and faces her. "The boy? That's done. I guarantee you, he won't bother Ann again. No, I'm making another call on Brenda Cady."

She points to the gun. "With that?"

"The matter has grown more serious."

Beverly once pressed her hand on the bare flesh of his abdomen where the gun's barrel is now making its own impression. Perhaps because she touched him there before, she can grab the gun. And do what with it? Run, run as fast and as far as she can and hope that even if he catches her he might be too exhausted to proceed with his mission? Or perhaps she can get a hold of his belt and haul him over to the bed. And if she can work that buckle . . . Oh, this is the thinking of a desperate woman! Beverly knows she has neither the physical charms nor the seductive powers to make him tarry, much less stop. She cannot, she has to admit, make him choose her.

"Don't," she pleads. "Please don't. Whatever your reason, set it aside. Please. If you go after someone with a gun, you could be the one who gets hurt. Or gets in trouble, bad trouble. *Please.* I don't want anything to happen to you."

Calvin looks steadily down at her, at this version of her he has never seen before, tear-streaked and begging like a child.

"All right," he finally says. "You come along, and after you see what I have to show you, maybe you'll feel different."

He leads her out of the house and across the back yard, and though with her long legs Beverly has always been able to match anyone's walking stride, she has trouble keeping up with Calvin in his march across the grass.

He enters the garage, and it takes a moment for her eyes to make the switch from the sun-blasted yard to the dark rafters and splintered studs of the garage.

"Come here," he says sternly from the back of the garage.

As she walks toward him, the garage's assorted smells take turns assaulting her senses—weed killer, oil, dry rot. Gasoline.

Calvin points down to the gas can. "This is what we're dealing with."

She's not sure what she's supposed to see.

"*This*, God damn it!" He squats and lifts a string that's coiled next to the red can. For her inspection, he drapes the string over his finger.

"I . . . I'm not sure what you're showing me."

"A bomb. The sonofabitch made a bomb, and this was supposed to be the fuse." He stands stiffly, still holding the string. "He had one end of this in the gasoline and the other end over in your lilac bushes. That's where he likely planned to light it. And then run like hell."

Beverly has trouble comprehending what he's showing her. It's frightening, of course—it *is* a bomb, after all—but there's also something preposterous about it. In its overelaborateness, it reminds her of her sixth graders, how the boys are always hatching ingenious schemes of destruction and revenge. *Wouldn't it be neat if we dug this trap, real deep and at the bottom there'd be these poison stakes and over the top* . . . But they never implement any of these plans; all the satisfaction comes from talking about what they *could* do.

"Would this . . . would it have worked?" she asks Calvin.

"Probably not. The string isn't fuse material, and it isn't likely it would burn that distance. But that's not the point, is it? You've got someone out there who's not content just to barge into someone's house and scare the hell out of folks. Now he's looking to make good on his threats."

"You think Brenda Cady's husband did this?"

"I'm damn sure of it."

"So you're . . . What are you going to do?" She hopes that if she forces him to declare his intentions, to move them from the dark tangle of his brain to the open air of speech, he might realize how inappropriate they are and then he'll slow down or back off completely.

"I'm going to do the job I was hired to do," Calvin says.

"Hired? Hired! Who *hired* you? You're here to watch your grandkids while their parents are out of town. You're a babysitter! You're not some kind of gunfighter here to clean up the town!"

He says nothing but merely glowers at her. In the dim light of the garage, his eyes gleam like a polished, sharpened tool. She knows she hasn't made any impression on him whatsoever.

"Call the police," she says. "It's their business to handle matters like this."

He digs into the pocket of his Levi's and brings out the keys to his truck. "I have to go."

It's about as much reply as she expected, but then she knows by now how his counter argument would run: *The police? This is no job for the police. They're bound by the laws of the civilization they've sworn to protect.*

"I'll go with you then."

He shakes his head, a little sadly she thinks. "Not this time."

"I'm afraid of what could happen," Beverly says. "To you." The last two words she speaks softly.

He nods gravely, as if he knows as well as—better than—she the import of what she's saying. And of what she is *not* saying: This time you might not get away with murder.

"I've got to get this done," Calvin says.

He has taken years off Beverly's life, back to a time when passion and desire ran as hot in her as a fever. And now he's taking her back even further. She feels like stamping and screaming, Don't go, don't go! Please, Calvin! I don't want you to go! Not that she believes he'd be any more susceptible to a child's tantrums than to an aging woman's importunities of love.

She steps aside so he won't have to walk through her on his way to climb into the truck.

The engine coughs to a start, and then in that grinding interval while Calvin tries to get the correct gear to engage, Beverly jumps behind the vehicle, and gets one foot up on the bumper, in the process feeling the truck's tired springs sag with her weight. With both hands, she grabs the top of the tailgate and is about to climb into the back of the pickup when Calvin sees her in one of his mirrors. He yanks on the emergency brake, gets out of the truck, and grabs Beverly around the waist before she can get her leg over the gate.

"I said, *Not this time.*" He tries to pull her loose, but she holds onto the truck's hot metal as if she's hanging over a precipice.

"Come on. Down you go." He isn't tugging as hard as he can. Like a parent, he's trying to use force and restraint simultaneously.

"All right, Beverly." He speaks her name, his voice so soft that she can allow herself to believe his will is weakening. If she just keeps holding on, perhaps he'll relent and let her go with him.

But then he lifts her up and away from the truck with such ease that Beverly can't help but make the comparisons—he carries sheep to shearing and wrangles calves to branding.

Beverly doesn't struggle. She can tell he's trying not to hurt her. He's also trying not to let his hands come up too high near her breasts or drop below her waist. He can't take a chance on confusing her—or himself—about the nature of this touch. He carries her into the shade of the lilac bush, and there he sets her down gently. He continues to hold her, but Beverly knows it's not affection that causes him to linger. He's trying to convey to her—without words since he's wary about the power and efficacy of them—that it's essential she make no more effort to follow him. If he could, he'd probably chain her to the spot. But why not take the animal metaphor in another direction—why doesn't he simply command her: Stay! Stay!

"I mean it," Calvin says sternly, and then he backs slowly from her, watching to make certain she doesn't make another attempt to come after him.

Among the virtues that humans and animals are likely to share, Calvin Sidey probably values none more highly than obedience, at least among women. Beverly knows that, so she doesn't move while he climbs back in the truck and drives away. She remains perfectly still and listens as gravel pings against the truck's undercarriage and the gears clash and the transmission whines. She doesn't move as the cloud Calvin left in his wake drifts back to her, and she knows that his dust would adhere to her tears and together they'd leave their own dirty trail on her cheeks. Beverly stands exactly where he put her until she can be certain he's exited the alley.

Then toward her house she runs, and the motion reminds her exactly of another time when she lifted her legs and pumped her arms with the same frustrating feeling of not being able to move fast enough. She had been on playground duty during the lunch hour when she looked out toward the swings and jungle gym just in time to see a little girl topple backward from the top of the slide. Beverly raced across the playground to the child, although she knew—she *knew*—the girl could not have survived the fall (but she did, and with no injury worse than a broken ankle). Beverly runs now with the same certainty—that someone's life is in jeopardy. She just isn't sure whose.

Her keys are not hanging on the hook next to the door leading to the garage, and that can only mean that Adam has once again taken her car. Nevertheless, she jerks open the door to verify that her car is gone. And it is. The garage is empty.

Adam's Chevrolet is parked at the curb, but that probably won't help her—even if she could find his keys, she'd no doubt be getting behind the wheel of a car with an empty gas tank, the usual reason for him to take her car.

Beverly stands in her kitchen with her palms to her temples, wishing that by pressing hard on the outside of her head she could stop the whirl of thoughts on the inside. Should she call the police, give them a description of Calvin Sidey and his truck, and say that he must be stopped and saved from himself? Should she phone Brenda Cady and warn her to leave her house immediately, that she and her boyfriend and possibly even her son are in imminent danger? Should Beverly call Gladstone's one taxi and have him take her to Brenda Cady's address, hoping that whatever Calvin has in mind to do he might talk before doing it? The absurdity of that thought propels Beverly into action.

She hurries down the stairs to the basement, and this time the sight of the mess Adam lives in does not merely irritate her; it fills her with despair. How can she hope to find car keys among the dirty clothes, scattered books and papers, twisted sheets and bedclothes? She can't help but compare this scene with the spartan order of Calvin's makeshift basement bedroom.

Thoughts like this, to say nothing of a mother's disappointment with her son, are, however, a luxury she can't afford, not now. She's on her way to search through the pockets of a pair of jeans Adam has worn recently when her eye falls on the only neatness in the room—a stack of paper beside the typewriter. This must be Adam's novel. But more important is the set of keys serving as a paperweight for the manuscript pages.

Beverly is up the stairs and heading for Adam's car when she realizes that she read more than the words *Chapter One*. Embedded in her consciousness is Adam's first sentence: "The stranger rode into town with a grudge and a gun, a Colt .44 with a bullet in every chamber." She can't criticize her son for taking her car, but she's exasperated with his prose. You don't need *gun* and *Colt .44*, do you? And *a bullet in every chamber*—wouldn't that be understood? Or is he trying for some special emphasis? The economy and alliteration of *grudge* and *gun* is good though, she has to admit.

Adam has left the car parked in the sun, and the interior is so hot Beverly can only touch the steering wheel with her fingertips. She starts the car, and just as she suspected and feared, the needle is on *E*. The Texaco station is on the way to Brenda Cady's. If she gets that far without running out of gas, she can stop and ask for a dollar's worth of gas and hope those extra minutes won't mean the difference between life and death.

THIRTY

|||||||||||||||||||||||||||||||||||||||||||||||||

While the minutes and hours creep along, and Marjorie imagines where Bill might be along the road to Gladstone, she keeps berating herself for not sending him on his way with a very specific instruction. She doubts that her husband will know to do this on his own, and she's certain that her father-in-law will not. As eager as Bill was to get going, she should have detained him for a moment longer and said, Hold her. When you see Ann, before you say a word to her, before you ask her what happened or how she's doing, *hold her tight*. You might look at her and see a woman, but she's still girl enough to need her father's arms around her . . . almost as much as she needs her mother's.

And then Marjorie has to face a hard truth and a harder admonishment: If she had not chosen this operation—yes, chosen, she chose it—she would have been there to comfort her daughter herself. Although Ann is strong enough, healthy enough, to recover from her injuries and any fright she might have received, she'll still want, though she might not consciously know of this desire, to have her mother at her bedside. God knows, there were times in the past, when Marjorie needed hers, but that was not to be. Indeed, Marjorie couldn't even reveal to her mother how anguished she, Marjorie, was. When Tully died, Marjorie's mother was relieved, even if she didn't say this out loud; the worst day of Marjorie's life was an occasion for quiet rejoicing for her mother and father, and Marjorie knew it. The thought that Mrs. Randolph might have put her arms around her daughter and tried to console her in her grief would be laughable if it weren't so sad.

Visiting hours arrive, and Carole, almost as though she knows her sister needs to be distracted from her worry and guilt, enters Marjorie's room. Carole is carrying a paper bag that she sets down on the nightstand. Marjorie asked Carole for cigarettes and lip balm, but the bag obviously holds something else.

Carole reaches carefully inside and lifts out first one then another tall Dixie cup. Carole's fingers leave prints in the frost that coats the waxy containers.

"Milk shakes!" Carole announces in a triumphant whisper. "From Dunn's Dairy—they have the best ice cream in Missoula. I thought you deserved something extra special for all you've been through."

She unwraps a straw and sticks it in one of the shakes and hands it to Marjorie. "They're both chocolate. And I practically broke the sound barrier driving here, so they'd still be nice and thick."

Marjorie takes the cup, although she has no particular interest in or appetite for a milk shake. But this is typical of Carole, who often hides her own enthusiasms by pretending they belong to others. When Marjorie and Bill drove up to Carole and Milo's, Marjorie noticed that the house had recently been painted a pale lavender. But as hideous as the color was, Marjorie recognized it as a shade Carole had been fond of since childhood. Yet the first thing Carole said when she greeted Bill and Marjorie was, "Well, what do you think of the color? I wasn't sure, but Milo insisted." And even more than the color of lilacs, Carole loves ice cream in any of its forms.

Marjorie draws on her straw, but the first sensation of the cold, creamy paste hitting the roof of her mouth is too much, and she has to put her cup down.

"You don't like it?" Carole asks. She has already taken the lid off her cup.

"It's delicious," Marjorie says, but leaves her milk shake on the tray.

The sisters do not converse while Carole works expertly on her milk shake, using her straw like a spoon and lifting up one dripping, carefully balanced mouthful after another. Finally, the cold must get to her as well, and she slows down. "You know what I was remembering on my way over here today?"

Marjorie shakes her head, a maneuver she performs with caution.

"I was thinking about Grandpa's funeral in North Dakota and how we got such a late start coming back."

"Mm-mh. What about it?" She doesn't mean to sound brusque, but she wishes Carole would leave. If Marjorie confesses that she's having difficulty concentrating on anything but Ann's accident and Bill's journey back to Gladstone, Carole will simply offer the advice that Marjorie won't be able to take: Just think about something else.

"Do you remember where we stopped to eat?" She doesn't wait for Marjorie's answer. "It was at a supper club just outside that town—what was it? Valley City? The restaurant was up on a hill, I remember, and it was the first time in my life I ate prime rib."

Yes, that's her sister all right, thinks Marjorie. Of all the firsts that can be experienced in a life, how many people recall the first time they ate a particular cut of beef?

"What do you think was going on with Mom and Dad on that trip?" Carole asks. "I mean, we *never* stopped for a meal when we traveled. It was always a packed lunch of an apple and summer sausage sandwiches. I bet Dad paid more for our supper that night than he paid for any meal in his life. Do you think he inherited something? Could we have been celebrating that night?"

"I'd find it hard to believe that Grandpa died with much of anything to his name," Marjorie says. "They sold the farm years before and were living in that dingy little apartment."

"I suppose. But do you remember anything about Mom and Dad that night? How they were acting? If they said something about the occasion?"

Marjorie does have a memory of that night, but it has nothing to do with her parents or their demeanor . . . There was a bar connected to the dining area, and to get to the restroom you had to pass through the bar's smoke and undergo the scrutiny of a group of rowdy businessmen. When Marjorie walked past them the first time, they fell silent, and Marjorie felt their eyes on her. She was only sixteen, but she had grown accustomed to the way men stared at her. To the funeral she had worn a dress handed down from a cousin, and though it was navy blue and buttoned to the throat, Marjorie remembers that it felt tight. On her way back from the restroom, she heard one of the men say, "Slow down, miss. Stay a while." She kept walking, and another man made a clicking noise with his tongue. She was not offended, but neither was she flattered, and not until she was back at the table, back in the company of Carole and her father and mother did it occur to Marjorie that those men had not known she was with her family. Neither did they know her age or that the expression on her face was the lingering remnant of a sulk she had been in since they left Gladstone.

Marjorie was in love with Tully Heckaman, and she hadn't wanted to leave him, not even for a couple days, not even for her grandfather's funeral. Neither her parents nor Carole knew yet that she had been dating Tully, much less that only a few days earlier she had let him touch her bare breasts—her own "first" to remember. They certainly couldn't know that just thinking about his touch was almost enough to bring back the sensation, a tingling Marjorie likened to the sun's heat pooling on her bare skin. Oh, so much of her life then was secret and unknown—not only to strangers, like those men in the bar, but even to the people closest to her, her family seated around the table.

"To tell you the truth," Marjorie says to her sister, "I don't remember that night at all. I mean, I know we went to the funeral. I know that as a fact, but there's nothing to go with it. It's like the images, whatever they were, have been snipped out of my head."

Carole stops slurping her milk shake, and worry replaces her look of pleasure.

"The doctor said it could happen," Marjorie explains. "That I might have some memory loss as a result of the, you know, the surgery."

She's not lying. Memory loss is one of the side effects, whether permanent or temporary, that Dr. Carlson told her she might undergo. And though Marjorie's memories are intact, as far as she can tell, she has decided—and the decision is fresher than her milk shake—that she'll use the doctor's words to her advantage. If Marjorie is ever questioned about something in the past that she doesn't wish to share—her relationship with Tully Heckaman, for example—she will claim that she doesn't remember what her interrogator, whether it's Carole or Bill or one of her children or a complete stranger, asking about. A simple shrug might allow her not only to hoard her history but also to keep a part of her secret self inviolable.

"And that's happened?" Carole asks, continuing to look at her sister with concern. "You've lost your memory?"

Marjorie has done too good a job with her deception. Now she feels sorry for Carole and has to console her. "Well, not *all* my memories."

"What don't you remember?"

Before Marjorie can answer, Carole realizes the absurdity of her question. "Of course—you can't remember what you can't remember!"

At that, they both laugh, and for a moment Marjorie *does* forget. But only for a moment. In the next instant, Marjorie's concern about Ann returns, hitting her as suddenly as an ice cream headache.

THE HIGHWAY DROPS DOWN out of the hill country. The land flattens. The pines give way to a few scattered stands of hardwoods, but soon they vanish too. Now there's nothing but mile after mile of grassland—bluestem, bluejoint, blue grama, so-called—yet the only blue available to sight is the sky's, a pure and topless blue that seems to rise all the way to God.

On the wall of his office, Bill Sidey has a calendar given to him by his insurance agent, and every month features a different photograph of the Montana landscape. As he speeds toward Gladstone,

Bill thinks of how false is the picture that depicts a scene similar to the one he's driving through.

The photograph is contained, limited, but if this landscape conveys anything at all it is boundlessness. And while a picture can give the impression of space, it can't communicate what time means to this country. You can walk, run, ride, drive, even fly over this region, and your journey will seem to go on and on and on, world without end.

Ahead, on a hill, and not a hill really but only a little lift in the land, as if the earth drew a breath and swelled, there's a ranch. From down here on the highway the ranch house and outbuildings look like parts from a children's game, pieces to be moved around a board, though Bill knows it's quite possible the actual structures have hunkered on that hilltop for a hundred years, and the inhabitants have watched other generations arrive and depart, with only failure to separate their coming from their going. Or maybe the ranch has only been there a few years, the spot chosen for no reason so much as its distance from other human beings.

No matter how long they've been there, the people who live out here believe that whatever life demands of them they can meet it on their own. And perhaps they can. But Bill Sidey knows he's not cut from that cloth. The infinite sky that inspires certainty in some people breeds doubt in him, and he's never been sure what the truth of human endeavor is: Are we meant to do it on our own or with the help of others? He wishes he could arrive at an answer before he enters the Gladstone city limits.

THIRTY-ONE

||||||||||||||||||||||||||||||||||||||||||||||||||||||||||||||||||||||||

Will, Gary, and Stuart are fishing for bluegills and crappies in the Elk River. Well, Will is fishing for bluegills and crappies. While his friends throw spinners and spoons out into the faster water, hoping to lure a northern or a big bass, Will has been assigned to this back bay where his bobber and red worms are better suited for calmer waters and where there's no danger that his drifting line can become entangled with Gary's and Stuart's.

The indignity of being relegated to this spot is the second reason for Will's anger. He has smoldered for days over their plans to spy on his sister, and now that Will has his own counterstrategy in place—the fuse waiting in the driveway dust—Stuart and Gary have said no more about Ann and have not repeated their request that Will alter the draperies in his house to allow them to gaze at his sister without impediment. They seem to have forgotten the matter entirely.

Finally, when Stuart lets out a whoop and holds up the northern—close to two feet of fish, its long, slender body flashing silver as it wriggles in the sunlight—Will decides he's had enough. He reels in his line and tears the fragment of worm off the hook. He pinches two chunks of lead split shot on the line only an inch from the hook, and he doesn't bother putting another worm on the hook. He climbs off the log he's been fishing from and walks down the pebble-studded sand toward the bend in the river where Gary and Stuart stand. Stuart has retrieved his lure from the fish's mouth, put his catch on the stringer, and is already prepared to cast again into the fast-flowing water.

When Will comes within thirty feet of his friends—close enough, he thinks, to cast with reasonable accuracy—he brings his rod back, sidearm rather than overhead, and sends line, sinkers, and hook flying toward Stuart, the closer of the two boys.

He hits his target but to no effect. The line unfurls near Stuart's waist, but the hook merely scrapes against his jeans. Stuart feels something, and he looks down, but Will is already reeling in his line, preparing for another cast.

"Was that you?" asks Stuart. "What the hell are you doing?"

"Trying to catch something," Will answers.

"Jesus. You ain't going to catch it over here. Don't you know where the fucking water is?"

Gary seems to understand better what Will's intentions are. "Cut it out, Will," he says, flipping the bale on his reel closed and lowering his rod.

"I'm not trying to catch a fish," says Will. "I'm trying to hook a shithead."

He has his rod drawn back, this time for an overhead cast, when Gary starts running toward Will.

"Will, God damn it! Don't do it!"

Stuart, however, is concentrating on his line, in reeling in his lure with a stuttering rhythm to fool a fish into believing a piece of shiny metal is an easy prey.

Will lets go his weighted line, and as soon as it begins to arc through the air, as balanced and swift as an arrow, he feels sure his aim is true.

The hook catches Stuart in the softer flesh of his arm, above his elbow, but when the barb goes in, he doesn't startle or flinch as if he's been stung. He simply drops his rod and reaches across to the line connecting him to Will. Stuart tears the hook out of his arm, a long strand of blood unspooling in its wake. Then, holding onto the line, hand over hand Stuart begins to haul Will in. "You little fucker—c'mere!"

Seen from a distance—like a hawk's, coasting on the warm wind high above the river—it may seem as though Will is simply walking toward his bleeding friend. And once he's no more than a fishing rod's distance from Stuart, Will wonders why he didn't just drop the rod or at least resist, or to dig his tennis shoes into the sand or even to tug back against Stuart's pressure. And then Will knows. He wants as much fight as he can get, and he starts things off by launching a looping right hook at Stuart's rage-clenched face.

The punch never lands, though Will doesn't know how Stuart ducked or intercepted it. He doesn't know because Stuart's blow to Will's diaphragm knocks not only air out of him but awareness, and he has no space in his consciousness for anything but the desperate attempt to draw air into his lungs.

Will catches his breath, but he barely has time for a single gasp when Stuart wraps him in a headlock. Will's neck and face are squeezed in the crook of Stuart's right arm—the arm pierced by Will's hook—and he knows that his face is probably being smeared with Stuart's blood. Will has seen Stuart scuffle and fight often enough to know his preferred strategy—immobilize the opponent with a head or neck hold and then pummel away with his free fist. In preparation, Will grabs Stuart's forearm, less for the hopeless task of loosening Stuart's grip and more for getting his hands up to protect his face when the punches come.

But they don't come. This isn't going to be anything like the battle Will fantasized about, one in which he would be obviously outmatched yet his rage and his nobility—yes, yes, what other word would describe his willingness to fight for his sister's honor?—would give him a strength that he had never owned. In actuality, this fight—is it even right to call it that when one combatant is able to exert his will without opposition?—is a return to the powerlessness of infancy when you have neither the size, strength, nor language to affect, in any way, a world that can move or ignore you as it pleases.

Will is not being struck because Stuart has another punishment in mind. Stuart is hauling Will in a direction Will can't even determine. He can't see anything but Stuart's legs, feet, and the ridged sand below.

And then that view changes. The sand turns dark, then wet, and then they're in the water, the river so instantly icy around Will's ankles it feels as though he's stepped into traps that spring shut on him. But the water is soon flowing over his calves, then splashing above his knees, and when it rises to his crotch he can't be sure if it's the cold water that makes him want to gasp again or the even icier realization of what is about to happen.

Stuart is going to drown him.

Does that thought arrive the second before Stuart begins to lower Will's face toward the river, its surface barely wrinkled considering all the dark turbulence below? Or does Will have to glimpse the water coming closer to his mouth and nostrils to know what Stuart intends?

Will pulls and scrapes harder against Stuart's forearm, but not with the hope that he can escape Stuart's grasp. Realism now has as tight a hold on him as Stuart, and in Will's mind Stuart's strength has assumed the same implacable strength as the river. But Will wants at least to free his mouth so he can speak.

Will wants to make a joke.

He isn't sure if he can quite present the situation as hilarious, but he can certainly make a number of ironic, mordant observations, the total effect of which might be humorous. He can say the fisherman, not the fish, has been hooked—the fish has its revenge! He can point out that Stuart hasn't hooked him—Stuart has *crooked* him, caught Will fast in the crook of his arm. And isn't it funny that fish die when they're kept out of the water—they drown in fresh air!—whereas Will is about to die because he can't breathe in water? If he could get his mouth free—lips and tongue would be enough—to make these words, and with his words alter the mood of the boy about to kill him, then Will could control his fate. This is the only real strength and power he's ever had. To think that only days ago he believed he could make his way in the world, survive, like his grandfather, with the prowess of his physical being! If Will Sidey has a life beyond this day, this hour, it will be without any cowboy illusions.

And here is an observation he's sure he would never be able to share with anyone—this water tastes of its opposite element. When

Stuart pushes Will's head under, Will tries to hold his breath—*Don't breathe in water!* he tells himself. *Don't breathe in water!*—but the river, with the force of its current, pries his lips apart and flows between his clenched teeth and, wonder of wonders, the water tastes of dirt! The discovery is so marvelous that Will can't be sure if it might not be his sharpest grief—he'll never be able to impress anyone with this special knowledge: The Elk River chews its way through Montana's landscape, and by the time it swallows Will, it has hundreds of miles of dirt, sand, and grit, and if you put your own mouth into this churning, yellow water you'll be reminded more of garden loam than anything that flows from the kitchen faucet.

But this taste is soon replaced by the scalding, sour panic of vomit, and when Will has to cough that out—*One more discovery!* He can drown from the liquid inside him as easily as that on the outside!—in its wake the river rushes in, and Will feels his life's borders being washed away in the rush of the current.

The Gladstone Municipal Pool opened three years earlier, and from the day of its opening, Will and his friends were there almost every summer day. Yet for all those hours spent in the pool, Will never dared to open his eyes under water. He couldn't do it in his own bathtub, so he certainly couldn't do it in that water stinging with chlorine. But the next summer, the very first time he jumped into the pool it was with his eyes wide open; over the winter he had forgotten his fear. He'd stay under water for as long as he could, watching the bobbing, kicking, sometimes flailing bodies of the other people, kids mostly, who had no idea they were being watched below the water line. He cherished his invisibility, his ability to be there yet not there. He kept waiting for a dangerous situation to develop—one of the little children sinking to the bottom of the pool perhaps—and only Will with his special vantage would notice, prevent the tragedy, and be hailed as a hero.

The muddy Elk River is as dark as coffee, of course, and Will can see nothing. But then why would he? On this occasion, his life is the one that's dissolving, and the river's murk is indistinguishable from that other darkness that will hold him down forever.

THIRTY-TWO

Brenda Cady must be inside her house—Beverly can hear her little boy crying, a persistent, desultory wailing.

And there's the push mower, abandoned in the middle of the brown patchy yard. Was Brenda interrupted in her work by Calvin Sidey? Was she lying unconscious inside, knocked out when she refused to give Calvin the information he demanded? Is that why her little boy is crying—because he can't rouse his mother? Is it possible that Brenda, that both Brenda and her boyfriend, are lying inside on the floor . . . ? Beverly bangs on the door so hard her knuckles hurt, but it helps distract her from these dark premonitions.

She jumps off the concrete slab that serves as the step to the front door, and heads toward the backyard, hoping she'll discover Brenda there. Or perhaps Beverly will find a window that will allow her to peer inside.

Beverly has not turned the corner of the house, however, when the front door opens behind her and a voice stops her. "Hey! What the hell are you doin'?"

She pivots and sees Brenda Cady standing at the door and shouting at Beverly through the screen. Brenda is dressed in a bandanna-print dress and its elasticized top leaves her shoulders and upper chest bare. Near her neck are a series of bright pink blotches, exactly the kinds of marks that a man's fingers would make digging into flesh. Below her right eye is a similar patch of discoloration. That area looks swollen too, as if she might have been slapped or punched. And her lower lip—it looks puffy . . . The scene leaps unbidden to Beverly's mind's eye—*Calvin grabbing Brenda Cady, slapping her across the face, ready and willing to do more if she didn't tell him where her husband could be found.*

"I know what you're doing here," Brenda says when she recognizes Beverly. "But you can turn right around. He ain't here."

"He was—?"

"He left about ten minutes ago and good riddance."

Ten minutes . . . If Beverly had not stopped at the Texaco station and bought gas, she would have been here in time. But in time for what? To stop him? She has already failed at that endeavor.

"He's crazy, you know," Brenda Cady says. "Your husband. Crazy mad and mad crazy. And he's going to get what's coming to him."

"Did he want to know where your husband is? Is that what he came for?"

"Lonnie? He ain't my husband. My choice, not his."

Now Beverly wishes she too had corrected Brenda's misunderstanding; it might have established a useful commonality between them, but at the time—on the instant, in fact—she felt that to deny Calvin as her husband would have been disloyal.

Brenda opens the screen door and walks out toward Beverly with a stride that's so languid and self-assured it's vaguely threatening. If she approached Calvin in that manner, it was no wonder he struck her. But Brenda seems to know that Beverly has no choice but to stand still and accept whatever abuse Brenda wishes to bestow.

Beverly wants to ask how long Brenda held out before Calvin got from her the information he wanted, but instead she asks, "Where did he go?"

"Lonnie? Or your man?"

"Mine." At the single word Beverly feels her eyes grow warm with tears. She hopes Brenda doesn't notice, for this tough-talking young woman would surely regard tears as weakness.

"Not that it makes much difference." Brenda Cady puts her hands on her hips, a defiant stance she hadn't assumed in front of Calvin, of that Beverly is sure. "That old man is going to get himself stepped on and squashed flat."

"Please," Beverly says. "Just tell me where I can find him."

"Why? So you can try to save him? That old man deserves whatever he gets. He should know better than to mess with Lonnie Black Pipe."

The name is familiar to Beverly. Lonnie Black Pipe has a reputation for being a troublemaker, someone whose temper has landed him in jail on more than one occasion. Beverly wants to say something in Calvin's defense but nothing comes to mind but the kind of remark a child might make boasting about his father. *Your man's a bad Indian? Well, mine's a cowboy.*

Instead, Beverly says, in a voice almost too soft for the out of doors, "He's got a gun."

Her statement elicits exactly the response that might be expected. Brenda Cady's eyes blink as if she has not heard the word *gun* but its sharp report. "Are you sure? I didn't see no gun when he came to the door."

"Believe me," Beverly whispers.

Brenda Cady looks back over her shoulder as though she needs to see the site of her conversation with Calvin in order to recall its contents. "The Wagon Wheel. Lonnie likes to play pinochle there."

"The Wagon Wheel—that's down by the depot?"

Brenda nods. "A gun. Would he use it?" Apparently Brenda is new enough to Gladstone that she has not heard any Calvin Sidey rumors.

"Why don't you call the Wagon Wheel—talk to your Lonnie. *Tell him to leave the bar.*" Beverly is already backing up toward the car.

Brenda shakes her head strenuously. "He won't do it. He won't run from any man."

"It's not running, it's . . . Say something else then. Tell him you have to take your boy to the doctor, an emergency. Tell him *something.* Just get him the hell out of there!"

Beverly turns and runs toward Adam's car, parked haphazardly at the curb. But before she speeds toward Northern Pacific Avenue and the Wagon Wheel Bar she has to know if the man she'd be racing toward is worth any of her efforts. She turns back toward Brenda Cady, who is still standing on her weed-choked lawn, squinting and staring up the street as if future events are already in place, located in the sun struck distance and available for sight.

"What did he do to you?" Beverly asks. "Calvin Sidey. To make you talk—what did he do?"

"Calvin . . . ? Is that his name? That old man? What the hell are you talking about?" And then she must realize what Beverly is referring to because her hand grazes the spots on her face where bruises would soon show. "This? He didn't do this. I'd like to see him try. No, this was Lonnie. Sonofabitch."

Beverly hurries toward the car once again, and though her heart is still weighted with dread, it's lighter than it was only seconds before.

THE SUN'S BRIGHTNESS BURNS Will's eyes in a way that chlorine never does. Will squints and turns his head, and when he does, someone kicks the bottom of his foot and says, "Hey, stay awake."

The voice comes from above him, and in his disorientation Will wonders if the same sun that's trying to burn out his eyes is speaking to him.

Then another voice: "Come on. You puked up the whole goddamn river practically, so you gotta be hungry. Get up off your ass, and I'll buy you a hamburger. At Groom's."

Is that Stuart talking to him? But Stuart was trying to kill him, not feed him. And Stuart knows that Will's parents don't like Will to patronize Groom's. Few parents want their children there. Groom's is on Northern Pacific Avenue, across from the train depot, the only eating establishment on a block that otherwise is nothing but bars, and those are the saloons that cater to the serious drinkers and the down-and-out drunks, the bums who ride in on boxcars and cadge a drink before jumping another freight. The Groom's hamburgers that most families in Gladstone eat come into the home in a white paper bag, picked up by fathers so that wives and children don't have to venture beyond Woolworth's when they're on Northern Pacific Avenue.

"But if we're goin' into town," Gary says to Will, "you better dunk your head in the river again. You got throw-up in your hair."

Will manages to sit up, but when he does his stomach lurches, his head feels as if it's being squeezed, and he coughs so hard his sides ache.

"I shoulda' drowned you, you little fucker," Stuart says. "What the hell was the idea with the hook?"

He squints up at Stuart, who is not looking at Will at all but is nonchalantly pinching blood out of the little tear in his arm.

"I guess you looked like a big fish to me."

Gary says, "You're lucky I pulled him off you. He really would've liked to drown you."

"Nah. They would've sent me to reform school. A little shit like him ain't worth it."

Will tilts his head to the side, and though he can hear a faint gurgling, no liquid drains out. "You could've just said I drowned accidentally. Like the current got me or something."

"Don't give him any ideas," says Gary.

Stuart stops squeezing his wound and shakes his arm as if he's trying to restore feeling. "I'll remember that if I ever decide to drown you again."

"Is that why you said you'd buy me a hamburger? 'Cause you almost killed me?" The taste of silt is still strong on Will's tongue, and when he closes his mouth, sand crunches between his teeth.

"How about you shut the hell up and stop asking your goddamn questions. I ain't so sure the river isn't still where you belong."

Will isn't sure either. He has gotten to his feet, but he feels unsteady, as though the current is still tugging at him. And now he can tell that water is dammed in both ears. To hear the water rushing inside and outside him is more than disconcerting. The river has almost taken his life—will he never feel right outside its waters? Tonight he'll lie down in his own bed—will he feel the river's motion as soon as he closes his eyes? Will he ever have another dream through which the Elk River's dark waters don't flow?

THIRTY-THREE

Jesus, Calvin thinks, is there a bar anywhere on the planet that doesn't stink of stale beer, stale cigars, spilled whiskey, and unwashed men? The Wagon Wheel might be new to Gladstone since Calvin moved away, but this bar is no different from those he leaned against in his drinking days. The haze of cigarette smoke, the dim light, the dark glitter of bottles lined up behind the bar—oh, yes, Calvin is right at home here. Over by the begrimed window where there's enough light for them to see their cards, four men are playing pinochle. At one end of the bar a solitary drinker is hunched over the *Gladstone Gazette*. At the other end, three men in suits and ties are loudly arguing over a political issue that might or might not have a solution, but either way it sure as hell won't be found inside the walls of the Wagon Wheel. A young cowboy and a woman old enough to be his mother are hanging over the jukebox as if they believe moony looks are enough to play any song.

The bartender, a burly young fellow with a bushy mustache, slides down to where Calvin Sidey stands.

"What can I do you for," asks the bartender. Then he takes one hand off the bar, ready to reach for a glass, as if he's been in the business long enough to know what a man like Calvin Sidey comes in to drink. A shot of Old Crow.

"I'm looking for a man who spends a lot of time here—"

But before Calvin can ask for Lonnie Black Pipe, Calvin's own name is called out.

"Cal? Cal Sidey?"

In the whiskey light of the Wagon Wheel, the little man who's tottering toward Calvin looks like a character from a fairy tale, a hunched-over white-bearded gnome complete with a hand-carved walking stick that might turn into a snake if he throws it to the floor. Nothing about the old man is familiar to Calvin, who wants to turn back to the bartender and to his reason for being in the Wagon Wheel.

"Judas Priest," the bent old man says, his voice high-pitched and wheezy, as if every sound he makes has to squeeze through a too-small opening. "Cal Sidey. I heard you was dead."

"Not hardly."

"I even heard tell how it happened. Dropped dead of a heart attack out in the middle of the prairie and not found for days."

"Maybe someday," Calvin says. "Not yet."

"By God. Calvin Sidey. I'll be go to hell."

"And maybe that too," Calvin says, and steps back to the bar.

"You ain't got any notion who I am, do you?" the old man asks. "Not a notion."

To the bartender, Calvin says, "I'm looking for—"

"Roland Sill," the old man says, his voice raised as near to a shout as it will come. "Eh? Now you remember?"

"I remember you," Calvin says.

Pauline had been fond of Roland Sill, a rag peddler whose horse-drawn cart clattered up and down the streets of the town, loaded with pots, pans, and the scraps and bolts of the fabric he bought and sold. Roland and his brother lived in a shack just outside Gladstone. They were Jews from back East, some people said; Gypsies, others said. But as long as Roland bought and sold at fair prices, his origins didn't much matter.

Calvin knew from Pauline that Roland Sill came from Montreal. One day Roland greeted Pauline in her native language, and she was so delighted to hear and speak French that she invited Roland over. There he became a regular visitor, sitting at the kitchen table, drinking tea, smoking his pipe, and gabbing away with Pauline in a language that Calvin could only understand a few words of, at least as those two spoke it—as rapidly as birds trilling in the trees.

Calvin walked in on one of those conversations one day, and for some reason he thought they were talking about him. And laughing. To Roland Sill, Calvin said, "Don't you have work to do?"

Roland heard the tone in Calvin's question and he jumped to his feet. "Yes, sir!" But on his way out the door, he said quietly to Calvin, "You got nothing to worry about from me, brother." Even then, Roland Sill was a wizened little man who walked as if he were carrying a heavy bundle of rags on his back.

It looks as though Roland Sill's burden, like every man's, has only gotten heavier over the years. He's so bent over that it's all he can do to shift his gaze from the Wagon Wheel's dirty floor up to Calvin Sidey.

"I remember you," Calvin says again. "How have you been, Roland?"

"Pas mal," says Roland. "Better if you let me buy you a drink."

"Maybe another day. I'm here looking for a man. Lonnie Black Pipe? You know him? Have you seen him around?"

From behind Calvin comes a voice. "You found me."

Calvin turns, and for an instant he wonders if he's walked into a circus. He took Roland Sill for a magic dwarf, and the man Calvin is facing now—the man who must be Lonnie Black Pipe—has a face so hideously scarred he could be a freak show attraction.

"You're Black Pipe?"

"Everybody here knows that. What they're wondering is, who the hell are you?" Lonnie is dressed in black, from his boots right up to a big, flat-brimmed hat. He takes the hat off now and sets it carefully on the bar. On half his skull black hair grows in a thick mat; on the other half, the half glistening with the same burn scars that cover the left side of his face, a few tufts of hair sprout like weeds.

"And maybe the real question is," Lonnie Black Pipe says, "what the hell are you doing here?" Lonnie Black Pipe is a barrel-chested, big-gutted fat man, but he still looks powerful behind all that weight.

Calvin wishes now that he hadn't left the gun in the truck. He hadn't brought it in the first place thinking that he'd use it, but he wanted to make an impression, an unmistakable, unforgettable impression, and nothing does that quite like the round black vacancy of a gun barrel. But as he was driving here, he was arguing in his mind with Beverly Lodge, and she must have won the argument because, when he parked the truck, he put the gun back in the glove box.

But he can't go back outside, retrieve the pistol, and then return to the bar and resume the conversation.

"I'm here with a message," Calvin says. "For you." A message. It was exactly what he said to that kid. What the hell. He's been looking for a way he can be of some use in his old age, and maybe he's found his occupation. Calvin Sidey, messenger.

Lonnie Black Pipe laughs, or as close as he can come to a laugh with that twisted mouth of his. "Like Western Union, you mean?" He looks around the bar as if he knows he's performing and he wants to make certain the audience is attentive.

"I found your goddamn bomb, and you're lucky I didn't go to the sheriff with it. But don't think you're getting off. If you so much as go near the Sideys or their property, you'll wish you were behind bars so you don't have to deal with me."

"A *bomb*? What the hell are you talking about?"

"You know damn good and well. Out back by their garage."

"You listen to me. Does this here look like the face of a man who's going to fuck around with a bomb? If I got a problem with you— and I can feel one coming on pretty goddamn fast—I'll let you know to your face. What the hell do I need with goddamn bomb? *Shit.*"

"I'd be impressed with that line of talk if I didn't know you for a man who takes up his argument with women, shouting and scaring the hell out of them in the process. That's my idea of a bully and a coward."

Lonnie Black Pipe twists around in order to address everyone in the bar. "Does *anyone* here know what the hell he's talking about?" He gestures to the bartender. "Randy—hey, Randy. You let a crazy son of a bitch in here, you know that?"

Randy says, "Take it easy, Lon."

"*Me?* Me take it easy? This crazy bastard comes in here talking about bombs, but I'm supposed to take it easy? The hell."

Calvin breathes a little easier as he listens to Lonnie Black Pipe. A man innocent of Calvin's charge would register more outrage and wouldn't be talking as much as Black Pipe is. What's more, Calvin called him a bully and a coward, and Black Pipe let that pass. Calvin guesses that his point has been made, and this little dance will soon be over.

"You heard what I came here to say. You'll stay away from the Sideys."

"Mister, I'm running out of patience here. Now, I don't know if you got me mixed up with someone else or if you're just plain senile and don't know what the fuck you're talking about."

Then Calvin makes what he realizes almost immediately is a mistake. He points a finger at Lonnie Black Pipe and says, "You've been warned."

"You're warning me, old man?" Lonnie Black Pipe takes a step back, but there's no retreat in his movement. "You point that god-damn finger at me again, I'll break it off at the knuckle."

Then Calvin Sidey does another foolish thing, and again he knows how wrong-headed it is even as he's doing it. But he has his own problems with threats, especially when he's in the right, as he's certain he has been from the start with Lonnie Black Pipe, in spite of the man's denials.

Calvin walks up close to Black Pipe, lifts the finger that he's been warned not to point, aims it like a gun, and presses it right between the Indian's eyes.

Lonnie Black Pipe responds in a way that Calvin would not have predicted. He leans into Calvin's finger, increasing the pressure on his own forehead in the process. He smiles up at Calvin as if this turn of events delights him.

Calvin is about to back away, his point having been made, when Lonnie Black Pipe lifts his booted foot and slams it down hard on Calvin's foot.

For an instant, Calvin is pinned in place, and before he can pull away, Lonnie Black Pipe pushes him, but this is no ordinary shove. Lonnie Black Pipe slams his hands into Calvin's chest, and Calvin, unable to get both feet under him, loses his balance and reels backward.

Even as he's stumbling back, Calvin thinks, Don't go down, don't go down, don't go down. If he hits the floor and Lonnie Black Pipe remains standing, Calvin is sure he'll get his head kicked in.

Somehow Calvin is able to grab the raised edge of the bar and keep himself upright. He also regains his balance, and he's put just enough distance between himself and Lonnie Black Pipe that he's able to prepare for the charge that's coming at him.

By now, he realizes that this has been Black Pipe's strategy all along. An experienced bar fighter, Black Pipe must know how important it is to strike first and hard and keep the other man off balance. But by now Calvin has raised his fists and is ready for Lonnie Black Pipe.

The Indian also raises his fists, and he drops into a crouch. Calvin quickly develops his own strategy: he has a reach advantage, and he can use this to keep Lonnie Black Pipe from getting inside and pummeling him with body blows. But Calvin guesses too that Black Pipe is willing to accept five blows in order to land one of his own. Calvin will have to make certain that his punches are punishing enough to make Black Pipe reconsider. The problem is Black Pipe doesn't present much in the way of a target, nothing but the top of his head, and Calvin might break his knuckles on that big skull.

All conversation in the bar has ceased. The couple at the juke-box can save their coins. No one wants to hear any music. And the two men with their fists raised aren't dancing or circling. They aren't bobbing or weaving. They're waiting, waiting for the other to throw a punch or to show a weakness.

Calvin Sidey has been in his share of dustups over the years. The last time, unless you count the fracas with the boy this afternoon, was maybe ten, twelve years ago. But it's not just being older and out of practice that has Calvin worried. There's a look in Lonnie Black Pipe's eye that says he just might be enjoying this.

And here it comes—Black Pipe's shoulder hunches and it looks as though he's going to throw a hook. But no. It's only a feint. Yet it moves Calvin back another step.

"That's enough," Randy the bartender shouts. "God damn it. Take this outside or I call the cops right now. I don't give a shit if you split each other's skulls, but I'm not cleaning up the blood and puke in here."

Lonnie Black Pipe nods in understanding and starts for the door, all the while watching Calvin to make sure he follows.

Calvin drops his hands but only a little and heads for the sun-lit street and the violence to come. Most of the bar's patrons trail closely behind, including Roland Sill, hobbling as fast as his bent body will allow.

Over his shoulder, Calvin says, "Say something in French, Roland. Let me hear it one more time."

"*S'il vous plaît soyez prudent, mon ami.*"

Calvin hasn't understood a single word Roland Sill said.

Nevertheless, Calvin replies, "And au revoir to you," and pushes open the door.

FROM THEIR STOOLS AT the counter, Will, Stuart, and Gary blow straw wrappers at the *o*'s in Groom's, the chipped gilt letters decorating a high shelf. When one of the wrappers flies off course and lands on the grill, Mr. Groom barks, "What the hell are you trying to do—burn the place down?" Then Will and his friends move to a table by the window, but when Mr. Groom sees Stuart trickling sugar into his mouth directly from the dispenser, he slams his spatula on the counter. "Put that sugar down! Any more trouble from the three of you and you'll be out the door!"

So they try to behave themselves, but they aren't very successful. Will can't sit still but squirms to try to prevent his still-damp clothes from chafing and sticking to him. He half expects to be kicked out of the diner because the smell of the river and his own vomit still cling to him. Stuart, perhaps because the exhilaration of almost killing someone continues to throb in his veins, keeps finding any excuse at all to slug Gary in the arm or shoulder. Meanwhile, Gary, having assumed the role that's usually Will's, looks uncomfortable, as though he isn't quite sure he belongs in the company of the other two.

But when the waitress, a tall sharp-faced woman with small close-set eyes approaches the table, the boys restrain themselves momentarily. She holds her pencil poised over her order slips. "Okay, what can I get you honyockers?"

They agreed earlier on their order—three hamburgers with pickles and onions and three glasses of water. Stuart was adamant about not paying for soft drinks, French fries, or the deep fried onion rings, which are another Groom's specialty. But just as they're about to tell the waitress what they want, something outside appropriates her attention.

"Hel-lo," she says. "What do we have here?" Ignoring the boys, she calls over her shoulder to Mr. Groom, "El, you better come take a look at what's goin' on across the street."

Will turns to the window, but he can't see anything but parked cars, Northern Pacific Avenue, and its traffic.

Mr. Groom comes over to the table, and he instantly sees what he is supposed to. "Is that Lonnie Black Pipe? By God, that's trouble for sure."

Stuart almost knocks over his chair in his hurry to get to the window. "Lonnie Black Pipe? Where?"

"Should I call the sheriff, do you think?" the waitress asks Mr. Groom.

He hesitates for a moment before answering. "Nah. Let 'em go at it. Somebody'll come along and break it up sooner or later."

Will finally sees what everyone else is staring at. Across the street, outside the Wagon Wheel, a small crowd has gathered on the sidewalk. They encircle two men who are squared off like boxers, though their fists are held higher and closer to their faces than Will and his friends do when they pretend to box. One of the men drops into a crouch, and when he does, Will can clearly see that the other fighter is his grandfather!

For an instant he considers making an announcement of the fact—his friends might be impressed!—but since Will can hardly believe that it's so, he dashes from Groom's Diner and into the traffic of Northern Pacific Avenue.

Brakes squeal and horns honk, but Will keeps running, his hands covering the top of his head as if someone has just called out, "Heads up!"

Once he reaches the safety of the sidewalk in front of the Wagon Wheel, Will becomes a part of that group that has now grown larger. A few customers have come out of Bob and Goldie's, the bar two doors down from the Wagon Wheel, and four high school boys who must have been driving by and saw the possible altercation, have also joined the spectators. There are not so many people, however, that Will can't push forward to an unobstructed view.

He remembers—and recognizes—Lonnie Black Pipe from the day his father introduced him at the rodeo. But even without that memory, Will would know the man from town gossip. Lonnie Black Pipe, now there's an Indian you want to steer clear of. And the scars! Will can't imagine what it's like to go through life with a face so hideous that no one would want to look upon it.

The two combatants keep circling, one man occasionally feigning a punch just to see the other pull back. Although Lonnie Black Pipe is a good six to eight inches shorter than Will's grandfather—and looks even shorter because he's bobbing and ducking low—he seems confident and unperturbed. In fact, he's smiling, as though he's pleased to learn that this day has suddenly offered up something golden—an opportunity to give this old white man a beating.

Suddenly, as if a signal has been given, they come together in a flurry of punches. His grandfather bounces a straight right off the top of Lonnie Black Pipe's skull, but it's not enough to keep the Indian from boring in and slamming a blow to the ribs that brings a *whoof* from his grandfather.

Then their arms and torsos lock together, twirling away from the Wagon Wheel's front door, which is propped open and exhaling its stale beer and whiskey breath onto the summer sidewalk. As the two men move the crowd moves too, so synchronized they might all be part of the fighters' clinch.

Will can see both men, yet he can't tell exactly what the fighters are trying to do. They grunt and push and pull, but neither seems to be gaining any advantage. This isn't like any fight Will has ever seen, not on the playground or on television. How can they be struggling so hard, how can they be so intent on damaging the other, and yet so little is happening? There—Lonnie Black Pipe thrusts his head up, up, trying to butt Will's grandfather.

As they grapple, they fall against the Wagon Wheel's window, and Will winces as the glass shakes in its frame.

But the glass holds, and the two men slide and roll across the glass and then scrape against the Wagon Wheel's bricks. And then they run out of wall to hold them up. A narrow alley separates the Wagon Wheel from Houk's Auto and Truck Parts, and when the men come to that gap, one or both of them loosens his grip, perhaps to keep from falling.

THIRTY-FOUR

ow the hell did we get in this alley, Calvin
thinks. But more urgently he wonders how he
can get out, for he feels himself instantly at a
disadvantage. The space between the two brick walls is so narrow he
can't keep his opponent at a distance, and already Calvin feels Lonnie
Black Pipe's menacing heat closing in. Furthermore the sun's rays
have a difficult time finding their way in here, and in the dim light
Calvin can't see his opponent's eyes very well, and the way they
widen just before he throws a punch has been important to Calvin's
defense and counterpunching.

The crowd is making matters worse. They've followed the fighters, and now block the opening to the alley. They are strangely

silent, no one shouting encouragement, no one demanding that the fighters get serious, no one cheering one fighter or jeering the other. They're just waiting.

Calvin has a bad feeling about how he might leave this alley, but it doesn't take him long to run through the possibilities: he'll walk out or he'll be carried.

And because he'd just as soon the matter be decided sooner rather than later, Calvin throws out a left jab and follows it with a right hook. Lonnie Black Pipe easily blocks the jab with his forearm, and the other blow doesn't do much damage either. Calvin aims it at Black Pipe's temple, but it barely skims the top of the Indian's head.

The punches give Black Pipe something to think about, however, and he seems a little less determined to bore straight in on Calvin. Instead, he circles to his left, and as he does, he bounces up and down in his crouch. "Hey, old man," Black Pipe says, "you got your will made out?" This question seems to please the Indian, and he grins at his own wit.

Calvin says nothing but backs up a step, and when he does, something crunches under his boot. He tries moving to the side but now whatever is covering the alley floor is so thick underfoot that he has to drop his guard to steady himself. Fortunately an incinerator barrel is between him and Lonnie Black Pipe.

When Calvin glances down to see what he's walking on, he sees nothing but glass. Shards, slivers, jagged circles, beads, and chips of broken glass, green and brown and clear. Scores of beer and liquor bottles have been broken back here, perhaps hurled deliberately against the brick wall or smashed accidentally in careless attempts to throw them into the barrel.

"We can both walk out of here," Calvin says. He keeps his voice low; these are words meant only for Lonnie Black Pipe, not for the goddamn rubberneckers. "Your choice."

This remark seems to amuse Lonnie Black Pipe. He doesn't say anything, but his lopsided smile widens, and his fists now loosen and lower too. At the sight of that twisted smile and those open hands, Calvin allows himself to relax. Especially because Lonnie Black Pipe now moves away from Calvin.

But it's not because he too has grown tired of this fight; he is only changing his tactic, and Calvin doesn't understand that until it's too late. Lonnie Black Pipe grabs the rim of the trash barrel and topples it over. When Calvin skips to the side to avoid the tumbling barrel and the debris that spills from it—more broken bottles but with a few cans too—he stumbles and feels himself going down.

In the Wagon Wheel, he could urge himself to stay on his feet, but there he also found something to grab onto to stay upright. There's nothing here, but Calvin has another warning for himself—*Don't land flat!*—for if he does one of those daggers of glass might pierce his heart or lung or liver.

Calvin manages to twist himself to the side as he's going down, partly turning his back to his attacker in the process. He gets his hands out to break his fall, though he knows full well what the consequences of this action will be.

His hands, his hands from heel to fingertip, are pierced, torn, and sliced open, a sensation so specific that it separates itself immediately from the scrape of his skin across the concrete and cinders of the alley floor. But then the feelings merge, as the momentum of his hands pushes the glass deeper into his flesh and the rush of warm blood mixes pain with pain.

From behind Calvin, someone cries out, "Shit—he's down!" and for an instant Calvin wonders if that's his own voice.

But then he hears another—"Look out!"—and it can't be Calvin's own cry, because he couldn't warn himself before Lonnie Black Pipe's boot slams into his ribs.

With the pain from the kick—oh, God *damn*, here's another one!—comes an even sharper pain when he tries to breathe, and whether in or out makes no difference. Was that snap from a rib breaking?

The shadows in the alley grow. The crowd recedes and falls silent. Not even the broken glass surrounding him gives back any light. He's losing consciousness, but Calvin can't seem to stop his drift toward darkness. He's on all fours, glass grinding into his hands and knees, and now if he collapses completely, his face and chest will be unprotected. Despite the pain, he tries to push himself up. Nothing happens. It's as if every muscle has been sliced free of bone, and he's left with nothing but desire *get up, get up, get up.*

Suddenly Lonnie Black Pipe is squatting right in front of Calvin, so close Calvin can smell the Indian's sour breath. Black Pipe grabs Calvin's hair and lifts his head so Calvin can see what's in Black Pipe's hand. It's a broken beer bottle, and Lonnie Black Pipe holds it by the neck, its jagged points glinting like knives.

"Hey, look up here," Black Pipe says. "Somebody just told me who you are. And if you wasn't Bill Sidey's old man, I'd slice your fucking face off. You hear me?"

Blood is smeared across Black Pipe's face, the result of a still-dripping bloody nose. The sight gives Calvin a little shiver of satisfaction, both because it means at least one of his punches did some damage but also because that bright scarlet is a sign his vision is clearing.

Black Pipe yanks Calvin's hair and asks again, "You hear me?"
Calvin nods as best he can.

Lonnie Black Pipe stands up, glass crunching under his boots.
He tosses the broken beer bottle aside, and it lands with a melodic
ping completely at odds with the purpose Black Pipe was going to
put it to. "Now get the fuck out of here."

Calvin braces himself for another kick, but it doesn't come.
A moment later, Lonnie Black Pipe walks away, and it sounds to
Calvin as though the Indian is being congratulated for "showing
that old man what's what." There was a time here in Gladstone,
Calvin thinks, when an Indian who so much as looked the wrong
way at a white man might have been beaten within an inch of his
life, or several inches beyond. Well, that's progress, Calvin supposes.

Then, while Calvin is still trying to find a way to get up, while
his boots are scrabbling ineffectually in the glass and cinders, a man
wraps his arms around Calvin's midsection, and helps him to his
feet, a gesture he's grateful for, despite the pain it causes him. Yes,
he's sure of it; his ribs must be broken.

Once Calvin is standing, the man continues to hold on to him.
"Easy, mister," the man says.

Calvin leans back to get a look at the man who has come to his
rescue. A burly, bespectacled fellow in a powder-blue Ban-Lon, he
looks to be close to Bill's age, and Calvin is about to ask him if he,
like Lonnie Black Pipe, also knows Bill Sidey, but then Calvin stops
himself. His mind's still not quite right, and he'd better keep his
mouth shut until he can be sure it won't be nonsense that spills out.

"Just hold on," the man in the blue shirt says. "We'll get somebody to call an ambulance."

Calvin takes a couple of unsteady steps. The man in the blue shirt keeps his arms out as if Calvin is a toddler who might fall at any moment.

"I'm all right," Calvin says.

"Mister, you might be a lot of things, but all right isn't one of them." His blue shirt is streaked with Calvin's blood.

"I don't need the ambulance," says Calvin. He's moving now, and the momentum of one small step after another seems oddly to steady him. He walks out of the alley, and when he does, the rays of the late afternoon sun hit him so hard he has to look away. But more light is another help. Calvin is sure now that both the darkness of the alley and of unconsciousness are behind him. The small crowd parts to allow him to walk farther from the alley and the site of his beating and humiliation. Even the man in the blue shirt now leaves Calvin alone.

To help stop the bleeding, Calvin holds his hands high and out in front of him. In the heel of his left hand, a piece of brown glass protrudes, and a scrap of the bottle's label still adheres to the glass. Schlitz. Calvin plucks out the glass and lets it fall. If an ambulance is coming, its driver hasn't turned on the siren. The only sounds are the usual rush of traffic, and an occasional *ooh*—half gasp and half moan—when someone sees Calvin's hands.

WILL KNOWS HE SHOULD do something, but what? He couldn't see what happened in the alley, but it must have been awful, awful, awful, because his grandfather is limping and dripping blood, and when he walks out into the light his face is as gray as the sunstruck sidewalk underfoot.

"Grandpa?" Will says, but he barely whispers the word, and he knows that his grandfather can't hear him. What if his grandfather asks Will for help? Then what would he do? He can't stop his grand-father's bleeding, and he can't stop the man, the gruesome-looking man, who did this to his grandfather. Lonnie Black Pipe is walking back toward the Wagon Wheel in the company of two men who are laughing and patting the Indian on the back.

Will looks around for Stuart and Gary. If they also crossed the street to watch the fight, maybe Will can ask them what he should do. But everyone who gathered for the spectacle is drifting off now, so that Will stands alone in front of the door of Houk's Auto and Truck Parts. From inside the store comes the smell of rubber tires and motor oil.

Will is usually unable to look at any blood or gore—a run-over dead squirrel in the street can literally sicken him—but strangely the sight of his grandfather's cuts doesn't bother him. While Will is pondering this change in his nature and wondering if it's a conse-quence of having been submerged in the river's muddy water and believing that he was going to die, his grandfather suddenly stum-bles. He doesn't fall, but he stops, and he seems not only to have lost his energy but his way. He takes a breath, and Will can hear the hiss when his grandfather inhales. Then Calvin shakes his head as if to clear his vision, and when he looks around to get his bearings, he sees Will.

"Grandpa," Will says, loud enough this time to be heard.

"Will, what are you doing here?"

"I saw you," Will says.

"Well, you weren't supposed to." His voice is a low-pitched rasp and not much louder than Will's whisper. "Now you better get on home before you see something else you shouldn't see."

"Your hands."

"Nothing a little iodine and a few Band-Aids can't take care of."

"Can I help you . . . ?"

His grandfather shakes his head, and with that tight-lipped gesture he begins to move again, his first step a lurch in the direction he was headed in before.

Will waits a moment, then follows. Soon he sees where his grandfather is going—toward his truck, parked in the lot of the Northern Pacific train depot. Will runs ahead of his grandfather, and when he arrives at the truck, he puts his hands on the door's hot metal as if he's touching goal in a game of tag.

Once he catches up with his grandson, Calvin Sidey says, "You want to help? Reach into my pocket here and get out the keys and unlock the door."

His grandfather's T-shirt is smeared with red, but Will can't see any blood around the pockets of his grandfather's Levi's. Still, Will's careful as he reaches in for the keys. When he extracts them, he starts to walk around to the driver's side.

"No," Calvin Sidey says. "Open this one," meaning the closer passenger door.

Will does as he's told. When he opens the door, the heat that had been stored in the truck rushes out like a hot sigh. Will climbs in.

"Huh-uh," his grandfather says. "Out."

"I'll ride home with you, Grandpa."

"Out," Calvin Sidey says again.

Will jumps down from the truck, landing on asphalt that feels soft from the day's heat. Then Will has to step aside so his grandfather can reach inside the truck. Blood drips on the seat, but Calvin Sidey doesn't seem to care. His grandfather opens the glove compartment and takes something out, and Will gasps when he sees what it is. A gun, a pistol. Unlike many of his friends, Will doesn't have much experience with guns. He doesn't own one, he doesn't hunt, and he's never even fired a gun, not a shotgun, not a rifle, and certainly not a pistol. The weapon in his grandfather's hand is an automatic, Will thinks. Like soldiers have in the World War II movies. His grandfather has trouble holding the pistol, and if he weren't able to loop his finger through the trigger guard, it would probably fall to the pavement.

Thus armed, Will's grandfather heads back exactly the way he came, and though he certainly must know where he's going, if he were lost he could follow his own blood trail.

Will has no doubt of his grandfather's destination either. He's going back toward the Wagon Wheel to take revenge on the man who beat him. Will looks around frantically. There aren't many people on the street, but the few who are present, lingering outside the bar or walking to one of the other bars or businesses in the neighborhood, pay no attention to the old man and the boy making their way down the sidewalk in a strange slow dance. Does no one notice that this bloodied old man has a gun in his hand? Shouldn't someone stop him? Where's that man in the blue shirt? Earlier he was going to call an ambulance—will he call the police now? If someone doesn't do something, his grandfather will walk into the Wagon Wheel and shoot Lonnie Black Pipe. And then not only will the Indian be dead, Will's grandfather will be arrested, tried, convicted, and sent to prison. Or worse . . . One of the older boys, Larry Jenkins, whose father is a lawyer, told Will and his friends earlier in the summer that Montana still has the death penalty, and the method of execution is hanging!

Someone has to save his grandfather from that fate, and since no one else seems available for this duty, Will steps forward.

"Grandpa," Will says, stepping alongside his grandfather and matching his stride to the old man's. "Don't, Grandpa."

Calvin Sidey doesn't acknowledge the boy but continues to stumble forward.

"Grandpa," Will says again, tugging at the hem of his grandfather's T-shirt.

His grandfather stops and looks down, "Go home, boy. You hear? Go home, God damn it." Then the old man starts walking again.

Will has to stop his grandfather, he has to. If he doesn't, the whole family will be destroyed. To be a Sidey will mean something shameful, and they'll have to leave Gladstone and move to a place where no one knows that Will Sidey's grandfather once walked into a bar and shot a man dead.

Will grabs the pistol and tries to pull it from his grandfather's hand. After the briefest moment of resistance, it comes out with surprising ease, as though the blood has greased the way.

"Hey," Calvin Sidey says, but by now Will has skipped a few feet away and out of his grandfather's reach.

The gun's grip is warm and wet from his grandfather's blood. It is also surprisingly heavy, and Will raises and lowers his hand a few times to try to familiarize himself with its weight. Then the realization of what he's holding—and that he really doesn't know how to work it, or, even more startlingly, that he doesn't know how to keep it *from* working—makes him lower the gun, keeping it close to his side.

"Give it here, boy," Calvin Sidey says. "Before you hurt yourself."

Will shakes his head and continues to back away from his grandfather.

Calvin Sidey tries to quicken his step in pursuit of his grandson, but the effort costs him. He winces and stops so abruptly you'd think he was pulled up short on a leash. His next move is not toward Will. He staggers toward the street and sits down heavily on the curb. With his feet in the gutter, he hangs his head and lets out a groan that frightens Will. Is his grandfather going to die?

That terrifying thought barely has time to form itself in Will's brain when he hears someone call his grandfather's name. Will looks in the direction of that anguished shout. Mrs. Lodge is running toward them, her cheeks flushed and glistening with tears.

When she reaches grandfather and grandson, her first question is to Will, spoken through her ragged, panting breaths. "Are you hurt, Will?"

He shakes his head.

Although she can't know anything about what has happened, she must realize what might happen, so she says to Will, quietly but firmly, "Hand me the gun, please. Quickly."

Will does as he's told.

Once the pistol is in her hand, Beverly Lodge does not hesitate. She steps over to the sewer opening set in the curb and drops the gun through the hole. As the pistol's steel bounces off iron and concrete in its clattering fall, an echo almost like a far-off bell rises to the street.

Only then does Beverly Lodge turn to Will's grandfather, and her single word, "You," sounds as though it could be the beginning of a scolding.

Will's grandfather doesn't say anything, but he lifts his lacerated hands toward her. At that moment Will believes that his grandfather is asking for help from the only person he'd ever ask.

Beverly Lodge's "Oh!" is such a piercing cry, Will is surprised people don't stop their cars or run from nearby buildings to see what's wrong.

But Mrs. Lodge sees what must be done. She lifts her dress and enfolds those bleeding hands in the material. She's standing right there on Northern Pacific Avenue, her dress raised so high anyone can see her legs and maybe even her underpants, but Mrs. Lodge doesn't seem to care. She just stands close to his grandfather and holds his hands.

"Will," she says, "go into that business there and ask them to please call an ambulance. Right away, Will. *Right away.*"

THIRTY-FIVE

Bill pauses at the top of the stairs, then bends down in order to see as far as he can into the basement. Yes, it looks as though his father's light is on. Well, Bill might as well get on with it. He grasps the handrail and begins his slow descent. When he reaches the bottom step, he can see that, yes, his father is awake, awake and watching his son approach.

His father is lying on his bed and smoking one of his hand-rolled cigarettes. Bill can't understand how his father is able, with his heavily bandaged hands, to manage the delicate process of filling a paper with tobacco, rolling it, then striking a match and lighting it. As it is, Calvin must hold the cigarette with the tips of his fingers, the only part of his hands not wrapped tight with gauze and tape. And taking a drag from the cigarette is a delicate, awkward process since his lip is still split and swollen.

Bill walks over to the bed and looks down on his father. "How are you doing, Dad?" The white bristle of his father's unshaven whiskers add to his ashen look. "Would you like me to shave you?"

Calvin scrapes up and down his cheek with his fingertips. "No need. I'll just let it grow."

"Well, you let me know. By the way, Mrs. Lodge is upstairs. She'd like to see you."

"Tell her I'm sleeping."

"I'm sure she'll come back," Bill says.

"Tell her I'm sleeping then too. Or on the toilet. I don't give a damn. Or come right out and tell her I don't want company. And especially not hers. That ought to do the job."

"She seems to think there's something between you."

"Does she."

"Well? Is she right about that?"

"Maybe you should be talking to her."

The nutty sweet aroma of his father's tobacco fills the basement. It's a smell that not only does not belong in this place that's usually redolent of damp earth and mildew but seems also reminiscent of another time, not summer but fall or winter and fallen leaves and wood fires. But Bill knows that now he's allowing a pleasant odor to make him nostalgic for a time that never was. He reminds himself of what he must do.

"Dr. Ellingsrud called. He thinks you still belong in the hospital. Hematuria can be a serious matter. When was the last time you urinated, Dad? Is there still blood?"

Calvin waves off this concern. "I've pissed blood before. A horse once threw me and I hit a fence post on the way down. Took damn near a month before my water cleared."

"All right, Dad." Bill sighs and the fog of cigarette smoke wavers. "All right. But let me know if it doesn't get better. Would you do that?"

"I'll let you know if there's something to worry about."

"He's concerned about infection too. He wants you to watch for—"

"I remember. I was there, you know. I heard everything he had to say."

Bill nods slowly, trying to hold on to his patience. His father has been through an ordeal, and the evidence—the cuts and bruises, the bandages and the antiseptic—is there for anyone to see. But Bill knows that the psychological damage is probably worse, though that's invisible, unless you know, as Bill does, to look at—and beyond—the curt responses and the averted gaze, the body not just prone but its energy all but vanished. "There's something else we need to talk about."

Calvin finally looks at him. "Then let's get to it."

Bill starts to sit down on the edge of the bed but then thinks better of it. He clears off the chair beside the bed and situates the chair so that he and his father are facing each other. He places the ashtray on the bed beside his father, and only after all these preliminaries are out of the way does Bill finally say, "You'll have to leave here."

His father shifts as if he's determined to rise right at that moment. "No, no," says Bill, and reaches out a hand to hold his father down if need be. "No. Not now. Not until you're healed. Not until the bruises fade and the stitches are out. But when that day comes, you'll have to go."

"You don't have to worry on that account. I packed light for this trip. I'll head back as soon as I can wrap my hands around the steering wheel."

"I don't mean leave town, Dad. I mean you can't stay *here*. In the house. Though I suppose since it's still in your name, if you wanted to, you could send us on our way."

"Jesus, that again? I told you: I make no claim on this place."

Bill looks down at the basement floor. "All right, Dad. I remember."

"So you're kicking me out," Calvin says. "Good for you."

Still staring at the floor, and the cracked, curling linoleum, Bill thinks, What shabby surroundings. But he won't allow himself to be deterred. "Not out of Gladstone, Dad. I want you to stay in town. I'll help you find an apartment, or even a house if you'd rather. But some place close enough that Marjorie or I can look in on you. Or Mrs. Lodge."

"I can take care of myself. Besides, town life doesn't suit me."

Bill can't help himself. "Any town or this one?" He immediately shakes off his own question. "Never mind. It doesn't matter."

"You're right. It doesn't."

Bill takes a deep breath. "You didn't ask, but I need to tell you why I don't want you living here, under this roof."

"Fire away. I reckon this is what you made the trip down here for."

"I don't want you around the kids. I don't want them seeing how you handle life. Or *don't* handle it. I don't want them getting the wrong ideas about how we're supposed to get through our troubles, with bluster and threats and fists. Or worse. You go charging off all on your own without making sure of the facts, without seeing if you need reinforcements, without even checking to see if someone else should be brought in on the matter. You just assume you're the one who's supposed to take care of whatever needs taking care of. Ann and Will look at you and your life, and they're liable to learn the wrong lessons. What's more—"

Calvin Sidey makes a slashing motion with his hand to stop his son from going on. "That's enough," he says. "I might have fucked up six ways to Sunday, but that doesn't mean I have to lie here and listen to a lecture. You made your point. I'll be moving on as soon as I'm able. Now why don't you go on back upstairs? I'm tired, and you've got a message you need to deliver to Mrs. Lodge before she comes charging down here. From what I can tell, she's not a woman easily put off."

Bill hasn't said all he hoped to say to his father, but that, he realizes, is a feeling he'll always carry with him.

He stands and backs away toward the stairs. "Do you need anything else tonight?"

Calvin Sidey reaches across and stubs out his cigarette in the ashtray. "Not a damn thing."

The cigarette is extinguished. Bill's foot is on the stair. His speech is delivered. But with his back to his father, Bill Sidey says, "And I don't want you smoking in bed. Not under my roof."

BEVERLY LODGE IS SITTING quietly at the kitchen table, but when she sees Bill Sidey come up from the basement, she gasps. He's wearing a look so stricken he might have discovered his father's dead body down there. "Is he—" the words are out before she can stop them.

"I think," says Bill, "he needs to sleep. He's done in."

"If I could just see him for a minute . . ." Beverly hears the pleading in her voice, but there's nothing she can do about it.

Furthermore, she no longer cares. If Calvin has done anything to her, it has been to render unimportant what once might have mattered so much to her. And what is that something? Only her pride and all that goes with it.

Bill shakes his head slowly.

"He doesn't want to see me."

"Once he gets rested up, once he gets his strength back . . ."

Beverly almost laughs at the moment's irony—the son is intent on sparing the feelings that the father doesn't give a damn about. "Please. You don't have to say any more. He doesn't want to see me. I understand." She stands and straightens the strap of her sundress that keeps slipping from her shoulder.

"I don't know what to say," Bill says, and smiles weakly. "He's not worth it, you know."

Beverly turns up her palms. "Yet here we are."

And then Bill Sidey must feel remorse for what he's said about his father. "I think he's still feeling a little embarrassed about everything," he adds. "He's not a man who's accustomed to—"

"I understand," Beverly says again. "I may have only known your father for a few days, but I've come to understand him very well." What she doesn't say however is that since Calvin came to town and turned his gaze on her, Beverly Lodge's own being has become incomprehensible to her.

This brings a wider smile to Bill's face. "Really? I've known him a long time, and I can't say I've come close to understanding him."

"Well, parents always keep a part of themselves away from their children. You know that."

"I do," Bill says. "I do indeed. And then the kids return the favor tenfold. If Ann had only said something to me or her mother about what was going on. Though I did think it strange that we hadn't met this boyfriend. And what the hell set Will off on his wild thinking I'll never understand."

Beverly shrugs, and even that little motion causes the strap of the sundress to slip from her shoulder again. What a fool Bill Sidey must think she is, coming over with her lipstick and rouge and flirty dress to see an old man with his hands bound up like a child's so he can't get into any more trouble, an old man who doesn't even want her in his presence.

"Little boys' minds," she says. "I've watched them operate in my classroom for years, but I can't say I begin to comprehend them."

"But a prowler? He thought there was a *prowler* in the neighborhood, someone who was hiding every night in our garage? If he'd only said something about his fear, we could have told him there was nothing out there."

"And maybe he liked scaring himself with his made-up fears."

"Yes, maybe he did."

Dirty dishes are stacked in the sink, and Beverly has to resist the impulse to go over there, run some hot water, and start in on them. "When did you say Marjorie's coming home?"

"Day after tomorrow. Carole and her husband are bringing her."

"She's still recuperating, I'm sure. I'll be happy to come over any time to help out. When you have to go to work, for instance. And you can tell your father I'll stay upstairs if he's worried we'll accidentally bump into each other."

"I appreciate the offer. But Carole's going to stay for a few weeks. She seems to be looking forward to the opportunity to baby her little sister."

"Well, you know where I am," Beverly says. "If there's anything you need, anything at all, don't hesitate to knock on my door." She's about to open the screen door and walk out of the Sidey home, but she pauses to say, "And tell that stubborn father of yours . . . Oh, never mind. There's no telling that man anything." And she pushes through the door before a hot rush of tears can add yet another measure to her humiliation.

CALVIN SIDEY IS CONDUCTING an experiment. He's sitting on the edge of the bed and holding a copy of the poems of Catullus. He has flexed his fingers often enough that the tape and gauze wrapped around his hands has become pliable. He wants to see if he can turn the pages, and because this collection is printed on Bible paper he finds he can. As he swipes one thin, silky page after another, he stops, as he so often does, on the death of Lesbia's sparrow.

His concentration is so complete that he doesn't notice that his granddaughter has come down the stairs.

From across the room, she says, "Grandpa?"

He closes the book. "You're up mighty late tonight, aren't you?"

"I slept pretty late this morning," she says. She hunches forward and squints as if she has trouble seeing through the basement murk, but she keeps her distance.

"Good to be out of that hospital, isn't it?" He wants to encourage her to come closer, but he doesn't know how. "How's that arm doing?"

"It doesn't hurt much." She takes a few steps toward him. "How about your hands?"

"No, not much." He holds up his bandaged hands. "Just feeling a little clumsy."

She takes a few cautious steps forward. Calvin tries not to move, as if his granddaughter were an animal easily spooked.

She smiles and asks, "Are you growing a beard?"

He raises his chin and pretends as though he's grooming his whiskers. "I might do just that. Maybe by Christmas time I'll be able to play Santy Claus."

"Are you staying in Gladstone? I heard Dad talking to Mom earlier and he said he asked you to stay."

"We'll see."

"I hope you do," she says. "Will does too. He won't say so, but I know he does."

"Well, that's nice of you to say. I appreciate that." What if he motioned for her to come over and sit down? Would the gesture seem frightening, coming as it does from someone who looks as though he has paws for hands?

"And no matter what," she says, "I wanted to say thank you. For what you did. For how you helped me with, you know, with him."

"You have any more trouble with that fellow, you tell your father. Hear me? He'll know what to do." He hadn't meant to sound like a scold.

She nods and steps back. "I better go back up," she says. "Good night."

As she heads up the stairs and disappears into darkness, the words that Calvin Sidey would never speak come to him at last: *And don't you stop until you find someone who'll write poems for you.*

CALVIN SIDEY HAS INDEED packed light for this trip to Gladstone, yet when he quietly climbs the stairs from the basement, his suitcase is heavy enough that he can feel a couple of the stitches in his hand pop loose from the weight. But he's not about to let that slow him down. He goes out the back door, careful not to allow the click of a latch or the creak of a spring give him away. Into the night he goes, hurrying across the lawn and toward his truck.

He waits until he's inside and behind the wheel before inspecting his bandaged hand. In the dark, the fresh blood soaking through the bandage looks black, but the dark stain isn't any larger than a fifty-cent piece, so the bleeding can't be very serious. Calvin makes of his left hand a clumsy claw to encircle the steering wheel. With the heel of his right hand, he maneuvers the gear shift, and he feels again a tug at his sutures and perhaps another gives way. If he were staying in Gladstone, he might look up that young doctor and tell him, Look here, you're going to have pull your stitches tighter and knot your thread more securely. You don't want your patients springing leaks.

But that lesson will have to be left to another patient. Calvin is as good as gone, escaping yet again from this house, this town, this world. He puts in the clutch, and lets the truck coast down the alley. Only when he's well away from his son's and Beverly Lodge's houses does he turn the key in the ignition and allow the engine to roar to life.

Ave atque vale.

ACKNOWLEDGMENTS

First of all, thanks to my wife, Susan. This book found its way to publication only because she continued to believe in it, even when my commitment wavered. Her faith was seconded by PJ Mark, my extraordinary agent, and I thank him for his kind honesty, intelligence, and friendship. I'm fortunate to work with Kathy Pories, an editor whose keen eye is matched only by her understanding heart. I thank her and Elisabeth Scharlatt, Ina Stern, Craig Popelars, Lauren Mosely, Jude Grant, Emma Boyer, Brooke Csuka, Debra Linn, Anne Winslow, and everyone at Algonquin Books who worked to make this book better and to help it find an audience.